*For the first time ~~in one volume,~~
two beloved Regency classics
from two of the genre's masters. . . .*

ELIZABETH'S RAKE

Praise for Emily Hendrickson

"Emily Hendrickson delights. Never pass up her books."   —*Affaire de Coeur*

"Regency perfection."   —Sandra Heath

and

CUPID'S MISTAKE

Praise for Karen Harbaugh

"[*Cupid's Mistake*] is peppered with witty dialog and humorous repartee."   —*Library Journal*

ELIZABETH'S RAKE

EMILY HENDRICKSON

—— and ——

CUPID'S MISTAKE

KAREN HARBAUGH

A SIGNET BOOK

SIGNET
Published by New American Library, a division of
Penguin Group (USA) Inc., 375 Hudson Street,
New York, New York 10014, USA
Penguin Group (Canada), 10 Alcorn Avenue, Toronto,
Ontario M4V 3B2, Canada (a division of Pearson Penguin Canada Inc.)
Penguin Books Ltd., 80 Strand, London WC2R 0RL, England
Penguin Ireland, 25 St. Stephen's Green, Dublin 2,
Ireland (a division of Penguin Books Ltd.)
Penguin Group (Australia), 250 Camberwell Road, Camberwell, Victoria 3124,
Australia (a division of Pearson Australia Group Pty. Ltd.)
Penguin Books India Pvt. Ltd., 11 Community Centre, Panchsheel Park,
New Delhi - 110 017, India
Penguin Group (NZ), Cnr Airborne and Rosedale Roads, Albany,
Auckland 1310, New Zealand (a division of Pearson New Zealand Ltd.)
Penguin Books (South Africa) (Pty.) Ltd., 24 Sturdee Avenue,
Rosebank, Johannesburg 2196, South Africa

Penguin Books Ltd., Registered Offices:
80 Strand, London WC2R 0RL, England

Published by Signet, an imprint of New American Library, a division of Penguin Group (USA) Inc. *Elizabeth's Rake* and *Cupid's Mistake* were previously published in separate Signet editions.

First Signet Printing (Double Edition), February 2005
10 9 8 7 6 5 4 3 2 1

Elizabeth's Rake copyright © Doris Emily Hendrickson, 1993
Cupid's Mistake copyright © Karen Eriksen Harbaugh, 1997
All rights reserved

 REGISTERED TRADEMARK—MARCA REGISTRADA

Printed in the United States of America

ELIZABETH'S RAKE

To my dear Kirsten,
the finest assistant a writer could desire.

1

"I MET THE most divine gentlemen while at Emma Fenwick's for tea," Hyacinthe cooed, trailing her soft woolen scarf of peacock blue paisley behind her as she drifted across the room of her aunt's country home.

The small morning room at Montmorcy Hall was a favorite gathering place for Lady Montmorcy, her daughter Chloe, and two nieces who lived with her, cousins Elizabeth Dancy and Hyacinthe Dancy. They were daughters of her two brothers, and while quite unlike, she considered them charming additions to the household.

This February day proved no different. Outside, a strong breeze swept the Surrey countryside, and it looked to rain before long. Inside, a cozy fire warmed the air and cheered the eye.

Elizabeth Dancy gave her cousin an impatient glance from troubled blue-green eyes before returning to the difficult execution of a winter scene on the copper plate before her. "Lovely," she murmured, quite accustomed to Hyacinthe's transports of fancy after several months of her company. How Aunt Bel tolerated it was a mystery to Elizabeth.

"Well, and you ought to have been there." Hyacinthe preened before the mirror above the fireplace before making her next announcement.

Knowing what was expected of her, Elizabeth dutifully asked, "Why?"

"Well . . . the Marquess of Norwood, for one. And"—Hyacinthe darted a complacent look at her favorite cousin—"the Viscount Leighton as well."

The immediate stiffening of Elizabeth's spine gave the only clue of her reaction to this news. Drat and double drat, she fumed silently. She had escaped from London hoping never to see the man again. And here he popped up almost on her aunt's doorstep. She had avoided his calls, claiming the headache. What would the rake want with her, anyway? Their friendship in London had not flourished.

Fixing her dear cousin with the blandest of looks, Elizabeth said mildly, "How nice." She hoped her clenched jaw allowed her to be understood.

"Nice! That is all you can say to having two of Society's most desirable bachelors practically under our noses?" Hyacinthe ceased her posing and dropped into a chair close to where Elizabeth worked at her engraving.

"I am not interested, at least not in those gentlemen," Elizabeth said quietly. "You may have both of them with my blessing. I do not care for rakes," she added, thinking of Lord Leighton, "nor do I long for a title. A simple life in the country is all I desire." And, she added to herself, a man who does not stir up such scandalous yearnings within.

"Oh, mercy," Hyacinthe said in disgust. She looked at her dearest Aunt Bel for support, and received a cautioning nod.

Isobel, Lady Montmorcy, widow of the esteemed Marquess of Montmorcy, had welcomed her nieces into her Surrey home to keep her daughter company. Not yet out, Lady Chloe Maitland ached to rush to London to make her come-out and find a husband, not necessarily in that order. Lady Montmorcy hoped that her nieces would provide distraction.

"I think it is marvelous!" Chloe breathed, her eyes wide with the excitement which might be expected in a seventeen-year-old girl.

"They will scarcely bestow a look on a girl barely out of the schoolroom," Hyacinthe said in deprecating accents.

Elizabeth tossed her younger cousin a sympathetic glance, then added, "You would not wish to be thought *coming*, Chloe. I know you are impatient, but your time will arrive, and you had best savor every day, not wish it gone." Elizabeth spoke with the wisdom that comes with being nineteen and having a Season behind one.

"True," added Lady Montmorcy, looking thankful that her nieces were the ones to pour cold water on the impetuous Chloe's auburn head, and not herself.

"Elizabeth has had a Season, and she did not accept anyone. I do not see how you could pass up several proposals," Chloe said, giving her cousin a reproachful stare.

"I knew we should not suit." Elizabeth glanced up, then resumed her work with a somewhat faster heartbeat. How could she have accepted anyone when she nurtured a highly improper *tendre* for the most shocking rake in all of London?

"Well, I shall find someone, I can assure you of that," Chloe declared in ringing accents. "I have no wish to dwindle into a thornback." Then, giving Elizabeth a stricken look, she added, "Not that you fall into that group, for you are too young and beautiful. It will be years before you are past praying for." That these words were scarcely better was brought home to her by the frosty glare from her mama. It wouldn't do to be thought an old maid when one was nineteen.

"You met Viscount Leighton before, Elizabeth, didn't you?" Hyacinthe said. "I recall that he served as groomsman at Victoria's wedding. Since you were also an attendant, I fancy you first met him then? Or perhaps at one of those many parties you attended?"

"I cannot understand why you did not come to London yourself," Elizabeth said, hoping to change the subject.

"I detest the city. The air is injurious to the health and the atmosphere not to my liking. I far prefer life in the country." Hyacinthe tilted her pert nose a trifle, while staring off into the distance.

"Where she could be a queen bee," Chloe added, giggling at the scowl directed at her from her mother.

Ignoring her teasing, Hyacinthe returned to her original topic—the gentleman from London.

"But you did meet Lord Leighton? Did it have something to do with the daring deeds Victoria performed?"

"Yes," Elizabeth admitted.

Chloe frowned. "You have said nothing about it. Explain, if you please. I hate not knowing things."

"Victoria served as a government spy while doing her

sculpting," Elizabeth revealed. "That is how she met Sir Edward. I fear I did no more than engrave banknotes for our spies to use in foreign countries. Only Julia did not join us. We all learned a bit about codes and ciphers, spy work in general. It is not as exciting as one might think."

"I have a feeling there was a great more involved," Hyacinthe murmured, directing a curious look at her mild-mannered cousin.

"I believe we ought to invite both of the gentlemen to the Valentine's Day ball you are to give, Aunt Bel," Hyacinthe coaxed with demure propriety. " 'Tis my understanding that while Lord Norwood is but visiting in this area, Lord Leighton is a resident."

"He is the son of the Earl of Crompton," Lady Montmorcy said with a hint of curiosity in her voice. "But he has not frequented his father's company for some time. Once a young man has a taste of London, he is seldom found languishing about the family estate . . . unless he has come to grief. Elizabeth?"

"If the gossips are to be believed, he is the worst rake in London, ma'am."

"A rake!" Hyacinthe uttered in ringing tones of horror and fascination.

"I wonder what has brought him home, then." Lady Montmorcy gave Elizabeth an expectant look, like an inquisitive robin listening for the sound of a meal.

"It was my impression that his father is ill, ma'am."

"Ill? Oh, I do hope not." Lady Montmorcy subsided into solemn reflection that lasted some moments.

Elizabeth wondered at the wistful smile that lingered on her aunt's face, but said nothing, pleased to have the attention turned elsewhere.

"Well, perhaps he will not attend, but would it not be proper to send invitations to them both?" Hyacinthe queried in dulcet tones that fooled only her aunt, who thought her the epitome of propriety and grace.

"I doubt they would wish to join in anything so terribly countrified," Elizabeth said in an offhand manner, as though it mattered not the least to her if the dashing beaux from London crossed the Montmorcy threshold to attend the annual Valentine Day's ball.

She had purposely avoided Lord Leighton from the

moment she had glimpsed his tall, handsome figure on the main street of the nearby town. Recalling he had left London to visit his father, she prayed that august gentleman had recovered, and that Lord Leighton was merely pausing nearby. It had meant some skillful dodging, paying a call or two she'd not intended, and shopping for things she'd not the least notion of buying as a means of evasion.

At last she decided to remain at home. It had not been easy. And now, to have him right in the house? At the ball? She knew her aunt and all the wild superstitions she believed. What did she think happened on Valentine's Day? Elizabeth knew enough to be extremely wary.

"Do as you wish, of course," she offered quietly. Then, deciding she had best be prepared, she continued, "What traditions do you hold for that day, Aunt Bel?"

"Oh, there are a number of delicious beliefs, my dear. Let me see . . . well, there is the matter of the first man you see on that day. The custom varies, but *I* believe that the very first man an unwed girl sees on that day will be her husband."

"I thought him merely to be her valentine for that day," Elizabeth objected in what she hoped was a reasonable manner.

"No, no," Aunt Bel denied firmly. "I have seen it work many times, although not for Chloe, but she is too young as yet." She gave her precious girl a fond look.

Hyacinthe sat up with a calculating expression on her face, but erased it when she caught Elizabeth watching her.

"I believe I shall remain in bed the entire day, if that is the case," Elizabeth said at last, giving up on guessing what might be going on in Hyacinthe's mind.

"I shan't," Hyacinthe said firmly. "I shall address the invitations right now, and hope they will not be offended at the lateness. The ball is almost upon us, and I think they ought to see that there are acceptable entertainments to be had in the country as well as in London."

Elizabeth repressed a sigh and bent to her work. It was a foolish dream for Hyacinthe to fancy they might compete with a London hostess, not to mention the extraordinary diversions found in the city. Elizabeth had missed

Lady Tichbourne's *conversaziones* and the other gay amusements she had known in London. But, she reminded herself, her expulsion from that mad whirl was voluntary. She had fled—for Lord Leighton had merely teased her when Elizabeth wanted something else entirely.

With Victoria on her way home from her wedding trip, and Julia at Viscount Temple's country estate, Aunt Bel's home proved just the right sort of haven. Or had.

Elizabeth could execute her engravings while deep in the country as well as in the heart of the city. The commission from Mr. Ackermann for a series on country life was a godsend. It gave her an excuse for doing something she enjoyed, and permitted her to refrain from going about with her cousins if she chose. Memory of Lord Leighton's stolen kisses had haunted many a night's sleep. The wretched man most likely had forgotten all about them. Not so Elizabeth.

"Is that a skating scene, Elizabeth?" Chloe said, frowning over Elizabeth's shoulder at the lines being cut into the copper sheet. "I do hope we can go skating this winter. Last winter was too mild. But if the cold weather continues, we just might."

"I think it would be lovely if we could have a skating party in that event," Hyacinthe said, folding her hands properly in her lap as she bestowed a demure look on her aunt.

"I suppose so," Aunt Bel said without a great deal of conviction.

"Is everything ready for the ball? What decorations do you plan this year, Aunt?" Elizabeth prompted, again hoping to change the subject.

"Nothing terribly unusual, I fear. I have had the footmen set up the cupids in the ballroom, and Hyacinthe and Chloe are nearly finished with the satin hearts. There will be flowers from the greenhouse, and the cook is making a confectionery heart from spun sugar."

"Ordinary, indeed. I vow it will look splendid. I'll have you know that the white and red satin hearts are quite exceptional," Chloe declared stoutly.

"I feel certain it will be the best yet," Hyacinthe added, throwing a significant look at Elizabeth.

Not misunderstanding the matter in the least, Elizabeth responded, "You know an invitation to your Valentine's Day ball is eagerly sought by everyone who is anyone, Aunt Bel. I venture to say this one will top them all."

"If only people are not too tardy," her aunt replied, taking note of the time on her locket watch. "I do not approve of this Town fashion, arriving late to functions." She rose, glanced at Chloe, then said, "I had best confer with Cook again," and marched out of the room with a militant expression on her face.

"I vow, Chloe, even if she is your mother, there are times when Aunt Bel positively gives me the shivers," Hyacinthe declared.

"I think we ought to write down a list of all her superstitions so we shall be prepared," Elizabeth said. "Chloe, my love, be an angel and find a paper and pen. You ought to know them nearly as well as your mother, and I would be aware of what to expect." Elizabeth fixed a compelling gaze on her cousin, who obediently rose to do as bidden.

"Pansies and verbena she believes to be love potions," Chloe began.

"Thank heaven it is February," Elizabeth declared.

"Well, you already know about the first man you see being your future husband. Are you really going to remain in your room, Elizabeth?" Hyacinthe said with an appraising gaze.

"Perhaps," Elizabeth replied in a noncommittal tone.

"When is your birthday?" Chloe inquired, while drawing little hearts around the edge of the paper.

"Mine comes in April, while Hyacinthe's is in March. Why?" Elizabeth knew that her aunt believed all sorts of things, and one could be entertained for hours listening to her ramble on. She appeared to believe in every one of her collection of superstitions.

"Mama says April has a precious stone, the diamond, which stands for innocence. March has a bloodstone, which means courage and presence of mind. I should say that fits Hyacinthe admirably. I have yet to meet anyone with more presence of mind."

"Chloe," the redheaded Hyacinthe cautioned. "That is nonsense, no matter how pretty it sounds. What else?"

"Mama says that two lovers can find out if they will suit by going out at night and picking a flower. If the stem is straight and smooth, their lives will be like that. But if the flower is crooked or spoiled, take caution." Chloe's eyes twinkled with delight. "And she also says that if you eat a piece of bride's cake before you go to sleep, you will see a vision of your future husband."

Hyacinthe and Elizabeth exchanged guarded looks. Elizabeth tried hard not to laugh; Hyacinthe appeared to reflect on the subject.

"Did you know that if you put a clover leaf in your right shoe, the first man you meet will be your love? Or at the very least someone who has that name," Chloe continued, aware that her cousins did not agree with their aunt's little notions. "Of course, you might recite a special verse first. It goes—"

"Spare us, Chloe. Since it is mid-winter, 'tis unlikely we shall find a clover leaf. And we have other things to concern us." Hyacinthe ruthlessly stopped Chloe with her words, and the younger girl subsided warily.

"Well, Mama may follow tradition and have each person draw names as they enter the ballroom, the girls to be paired with the young man whose name she's drawn."

"I think that might be horrid," Hyacinthe observed.

"Not if your valentine presents you with a lovely gift, as is custom here," Chloe replied. "Last year Mama received some very pretty gloves from her valentine, Mr. Smithers. He also sent her a very lovely valentine, embossed on paper from Dobbs, and very gallant it was, too. Although it was folded like a letter, it had hearts and cupids with love knots on it. I fancy I should like one like that, for it is superior to homemade ones, do you not think?"

"It is the message and intent that is most important, I suppose," Hyacinthe murmured.

"The homemade ones require talent as well," Elizabeth added. Relieved to find no other superstitions associated with Valentine's Day, she was only too willing to put aside her nearly finished engraving and join in completing the plans for the ball.

"Is it agreed that we shall extend invitations to Lord Norwood and Lord Leighton? Aunt Bel will be in alt if they accept, and surely they must, for anyone can tell them that her ball is most delightful." Hyacinthe cast a cautious glance at Elizabeth before proceeding to address two invitations in her flowing copperplate. "I shall send one of the footmen with these."

"You sound as though you will take no chances," Elizabeth joked.

"Indeed," Hyacinthe murmured as she gathered up a few papers with notes for the party before leaving the room. She paused at the door. "Is Norwood a rake as well?"

"I suspect he is." Weren't they all? Elizabeth could only hope that the illness that had affected Lord Crompton and had brought Lord Leighton on the run was serious enough to keep the young rake from attending the ball.

Excitement ran high the following day when formal acceptances were received from both gentlemen.

Aunt Bel studied Elizabeth before offering her thoughts. "I believe we shall have the cream of parties, my dears. There is not a mother around who will fail to see that her children attend. The young ladies should hope to catch the eye of the titled gentlemen, the young men would strive to learn the manners of a London beau."

"Even if he is a rake?" Elizabeth kept her eyes on her plate, pushing around the buttered eggs that had appealed to her a short time before.

"A titled, wealthy rake is always forgiven. Besides, everyone knows that a reformed rake makes the best husband," Aunt Bel said complacently.

"Another of your beliefs?" Elizabeth nudged her plate away, concentrating on the scrap of toast in her hand.

"I have seen it happen more than once." Lady Montmorcy finished the last of her chocolate, then consulted the locket watch she always wore. "Time to attend to the acceptances. I suspect others will quickly learn of our important guests. Word does spread. Not that our little affair would not be well attended all the same. I like to think the ball relieves the tedium of February. I only hope it does not snow.'' This last remark was said with a worried glance out of the window.

Elizabeth rose from the table to walk to the windows. Outside the gray skies did not hold the promise of fair weather. "It may wait, or possibly it will rain, and I doubt that will be any more welcome. The roads are bad enough as they are.''

"Are London streets better? Neatly cobbled and even?'' Chloe demanded to know.

"Cobbled, yes. Better? No. They smell, and are anything but even. One endures what one must, I expect.''

"How can you like the spring in London if it smells?''

"It is the company, love, not the condition of the streets,'' Elizabeth said, then chuckled as she recalled the many times she and Victoria had dashed madly about London while using their individual talents for the government. Did she miss the excitement, the daring subterfuge? She wasn't sure. She had welcomed the quiet haven at Aunt Bel's, but now sensed all was due to change.

She expressed as much to Hyacinthe when they went up to bed the evening before the ball.

"It is far and away the silliest thing I have ever heard,'' Hyacinthe scolded in her pretty manner.

"I cannot help it,'' Elizabeth replied slowly. "I have this feeling, a sensation of complete reordering.''

"Well, I am going to put up my hair in papers and retire for the night. I rather envy those chestnut curls of yours. You do not have to sleep with little knobs all over your head beneath a nightcap. Do you know that I have the prettiest collection of nightcaps? Mine are all embroidered and trimmed in lovely lace.''

Near Elizabeth's door they were confronted by the sight of Aunt Bel directing several maids. They were carrying Elizabeth's clothes from the green room, where she had been residing. Hyacinthe's maid was carefully transporting all of her belongings across the hall to the green room.

"What is this, Aunt Bel?'' Elizabeth demanded.

"I have decided that the pink room is to be yours, Elizabeth. The green one is more for Hyacinthe. Her unfortunate coloring, you see.''

"I see nothing unfortunate about lovely red hair and

beautiful white skin, even if she does have a freckle or two," Chloe stated in ringing terms as she joined the others.

"You do like pink, even if you wear aquamarine most of the time?" Aunt Bel said with an anxious look at Elizabeth now that the deed was done.

"Of course, Aunt, it will be fine, as long as Hyacinthe does not mind," Elizabeth said, trying to soothe her aunt.

"I had this vision, you see. It clearly told me to switch you girls." Aunt Bel stared off into space a moment before returning her attention to the maids.

"Who are we to argue with a vision?" Hyacinthe said with rare good humor.

Elizabeth suspected that as long as Hyacinthe's clothes were in order, and the bed comfortable, she really did not mind. "I fancy you will like the green room, Hyacinthe. The view is ever so pretty and the sun warms you in the morning."

Aware it would not be proper to make a fuss, Hyacinthe smiled and strolled into her new room.

Elizabeth watched until the door closed, then turned to her aunt. "Is that the real reason for the change? Not that I mind, for 'tis a lovely room. But it has been hers all these months."

"She misses her parents, it will keep her mind occupied."

"They have been gone over a year now, she is out of mourning. I suspect the advent of two qualified London beaux will more than keep her busy."

"She is exceedingly proper, and is not given to the ruses taken by other young ladies," Aunt Bel assured.

Elizabeth wondered how her aunt could be so blind, then shrugged off the feeling that Hyacinthe was being catered to while she, who'd lost her parents many years before, was not.

Actually, the pink peony room, as Aunt Bel delighted to call it, was more to Elizabeth's taste than the green jade room. Around her, the walls bloomed with luscious peonies amid oriental traceries of leaves and vines. The bed hangings were a deep peony pink that ought to have clashed with her hair but didn't. On the floor, a thick carpet with the same colors woven into peonies on a pale cream background looked lush and inviting.

The wardrobe doors stood open, revealing the rows of gowns in the aquamarine Elizabeth favored. The color matched her eyes, she'd been told often enough, and it was one of her few points of vanity. The aquamarine was also reflected in touches here and there about the room, much better than the conflicting jade.

The tap on her door some minutes later was not totally unexpected.

Hyacinthe stuck her head around the door, then slipped inside. "What do you make of this exchange?" She spread her arms out to encompass the room.

"One of Aunt's little oddities. I trust it does not upset you?" Elizabeth eyed her cousin with a few misgivings. Hyacinthe might not throw tantrums, but she could make life very unpleasant if she decided to be annoyed.

"Mercy, no. But it is strange. One never knows what Aunt Bel will do or say next." Hyacinthe prudently seated herself on a slipper chair of rich peony velvet.

"Which makes for a life that is never dull, at any rate." Elizabeth chuckled at the grimace that crossed her cousin's face.

"I know you were teasing when you said you intended to remain in bed all day tomorrow. But really, you do not fear that Aunt Bel truly believes in that nonsense?" Hyacinthe leaned forward, studying her cousin's expression intently.

"I believe she does, but what she might do at the ball, I cannot say. She is not predictable," Elizabeth concluded in a great understatement of the matter.

"I have noticed that you have behaved a bit peculiarly these past weeks. Even before I noticed that Lords Leighton and Norwood were in the vicinity." Hyacinthe studied the toe of her embroidered slipper, assuming a very nonchalant mien.

"I'll admit I was taken aback to discover Lord Leighton was in this area," Elizabeth confessed.

"Do I detect a romance?" said the ever romantic Hyacinthe, perking up to watch her cousin as she brushed her curls, preparing for the night.

"That is absolutely the most utter nonsense! He treated

me more like a sister. Lord Leighton is a monstrous tease. What a pity he did not have a string of siblings upon whom to vent his inclination—not that they would have enjoyed it any more than I did," she concluded acidly.

"You do not like him?"

"I loathe the man," Elizabeth declared, although quietly, and with less conviction than she ought.

"Fascinating."

"Do not tell me that hate is akin to love, for I'll not listen. Julia reminded me of that before I left London."

"Your sister is most likely right, having been married and all. Marriage makes a woman a woman, or so my mother always said," Hyacinthe murmured wistfully.

"Go to bed, Hyacinthe. I am worn to flinders what with the preparations for the ball. I should think you would be, too." Elizabeth made shooing motions with her hands, but wore an affectionate look on her face that belied any cross feelings.

"I shall see you in the morning. Be careful who you meet after midnight!" Hyacinthe giggled and fled to her room.

Alone, Elizabeth felt free to indulge in singing a little tune. As customary, she tucked her pistol beneath her pillow, something she had done for the past few years. A life in London that had been filled with spies and daring deeds had prompted her to keep the gun handy. Even though all that was behind her, old habits died hard.

She crossed to open the French window a crack, inhaling the crisp, cold air with relish. The windows led to a charming balcony. At least it likely seemed such in the summer, when the wisteria bloomed. There was no one out there now to hear her, for she was a dreadful singer, having what her family tolerantly referred to as a tin ear.

The melody was one she loved, and wished she could have done justice to, but alas, she couldn't. So she sang and hummed in the privacy of her room.

A glance in the looking glass told her that her nightgown draped quite nicely about her in sheer cambric folds, its tiny bodice covered in exquisite embroidery. Over her head she pulled a dainty nightcap of lace and

cambric, tying the ribbons neatly under her chin before
crawling beneath the covers.

She had barely drifted into a good sleep when she heard
it. A noise.

Suddenly alert, she stealthily sought the gun beneath
her pillow. Her fingers groped for the not-so-very-small
firearm. A crack shot, she knew how to handle the
weapon once she had it balanced in her hand.

She waited, scarcely daring to breathe.

Another sound, a scraping noise that one might make
while floundering about in the dark.

Elizabeth took aim at that noise, then cautiously waited
to see if the intruder would identify him or herself.

Silence. Then another soft bump and a muttered curse.

Elizabeth was correct. Danger lurked, even in the heart
of the country. She wavered in her resolve, reluctant to
shoot yet fearful of what might befall her if she called
for help. The intruder might attack her before help could
come! She had never thought to actually shoot *at* someone, only fixed targets, tame round objects stuffed with
straw. Too terrified to cry out a challenge, she knew she
must defend herself the best she could.

Taking a careful breath, she squeezed the trigger,
knowing she had but one chance to hit her target. A muffled cry told her that her shot had struck its quarry. Another sound prompted her to believe the person had fallen
to the floor. With trembling fingers she placed the gun
on the table, lit her bedside lamp, then slid from beneath
the covers.

It was then she discovered the identity of her victim.
"Lord Leighton! Oh, jiminy!"

Elizabeth dropped to the floor, heedless of the impropriety of her dress or her isolation with the man she'd
assiduously avoided. Blood seeped from the wound on his
arm, and he looked to be in frightful pain. "Confound
it," she murmured as she rolled his lordship over to better examine the damage. What a pickle!

"All I wanted was a chance to talk with you," Leighton protested, his words slurred, to the apparition in
snowy white who hovered over him like an angel of
mercy. She missed the appreciative gleam that sparkled

in his eyes as he viewed the sheer cambric-veiled figure of the well-endowed Miss Dancy.

"You might have presented yourself in the drawing room, sirrah," Elizabeth snapped, albeit quietly. She could scarcely miss the alcoholic fumes that emanated from his lordship. The man was foxed!

"And be informed you were not at home? You have avoided me at every turn." He winced when she tugged the sleeve of his coat, pulling it from him with none-too-gentle jerks. "That hurts," he complained.

"And so it should. You have been shot," she reminded him, quite unpitying in her care. "And you are most improper, creeping like this into the bedroom of a young woman."

Then she remembered that this room had belonged to Hyacinthe until this evening. Her heart felt crushed as she considered the implications of that, even as she sought a pad with which to stanch his bleeding.

The door flew open and her aunt charged into the room, a poker in hand, her dressing gown flying about her. At the scene before her, she halted abruptly. "What's this?"

"It was an accident, ma'am," Elizabeth said, trying to figure out how she and Lord Leighton might extricate themselves from what she was rapidly coming to see might be a very tricky situation.

Her aunt consulted the mantel clock. "After midnight!'Tis Valentine's Day! You have just shot your future husband, my dear girl!''

2

Pandemonium broke loose.

A wide-eyed Chloe peeped around the door, Hyacinthe right behind her, both arrayed in voluminous white nightrobes with dainty caps tied neatly under their chins.

They were quickly followed by Gibbons, Aunt Bel's odd butler, clad in an awesome plaid flannel robe of generous proportions, and the first footman, James, attired in a hastily donned shirt and breeches. The latter two properly kept their curiosity under control.

Elizabeth threw Gibbons a wild glance, wondering if he would rise to the occasion. "Do find a doctor, or at the very least someone who knows more about medicine than I do."

"Here, here," murmured the injured Leighton. He shifted his position and placed his head on Elizabeth's lap. When she sent him a startled look, the one she received in return was limpid with innocence. "I am in great pain," he added sadly, then winced as she moved.

Elizabeth spared him a dark glance that told what she thought about his uttering a word one way or the other.

Before the plump, absentminded Gibbons could act, he was thrust aside by Purvis, Aunt Bel's formidable abigail. Her flowered chintz robe wound snugly about her spare frame, tied in place with a no-nonsense belt, and a lone braid of an odd shade of gray hung over one shoulder. Her nightcap was a prim muslin, with the barest frill, and tied precisely beneath her chin. She carried a neat basket from which she began to extract various dreadful-looking objects.

"All of you, out!" she declared in a brisk voice, seeming pleased to be in command. She placed a restraining hand on Elizabeth's arm, adding, "Except you. You have sense." From Purvis, that was high praise.

The onlookers, disappointed that they had to wait for explanations, drifted away from the scene to confer in soft accents down the hall.

Feeling sorry for Lord Leighton, even if he had entered her room in a havey-cavey manner, Elizabeth deftly eased him from her lap, ignoring the look of reproach he bestowed on her. She tucked a pillow beneath his head, wondering aloud, "Would it not be better to place him on the bed?"

Purvis surveyed that piece of furniture, then nodded. "He ought to be able to manage that distance, surely."

The patient made an inarticulate sound that both women ignored.

"Up with you," Purvis said to the unfortunate fellow, then firmly guided him to the bed with Elizabeth on his other side.

His right arm curved around her slim shoulders and pulled Elizabeth extremely close to his side. She considered giving him a sharp set-down, then chided herself for that unkind thought. The poor man could scarcely behave in an unseemly manner when he was in such pain, much less have amorous notions. As though to emphasize this, he groaned when Purvis nudged him against the edge of the bed. Elizabeth felt his body slump against her as Purvis threw back the covers. Those strange stirrings deep within her began to flicker again, and she ruthlessly thrust them aside, wondering how on earth she could feel like this at such a moment.

Instead she slipped her arms about him to offer support, pressing her slim body against his side to keep him from toppling over. To compensate for shooting the man, she tenderly helped him stretch out, noting how tall he was, how broad were his shoulders with his coat tossed aside. No padding needed in his coats.

With a speaking glance, Purvis thrust a robe into Elizabeth's hands. Impatiently she donned it, then returned to her duties.

Tucking her very own down pillow under his head, she then assisted Purvis in cutting away the left sleeve of his shirt, firmly nudging away any reactions to all that bare flesh. A young lady was rarely exposed to naked limbs.

With surprising skill Purvis set about examining the wound. She barked out an order for brandy, insisting Lord Leighton needed it. Elizabeth went to fetch it, glad to be away from the sight of all that blood for a moment. Wonder of wonders, James stood outside the door with a decanter of the late Lord Montmorcy's best on a tray. It took but moments to pour a glass for Lord Leighton, not that she felt he needed one.

Leighton drank deeply, then gave Purvis a grin. "Do your best," he said, his voice oddly faint to Elizabeth's ears, which made her feel even more wretched. She averted her eyes from the sight of Purvis cleaning the wound.

In the twinkling of a bedpost, Purvis completed her examination. Her self-satisfied grunt brought Elizabeth's gaze back to her. As though in response to an unasked question, Purvis glanced up to meet her eyes. "My previous mistress had a husband who liked to duel."

Elizabeth considered that statement in silence, assisting Purvis with what she required, while avoiding the sight of his injury. Taking the water pitcher from the dresser, she poured some of the cool liquid into a bowl. Then soft cloths, jars, and bottles were extracted from the depths of the basket, to be used and replaced in order.

When Elizabeth risked a glance at their patient, she met his eyes. His low moan of pain tore at her heart and she looked away.

The sight of all the bloody water and the stained cloths turned Elizabeth's stomach, and she felt utterly miserable. When he looked at her, she could have wept with vexation, for his gaze held no reproach, only appeal.

At last, Elizabeth surveyed the bandaged man who occupied her bed. That dark hair flopped in a frightfully endearing manner over his pale brow. She succumbed to the temptation to brush it off his forehead. To her consternation, she found her eyes caught in his steady gaze.

"I am sorry, sir. Never mind that you did ask for trouble, entering the house like that." She folded up the last of the bloodied cloths, placing it atop the stack.

Purvis gave a snort, adding, "Young men will do strange things around St. Valentine's Day, won't they?" She tidied the table and bed, then surveyed her patient.

"I doubt that had a thing to do with this nocturnal call, however," Elizabeth said in reply. Worry flooded her being as she continued to look at the silent man on her bed. "I shall sit up with him for what remains of the night. After all, it is my fault he is wounded." Her eyes added the rider that he would not be in her bed if he had gone about the call in a proper manner.

Aunt Bel materialized at her side, studying Lord Leighton with shrewd eyes. "I believe that would be permissible. You are betrothed as far as I am concerned." To his lordship she added, "You have fulfilled my vision, sir, but you might had arrived at a more proper hour."

She motioned James to her side, then watched as he removed Leighton's boots and settled the man more comfortably. Ignoring Elizabeth's sputtering, Lady Montmorcy organized the room, seeing that her niece had all she needed, then retired.

Once alone, Elizabeth met Lord Leighton's drowsy gaze with trepidation. Swallowing with care, she said, "We are not, you know. She fancies the notion tonight." She spared a glance at the mantel clock, then continued, "I shall convince her later that it is all a hum."

She paused by the side of the bed and admonished him, "What an exceedingly foolish thing to do, to be sure."

"It seemed like a good idea at the time. After all, Romeo tried it," he murmured groggily. "Didn't expect a gun."

"What with all that went on while I was in London, with those intruders, I find I have peace of mind with it under my pillow."

"I see."

"Besides, *I* was not the person you intended to see this night," Elizabeth observed primly, annoyed at the feeling of ill-usage that grew within her.

"And who did I plan to see?" he inquired.

"This was Hyacinthe's room until this evening. She is the woman you aimed to call upon."

"Rubbish." He stirred, then groaned. His sigh and

look of reproach brought Elizabeth to his side with a cloth wrung out in cool water. She gently wiped his brow, then offered him a drink of water.

"Hush, now. We can discuss this in the morning. You are in no condition to make sense of anything at the moment."

She watched with a kind of satisfaction as the potion Purvis had given Lord Leighton took effect. Those absurdly long lashes drifted down over ashen cheeks, and in minutes he slept.

Three of the clock, and bitterly cold out. She wrapped the robe Purvis had fetched her more tightly about her, then strolled to the fireplace. She placed another scoop of coal on the fire, stirring the blaze absently. The flames leaped higher, and she relished the warmth. The French windows were now shut tightly, and shut they would remain. She wanted no chill to injure his lordship.

Turning, she studied the man in her bed. He looked different now as he slept beneath the prim white covers. Innocent. Vulnerable. Odd, she had never associated those words with the rake she considered him to be. While in London he had teased her unmercifully, or at least, she amended in all fairness, he had teased her with the good-natured toleration of an older brother.

He had driven her quite mad with all those taunting glances, the words meant to mock her. And as for those kisses he had stolen while at the Fenwick's ball, well!

And now he sought her dear cousin, Hyacinthe. Regardless of his protests, she knew better. He must have bribed one of the maids to reveal the location of her cousin's room. Hyacinthe, with her glorious red hair and green eyes and flawless skin—but for two or three freckles that only added to her appeal.

What would happen later this day at the ball? Elizabeth wondered suddenly. She could scarcely attend, with a wounded man in her bedroom, a man *she* had injured. If word of this reached the local society, tongues would flap like a flag in a stiff breeze. At least her sister Victoria was still abroad and Julia off in the country.

What her brother Geoffrey might say didn't matter. As far as she knew, he still remained on the continent with Wellington. Her thoughts turned to where he served.

Elizabeth doubted for a minute that the peace negotiations with Napoleon at Châtillon would prove fruitful. She didn't trust the Corsican one bit, and hoped those who dealt with his generals didn't either. But Lord Castlereigh was no fool, and likely to see through any ruse the French might think up.

As to the rumors abounding that Napoleon was dead, Elizabeth doubted those as well. It would be too convenient for so evil a man to simply die just like that.

Leighton stirred, and Elizabeth immediately forgot her gloomy contemplations to check on him. He was slightly warm, but not alarmingly so. She wrung out the cloth and set to cooling his brow.

And so the hours passed with Elizabeth soothing his brow, keeping close watch over her rake.

When Purvis briskly entered the room to inspect her patient, she gave Elizabeth a grim smile of approval. "I told her ladyship you'd do just fine as a nurse, and so you did. You've learned well. She has decided he must be moved across the hall to the blue room. James is coming up, and we shall effect the transfer shortly."

A dismayed Elizabeth gave Lord Leighton a concerned look, wondering how he would stand such a move.

"It is not seemly that he be here in what is, after all, your room. The other is ready for him. Ah, here is James now." Purvis turned to greet him, giving softly voiced instructions that apparently met with his approval.

When Elizabeth glanced at the figure on her bed again, she met his bemused gaze with a fluttering heartbeat. Those eyes had such power to disturb her, even when he was half asleep. Aware he had needs that could not be cared for by herself, she greeted the news that his valet would be sent for with great relief.

"Until he arrives, James will stand as attendant for his lordship," Purvis declared.

With that bit of information, Lord Leighton was eased from the bed and assisted out of Elizabeth's bedroom and across the hall. It was not far, but she could see he leaned heavily against James as they shuffled to the blue room. How odd that such a small wound should be so utterly debilitating.

The door closed behind the men, and Elizabeth stood

uncertainly in her doorway, feeling somewhat foolish to be seen staring at the slab of wood, yet unable to move.

The rustle of skirts roused her from her abstraction. Chloe and Hyacinthe descended upon her with soft exclamations of concern, and unconcealed curiosity.

Determined to keep the matter as unromantic as she could, Elizabeth said, "It was all a hum, you know. I believe I mentioned he is the greatest tease in all of London. I daresay this prank will cause him to think before he tries such again." Elizabeth strolled back into her bedroom, glancing longingly at her pillow, wishing she might crawl beneath the covers and sleep for a week.

"A prank?" Hyacinthe said, looking puzzled. "He strikes me as being past that sort of thing. I cannot agree."

"Nor I," added Chloe, a dreamy expression on her sweet face. "It is far too romantic, the handsome nobleman who climbs the vines to see his true love." Her dramatic sigh caused Elizabeth to seethe. "And just to speak with you?"

"It is not romantic in the least. Oh, he is the most vexing creature alive!" Her eyes sparkled with indignation and something else neither of her cousins seemed to identify.

"Dear Elizabeth," cried Chloe, much affected by the thrilling event which had occurred in her dull life, "you are worn to flinders, and we stand here nattering on like a tea party. Forgive us, do."

Hyacinthe also recognized that her cousin needed sleep more than a coze and returned to the door. "We can discuss this later. I should like to know what it was like to nurse such a handsome man through the night."

That was precisely what Elizabeth wished to avoid until she had consulted her aunt, and possibly talked the problem over with the invalid in the room across the hall. She crawled beneath the covers of her bed, inhaling the oddly comforting scent of brandy and sandalwood that remained from the previous occupant.

Some hours later, feeling refreshed and well rested after her sleep, Elizabeth dressed herself in a warm gown of an unusual berry red color. Draping a cream wool shawl over her shoulders, she peered around her door; then seeing not a soul around, she ventured into the hall. Tiptoing to the door of the blue room, she paused, listening.

Not a sound.

Depressing the door lever, she peeked inside to see his lordship propped up against several pillows. The snowy sheet was tucked neatly about him. He was now dressed in a proper nightshirt. And he looked bored to death.

"Come in," he whispered. "I trust you have satisfied yourself that I still live, no thanks to you."

"Good morning." She noted his wince and recalled the brandy, not to mention the pungent odor he had brought with him. Bristling with irritation, she thrust the door open wider, leaving it ajar, then stepped closer to him.

The blue silk hangings on the walls matched those draped over the bed. The carpet was a dull mixture of blues and tans, and added to the masculine appearance of the room. All this she ignored, concentrating on the man.

"You know full well that if you'd not had the hare-brained notion to call upon Hyacinthe in the middle of the night, we should not be in this pickle now." There. It was out in the open. She waited to see what he would say in his defense.

His stare was quite disconcerting, she decided after a few moments had passed. "Well, have you nothing to say for yourself?"

"I have a better understanding of what a fellow who has been tried and judged before opening his mouth must feel like. You have it all wrong, you know," he said softly.

"Until last night, Hyacinthe occupied what is now my room. Aunt Bel had a vision, you see, and decided we must change rooms," Elizabeth added by way of explanation, although why it was needed, she wasn't sure. "Your informant could have no way of knowing of that change, surely?"

"I had no informant, other than the knowledge that you resided with your aunt in this house. You gave me the information yourself,'' he proclaimed with satisfaction.

"I have not seen you in months, sirrah.'' She had been unable to conceal a start of surprise at his words. "There is no way that you might have learned such from my lips.''

When he shifted his gaze from her eyes to her mouth, Elizabeth groped about for a chair and sank down upon it, her knees feeling oddly weak.

"I have been trying to see you for an age, it seems. I need your help.''

This pronouncement brought Elizabeth a feeling of alarm. "You *needed* to see me?''

"Indeed. And as for your location, I heard you singing in your room, and knew it could not be anyone else. I recalled your rather, ah, unique voice.'' He gave her a faint grin, and Elizabeth shifted back against the chair.

Nodding somewhat regretfully, she said, "That has the ring of truth, for I was singing before I went to bed. You ought not have been in the cold for so long. You must have waited a long time while I went to sleep.''

Her scolding brought a wider grin. "That wisteria vine is handy. I managed to climb up and down with ease. Your aunt ought to have it cut back, for it makes it far too simple for a thief to enter the house.''

"As you did,'' she reminded him.

"Quite so. Now that we have settled the matter of the not-mistaken identity or mixed-up rooms, shall I reveal why I was bound to see you?''

She gave him a judicious look. While dying to know what had prompted such drastic action on his part, she feared he would overdo, and subside into a decline. "If you are certain it will not make you tired, I should like to comprehend such outrageous behavior.''

"Not going to make this easy, are you?''

"No.'' She clasped her hands in her lap, and waited with outward patience.

"I needed someone I could trust and depend upon. You know I came here because my father was unwell. Dr. Dibble has done what he could, but . . . It's all dashed peculiar. I need your help.'' He gave her a beseeching look, glancing pointedly at his wound as though to remind her that she owed him something. "He should be improving, yet he declines."

Any romantic notions Elizabeth might have harbored sank at once. "How can I help? I am not a nurse, although Purvis has tried to train me." She frowned at him, puzzled.

"My father has always had a constitution of iron, but lately he has failed badly. I fear something havey-cavey is going on. Pretend to nurse him, but I want you to keep your eyes open. I suspect everyone, but I can trust you."

She blinked at this encomium from a man who usually teased her to death.

"I knew you had aided the government before coming here. I have not forgotten your engraving banknotes. When Edward told me I was amazed at your daring. I figured that someone who knew how to hold her tongue and had a lively curiosity would be ideal."

"Ideal for what?" Elizabeth asked warily.

"I had hoped to take you over to Penhurst Place, to see what you might uncover," he repeated patiently.

Even as he spoke, Elizabeth realized that while she had conversed with him, he had abstained from his previous mocking manner in London. Rather, he treated her more like an equal, or at least like someone who possessed a particle of sense. Yet she wavered, aware others would deem her behavior improper.

Apparently mistaking her hesitation for a refusal, Lord Leighton continued his appeal: "Could you go to the house, bring the message to my valet, and inform my family I shall be gone for a bit? At least Sidthorp, our butler." He did not explain why the butler rated such attention. "I had thought you might tell your aunt that I have need of your nursing skills. You might come with me when I return home."

He glanced at his neatly bandaged arm and added, "I ought to send Purvis along. Perhaps she could determine what ails my father. Dr. Dibble certainly is puzzled, not that Father permits him around all that much. Detests the man. Calls him a quack."

Considering his request, Elizabeth found it impossible to deny. Not only had she been bored, she did not welcome the idea of attending the Valentine's Day ball and be subjected to the inevitable gossip that must be circulating by now, given the nature of things and the way servants talked.

"I shall be glad to do as you request. At least, I shall see that your valet brings what you wish, and I will inquire after your father." She felt dreadful about shooting Leighton, and felt she ought to make amends. She rose and walked to the door, pausing there to add, "I shall also attack Aunt Bel, to explain why we simply cannot be wed. This silly superstition about marrying the first man one sees on Valentine's Day is just that—silly. I doubt if you wish it either." Not wanting to hear him agree with her, she held up a finger for silence, then went on. "You had best rest now, for you must be fearfully tired after all that explanation."

Not waiting for a reply, she left the room, unaware of the sly grin on his face, closing the door quietly behind her before swishing down the stairs in search of her aunt. One thing at a time.

She ran her to ground in the room given over to the ball. Actually, it was three rooms that opened on to one another. Sliding panels could be pushed back into slots so that the area could become one huge room, as now. It was an eminently practical arrangement, offering flexibility without the problem of having an enormous room delegated to being a mere ballroom.

"Aunt, we must talk, if you please." Elizabeth did not have high hopes of making her aunt see sense. When Aunt Bel became convinced of something, that was usually it.

"Naturally, dear girl. You wish to establish a wedding date, one that will be good for a woman born in April. May is unlucky. Best consider June. Monday for wealth, but Wednesday is the finest of all days to be married."

"No," Elizabeth cried in frustration. "Not in the least. You must see that this entire situation is impossible. You cannot force his lordship to wed me merely because he stumbled into my room after midnight."

"I could do that even if he stumbled into your room *before* midnight. 'Tis not the thing, you know." Her look of reproach brought Elizabeth to a halt. "Propriety!"

"I do not wish a forced wedding, Aunt Bel," Elizabeth replied through clenched teeth. While she might be compromised, just how many knew? Compromise be damned.

"Nonsense. You are of an age to be married; he is a handsome young man with a tidy fortune who needs a wife. What else is there to consider?"

"Why not try a different custom?" Elizabeth begged, bringing forth the one she'd gleaned from one of the maids. "Each girl may write the names of three beaux on slips of paper, wrap each in clay, then plop the clay balls in a bucket of water. The first to bob to the surface will be her valentine. It would be different," she concluded with hope in her voice.

Aunt Bel stared off into space for a time, evidently considering the custom from every angle. "Noooo, I think not. Besides, Leighton's name would likely be the one to pop up, anyway. I take these things seriously, you see."

Exasperated beyond belief, Elizabeth frowned, then replied, "I shall not marry the man, you know. Geoffrey has to give his consent, and he will listen to what I say." She actually didn't know that for a fact, since it had been a long time since she had talked with her brother. But she hoped he would pay heed to her reasoning, and have no more liking for a forced marriage than she did. If she could reach him before Aunt Bel acted.

"By the bye," Elizabeth said before she disgraced herself by losing her temper with her aunt, "Lord Leighton has requested that I check on his father, and also bring a note to his valet for certain things he wishes to have. His family needs to be told of this, and I am the most likely one to bear the news. Will that be acceptable, ma'am?"

"By all means. Be sure to take Rose with you."

Elizabeth welcomed the presence of her maid as a buffer against whatever might befall her at Penhurst Place. Although what that might be, she couldn't guess.

Leaving her aunt directing the placement of satin hearts, Elizabeth recalled she had yet to consume any food that day. She wandered to the breakfast room, where she found a selection of cold meats and rolls, a salad of sorts, and a torte set on the sideboard for anyone who wished a nuncheon. She filled a plate, then sat at the far end of the table by the window, where she could look out at the dreary scene. If it did not snow it would be a wonder, for the leaden skies looked ready to dump several feet of the stuff before nightfall.

"There you are!" Hyacinthe declared as she peeped into the room. She marched in, remarkably as her aunt was wont to do, then plumped herself down at the table. "I must hear all!"

"Precious little to tell," Elizabeth replied after a bite of cucumber pickle. She surveyed the assortment of food on her plate, and assembled a sandwich to facilitate the consumption of it.

"But what happened? That is, before the gun went off? Did he ravish you?" she concluded, having only a vague notion of what this meant.

"No," Elizabeth asserted, having a much better idea of things. "I heard a sound. I was afraid, so I withdrew my pistol from beneath my pillow. When I heard the third sound, I fired. And hit his lordship," she concluded with a grimace. "The dratted man ought not have been in my room."

"You seem rather unfeeling, cousin dear." Hyacinthe studied her cousin with an assessing gaze.

"Actually, it was utterly beastly. There was so much blood and his wound looked awful." The sandwich, at first eagerly contemplated, was placed on her plate and pushed away. "I cannot bear to think what he must have suffered, all because I avoided him at every turn. He was right, you know. I would have refused to see him if he had presented himself at the house. So, in effect, I drove him to climb up to my room."

"Mercy." Hyacinthe sighed at the drama that had unfolded in her mind's eye. "Now what?" she demanded impatiently.

"Now I shall do as I promised. I am traveling over to Penhurst to deliver a number of messages. His family must be told he will be away for a day or so. I dread informing them of the shooting. If his valet has not already left, I have instructions for him as well." Elizabeth glanced out of the window once more. "I only hope that the weather will hold until I return."

"And then?"

"Why, you shall be the belle of the ball, and I shall tend the invalid." It sounded about as appealing as a jail sentence. But, Elizabeth realized, she would have the rake in her power. And that thought was oddly pleasing.

3

ELIZABETH SLIPPED SURREPTITIOUSLY from her room, down the stairs, and out to the stables. The house had been at sixes and sevens between last-minute preparations for the ball—which Aunt Bel would not dream of canceling, even if Lord Leighton lay wounded on a guest room bed—and watching over his lordship. It must be admitted that the latter task fell to Purvis, who assumed the job with obvious relish.

The entire house knew of the shooting and subsequent betrothal of Elizabeth and Lord Leighton. Although not a word came directly to her, she could tell by expressions, the looks that followed her wherever she went.

At the thought that she might be forced to wed the rake, Elizabeth sighed. That was not what she wished. Not in the least. She would plot and scheme, and if worse came to worst, she'd run off. Julia and Victoria would understand.

Thankful her aunt was preoccupied, and that she need have no worry for Lord Leighton, for Purvis was the best possible nurse, Elizabeth urged Rose along to where the carriage ordered some time ago now awaited them.

"Hurry, Rose. I've no wish to be pressed into service by Aunt Bel with a last-minute commission."

"Yes, miss." The maid timidly climbed in beside her mistress, then settled uneasily in the corner of the gig as they set off smartly down the drive. "You plan to live at Penhurst after your weddin'?" Rose ventured to ask in a small voice.

"I fancy that Lord Leighton would wish me to remain there," Elizabeth replied, thinking that his rakish lordship would most likely consign her to the country forever if he was compelled to marry a slip of a girl like herself.

Then, realizing that Rose felt threatened, Elizabeth added kindly, "No matter where I am, you shall go with me if you wish."

The shy young maid, her eyes large with joy, murmured, "Oh, thank you, miss." She drew farther back against the cushion, her face rosy with relief.

The road that led to Penhurst Place was most impressive, Elizabeth decided as she drove the gig along the back roads. She studied the land they passed. Pretty cottages and farms revealed the excellent stewardship her sisters had mentioned when they scolded her for not enticing Lord Leighton into a parson's mousetrap. Since his lordship behaved well in their presence, they could scarcely be expected to understand how he teased her, or how she hated it.

At the rather plain but elegant brick gate, she paused while the caretaker opened it for her. Then, with a flick of her reins, she continued to proceed along the avenue to the front entrance.

The house was beautifully situated on the crest of a hill, with a fine view to the south of the Ranmer woods across a pretty valley. She considered the pleasant two-story building, built of mellow, saffron-hued stone. It seemed small for an earl. Perhaps it was but one of his residences, maybe a favorite? Come to think on it, the house looked very new, with no ancient ivy clinging to the walls, much less the sturdy wisteria vines her aunt's house wore.

With Rose trailing behind her, Elizabeth braved the front door, glancing back at the lad who walked her horse and carriage. Then the door opened silently, and a portly man appeared, a questioning look in his eyes.

"Sidthorp? I am Miss Dancy. I bring news that Lord Leighton was wounded last evening. He remains at Montmorcy Hall. I have brought a message for his valet, and wish to inform his family of the event." The terse description of his home had included the names of pertinent servants. "Is Hadlow about?"

"Lord Augustus and Mr. Percy are out at the moment. Hadlow is here. I trust his lordship is not seriously injured?"

"No." At least she hoped not.

Upon learning the valet had not departed for her aunt's home, Elizabeth asked to speak with him. She followed Sidthorp across the elegant, high-ceilinged hall, and along a paneled corridor that opened on one side onto a central courtyard. Sidthorp showed her in to a charming drawing room, leaving Rose behind to wait in a quiet alcove in the hall.

Left alone, Elizabeth surveyed the room where Lord Leighton must have spent some time as of late. It seemed odd to have the drawing room conveniently situated on the ground floor. French doors opened out onto a gallery that ran the length of the house, with a southern view of the pleasant valley.

Over her head carved and gilded paneling indicated that the earl had spared no expense in decorating his new house. Gilt lavishly adorned the pretty panels painted with cherubs. She was pleased to see that the furnishings were placed where they might be used, rather than lined stiffly against the wall, as had once been the custom. The crystal chandelier must be beautiful in the evening when lit for company, for even now, rainbows danced as the prisms caught the daylight.

A stir at the door brought her whirling about. Her first impression of the valet was that he would never get along with Purvis. He looked to be as strong-willed as the abigail, and twice as despotic.

"Hadlow, his lordship is anxiously awaiting your arrival. I brought a list of items he wishes to have you take him." She handed the slip of paper to the valet. "I trust the earl is well?"

The narrow glance from the valet did little to reassure her. "He is rather poorly at the moment." Then he left.

Deciding that her best course of action was to see for herself, Elizabeth crossed the room to make a stately progress along the corridor to the front hall. Sidthorp conducted her up the stairs to the bedchamber. Bowing, he left her standing before the door. She rapped gently. A thin face appeared when the door cracked open.

"I wish to see his lordship. Lord Leighton wants to know how he is."

"He sleeps now, miss. Tell his lordship he be unchanged."

Accepting his reluctance to permit a stranger inside, she nodded, then returned to the hall, where she found Rose.

Somehow the sight of her gig before the house did not surprise her in the least. With the earl ill, it was highly unlikely that any caller would remain for long.

While she and Rose jogged along back to Montmorcy Hall, she examined the situation from every angle and decided the entire matter was beyond her.

When she entered her aunt's house, the place was in a well-ordered hubbub. Footmen and maids bustled about, intent on their missions. Upstairs, she noted all the closed doors along the hall, and surmised that the occupants were either resting or preparing for the ball.

Elizabeth elected to do both. Her gown of coral silk was not new, but also not seen by anyone likely to attend this evening's function. And since she would most probably be required to dance attendance upon Lord Leighton, she really didn't care what she wore.

The dinner gong sounded precisely at six of the clock. After months of her aunt's company, Elizabeth rushed to gather her reticule and hurry down the stairs. There would be no dallying about, no waiting for a tardy guest. Aunt Bel would take a look at that locket watch she wore every waking hour of the day, and at five past the hour, head into the dining room. Woe betide a latecomer.

Outside the drawing room door, Elizabeth caught up with Lady Chloe and Hyacinthe, who appeared to be leisurely strolling into the room while deep in conversation. At the sight of Elizabeth, Hyacinthe broke off.

"I looked for you this afternoon. Wherever did you go? It was as if you vanished into thin air."

Gratified that her disappearance had proven so effective, and that not one of her aunt's capable servants had found her out, Elizabeth smiled, then murmured, "I had a brief errand to perform."

"For Lord Leighton?" demanded Lady Chloe in a breathless voice.

"More or less. Do you know, I do believe the weather is going to hold. Although the clouds are rather murky and look as though they might prove nasty, they won't."

"I wouldn't either, if it meant risking Mama's wrath,"

Lady Chloe retorted, then darted a glance at her formidable parent.

Elizabeth reflected that it was quite odd how that dainty woman, who looked as though she wouldn't harm a gnat, could have everyone quaking in their slippers at her merest frown. Perhaps it was her habit of checking her locket watch, demanding punctuality, and nicely getting her way in practically everything.

Which brought Elizabeth back to the riddle she'd been trying to solve all day—that ludicrous insistence that she wed Lord Leighton merely because he was the first man she had seen after midnight on St. Valentine's Day. Or did Aunt truly feel Elizabeth was compromised beyond redemption? That she must wed? Her aunt had uncommon persistence. What she wanted, she got, willy-nilly. And she wanted a wedding.

Perhaps later on, after dinner, Elizabeth could slip up to his lordship's room to discuss their counterattack. They needed to plan, put their heads together, and decide how best to change her aunt's mind. It could be done. Otherwise, it was a middle-of-the-night flight for Elizabeth Dancy!

He might be a viscount and wealthy and handsome as a hero in a novel, but he was a teasing rake, and she wasn't going to have him. Not as hers. If she decided to wed, it would be to someone who cherished her, whom she loved. The gossip she'd heard while in London about Lord Leighton's wild escapades and his bits o' muslin had scandalized her.

With her resolve firmly fixed, she sat down to dinner with an easier heart, ignoring those nigglings of disquiet that entered her mind whenever she glanced at her aunt's placid face. She knew that behind that amiable facade hid an implacable will. Still . . .

Hyacinthe was in alt to be seated beside the Marquess of Norwood. Lord Norwood's Brutus cut displayed his blond locks admirably. The black velvet coat he wore to such advantage complimented his fair looks. That his cravat was a trifle too high for Elizabeth's taste, or the blood red ruby set in the center of it a bit too large, did not matter. Hyacinthe seemed enthralled.

Down the table from where Elizabeth sat between

Squire Littledale and Mr. Beamish, Lady Chloe could be seen—when Mr. Beamish turned aside—happily chattering to the youngest of the Harlowe family, John. That connection would not be approved, since he had not a feather to fly with and would most likely be placed in the church. Since clergy were not known to be plump in the pocket, Aunt Bel would maneuver him to the outermost. Of course, had Harlowe sufficient connections so as to obtain several livings in prosperous churches, which naturally would be handled by an impecunious curate, John might do well enough. But Elizabeth suspected her aunt would look higher for Lady Chloe.

Leaving the gentlemen to their port, Elizabeth drifted after the ladies, Aunt Bel charging in the lead, to the drawing room. They congregated there for a short time before going on to the ballroom. Exclamations of delight at the lovely decorations were heard from all. It was there the gentlemen shortly joined them.

Two dances were all Elizabeth was to be allowed. Mr. Beamish requested one, John Harlowe the other. Aunt Bel summoned her with a faint nod, then ordered, "I would that you attend Lord Leighton. The poor man must be bored to death. He would be gracing our ball had you not acted so precipitously. I trust you have stored your gun in a more appropriate place by now?"

"Yes, I have, Aunt Bel. You wish me to entertain Lord Leighton? In his bedroom?" Elizabeth whispered the last sentences lest someone overhear and make the worst of it.

"Indeed."

Taking an irate breath, for she hated to leave the gaiety for the sick room, yet knowing she must do as her aunt thought best, Elizabeth left. Never mind that she had originally intended to do just this. She disliked being ordered about.

The upper floor was silent, the rooms deserted, with only faint strains of music creeping up the stairs and down the hall. One could hear a wisp of laughter, a snatch of melody, the murmur of conversation, but all muted, as though from a great distance.

His door stood ajar, and Elizabeth paused after touching the lever, wondering if she might sneak away and later pretend he had been asleep.

"Come in, whoever you are. I vow, the veriest tweenie would be welcome" came an irritated voice Elizabeth had grown to recognize.

"Aunt Bel sent me up here to look after you. Where is Purvis? Or Hadlow?" Elizabeth had hoped the abigail would be there, to keep him from his teasing worst. His valet was another matter, and she could not like the man.

"Ah, the treasure. Purvis decided I may be left alone for the nonce, and has taken herself off to the kitchen. I suspect she intends to brew up some more vile concoctions to pour down my throat. Hadlow returned to Penhurst for the moment. He decided I required a change of clothing."

"You look well enough, sir."

"So timid? Is this indeed the fearless woman who shot the intruder who dared to enter her holy of holies, her bedchamber?" His voice mocked her, while those unusual hazel eyes looked almost black in the dim light. They had a slight tilt to them, which added to that rakish image. Quite devilish he was, and his glance turned her legs to mush.

Elizabeth favored him with a narrow-eyed glare as she groped for a straight-backed chair to ease down upon. "It could have been an intruder, a thief . . . or worse." She could feel her cheeks grown warm at his speculative look.

"Worse you definitely do not want."

"Aunt Bel insisted I spend time comforting you, as I am responsible for your being here, instead of gracing the ballroom." Her tone clearly revealed that she, at any rate, doubted his ability to grace any place well.

"Hm."

She considered him a few moments, then said, "If we were smart, we would be figuring how to spike Aunt Bel's guns, instead of sparring like this. I mean, you cannot wish to marry me and, as I have stated several times, I do not wish to marry you."

He looked affronted.

Elizabeth repressed a smile. "I did not tell anybody that you were, er, disguised when you entered my bedchamber. Perhaps I ought to have revealed that in aid of our release.''

"Foxed? No. Well, perhaps just a trifle in my cups. Dutch courage.''

"You? I do not believe that taradiddle for a minute. I rather suspect this piece of mischief popped into your mind, and you blundered into my room on the spur of the moment. I trust that in the future you will be less impetuous.''

His silent perusal of her unsettled her considerably, but she kept her chin up, returning his look with what she hoped was cool detachment.

"Actually, I have been doing a good bit of thinking about that. Goodness knows, I have had more than enough time to solve any number of problems.''

"And?'' she replied with a great deal of hope in her voice. If only Lord Leighton were not quite so handsome, or possessed of so many other admirable qualities that would likely be thrown in her face again and again when she broke off with him.

"I have an idea.'' He flashed a grin at her that made her wonder at her resolve, and her ability to keep it.

"Please do go on. I cannot bear the suspense.''

"You won't like it,'' he prophesied. "I propose that for the time being we allow this foolish arrangement to stand.'' He held up a hand when he saw that her bosom swelled with indignation. "Allow me, please, to finish? I came here to obtain your help, and your help I shall get—you owe me, remember?'' When she subsided, he continued. "If we are engaged, no one will think the least of it if you go to Penhurst, spend time inspecting the house, becoming acquainted with the place where you will live someday. Correct?'' He ignored the fact that she'd been compromised by him.

Elizabeth nodded slowly. "I must agree your scheme has merits.'' Her guilt ate at her conscience.

"You needn't be so reluctant with your praise. I haven't heard anything better from you. While you are at Penhurst you can keep a weather eye on my father. I cannot fathom what has struck him down like this. Bloody mysterious. Never known him to cast up his accounts for so long, or be so dazed.''

"Filpot said there was no change in his condition. Hadlow said very little. I trust he told you more?" She raised delicate, inquiring brows, while folding her hands in her lap.

"Dash it all, I want to be there instead of languishing in this confounded bed." He balled his hand into a fist, gently pounding the bed in his frustration.

It seemed he truly cared for his father, and Elizabeth felt her heart soften, for she had precious memories of her own papa that she treasured. Any man who could reveal his affection for a parent in this day, when it was fashionable to act as though you somehow were created without benefit of such, must get her respect.

Then Elizabeth realized that all this talking had not been good for him. He could become feverish. Rather than ask him, for she well remembered how annoying it could be when ill to be constantly nagged about how one felt, she rose to do something about it. Crossing to the dresser, she found a basin filled with cool, lavender-scented water. Wringing out a small towel, she walked to his bedside, perching on the very edge of it.

His suspicious look cut her. With a deal of patience she softly said, "You are wearing yourself out with all this nattering. Hush now, while I talk for a bit." She stroked his brow with the scented liquid, soothing him, almost caressing him, if she'd but thought of it.

She concentrated on their joint dilemma. "I believe your plan might work. Aunt Bel muttered something about going to call on your father. I expect she will demand to see how he does, and I would not be surprised were she to gain entrance to the sickroom. Would you wish Purvis to have a look at him as well?"

"Your eyes are turquoise in this light," he said in a thoughtful voice. "Your skin is remarkably creamy, my dear."

"Except when you put me to the blush by absurd compliments, sir." She flashed him a look of reproof.

"I could do worse than marry you, I suppose. I doubt if any of my cronies would raise an eyebrow at the connection." He peered at her, a twinkle in his eyes, looking as rakishly fetching as any man she'd ever seen.

Elizabeth was utterly incensed. She allowed a few

drops of cold water to fall on his cambric-covered chest, the sheet somehow having slid downward. "I shall fulfill my share of the bargain and look after your father. But nothing more. I shan't marry you, sir. Not for anything."

"I'm such a good catch, how can you turn down marriage to me?" He affected a pout, and for an instant she had a glimpse of what he must have looked like as a boy. It took great resolve to resist his appeal, but he was most provoking.

She scowled at the plaintive note in his voice. She ought to pour the entire contents of the basin over his head. How dare the man propose marriage so casually? He was impossible. Rather than brush aside that appealing curl that had fallen over his brow, she rose and walked to the door, after dropping the cloth back into the basin.

"I shall pay my respects to Aunt and consign myself to bed. It will be a penance of sorts. On the morrow I will begin our plan."

"Before you leave, I have something for you. A Valentine's Day gift, if you like. I hope it pleases you. Over there, on the dresser. Open that package." He turned his head to watch her.

Disregarding his offhand presentation, she hastened to the dresser to pick up the rather large parcel. Sitting back down on the chair, she proceeded to undo the wrapping, exclaiming softly when she beheld what was inside.

"Good gracious! You ought not, you know. This is frightfully valuable." Perched in the tissue reposed an enameled gold singing-bird music box. The base, sides, and top were blue enamel. Wide gold bands trimmed the corners and the oval upon which the bird sat. Unable to resist, she wound up the music box and listened, utterly enchanted, to the sweet melody. "How lovely!" The smile beamed at his lordship was quite, quite bemused and delighted.

"I thought that since you are plagued with that infirmity of the voice, you might like a song sung on key."

Only the delicacy and great cost of the music box kept her from throwing it at him then and there. How like him to tease her about her lack of musical ability. Unwilling to let him know she was hurt, she smiled serenely at him.

"It is truly a marvelous gift, and I shall treasure it always. Would you mind if I conceal it from Aunt Bel for the nonce? We scarcely wish to add fuel to her determination to see us wed." At his nod she rose. "Thank you, Lord Leighton, for the valentine gift."

"I knew you'd be pleased, and so I sent a request to Hadlow to bring it along. Been in the family awhile."

His triumphant smile almost made her take back her words. What a devious man, to be sure. She turned to leave the room, the music box clutched tightly in her arms.

"And the name is David, you know. I think you had best learn to use it."

Compressing her lips and taking a deep breath, she nodded her good night to him. After first hiding the music box in her room, she sailed down the stairs to find her aunt. David, indeed.

The next morning Elizabeth discovered her aunt in the breakfast room, staring out of the window with a frown on her face. Beyond the panes of glass a few lazy flakes of snow sifted to the ground. Elizabeth believed that if her aunt frowned hard enough, the snow would cease, afraid to fall and vex that formidable lady.

"Good morning, Aunt."

"Bad weather to travel to Penhurst Place."

"You plan to go with me, then?"

Aunt Bel nodded. "I wish to see what Herold has done with that house. He was secretive about his plans, and with him not having a proper hostess, I've not had the chance to see it." She shot a sharp look at Elizabeth. "What did you think of the place?"

"Well, I saw nothing other than the hall and the drawing room. But it seems charming. The stone exterior is such a lovely hue of saffron, and the French windows in the drawing room seem most pleasing. Did you know the drawing room is on the ground floor? With doors that open out onto a very nice gallery with a delightful view?" Elizabeth reflected on the charming aspect of the room.

"Good thing you like the place. You'll live there soon enough." Aunt Bel consulted her locket watch, then stared out of the window again.

Elizabeth prudently refrained from disputing this statement. If she roused her aunt's suspicions, her plans could come to naught.

"We shall depart as soon as you have broken your fast. Hurry up, girl. We do not have all day. I fancy my drawing room will be full of callers this afternoon, paying respects after the ball."

"It was such a lovely affair."

"What do you know about it? You danced twice, then retired. Eat." After consulting her locket watch, Aunt Bel rose from her chair and sailed from the room in august dignity.

Elizabeth flashed a look of dismay after her closest relative of the older generation. There really was no one else she could live with, and Aunt Bel had a heart of gold. If only she did not also harbor such strange superstitions.

Having little taste for a meal, Elizabeth shortly left the room. In the entryway, she discovered her aunt attired in an attractive pelisse of dove gray trimmed in deep blue. A confection of blue feathers and gray ribands sat on her head, and made Aunt Bel look years younger.

"I requested that Rose bring down your pretty aquamarine pelisse and bonnet. No sense in going up just to come down again. Wastes time."

Rose timidly offered the articles, while Elizabeth reflected that it was as well she didn't care if she made an impression on the people at Penhurst or not. She'd not be given a chance to primp before leaving.

"I trust the household will be astir, Aunt? With a person as ill as the earl, they may be taking things quiet."

"We shall be ushered in," replied her aunt.

Of Lady Chloe and Hyacinthe, not a speck could be seen. Elizabeth suspected they still slept, relishing that delightful feeling after a ball at which one has been smashing and had masses of partners.

"I am pleased you have agreed to perform this nursing. Purvis declares you have been a fine pupil. You set a good example to the girls not only in this, but your acceptance of your lot. Your marriage to Lord Leighton will turn out quite well, I believe."

Elizabeth shot her a dismayed look. Why did she have the sensation of being trapped?

Before they could exit, a stir above stairs brought them to a halt. Both ladies paused in their steps as a polished gentleman slowly made his way with the aid of James down the stairs to join them. His wounded arm was cradled in one of Aunt Bel's less colorful scarves.

"Leighton! What's the meaning of this?" demanded Aunt Bel of her guest.

"Why, my carriage awaits us, my lady. I intend to go with you."

Elizabeth detected the faint bulge of his bandage beneath his superbly cut coat that indicated where his arm had been shot. Otherwise, he looked complete to a shade, and not the least in need of pampering. His color looked remarkably well for one who had suffered grievous injury.

"Good. That is, if you are in shape to travel," Aunt added. "The more you and Elizabeth are seen together, the better."

"But of course. May I call you Aunt Bel?" He bowed over her hand, smiling lazily down into her soft blue eyes.

Repressing a snort of disgust, Elizabeth eyed him with a jaundiced eye, then said, "Come, *David*, we had best be going. There is such a lot to be done, and no time to lose."

"I shall agree to that, my love." With that, he gestured her before him, and they hurried through the cold to the waiting carriage.

Once in the carriage, her feet on a hot brick, Elizabeth fumed in silence. Did he always have to get the best of her?

4

"You ought not have left your bed, sir," she began. 'I fear you are not strong enough." He sat opposite her in the closed carriage, next to her aunt. His wicked flash of a grin ought to have warned her.

"Why, after you cooled my fevered brow last evening, I slept like an infant. I feel certain that your ministrations did more than that vile brew Purvis poured down my throat." He behaved as though he had bested her again, with an odious grin on his face.

Elizabeth firmed her mouth, thinking of the dire things she would like to do to his lordship—like boiling him in oil, or something equally lovely. Her mind flashed to the nasty little comment he made the night before, saying that he could do worse than to marry her. Ohhhh, that abominable male conceit of his. It was not enough that he had to be the most handsome man about, but he must tease her into a muddled heap of sensibilities.

What a lowering reflection to be considered as nothing more than a passable connection. Well, she would just keep that lovely music box he gave her last evening. If she must end up on the shelf, the lovely tinkling music would serve to remind her how she got there. She surveyed the gentleman across from her coolly.

"Forgive me for my concern. You seemed a bit pulled this morning, and I naturally believed you to be suffering from the effects of your wound. 'Tis unlike you to look so weak and worried." She bestowed a sugary smile on him, demurely folding her hands in her lap. It was as well, for she dearly wished to punch him on the jaw, as her brother had taught her years before.

Leighton's gaze narrowed, and that devilish smile disappeared. Uncertainty flared in his hazel eyes for a moment, much to her satisfaction. Oh, to strike a blow against all gentlemen who delighted in teasing poor defenseless girls! She quite forgot her lethal little gun that had wreaked such disaster on his lordship two nights ago.

"I declare, sir," she continued sweetly, "I hope you intend to go straight to your bed when we arrive at your home. It would be dreadful if you took a turn for the worse, what with being your father's only heir and all."

He frowned at her, and Elizabeth repressed a smile.

"I believe there are a number of hopefuls in the offing, in the event I go aloft without an heir of my own," he replied in a repressive tone.

It would serve him right if—after she gave him the mitten quite properly—he was unable to find a woman who'd accept him. For that matter, could he ever be serious long enough to make a suitable offer? Casting a doubtful look at him, she decided he would most likely tease his way into marriage, as he did other things. Providing, of course, that he ever got around to it. She'd wager that marriage was not high on his list of things to do.

"Children," began Lady Montmorcy in her most quelling manner, "I believe you had best cease this sparring. Lord Leighton, I should like to know more about this illness that has struck your father."

"Dashed odd thing," Leighton replied. "My father has always been healthy, never sick a day. And then, little by little he became ill, and before long he was in bed, feeling wretched."

Elizabeth noted his apparently sincere worry, and reflected that there definitely seemed to be a serious side to Lord Leighton, or David, as he had insisted she call him. She was skeptical as to how deeply it ran.

"I recall Crompton as being fit as a fiddle," Aunt Bel commented as she stared off into space. "Always on the go with the goers, and never one to malinger." She shook her head in dismay. "Puzzling."

"Quite so, Lady Montmorcy," Leighton said in that persuasive manner he possessed in such abundance. "That is why I hoped to enlist Elizabeth's help. There appears to be a mystery here. She performed noteworthy assistance to the government, and may still be engaged in helping their efforts, for all I know. At any rate, since we are betrothed, it would be acceptable for her to spend time at Penhurst Place assisting me, would it not?''

Aunt Bel frowned slightly, then her brow cleared. ''I believe it would be most proper. After all, she did you an injustice, shooting you like that.''

''Aunt Bel,'' Elizabeth protested, ''he broke into my room in the dead of night. For all I knew he might have been a robber . . . or worse! What was I to do? Meekly permit him to do as he pleased?''

''Elizabeth Dancy'' came a scandalized retort.

His lordship's grin was quite the most odious one yet. Elizabeth knew she blushed, most likely a fiery red, and contained her anger just barely. Trust the two of them to put the worst possible construction on her words.

The two younger people avoided further quibbling by their providential arrival at Penhurst Place. Aunt Bel surveyed the neat brick gate with a shrewd eye, then scanned the orderly avenue to the house with an astute knowledge of what it took to keep an estate in such excellent repair.

''You have a good steward, Lord Leighton,'' she commented.

''A cousin, Jeremy Vane. My father took him in some years ago, training him in estate management with the hope that some day Jeremy would have experience enough to command a good position.''

''Admirable,'' Aunt Bel said. ''Difficult thing for younger sons to find a niche for themselves.'' She sighed. ''I worry about my John. As an only son, he must assume his place before long. I trust his traveling will bring him home safe and sound soon.''

Lord Leighton gave her an inquiring look.

''John decided he wished to duplicate the journey his father had made years ago, haring across the Alps down to Italy. How he avoided the Frenchies, I don't know.'' She checked her watch, then added, ''Ought to have been home long ago.'' As though Aunt Bel thought her John would arrange his trip to her timetable.

''I feel certain cousin John is fine, Aunt Bel. He is as practical as even you might wish, and always manages to land on his feet no matter what happens,'' Elizabeth assured her.

The topic of the missing heir to the Montmorcy fortune was dismissed as the carriage drew up before the charming home of the Percy family. Or at least one of their homes.

Sidthorp ushered them in with a good deal more propriety than he had Elizabeth the day before. She surmised that Aunt Bel made all the difference.

"We are pleased to see you home, sir," he said to the Percy heir.

Lord Leighton gave him a lopsided smile, then removed his hat, handing it to the waiting butler. His gloves offered a problem his valet would solve later. "My father awake, do you know?"

"As to that, sir, you would have to see Filpot, his lordship's valet," he added for Aunt Bel's edification.

With an apprehensive glance at Lady Montmorcy, Lord Leighton said, "Shall you wish to go with me, my lady?"

"Most definitely," she declared firmly. Turning to Elizabeth, she added, "Wait for us in the library. We do not wish to overwhelm his lordship."

"Yes, do," Leighton inserted.

"Very well," Elizabeth said with resignation.

She watched the pair slowly make their way up the stairs until they reached the open gallery. They walked along the corridor leading to the south bedroom wing until they disappeared. She found the sight of Lord Leighton bending to listen solicitously to her aunt's conversation unsettling. Who knew what her dearest aunt poured into his ears!

Elizabeth turned to Sidthorp. "I believe I shall wish tea, if you please. I feel sure that Lady Montmorcy will as well once she has investigated Lord Crompton's condition."

The butler nodded, then ushered Elizabeth around the corner and down the corridor to the library. Just beyond an elaborate long-case clock, he showed her into an elegant room with book-lined walls.

The air of somber comfort must reflect the personality of the earl, for it certainly didn't his son. Elizabeth liked the neoclassical decor of the pleasantly airy room very much. She trailed a finger along the back of one of the many armchairs scattered about the room, casting an eye at the exquisite needlepoint covers with approval. She'd wager Leighton's mother had worked those. Or perhaps they had come from another estate, for one didn't often buy such delightful treasures that so well fitted the decor.

A writing table of the very latest design stood in the center of the room. Papers were strewn over the top, with a letter knife, a large seal, and red sealing wax in a clutter next to the inkstand. A tray with a pen and a knife for sharpening the quill sat by a silver-rimmed jar of sand. Quite evidently someone had been working here until a short time before. The pen point looked to need sharpening, and Elizabeth immediately decided that whoever used this desk seemed a trifle messy, and not as careful as he might be. Shouldn't those papers have been stored away from prying eyes? Not that she would snoop.

Dismissing the desk, she strolled to the first of the many bookcases set into the walls of the room. The latest works were found on the shelves at eye level. Above, she could see volumes in Latin and German. Walking on, she found a great number of books in French and a few in Italian. Evidently the Percys were a family well taught in many languages.

It did not help her to understand David any better, however. He remained as much an enigma as ever.

A pair of wing chairs flanked the fireplace, offering a cozy spot for reading or quiet conversation. The white marble fireplace was all classical elegance with fluted Ionic columns to either side. The portrait above the fireplace undoubtedly was a Percy, for he wore the faintly amused expression she saw so frequently upon Lord Leighton, not to mention the same brown hair and rich hazel eyes.

At that moment the door opened. She turned around, expecting to see Sidthorp with a tea tray. Instead she found a young man of moderate height, certainly shorter than David, Lord Leighton, who seemed to tower above everyone around. As matter of fact, this man seemed very much like David, only a faded shadow, not as handsome, or as personable. Confused, she raised her brows in inquiry.

"Miss Elizabeth Dancy? Sidthorp told me that we had guests. I am Jeremy Vane, cousin to Lord Leighton."

Elizabeth bestowed a welcoming smile on the gentleman. "How charming to meet you, sir. When we drove up to the house, we were much impressed by the landscape, giving evidence of your care."

His modest shrug could only be commended, she decided. He did not assume airs and graces unfitting a person so removed from the title.

"I appreciate all his lordship has done for me—the earl, that is. He has treated me like a son, and I do all I can to repay his faith."

"Praiseworthy, indeed, sir." She was at a loss as to what to discuss next.

Sidthorp solved the dilemma by entering the room with the tea tray. In addition to the generous pot of Bohea tea with the usual milk, sugar, and lemon slices, there were delicate lemon biscuits and treacle tarts.

"Lovely," Elizabeth said, recalling her slight meal before leaving Montmorcy Hall. In the process of arranging cups and saucers, she glanced up as the door opened once again.

"Jeremy! So you found our guest," Leighton said with a distinctly cool look at the steward.

"Not often we are treated to such a pleasantry nowadays," Jeremy replied evenly.

"Good," Lady Montmorcy said as she marched in behind Leighton. "We can refresh ourselves while we decide what to do. May I say that I find that man Filpot to be a nodcock of the first order, Lord Leighton?"

"You may," he said, sighing with apparent resignation. "Father refuses to part with the man, and indeed, he has been here a good many years. I'd prefer a reliable nurse, but that is not to be."

Aunt Bel exchanged a look with Elizabeth, one full of meaning.

"Would he perhaps permit me to look after him? Aunt Bel? What do you think?" Elizabeth ventured to say. "After all, if David and I are to be wed, I am like one of the family. How could he take exception to that?" She gathered, from the hard look directed at her by her dearest aunt, that Aunt Bel's efforts had come to nothing.

"Filpot would most likely be upset," Jeremy commented.

"Hang Filpot, the old fussbudget," David answered with a distinct lack of his usual charm. Indeed, he looked harassed and troubled, if Elizabeth was any judge. Perhaps his wound pained him. At least he had been able to obtain help with his gloves, and now was draped with a neat nankeen sling for his arm.

"I believe that keeping the room in utter darkness a bit rash," Aunt Bel declared. "Not to mention that potion he gives him. Seemed exceedingly nasty."

"That is the housekeeper's special remedy, my lady," Jeremy stated, looking as though he thought Lady Montmorcy might bite him. But then, she tended to have that effect on people, especially those of the lower orders.

"Hmpf," Lady Montmorcy replied, highly indignant that she had not been permitted to take charge as she longed to do.

Elizabeth had seen that look before, and decided she had best step in before her aunt said something utterly outrageous.

"If there is no other objection, I believe I would like to tend his lordship. Does that please you, David?" she inquired in dulcet tones for the benefit of his cousin.

She couldn't deduce what his reaction would be, for his face was in the shadows. However, he ultimately nodded his agreement. "As long as the arrangement meets with your aunt's approval." He turned to that lady to add, "Mind you, if the weather turns foul, she may not be able to return to the Hall for a brief time. Her maid will be with her, but outside the housekeeper and the maids, there are no other women living here."

"Lord Percy and his son ought to suffice. Neither cousin Egbert nor his father are precisely what you might call top-drawer, Lady Montmorcy, but they do well enough, I should think," Jeremy added, sharing an apologetic smile with Elizabeth.

"Fine. I shall return to the Hall and gather what I will need." Elizabeth resolved to consult with Purvis as well, once she had questioned Aunt Bel as to what she knew of the earl's condition.

Aunt Bel settled on one of the embroidered high-backed chairs to partake of her tea. Nothing could dissuade her from that important task. Sampling a tart, she daintily wrinkled her nose. "You will doubtlessly wish to find a new cook, Elizabeth, once you assume your position here. I believe this tart to be a bit off."

Elizabeth thought the milk a trifle sour as well, but didn't dream of complaining about it. Elderly ladies could get by with murder.

Once they finished tea, Elizabeth rose when her aunt decided to depart the house, following her from the library with a backward glance at Jeremy Vane. Perhaps she would enjoy his company while here. At least he did not intimidate her like his cousin. Nor did he appear to be the teasing sort.

"While you are in this house, you will please remember at all times that you are betrothed to me," David murmured in her ear, well out of her aunt's hearing.

"Whatever would I do that might call that into question?"

"I saw that languishing look at Jeremy. He doesn't have a feather to fly with, and is definitely not for you, my dear," David said rather close to her ear.

Elizabeth bristled at the tone of his voice. Of all the odious insinuations! As though she would set up a flirt with his steward. She had considered it might be nice to find a friend. Nothing more. Before she could reply to this insulting innuendo, the front door opened.

Two men entered the front hall. Both wore riding clothes and carried whips in their hands. They appeared to be amiably arguing about something. Upon seeing there were guests, and ladies at that, both halted in their tracks, the argument set aside.

Introductions were made, with Egbert appraising Elizabeth but thankfully not flirting with her. Aunt Bel studied Lord Augustus, as though searching for a hint of the man she had once known while in London years ago.

"Uncle Augustus, Egbert, I see you are enjoying the stables," Lord Leighton said in a voice that made Elizabeth glad she wasn't one of the men.

"Dashed fine lot of horseflesh, my boy. Dashed fine," replied the older man. He had the look of the Percys, but his skin was raddled, most likely from too much port, and his eyes above sagging pouches of skin looked cynical. While his clothing was spotless, the coat was several years behind the current styles and his vest amazingly plain.

Egbert glanced at his father and said, "That new mare appears to be an excellent addition, cousin."

"See that she remains that way, Egbert," David replied, giving his cousin a steady look.

With that, Lord Leighton ushered his guests to the closed carriage awaiting them in front of the house.

"You have done well, David," Aunt Bel praised, "in spite of that man Filpot. I shall feel better, however, when Elizabeth takes up her nursing duties. A pity your father would not allow Purvis to attend him."

"We have yet to see how he takes to Elizabeth," Lord Leighton reminded her.

"Everyone adores Elizabeth. Girl can charm a bird from a bush. I do not foresee any difficulty in *that* quarter. Perhaps she can succeed where the doctor has failed. However, I cannot say I have ever had much faith in Dr. Dibble." She glanced fondly at Elizabeth. "Just keep her safe, my boy."

Elizabeth shared a shocked look with Lord Leighton. What did her aunt think might happen?

"I had believed we would do rather better than that, my lady," his lordship declared.

"Fools frequently do. See that you remember that." She glanced at her locket watch, then turned to leave.

Elizabeth followed her aunt into the carriage, pausing only to inform Lord Leighton when she would return.

David watched the carriage roll down the drive with misgivings. Keep Elizabeth Dancy safe? The girl who so intrepidly shot at an intruder in the dark? He'd rather nurse a keg of blasting powder.

When he reentered the house, his relatives were nowhere to be seen. Trusting his memory, he ambled to the library door, where he found them inside. The remains of tea lay ignored while they sipped excellent port and discussed the morning's ride. He watched them for a moment before joining them. He took care to preserve his invalidish appearance.

"Pretty little gel. Pretty," Lord Augustus stated firmly, a twinkle lighting his rheumy eyes.

"Odd time of day to be paying a call, wouldn't you

say?'' Egbert added, unable to keep the curiosity from
his voice.

"Lady Montmorcy is a dear friend of my father's. Did
you chance to know her years ago, before she wed and
moved to the country, Uncle?'' David strolled over to
stand by the fire, warming himself, and wishing he might
rest. Although the injury was not as serious as he led
Elizabeth to believe, it did pain him some.

"Believe I did. Bound to. Knew everyone in those
days,'' his uncle replied, looking deeply into his glass of
port. "Am sure I did. Believe your father rather fancied
her at one time.''

"And you, Egbert? I vow I am surprised you had not
met Miss Elizabeth. She was everywhere to be seen in
Society last Season. Or do you prefer other company
while in the city?'' David suggested in an even tone.

An angry redness crept up on Egbert's face as he stared
at his cousin.

"Lightskirts. The boy enjoys his fun, David. Pity you
are not more inclined that way. Been Friday-faced ever
since you came home. Can't think why you stay. Ought
to find a good lightskirt to keep you company. Yes, sir,
a good lightskirt.'' Lord Augustus pounded his left fist
on the arm of the high-backed chair to emphasize his
point.

"I do well enough while in Town, Uncle, as you would
know if you ever went there. And you well know that I
am here because of the summons from Filpot. My father
is ill. Or had you forgotten?'' He studied the trio who
sat by the fireplace, the glow of the flames reflected in
their now sober faces. Jeremy had remained prudently
silent throughout their conversation, having nothing to
contribute, it seemed.

"He forgets now and again, David,'' Egbert said.

"We all do,'' David replied wearily. He began to leave
the room, then paused by the door. "Miss Elizabeth is
coming over later today. She will be looking after my
father. I want the three of you to keep out of her way. Is
that clear?''

They all nodded. David noted that Egbert looked exceedingly worried. Good.

* * *

At Montmorcy Hall, Elizabeth fended off questions from her cousins.

"I cannot see how Aunt Bel will allow you to visit a gentlemen's establishment, Elizabeth," Hyacinthe scolded.

"Somehow I doubt if I shall encounter them in the sickroom, cousin," Elizabeth said dryly.

"It sounds vastly romantic to me," Lady Chloe said in a breathy voice. "Fancy, nursing the father of the man you are to marry." A conscious look came over her face. "I do hope he does not die while you tend him. That would be dreadful."

"Indeed," Elizabeth replied with a wry twist of her mouth, rising from her chair by the fireplace. "I wish to consult with Purvis before I leave. Rose shall pack a small portmanteau for me, just in case the weather turns nasty and I cannot make my way home."

Lady Chloe dashed to the window to search the leaden skies. She shivered. "Oh, it looks bad to me. Purvis says she cannot recall a more vile February. I should say it is very likely you will spend at least one night there."

"I think it is all highly improper," Hyacinthe stated in the primmest of manners. "Nothing good will come of breaking Society's rules, mark my words."

"Do you intend to broadcast it to all and sundry, then?" Elizabeth inquired before leaving the sitting room.

"Hyacinthe," Lady Chloe rebuked, "they are betrothed now. I fancy that if Aunt Bel gives permission, it must be acceptable. And Elizabeth is a most agreeable girl."

"Perhaps too agreeable?" Hyacinthe suggested.

"I'll have you know that I have no desire to go to Penhurst Place, Hyacinthe. First, Lord Leighton requested that I assist him, then Aunt Bel as good as ordered me there. Since I am dependent upon her kind mercies, I shan't say no to her express wishes. Is that clear?"

"You met his cousin?" Hyacinthe said, her eyes calculating.

"Egbert Percy? Yes. Not a very prepossessing young man. An incipient fop, I'd say from what I saw. He cannot hold a candle to his cousin, Lord Leighton. Nor, for that matter, can his other cousin, Jeremy Vane.''

"My, what a lot of men!" Lady Chloe declared, her shocked eyes round with amazement.

"I believe I once read there is safety in numbers. His uncle, Lord Augustus Percy, lives there as well. I trust they will all behave like gentlemen. I doubt if Lord Leighton will do more than tease me. He seems to enjoy that a great deal.''

"How curious," Lady Chloe said in a wondering voice. "That does not sound the least lover-like.''

"Quite," Elizabeth replied, closing the door behind her as she left her cousins. Mercy, what an ordeal. Getting Purvis to share her knowledge of healing ought to be a snap compared to escaping from her cousins.

When Purvis was found at last in the still room, Elizabeth expressed her wish for healing potions. After explaining what she had learned about Lord Crompton from Aunt Bel, Purvis nodded sagely.

"Most peculiar. Can't say I could pinpoint the illness. If I could see the man. . . ?''

"Aunt Bel and Lord Leighton say that Lord Crompton will not have anyone else about. And Aunt Bel says the concoction that the cook makes him is a vile potion. Aunt said the smell made her feel ill. I'll wager you could do much better than that woman. Do you know her treacle tarts were off and the milk a trifle sour?''

"No!" Purvis declared in horror. "Well, and I shall do my best, Miss Elizabeth.''

With the honor of Montmorcy Hall at stake, Purvis set to work compounding her best restorative tonic. Once that was completed, she set to stir up other, more interesting potions. By the time two hours had elapsed, Elizabeth felt as though she might dabble in this sort of thing herself, for it fascinated her.

"Finished," Purvis declared, setting the last glass vial into the basket Elizabeth had placed on the table in the still room. "Remember, give him the tonic twice a day. And open the curtains. Poor man." Purvis tsk-tsked at the thought of a gloomy room, even if some of the best doctors urged such. She'd found a cheerful room to be better for health.

"Anything else?" Elizabeth began to fold a crisp white napkin over the contents of the basket, then paused as Purvis handed her a bottle of a brown substance. Frowning, she gave Purvis a questioning look.

"For Lord Leighton. I fancy his arm will be giving his a bit of bother. I showed that Hadlow how to dress the wound, but the man looks none too bright. You best see to it yourself."

Elizabeth meekly agreed, while wondering how in the world she was to get Lord Leighton to bare his arm so she might check his dressing, much less pour down his throat some of the stuff he declared to be utterly vile.

5

ON THE RIDE BACK to Penhurst Place, Elizabeth reflected on how life had changed for her since arriving to live with Aunt Bel. In the past Elizabeth had literally burst into a room, questions tripping off her tongue. A short time with her aunt had cured her of the habit. That, and having the correct and proper Hyacinthe around.

What with her aunt's penchant for punctuality, Elizabeth's habitual tardiness at meals had also been changed. She quickly learned that unless she arrived at the table promptly, she might not eat. Since that was also a habit she'd acquired over the years, she soon adjusted.

But now her punctual and proper aunt wanted her to violate all the dictates of society to tend a gentleman Elizabeth had never even met. To make it worse, she entered a household composed entirely of men, three of them close to her own age and eligible one way or another. Before leaving the house, she had turned to face Aunt Bel just inside the front door.

"How do you know I shall do the right thing? Or for that matter, how do you know I *can* do the correct thing?" Elizabeth inquired while being shuffled out of the door to the waiting carriage that would return her to Penhurst Place.

"You have become quite a sensible girl in the months since you came to live with me," Aunt Bel replied, patting Elizabeth's arm, while handing her the basket of herbal preparations Purvis had mixed for the earl and Lord Leighton. "I trust you to use your brains. You possess compassion along with your common sense. But keep your wits about you, for if that Filpot person is around, you shall have need of it." She watched as Elizabeth climbed into the carriage and the door was shut before scurrying back into the house out of the cold.

Not convinced her aunt was in the least correct in her assessment, but comforted by her words, Elizabeth settled back on the seat for her brief journey, tucking the rug across her lap for warmth.

How ironic it was that the one man in the world that she most wished to avoid should turn up, not on her doorstep, but in her bedchamber! She well knew that marriages often were compelled when a couple were found in a compromising situation. And with her in her nightgown . . . Mercy, he had looked straight at her! Perhaps he wouldn't recall the sheer cambric that permitted a shockingly intimate view of her person. And pigs might fly.

And . . . Aunt Bel still acted as though Elizabeth intended to marry Lord Leighton in due time.

When she sighed, Rose asked, "Be you troubled, miss?"

"Just a bit. I shall want you by me while at Penhurst Place. I cannot imagine what I shall encounter there. If nothing more, I want you to keep a watch on those valets. I do not like Hadlow, and I agree with my aunt that Filpot is missing something in his upper story."

"That Hadlow was right proper when he came to the Hall, miss. Treated us all with fittin' manners for a valet to a viscount, he did. Might not seem like a friendly fellow, but that wouldna' be right, you see. One must respect his position, he must." Rose nodded her head in a virtuous way, the single feather adorning her neat straw bonnet bobbing up and down in emphasis.

"Curious." Elizabeth found little comfort in this commendation, although she well knew that servants were not easy to fool, and that they were severe judges of character.

Sidthorp ushered her into the saffron-hued house with a much improved manner. Of course, he did not go so far as to actually smile, but at least he didn't look quite so forbidding. She handed her pelisse to Rose along with her bonnet and gloves. The basket she retained.

"This way, miss. Lord Leighton is in his room, but

he left instructions that you were to go directly to his father's room when you arrived.''

With Rose trailing behind, she followed the portly butler up the stairs and along the hall where her aunt and Lord Leighton had gone earlier.

"Is Lord Leighton's room in this wing?'' she inquired in what she hoped was a disinterested manner.

"Yes, miss. Last room on the left.'' The butler paused, rapped gently, then opened the door before them, quite some distance from Leighton's.

Elizabeth stood in her tracks, trying to adjust to the dark. For in spite of it being afternoon, it might have been night in there. "That will be all, Sidthorp.''

She must have sounded accustomed to giving orders, for Sidthorp left her immediately, even bowing. Elizabeth crossed to the windows and gently pulled the draperies aside to allow the winter light, such as it was, to enter. Then she turned to study the room while tying an apron about her waist. Although vast in size, it was simply yet elegantly furnished.

The enormous bed drew her attention. Nestled in the middle of the magnificent structure hung with royal blue silk that was embroidered with delicate gold threads lay a man. A very still man. Then he stirred.

Elizabeth hurried to the side of the bed, placing the basket atop the night table. "Sir? Is there anything I can do for you?''

It seemed to her that he fought to open his eyes. When he succeeded, Elizabeth suffered a shock, for David, Lord Leighton's hazel eyes stared at her from a lined face. Only there wasn't that familiar teasing present in them. They merely looked tired and ill.

Swiftly hunting through the basket, she found the tonic Purvis had prepared. In a trice Elizabeth had opened the bottle and poured a dose into a glass.

"Now, let me ease you up a bit. I shall have you feeling better in no time.'' He obediently drank the liquid, then studied Elizabeth with puzzlement.

"Who are you?'' he managed to whisper.

"Elizabeth Dancy. Lady Montmorcy's niece. I have come to nurse you. My aunt wishes you to be well, as does your son. For some peculiar reason they believe I can manage to persuade you to get better." She twinkled down at him, sharing the absurdity of a young woman convincing an old man he ought to live.

A ghost of a smile fluttered across his mouth, then was gone. "Amusing. Must know I like pretty gels."

The effort of that little speech exhausted the earl, and he closed his eyes to sleep once again.

She turned to share a concerned look with Rose, who set about tidying the room, muttering beneath her breath at the shortcomings of the Penhurst Place staff.

Elizabeth inspected the room. Aunt Bel had told her to dispose of anything that had come from the Penhurst kitchens or the valet. Elizabeth was inclined to agree after her own experience with both. She scooped up various evil-looking potions and proceeded to pour the contents out the window—after first checking to see that she wouldn't be dumping them on someone's head. She pulled the window shut quickly, grateful for the brief breath of fresh air.

That accomplished, she went about the room to check what else might be done, wishing she could give the place a thorough airing, for the stale atmosphere felt stifling to her, and it must to the invalid as well.

At last there was nothing left to do.

"Rose, I must also tend to Lord Leighton." The maid glanced with incurious eyes and nodded, accustomed by now to Elizabeth's ways.

She studied the potion Purvis had ordered her to give Lord Leighton with great misgivings. How could she dare to command his lordship to do anything? Then, recalling that she was responsible for his condition, she squared her shoulders and marched down the hall, bottle and spoon in hand, the ointment for his wound in her apron pocket.

At the last door on the left of the hall, she paused, then gently rapped.

"Enter."

Taking a deep breath—for she had never in her life gone into a gentleman's bedroom, except for her brother's and he didn't count—Elizabeth gingerly opened the door and peered in. He was alone.

She swallowed carefully, then stepped across the

threshold. She was inside. Holding the bottle and spoon before her as though to ward off any demons that might linger in a bachelor's bedroom, she moved forward.

"What the devil are you doing in my room? Elizabeth, you know you ought not be in here. Out!" he ordered, and not in a kindly manner.

His odious attitude, when she had come to administer medicine to him, and that not her own idea, firmed her resolve. "I have something for you."

"I have no doubt as to that, sweetheart. But I fear it will have to wait until this arm is better. You see, I'm a bit hampered in my movements." He gave her a caustic grin.

She knew she must be blushing. And it angered her even more. The dratted man could do it every time—disconcert her into a feminine flutter.

Annoyed, she did what she might not have had the nerve to do ordinarily. She marched to the side of his bed, poured out a spoonful of the "vile stuff," as he called it, then aimed the spoon at his mouth.

"If you think for a mo—" He was halted mid-speech when the spoon was deftly thrust into his mouth. She poured another and waited.

He glared at her. "You'll do it again, won't you? I pity our children."

Refusing to allow him to overset her again, she nodded. "Right you are. Open wide . . . sir."

He meekly obeyed, to her surprise. Finished with that task, she pulled the jar of ointment from her apron pocket. "Now to your wound."

"Hadlow will not like this," Lord Leighton prophesied.

"Oh, bother Hadlow," she said crisply, beginning to enjoy her authority in the sickroom. It did have merits after all. She could quite see how Purvis had become such a dictator. She rolled up the cambric sleeve of his nightshirt to a point above the wound, trying to be impersonal in her attentions.

The bandages unwrapped, she sucked in her breath when she saw the wound. While not actually nasty, it was scarcely a pretty thing either. She ignored his probing look and set about gently cleaning off the concoction

Hadlow had smeared over the injury, then replacing it with the mixture Purvis stirred up. In minutes she efficiently had his arm neatly wrapped. All that tending to the tenants at Montmorcy Hall had proven beneficial after all. She'd had training of a sort from a master, Purvis.

"Now then, you shall feel more the thing before you know it," she said as soothingly as she could. Then she recalled where she was and with whom. She took a step back.

He groaned.

Elizabeth immediately dropped the jar of ointment into her apron pocket and rushed to feel his brow. Staring down at his face, the closed lashes, she wondered what had happened. Purvis had not warned her that the "vile stuff" might affect him like this.

Wondering what she ought to do, she stretched out a hand to check his forehead for a fever.

His eyes flashed open. Before she realized what he was about, she found herself pulled down on the bed, falling against his body in a most scandalous way. Worse yet, his good arm snaked about her waist. In a trice she found herself being thoroughly and most adequately kissed. Warm little pulses went dancing up her spine, flittering along her nerves, until she was quite certain she would end up in a spineless heap on the elegant carpet.

Even though he had the full use of but one hand, he appeared to make good use of it, caressing her in delectable ways in improper places. Never had she dreamed anything could feel like this. And this was called lovemaking, she had no doubt. That seemed a rather prosaic word for such delightful passions.

This was *not* like the kiss at the Fenwicks' ball. There was no question in her mind he was an expert at this business. And she completely enjoyed being the recipient of his mastery. He smelled delicious, of sandalwood and something spicy. And he felt delicious, firm and muscular and somehow oddly comforting. She didn't care if she ever left this room.

He withdrew first, to her chagrin. She ought to have fought him, pounded at him, protested in some way, instead of meekly submitting. No, that wasn't true. She had not submitted. She had enthusiastically cooperated!

His satisfied smile was almost too much to endure.

"You, sirrah, are a cad and a bounder."

"You forgot scoundrel and rascal, not to mention rake."

"Those too."

She hardened her heart at the sight of the lopsided smile, the curl that flopped so endearingly over his forehead. "I had best leave. *Now.*" She slipped from his light clasp, rising to unsteady feet. She positioned the bottle that Purvis had sent on his bedside table, then turned away, hoping to calm her flip-flopping heart to normal.

"No. I want to give you something. Over there on the dresser. See the box? Fetch it . . . please?"

Unable to restrain her curiosity, Elizabeth did as bidden, telling herself that if she didn't, he might suffer a relapse. Returning warily to his side, she held it out to him.

He took the box, opened it, to extract a ring. An incredibly lovely diamond winked up at her from his fingers. A delicate gold setting surrounded it, and it was quite the most beautiful ring she had ever seen.

"You wish me to wear that?" she inquired with a mixture of horror and delight. "I daresay it's extremely valuable. I do not think I should," she said with an air of propriety.

"I found out your birthday is in April, and you are most assuredly an innocent. I believe this to be appropriate." He smiled a trifle grimly, then added, "Your presence here will be more readily accepted if you are seen wearing the family betrothal ring."

Her heart sank to her toes, although she knew that neither of them wished for the marriage. What a silly fool she was, to think for a moment that something else existed. This man was an experienced rake, a polished man about Town, certainly not interested in unsophisticated girls.

She accepted the ring, surprised to find that it fit her well. "How amazing. It fits."

His chuckle further unnerved her, and she backed away from his bed, glaring at him, lest she succumb to temptation. The trouble with resisting temptation is that it might not ever come again.

"I shall see you tomorrow?"

And then it might. Elizabeth nodded, totally unable to speak after her outrageous thought. She turned and fled the room, fuming at the faint chuckle that drifted after her.

Back in the earl's room, she found Rose standing at the foot of his lordship's bed, studying the man who lay so quietly.

"He be awful still, miss. Not natural-like."

"I know. I doubt if the tonic Purvis used is supposed to have that effect." Elizabeth walked closer to the bed, staring down at the earl with a frown pleating her brow.

"Reminds me of the time my brother got too much laudanum, miss. He lay just like that, in a stupor he was.

Elizabeth froze. Could it be possible that someone had drugged his lordship? But why? And who? She shook her head. Most unlikely. And yet, as she watched the spare frame, the barely rising chest, and flaccid countenance, she could not help but wonder.

A glance at the mantel clock revealed it to be time for dinner. She checked the earl's pulse and forehead, then slowly went from the room, leaving Rose in charge for the time being.

Once outside she encountered Filpot. His hair was neatly parted in the center and dangled about his ears, and his long legs were encased in modest black hose, with everything else he wore also in funereal black. The lanky valet glared at her.

"I shall return later to check on his lordship and give him his tonic. Nothing from the kitchen is to enter this room without my approval." Elizabeth folded her hands before her, hoping she could manage that quelling look her aunt did so well. "You may close the draperies this evening, but I want them open come morning. I shall be coming in to tend him then." Giving him a hard stare, Elizabeth calmly walked down the hall, then down the stairs to the ground floor.

Sidthorp stepped forward to offer his assistance.

"Going so soon, Miss Elizabeth?" Egbert emerged from the shadows of the corridor to her left.

"Mr. Percy. No, I remain for the time being."

"I see." He made her feel most uneasy, reminding her this was a predominantly male household.

"Come, have a glass of sherry with us. My father wishes to speak with you."

Recalling David's suspicions, she agreed, hoping to discover something useful about both of the Percys. Could there actually be someone in this house who wished the earl ill? Dead?

As preposterous as it seemed, she knew the expression "waiting for dead men's shoes" had valid grounds, and as well, arsenic was not called "inheritance powder" for no reason.

Darting surreptitious glances at Egbert while they walked down the corridor to the drawing room, she wondered about him and his ambitions. Did he desire a title? Wealth? Being a dandy could be vastly expensive. He certainly looked the fop this afternoon with his lilac pantaloons, primrose vest, and pale gray coat.

"My dear Miss Elizabeth," he said in a mocking manner as he ushered her through the drawing room door.

"Sirrah?" She raised what she hoped was an imperious brow at him, reminding him that he took a familiarity not granted.

He shrugged, not seeming the least affected by her words or expression. Apparently quelling took practice.

"Ah, so there you are." Lord Augustus Percy rose from his chair with a faint creaking of his corset. "Knew you'd come. How's my brother doing? Better, I hope. Rummy thing, getting poorly like that. Do the ticket, having you to look after him. Yes, sir, do the ticket."

"Stands to reason, Papa. A pretty girl by one's bed is sufficient to make one want to get well." Egbert cocked his head to one side, leering at Elizabeth in such a knowing way that she wondered if he had been in the hall while she attended to Lord Leighton. And kissed him.

"Right, my boy. Did you say m'brother is still among us?" Lord Augustus dropped back into the large high-backed chair near the fireplace, and peered at Elizabeth curiously.

"Yes, sir," Elizabeth said respectfully.

"Pretty behaved lass."

It was then Egbert spotted the engagement ring. He sauntered over to pick up her hand, ogling it most odiously, then displayed her hand to his father. "Well, well, dear cuz has not wasted a minute. Trotted out the family ring, no less. I trust you are honored, my dear."

"I am, indeed, sir."

"We are practically family. I insist we not stand on formality, and I claim the right to kiss the future bride." Egbert did more than leer at her, he stepped closer to her side, lifting a hand toward her face.

Elizabeth backed away from him, alarmed by his look of intent. A glance at his father told her to expect no help from that quarter, as the older man wore an amused and quite benevolent smile.

"I thought I told you to keep clear, Egbert," came a deep voice from the doorway. "Put one hand on Elizabeth, and you will suddenly find yourself in need of a new place to lay your head this evening."

Elizabeth relaxed. Although the words were spoken in a casual way, there was no mistaking the seriousness of the person who uttered them.

"Are you all right, my sweet?" David walked over to stand close to her. He effectively forced Egbert to retreat, to Elizabeth's relief.

"Quite. I believe Mr. Percy was merely teasing. It is a trait that must run in the family." She turned then, and saw at what cost he had come to her rescue. He looked pale, and she could detect the strain in his face.

"I shall join you." He drew her aside while Egbert replied to comments from Lord Augustus.

"You ought not be out of bed," she scolded.

"Hadlow informed me that he had seen Egbert, my most detestable cousin, hauling you off to the drawing room. I came to save you from a fate worse than death."

"Egbert?" she said, horrified at her escape.

"Any time spent in his company is regrettable."

"I can see there is no love lost between the two of you."

"Did you see my father?"

"Indeed, before I tended to you. If you hadn't put me so out of countenance, I'd have told you all about it," she couldn't resist saying. Then she grew serious. "I gave him the tonic, tossed all the other potions out of the window." At his amused expression she added, "I first checked to see if someone chanced to be outside."

"Any observations?"

"Rose made a peculiar comment. She said he reminded her of her brother when he had taken too much laudanum." Elizabeth studied the viscount, then gently nudged him onto one of the comfortable chairs on the far side of the room.

"Drugged?" He sounded as appalled as he looked. "But who? Or ought I say, which one?" he finished grimly, glancing at his relatives.

"It may simply be his illness. Perhaps after a good night's sleep, you will think of something. Or someone."

Before she could urge him to take better care of himself, and make a fool of herself by revealing her concern over him, Jeremy Vane entered the room.

"Miss Elizabeth. How charming to see you on this dreary day. I vow, it is like having the sun come out."

Elizabeth smiled at the modestly attired man, such an agreeable contrast to Egbert.

Not so Lord Leighton. He rose to his full height, frowned at Jeremy, then said, "No need to dump the butter boat over her, Vane. She is not only spoken for, but her fortune is only modest."

Jeremy drew himself up, nodded to Elizabeth, then joined the others, seeming unaffected by the snub.

"That was not kind of you," Elizabeth admonished quietly.

"I am not a kind man. Haven't you learned that by now?"

Not trusting that gleam in his eyes in the least, Elizabeth turned in a whirl to march up to her room. She would request a tray and avoid the entire Percy family.

She looked down when she reached the top of the stairs, and was surprised to find Lord Leighton standing in the entry hall, watching her.

"Oh, do get up to bed before you truly take ill."

"You care." He grinned at her, lazily walking toward the bottom of the stairs.

Elizabeth hurried to her room, closed the door behind her, then shut her eyes, totally exasperated with herself, not to mention that wretched man. Would she never learn to guard her tongue when near him?

"You prefer a tray up here, Miss Elizabeth?" Rose inquired at long last, seeing her mistress made no move to return downstairs. She had been put out of the earl's room by that Filpot, she explained when Elizabeth inquired.

"Indeed."

Crossing to the window, she studied the sky. Bleak gray skies were to be preferred to snow, she decided.

In the drawing room, David sank down upon a nearby chair, relieved to be off his feet. Not that his arm pained him as much as he implied to Elizabeth. He suspected that she would hightail it out of this house and back to Montmorcy Hall if she knew just how lightly he was injured. Oh, it looked rather bad, but in actuality it was amazingly mild. How fortunate Elizabeth had hit his arm, and with a gun not fully loaded. Hadlow assured him that the wound ought to heal nicely, with scarcely any scar.

"Had us worried, my boy," said his uncle when he realized David had rejoined them. Shifting in his chair drawn close to the fire, he studied his nephew from beneath his brows. "Dashed odd business, if you ask me."

"Perhaps a bit foolish. I have been trying to see Miss Elizabeth for weeks, and with the fortification of some excellent brandy I decided to beard the lioness in her den, or bedchamber if you will."

"Egad," Lord Augustus muttered while Egbert chuckled.

"As you know, I received a shot for my trouble."

"What the devil did you want to see her about that was so urgent you couldn't wait?" Egbert demanded when he could stop chuckling.

"It seemed like a good idea at the time. I wanted her to come nurse Father. That woman and her gin bottle was the final straw as far as a hired nurse. You must admit that Filpot has done poorly."

"Cannot abide that man," Lord Augustus grumbled.

"Nor can I," David replied. "However, he has been

with my father for ages, and so he remains. Perhaps Elizabeth will be able to counteract his influence.''

''The wound very disagreeable?'' Jeremy inquired from his chair to one side.

David looked down at the neat sling that covered his arm. Something told him that he had best be careful what he said about the injury. ''So-so.''

''Can only hope it doesn't turn putrid,'' Lord Augustus added in lugubrious tones.

''Amen to that, Uncle,'' David replied before rising. It was best he go to his room to keep up the appearance that his wound truly pained him.

''I always told you that your pranks would get you in trouble one day,'' Egbert said as a parting shot.

David considered the lingering kiss he had shared with the delightful Elizabeth and grinned.

6

ALL WAS SILENT the next morning when Elizabeth came down to break her fast. In the dining room, usually a pleasant place, the gloom outside seemed to have crept in through the windows and seeped beneath the doors.

"And a good morning to you," Elizabeth said to the sole occupant with determined sprightliness, although some of it was forced.

Lord Augustus surveyed the sky, then turned from the window. "Not good, not good at all," he said with a dejected shake of his head. "Weather turning miserable again. Best to remain inside." As if he jaunted about. "Known people to stray off the road in a snowstorm and freeze to death before help arrived. If one cannot see, one can hardly find the way."

He turned again to scan the clouds, speaking loud enough to be clearly heard although he was turned from her. "Good of you to stay. Proper gel. Worry about m'brother. You'll see to him right enough." There was a hint of a question in his voice she couldn't ignore.

Elizabeth buttered her toast, considering the previous day. In a mere few hours she had antagonized Egbert Percy, caused poor Jeremy to receive a tongue-lashing, and tumbled into Lord Leighton's arms. No, that was one arm, and she had assisted him, more's the pity. Proper girl? Hardly.

"I shall do all possible for the earl, you may be certain. It is a pity you are not as close as you once were. I wonder if a visit from you might not cheer him up."

"No. Not from me," he said with a trace of sadness.

She wondered about Lord Augustus. Why did he stay here when it seemed he and his brother had become estranged? It seemed most peculiar to her.

She would need to keep a sharp eye on all the inhabitants of this house. Could there actually be someone who would use poison on the earl? Was that why Lord Augustus persisted in staying? She stared at the man, lost in his unhappy reflections. What really went on in his mind? Poison? Her appetite suddenly fled, and she abandoned all pretense of eating, resorting to her teacup for a bit of warm comfort.

"Least he don't seem contagious. Bad to have you in any danger, proper gel like you," Lord Augustus said at long last.

A wry smile touched her lips. There was danger, and there was . . . danger. It seemed to her that Lord Leighton presented a peril of a serious sort. Or did he merely seek to provoke her once again? Exasperating, maddening man.

"Have you been at Penhurst Place very long, sir?"

"Dun territory, y'know. Some time ago. Just need a bit of time to come about. I will one of these days." His corset creaked as he joined her at the table. "M'home is lonely, don't you see? Wish things were different." He subsided into morose reflection again.

Elizabeth made a show of brushing crumbs from her fingers, then pushed away from the table. "I shall go up to see your brother now. Could I bring a message from you to him perhaps?"

"You are going now?" Jeremy Vane said in a dismayed voice. He stood poised uncertainly in the doorway.

"Only upstairs to stay with the earl."

He gave her a hesitant smile, then stood aside to allow her to leave the dining room.

She briskly walked to the central hall and up the stairs. Seeing Rose, she requested that she heat up a bit of the special broth for his lordship. Then Elizabeth marched down the south corridor to the earl's room.

She wondered what her reception would be today. If her suspicions proved true, and that repulsive Filpot was trying to do in his master, her attentions could save the earl's life. Feeling immeasurably better, she resigned herself to whatever came her way.

Sidthorp approached her. He had just come from the

earl's room, and she wondered if she dared to ask him what the mood was today.

"I trust that all is to your liking, Miss Elizabeth?" Sidthorp inquired. "You suffered no disturbance in your wing of the house?"

"Lovely," she assured him, a smile touching her lips as she considered her aunt's hopes. "A good sleep does much to restore one's spirits." It seemed Sidthorp was on the side of virtue. "May I go in to see the earl now?"

The butler rubbed his chin, then glanced about them. Nodding, he said, "Filpot went down to the kitchen not too long ago. I shall find some manner of delaying him, so you may investigate his lordship's condition without that, er, man about you."

Pausing, Elizabeth did something she normally would not have considered. She quizzed a servant. "Sidthorp, it seems that Filpot is not well liked. How odd the earl should be so devoted to the man."

"As to that, miss, his lordship is not one to make changes. Detests a deviation from the customary, you see."

That did not auger well for her assuming control of the sickroom. "Thank you, Sidthorp. I can only hope that I shan't find myself on the doorstep in a few minutes."

"Oh, he likes a pretty face, miss. Fact is, I believe I heard Filpot muttering a complaint to that effect when the staff ate their morning meal."

"Undoubtedly that is why I am here rather than my aunt." She made a rueful grimace at the thought.

"His lordship has avoided any attentions from ladies his own age." The butler shared a look of understanding with Elizabeth, then recalled the impropriety of the conversation about the same time she did. He turned and walked toward the stairs, while Elizabeth continued on to the earl's room.

She was to nurse an elderly man who was set in his ways and liked a pretty face, while avoiding entanglements with women his own age. A difficult task at best. Perhaps that was where Lord Leighton came by his inclinations? Like father, like son? She could just have well been describing David, Lord Leighton, come to think about it. He too seemed set in his ways, and he certainly liked a pretty face, if the gossips in London were to be believed. He was yet a bachelor, having eluded every matchmaking mama in Town. Only to be caught of his own doing.

Elizabeth giggled to herself.

"What a lovely sound so early in the morning."

She looked around from where she now paused before Lord Crompton's door to find Lord Leighton bearing down upon her.

"How are you this morning?" she inquired. "I trust you did not come down with a putrid throat, or something equally dismal, after your outing yesterday."

"Strange, whatever that vile stuff is that your Purvis concocted seems to work. I do feel more the thing today."

"Good, as there will be no repetition of yesterday." At his devilish grin she hurried on to say, "You shan't require my attentions."

He shifted his gaze to the door behind her, then reached around her to open the door. "Come, we had best have a look at the old boy."

She noted his face assumed a serious mien as they entered the bedchamber. Once inside he fixed a more cheerful look on his countenance, walking close to the bedside.

"At least the curtains have been opened, and the fire is not excessive. Quite pleasant, in fact." While she spoke she checked about the room, then walked over to join Lord Leighton at the side of the bed.

Reaching out her hand, she placed it against Lord Crompton's forehead, relieved to find there was no fever. A clean spoon lay on the table by the tonic Purvis had created. Elizabeth met the viscount's gaze before she picked up the spoon and turned her attention to his father. She measured the tonic into a glass, then leaned over the bed.

"Good morning, my lord."

He opened his eyes. "Ah, the pretty face," he said in a barely audible voice.

"I believe you are on the mend, sir." Elizabeth chuckled, then held the glass to his lips, urging him to swallow the tonic. He obeyed her, then sank back onto the pillows with a more alert expression on his face.

"About time."

"Good morning, Father," Lord Leighton offered. "Glad to see you look better."

"Odd that. Feel like I've slept a year."

Lord Leighton shared a look of consternation with Elizabeth. "Dr. Dibble found nothing amiss with you."

"Bah. Then why do I feel as weak as a new kitten, I ask you? I missed you—have you been ill?"

"Er, no. I ran into a slight complication."

Elizabeth decided to insert a comment. "He sought my help. I mistook him for a burglar and shot him in the arm."

"Good Lord!"

"It was a bit of a surprise." Lord Leighton cleared his throat before proceeding. "Also, Miss Elizabeth and I are betrothed, Father."

Surprisingly shrewd eyes surveyed Elizabeth from beneath a pair of shaggy brows. "Fell into a bumblebath, did he? Knew he would someday. Bound to. I believe it runs in the family."

"Something like that, sir. You see," Elizabeth said, deciding to confess all while the earl seemed in a good mood, "he happened to be in my bedchamber at two of the clock when I shot him. In the morning, that is," she added for clarification.

A ghost of a smile flitted across his lordship's face as he turned his gaze to his son. "Did it right and proper, eh?"

"Yes, sir. But my arm is better today." He gestured to the neat nankeen sling which supported his arm. Of Aunt Bel's print shawl there was no sign. Apparently seeing what Elizabeth noticed, that the earl showed signs of fatigue, Lord Leighton said, "Best get down to eat something before Elizabeth offers me some of your tonic."

Once he had left, Elizabeth set about smoothing the bed and checking the room as she had done the day before. She wanted to make certain that nothing from the kitchen had entered the room. No matter who might be trying to poison—if that was the case—it was better not to take any chances.

Rose slipped silently into the room with the broth. She handed the tray with the covered bowl to Elizabeth, then stepped back. "I'll just tidy up some, miss," she whispered.

"Care for a little broth, sir?" Elizabeth coaxed. "I should like to see you continue to improve. It does a nurse's heart good."

"I should like something more substantial, if you please," he insisted. But his voice was weak, and Elizabeth suspected he was putting on a good show for her benefit.

"Try this first. I promise you that I shall bring you hearty roast beef as soon as you may not take ill from it. Now, let me tempt you." She proffered a spoon, leaning over the bed to feed him.

A twinkle lit his eyes, reminiscent of the one she so frequently saw in David's. "That you might do, my dear."

"What a naughty man you are, sir," she whispered, so as not to shock Rose. She grinned back at him, then continued to feed him the contents of the bowl until all was gone. "There now, you shall feel better soon."

"Um," he replied, already drowsy.

"Sleep well." It wasn't necessary to speak in an undertone, as his lordship had returned to the world of sleep.

Elizabeth strolled to the fireplace, absorbing heat while indulging in a bit of reflection.

There were several prime suspects here. Lord Augustus, Egbert Percy, Filpot, Hadlow. Even the cook was not free from suspicion, Elizabeth thought with a grim smile, considering the deplorable meals at this house. She supposed she must include the innocuous Jeremy Vane, although she thought him unlikely. What could he possibly gain? Could there be anyone she had missed? Probably not. Egbert seemed the most likely, especially given David's aversion to him. But then, David did not care for Jeremy Vane either. She sighed with vexation. Was there ever such a coil?

One thing she needed to do was to find a book to read to his lordship. Now that he remained alert for longer periods of time, she hoped to entertain him with suitable material. What would he like?

The door opened, and Egbert Percy stepped into the room.

Elizabeth gave the earl a worried glance before walking across the room to meet his nephew. She intended to prevent him, or anyone else, from disturbing the earl.

"May I assist you in some way, Mr. Percy?" She made certain to keep him standing close by the door.

"I wondered how my uncle did this morning." He gave Elizabeth an uncomfortable look, and she wondered if that was the only reason he sought this room.

"Better, I think. He seems more alert, for one thing." She glanced at Rose, hoping the maid received the message she silently conveyed. "I was about to go down for a cup of tea. Rose will keep watch here. Shall you join me?" She bestowed an inquiring look on Egbert, then gestured to the door.

"Of course," he said politely.

It seemed that Egbert was not averse to playing the gallant. He placed her hand on his arm, chatting about the weather as they strolled down the stairs. Elizabeth felt quite in charity with him by the time they reached the vaulted corridor.

"Is there a garden out there in the summer?" Elizabeth inquired, studying the courtyard that was enclosed by the many-windowed corridor.

"Once there was. Lady Crompton had a fondness for flowers, I believe. Now there is naught but grass and a few bits of shrubbery."

"What a pity. I fancy that a bed of colorful blooms would look quite cheerful on a warm summer day."

Elizabeth guided him in the direction of the morning room in the back of the house, where Sidthorp had confided the earl's late wife had enjoyed spending her time.

Catching sight of one of the maids, Elizabeth sweetly commanded her to bring tea into the morning room.

"Avoiding your betrothed this morning? I thought newly engaged women couldn't wait to spend time with their sweethearts. It all seems dashed sudden to me." Young Mr. Percy stationed himself by the fireplace, watching Elizabeth with a narrowed, and somewhat hostile, gaze.

Sensing she skirted dangerous ground, Elizabeth pretended to examine a lovely painted screen near the window before replying to his comment.

"But we are sweethearts," she said, searching for a plausible reply. "We met in London, you know, at the Fenwick ball. I suspect it was love at first sight for both of us, at least it was for me. And I confess David seemed most enamored. Wherever I went after that, I seemed to discover him. He found me here in Surrey after I joined my aunt. How fortunate that she lives so close to his father. Most convenient for David and me."

She neglected to mention the vast amount of time before he had again sought her company. After all, she was embroidering the truth a great deal, so what did it matter if she did it royally?

"I still say there is something dashed peculiar about the entire business. I had not the least notion he'd formed an attachment."

"But then, you have never been in love, cousin," came a rich, smooth voice from the doorway.

Lord Leighton entered the room, crossing to where Elizabeth stood. He surprised her by touching her on the chin with one finger, then placing a gentle kiss on her lips. It was like a whisper of fire on her skin, singeing her lips with danger.

She knew he sought to prove the validity of their connection to his cousin, but she wished he hadn't kissed her. It stirred things best left alone.

"Good morning," she said, deciding to pretend they hadn't met earlier. "I trust it is agreeable that I have ordered tea. It is such a wretched day outside, and somehow tea always makes things better."

"Most acceptable. After all, my dearest, you will reign here one day." He settled down far too close to where she had sought a place on the settee. When he stretched his good arm out behind her, touching her back, she just barely refrained from jumping. That would never do—a proper bride to be did not flinch from the touch of her beloved.

"How do you feel? I notice you still use a sling." She

worried his arm was not improving. "Does Hadlow dress your wound properly as he ought?" She had a dim view of the valet's nursing abilities.

"I do well enough. He does not have your delicate touch, however." He shared a smile with her that sent tremors to her toes.

She noted the teasing twinkle in his eyes before he turned his gaze toward his cousin. Would she never remember that much of his behavior was due to his delight in teasing her? He could not be serious.

"Lingering about the house, Egbert? Thought you would be out on that new mare."

"Too cold by far."

"Ah, yes, the precarious health of the town beau."

Elizabeth decided to interfere. "Your father does seem to be doing better today, does he not?" She hoped her voice didn't squeak, but she feared it might, making her sound like a ninny.

"What's that? Crompton better? By Jove, that is good news." Accompanied by a creaking corset, Lord Augustus ambled into the morning room, seeking a chair next to the warmth of the fire. "Excellent, excellent. Best news I've had all day." He wheezed as he settled down onto the depths of the high-backed chair, giving Elizabeth a beetle-browed stare. When she tensed, David dropped his hand on her shoulder, bestowing a slight pressure on her.

" 'Tis the *only* news you've had this day, Father," Egbert said impatiently.

"What? Quite so, quite so. Nasty weather. Can't think but what it snows before the day is out, what?" Augustus frowned as he moved his stare to the window.

"Miss Elizabeth will grace Penhurst Place with her presence for more than a day if that is the case. These roads become impassable at the least bit of snow, you know," Egbert said, rather snidely, Elizabeth thought.

Jeremy paused in the doorway, a sheaf of papers in his hand. He gave David a hesitant look, then said most apologetically, "I'm afraid I need your signature on these, Leighton. With your father unable to run the estate, it dumps rather a lot on your shoulders."

Elizabeth smiled warmly at the young man, liking his shy manners. "Will you not join us in a cup of tea, sir?"

The maid entered at that moment, apparently having anticipated the gathering, for there were sufficient cups and a plate of macaroons as well.

At a slight nod from David, Elizabeth poured the tea, added milk and sugar as wished, then thankfully sipped her own, after noting that David had to remove that disturbing arm from her shoulders in order to consume his brew.

"He is feeling much better this morning, you will be pleased to know."

"How is that, Miss Elizabeth? From what I had heard, his lordship was sinking," Jeremy said awkwardly, shifting from foot to foot. He sipped his tea, watching Lord Leighton with a wary eye. The batch of papers was tucked beneath one arm, and Elizabeth wondered how long they would remain there.

How ill at ease he was, to be sure, she thought. Poor fellow, he must feel overshadowed just to be in the same room with Lord Leighton. She believed she had detected a faint family resemblance, however. His eyes were a rather insipid hazel, not the rich, deep tone she saw when she chanced to be entrapped by Lord Leighton's eyes. And Jeremy's hair was straight as an arrow, rather than possessing the charming curl his cousin owned, but it was a shade of brown not too unlike his cousin's.

"It is snowing out," announced Lord Leighton to no one in particular.

Desiring to put some distance between herself and the man who disturbed her, Elizabeth rose from the settee and walked to the window to watch large white flakes drifting down from the sky.

Jeremy Vane dropped all the papers to the floor, and they scattered about the room.

"Oh, dear," murmured Elizabeth. Quickly she placed her cup and saucer on a table, then assisted Jeremy in gathering them up. The poor fellow's face had flamed with embarrassment at the accident.

"Here you are. Such a tedious matter on a pretty, if cold, day. Leases and settlements. Victoria has tended to those while my brother has been away." She sighed, then caught an odd expression on Leighton's face that stopped her speech.

"Give me the papers, and I shall go over them in the library. It wouldn't do to get macaroon crumbs on them, would it?" Lord Leighton bestowed his lazy smile on all, then added, "Join me shortly, will you, Elizabeth? We have a small matter to discuss, if you please."

"Of course, David." She recaptured her cup, pouring a bit more tea for something to do with her hands while she thought. Jeremy had merely requested that David sign the papers, an administrative thing. Why was he placing the young man in an awkward spot by going over those papers? Surely he trusted his cousin to do his best.

Then she recalled how her aunt checked every piece of paperwork before signing anything, claiming she felt it best to know what went on under her nose. Elizabeth relaxed. David was trying to learn more about the estate, nothing more. But the very idea that he would treat his cousin like a mere employee bothered her.

Leaving Lord Augustus and Egbert to argue about how long the snow might continue, Elizabeth left the room. At the door to the library, she paused, then rapped sharply. The door opened before she could drop her hand.

"Good, you came promptly."

Elizabeth followed David over to the desk, wondering what this was all about.

"That young fool ought to know that I cannot sanction the authorization of these leases. It would be illegal. What kind of a spot is he trying to place me in, anyway?"

"I do not understand."

"Although I am the heir, it is not my privilege to approve these—according to my settlement—unless my father specifically allows it. He has not to this date. And I will not approach him about it at this time." David gave her a warning look lest she urge him to do just that.

"Perhaps you should talk with him about it?" she said anyway.

"And make him feel as though I believe he is about to snuff it?"

"I see." But she didn't, actually. She wondered if David was just trying to get at his cousin, whom he appeared to dislike excessively.

Seeking to change the subject, she said, "Do you have a copy of a good herbal in the house? Culpeppers perhaps? Or that new one, the *Family Herbal* by John Thornton? Aunt Bel has a copy and I think it quite good, for it deals with the medical properties of our English plants. Bewick has done excellent engravings which I very much admire," she concluded, wishing she might do such a volume herself someday.

He gave her an arrested look. "You believe there might be a clue in such a book?"

" 'Tis possible," she admitted.

David rose from the chair by the fire to wander along the shelves, touching a volume now and again.

Elizabeth joined in the search, hunting for either volume or anything like them.

He was awkward with only one hand and couldn't easily pull out books. She thought she could be of help if there was one he wanted to see, so she remained at his side.

Elizabeth noted various interesting volumes and pulled one out, thinking it might be good to read to the earl. As she did, another book fell to the floor. It proved to be a slim little volume.

"An Essay into the Operation of Poisonous Agents upon the Living Body," they read in soft unison, both horrified at the implications that began to hit them.

A chill crept over Elizabeth, and she shivered.

"Quite new, isn't it? Was your father interested in such as this?"

"Not that I know," David replied, meeting her eyes in an apprehensive frown. The teasing lights were gone now.

Egbert popped his head in to see what kept Elizabeth. "It's time for nuncheon, you two. Had a lover's spat?" His face wore a maliciously gleeful look, and Elizabeth longed to toss the book at his head.

"Merely looking for something to read later on. If I must spend the night here, I would enjoy a novel," she said instead.

He looked unconvinced, but could say nothing in the face of her declaration.

"Time we had some nourishment, my love," David

added. He unobtrusively tucked the slim volume in his sling. Then he drew Elizabeth along with him by the simple means of placing his arm protectively around her shoulder.

She supposed he said that for Egbert's benefit, although what possible difference it made whether his cousin accepted their betrothal or not, she didn't know.

"I believe I shall look in on your father first, if you do not mind. After all, I am here to nurse, not chat with you two. Rose will need a moment to herself as well. Please go ahead without me, for I might be awhile."

Elizabeth slipped from the room, leaving David and Egbert staring after her as she hurried down the hall and around the corner. With any luck, she could avoid the meal entirely.

The earl's bedchamber looked pleasant and warm, with the soft light flooding the room. Outside, a white world made it seem as though the room floated in space. It looked rather eerie, and Elizabeth rushed into speech.

"You had best get something to eat, Rose. But first, could you fetch me a shawl from my room? It is not precisely chilly, but the very thought of snow makes me cold."

"So, you return."

Whirling about, Elizabeth discovered the earl watching her. "You are awake!"

"For my sins, yes. What is that potion you poured down my throat?" His voice seemed stronger, and his color not quite so ashen.

"You sound like David. He loathes the potion Purvis sent for him." She lingered by the bed, watching him as much as he eyed her.

The earl chuckled, though it was faint and brief.

"Aunt Bel's abigail, Purvis, is marvelous when it comes to mixing up healing concoctions. I believe she is a frustrated apothecary."

The door opened and Rose entered with the shawl. Elizabeth thanked her maid, then requested that she heat more of the broth brought from Montmorcy Hall. "Best see to it yourself, then bring it up directly."

Rose darted an awed look at the figure lying in state

on the bed, then bobbed a hasty curtsy. "Yes, miss," she murmured before disappearing from sight.

It might annoy David were she to remain here, tending his father rather than joining them, but it gave her time to think.

While they waited for Rose, she held up the novel she had found just before the little poison book tumbled to the floor. "Why do I not read to you? This is a delightful book I feel certain you will like." She commenced to read at his nod. " 'It is a truth universally acknowledged that a single man in possession of a good fortune must be in want of a wife.' " His lordship nodded, and Elizabeth took them both into the world of Jane Austen's Miss Bennet.

When the soup arrived, Elizabeth reluctantly set aside the lovely book. She spoonfed his lordship the delicately flavored chicken broth. Once he had consumed what he could, she replaced the cover over the bowl, then set the bed to rights. She was about ready to go to her own lunch when Filpot entered.

The earl had shut his eyes, and there was nothing, other than the covered bowl on the tray Elizabeth now held, to indicate that he had been fed—or been awake, for that matter. She noted the valet's darting perusal of the room, and she hated to leave, but knew she must.

"I shall be back as soon as I can," she said quietly to the valet, hoping the earl caught her words as well.

Filpot frowned but could say nothing.

Nuncheon was over when she paused at the dining room door. In the kitchen she poured the broth into its jar. Then she supervised a light repast to her taste, and quickly ate it before returning to the library to seek out David. While hardly earth-shaking news, he would be pleased to know his father had consumed a bit of broth and enjoyed her reading.

"Where the devil have you been?" he snapped as she entered the library.

Her pleasure in the earl's progress dissolved at the cold expression on Lord Leighton's face.

"You will be pleased to know I fed your father a tidy amount of broth and read to him for a bit. We enjoyed our time enormously." She whirled about and marched to the door. A hand latched onto her arm, and she halted, waiting.

Heart beating madly, she turned to look at David. What did he want of her?

7

"PLEASE STAY. You may as well know I've a wretched temper when I have to deal with my uncle and cousins, particularly my cousin Jeremy." He stared down at her with an odd expression on his face, one she certainly could not fathom.

She eased herself from his clasp and slowly moved so that a table stood between them. "He seems most innocuous to me."

"He does, does he not?" David rubbed his chin with a speculative gesture.

"Why do they remain? Oh, I know Mr. Vane is your father's steward, but why your uncle and his son? Surely they could go home? If I am not being presumptuous," she added as an afterthought.

He strolled around the table, then drew her with him to the cozy arrangement of chairs before the fireplace.

"You know, I can see merits in marriage if it offers an arrangement like this, where a fellow may discuss problems with his wife." His eyes developed that familiar glimmer of teasing, and Elizabeth doubted his sincerity.

"I shan't comment on that, I believe," she replied.

He urged her down on the high-backed chair, then sat opposite, staring moodily at the fire. "My Uncle Augustus is really not such a bad sort of chap, a bit of a hanger-on, but he once he got along famously with my father. His son is another matter entirely. Father ordered Egbert to take himself off to London, or anywhere, rather than sponge on our estate. Quite created a chasm between the two families, or what is left of us. When Father became ill, Jeremy stayed on, claiming he could not leave at such a time when families must pull together. I suspect he lingers about waiting for the will to be read."

"What a ghastly thing to say." She reflected a moment, then continued, "But I believe I can see why you might feel that way." She thought a moment, then said, "Have you looked through that book we found? Is it of any value? Would it help someone who wished to poison another?"

"I should say a clever person could apply the lessons learned without difficulty."

"So all we must do now is figure out who bought that book, then plotted to murder your father."

"I knew you were a girl of uncommon good sense." He paused. "I really do not understand my antagonism to Jeremy. Perhaps it has something to do with all the time my father has lavished on him." He gave her a searching glance.

"And not you?" Elizabeth inquired with intuition. She could appreciate that David might resent the hours his father spent teaching estate management to Jeremy while ignoring his son.

"I did mention you are most perceptive."

"My father always favored Geoffrey over us girls. Although he is the heir, I suspect it had more to do with Geoffrey's amazing ability with languages. I do well enough with French and have a smattering of Italian, Julia about the same, while Victoria is close to my brother in her abilities, yet he favored his son." Elizabeth shrugged, then went on, "We all tried our best to please him, each of us perfecting a proficiency in some craft, and Mother seemed proud of us."

"But you craved a word of praise from your father?"

"Since you understand how I feel, then you know how I am able to sympathize with you." She gave him a dry look, then clasped her hands in her lap. "What do we do now?"

"I shall continue searching the house for evidence of the poison, and I should appreciate it if you would do the same. When you are not with my father, that is. I just wish I knew what I was looking for—precisely." He exchanged a rueful look with her and they both sighed.

"Which reminds me, why did you tell him that we are betrothed? You know it is not the truth, even if Aunt Bel insists we are to wed." Her annoyance had dissipated with time, but she was curious as to why a man who had so assiduously fought being leg-shackled was informing one and all about their bogus engagement.

"You are a remarkably pretty woman, my dear. And my father would wonder about your presence here, in a household of men, if I did not offer a plausible explanation." His grin was as devilish as his smooth words were prosaic. Those hazel eyes danced with an aggravating gleam.

Her pleasure at his compliment dimmed as she considered the practicality of his words. Speculating on what might lie behind that grin was something else.

"I wonder how long it will snow." Oddly enough, she wasn't worried about it. And she supposed she ought to be, had she an ounce of brains in her head.

"Regardless of when it stops, I doubt if the roads will be passable. Even London streets are a frightful mess when it snows."

"True enough." She rose, strangely reluctant to end their little interchange, yet knowing she must check on his father again. "You ought to find a reputable nurse, you know. I may do my best, but what if that is insufficient?"

"We *had* a nurse before you came. I found her raiding the gin bottle during the night and sent her packing." He had also risen and now stood close to her, looking faintly amused as she backed toward the door and bumped into the table instead.

"I understand that is not unusual." I ought to go, she reminded herself, yet she lingered, and she could not understand why.

"I shall attempt to keep my cousins out of your way." He fiddled with a leather bookmark that he'd found on the table, watching her face intently.

What was on his mind? Maybe he merely missed his London society, and perhaps his mistress? That thought so distressed Elizabeth that she turned to flee the room.

A hasty glance behind her revealed his lordship standing where she had left him with a thoughtful expression on his face. Face aflame, she hurried up the stairs and across to the south wing, where she could check on his father and be safe.

Rose met her breathless entrance with raised brows. "How is he?"

"Fine, miss. He's been restless, but I gave him some of the tonic, and he seemed to perk up, like."

Elizabeth walked over to the bed to study her patient. It was challenging to know what to do for someone who slept so much, especially when she was not skilled in nursing. Her lessons from Purvis had been too brief, she could see that now. But then, she was doubtlessly better than a nurse who indulged in gin.

With that thought as comfort, she sent Rose off to have something to eat.

Elizabeth was most curious who might have used that book on poisons. Perhaps the cook took it to prepare herbal potions in the still room, since Lady Crompton no longer was there to take charge.

"It surely cannot be as bad as all that."

She whirled about to face the gentleman who gazed at her from the depths of the enormous bed.

"I fear it is, sir. What with snow and trying to get you on your feet, I have my hands full." She held up her slim hands and smiled at his expression.

"I believe I feel better this afternoon. Shall you read me some more of Miss Austen's book?" His eyes had that appealing gleam so noticeable in his son's.

She promptly seated herself, opened the book to the marked page, and began. " 'But it must very materially lessen their chance of marrying men of any consideration in the world," replied Darcy.' " She raised her eyes to meet those of his lordship, sharing an amused look, then continued with the story. When it became necessary to light a lamp, he gave a sigh.

"Is it time for dinner?" he asked in a vexed tone.

Encouraged at what she took to be a sign of improvement, Elizabeth glanced at the mantel clock and agreed. "I believe it is. Goodness, the hours fly past when one has a good book." She placed the bookmark at where she had stopped, then rose. "I shall order some more of that special broth to be heated for you, and Purvis said you might have some of her special herb biscuits." Elizabeth turned to give the bell pull a tug.

"I only said that because I want to see you dressed for dinner."

She shook her head in dismay. "You are a wag, sir. I believe you are malingering here, and not the least under the weather." She tilted her head and flashed one of the Dancy smiles at him. She crossed to the bed and smoothed his covers, plumping a pillow to tuck beside him while bestowing a fond look on the gentleman.

"I think my son a very lucky man."

Elizabeth blushed, thanking her stars that Lord Leighton was not present.

"Never say that I do not have the best of taste, Father."

The sound of that rich voice came as a distinct shock to Elizabeth, and she found herself quite shaken.

"I am all agreement, son."

While Elizabeth went to the door to explain to Rose what was wished, she could hear quiet conversation between father and son.

It bothered her that David could slip into the room without her hearing a sound. After a spy had crept into their house in London, Elizabeth had slept with a gun beneath her pillow, but the gun was not here for tonight. And she wondered if she should have brought it.

"I am feeling so much more the thing that I believe Elizabeth ought to join you for dinner, David. Leave that shy little maid in here with me."

Unwilling to argue, Elizabeth instructed Rose on what to do. After explaining that the maid ought to consider his lordship like her father, it seemed she felt more at ease. By the time Elizabeth left the bedchamber Rose had proceeded to bully his lordship into consuming the broth and herb biscuits.

"Can you bear to join us for dinner this evening? I'll not like the notion of you hiding in your room just because my relatives put you in a quake. Or is it me you fear?"

"Neither, sir," she denied bravely. "I shall join you. Have you found any evidence of a poisonous substance?"

They continued to the head of the stairs in speculation. David had found nothing at all, to his frustration.

"I shall be down directly, when I freshen up." She took her leave, wondering how she was to manage her dress with Rose attending Lord Crompton.

Her gown lay neatly on the bed in the room Sidthorp had assigned to her. An open door revealed a small dressing room that also held a pretty cot suitable for Rose.

The decor of the bedroom looked to be the very latest designs, directly from London. Simple, almost austere, after Aunt Bel's rather ornate interior. Fluid curves and lovely woods graced the few pieces. The blue and cream with touches of gold on the walls and fabrics pleased Elizabeth very much.

The thought entered her mind that if she held Lord Leighton to his oft repeated declaration of betrothal, she would be mistress of this house. Then, as quickly as it had come, that idea was dismissed. But she had to admit that David did not appear the rake while under his father's roof. Although those hazel eyes did mock and tease her most dreadfully.

Even as she stripped her day gown off, then put on the evening dress suitable for a winter dinner with friends, she wondered how accurate the London gossips were. Her sisters had scolded her roundly for accepting the prattle of the London ladies as truth.

She had pinned her bodice in place and draped a modest string of pearls about her neck when the sound of the dinner gong reached her ears. Alone in this wing, she felt oddly shy walking along the broad corridor to the head of the stairs.

Below, she could hear voices, and once downstairs she drifted along to the drawing room whence they came. They were standing about, quite obviously waiting for her.

"Ah, Elizabeth. I have the good fortune to escort you to dinner. One of the times I appreciate my rank," David joked as he offered his arm.

"My lord, you do like to tease."

"You have mentioned that before. I know you have a sense of humor. Could it be *my* wit that you fail to appreciate?" He arched a wicked brow in mock dismay.

"My, the chit does have taste," Egbert murmured just loud enough for Elizabeth to overhear.

Dinner proved singularly uneventful. Seated at David's side, Elizabeth managed to do the food credit, although she felt the dishes lacked originality or taste. Several were overdone, others tasted most peculiar. Overcooked roast beef and bland apple pie, with other equally ordinary fare, must be to their liking, she thought, for all ate without complaint.

Following the meal, David excused them from the others, saying they wished to check on his father. Once up the flight of stairs, he paused before the door to the first of the rooms.

"This is not your father's room."

"Filpot just brought word that Father is sleeping nicely. I thought we might search this room while the others are below."

Suspicion flared up. "Whose room is this?"

"Jeremy's."

"Of all the foolish things to do, this is prime. If you *must* search here, do so when he is away from home. He could decide to come up at any moment."

"Quite so. Stand by the door and listen, I'll do a quick check." He placed his hand on the lever.

"I shall do no such thing. Come." She tugged his arm, to his obvious amusement.

He quickly walked with her from the room, then on down the hall to the end.

"This is your room, sirrah. I hardly think we need look here."

"More's the pity. I wondered if you needed to have a look at my wound."

She pursed her mouth in speculation, then chided herself for a suspicious mind. Of course his wound needed inspection. She ought to have thought of it without his prompting.

He whisked her inside even as he pulled off his coat.

Elizabeth sighed inwardly when she observed how well formed Lord Leighton was. He certainly stripped to advantage, as Geoffrey would say.

Once David's shirt lay discarded on the chair, she efficiently removed the bandage to study the injury. Thank heaven she had only put in three-quarters of the powder normally used in the gun. Not only had it lessened the force of the bullet, but it meant that the wound had healed better, with less tearing of the skin.

It took but a short time to make her examination, gently smear some of Purvis's compound on his arm, then bind the wound once again. She concentrated on her task, determined to ignore his proximity and the feelings he stirred within her. She glanced at the open door. Why that ought to make her more assured, she didn't know. She felt quite certain that if he wished to make improper advances to her, whether the door stood ajar or not wouldn't affect him in the least.

She gave the finished bandage a light touch. "There, now, it looks much better today. You heal well, my lord. In time the scar will scarcely be noticeable."

"I trust my wife will not mind it, then." He pulled his fine cambric shirt over his head, wincing at the strain on his arm. He managed the three buttons concealed beneath a modest frill. Fortunately, his collar points were not as high as Egbert favored.

Elizabeth knew she ought to leave the room, but she had never been privileged to observe a gentleman in the process of dressing before, and it fascinated her. He fumbled with his cravat, then gave up, tossing it aside.

"Shall I call Hadlow?" she offered.

He nodded regretfully. "I cannot manage yet. But soon." His eyes held a message, but it was one she was reluctant to read. "I shall see you downstairs."

Put totally out of countenance by his quite proper observation, Elizabeth blushingly escaped, pausing to check on the earl. Leaving Rose capably standing guard over his lordship, she returned to the library. Her face burned with embarrassment at her behavior. Why, a lady simply did not stand by while a gentleman restored his attire. She knew better.

While she waited, she perused the shelves again for some sort of herbal. She wanted to help if she could.

By the time David joined her, Elizabeth's equanimity was somewhat restored, and it improved by the simple matter that he did not tease her about her folly.

When David entered, he closed the door carefully be-

hind him. The familiar twinkle returned to his eyes as he
surveyed Elizabeth perched precariously on the library
steps.

"I am discouraged," she admitted, wiping a stray hair
from her forehead while surveying the area she had managed to cover. She reached to replace a book, offering
him a scandalous view of a neat pair of ankles. When
she realized what she had done, she moved suddenly, and
the library steps tilted to a perilous degree.

David left his place by the door and rushed to steady
her, both arms reaching for her lest she tumble.

Embarrassed at her silly display, she averted her face.
Fortunately, he said nothing about her impropriety.

"After studying that book you found, I have been over
most of the rooms in the house," he said. "I hoped to
find evidence, but all I find are cobwebs and dust."

"It must be very discouraging for you." She felt her
face lose some of its heat as he ignored her display of
ankles.

"However, since he appears to respond well to the
tonic Purvis sent and the broth you brought, I am convinced we are on the right track. If we can just keep the
would-be poisoner from finding out that Father is well
on the mend. Let him think the progress is nil, or very
slow. What do you think?"

"I am not skilled in dissembling, but I could try. This
cannot help but worry you."

"Indeed," he said wearily. "I believe we owe ourselves a respite, since he improves. Tomorrow, providing
the cold weather holds, we ought to try a bit of skating.
Do you indulge in that sort of thing?" He ran his fingers
through his hair, the baffled expression replaced by one
she thought calculating.

"I cannot say I have," she replied cautiously. "Hyacinthe and Lady Chloe spoke of a skating party."

"Then, by all means I shall teach you. I am reckoned
to be a dab hand at skates," he said with modest pride.

"Even with one hand?" she teased. Let him have a
taste of what he did so well.

"Still at it, you two?" Egbert's sneering voice cut between them like a knife. "I should like to know what
attracts you to this particular room." He gazed about as

though searching for the clue. "Although I have heard a library is a favorite place for lovemaking among betrothed couples. So much can be conveyed across the pages of an open book, don't you know?"

Utterly outraged at his assumptions, although she knew she invited such by her behavior, Elizabeth straightened and prepared to give him a blistering set-down. A nudge in her back stopped her.

"We have been merely looking through the books. Did you find something to read, Miss Elizabeth?"

She smiled. "As a matter of fact, I did. 'Tis a book I have long wished to read, *Self-Control* by Mary Brunton. It is reputed to be a good tale of the triumph of virtue over passion." With that crisp statement she whirled about and pulled the volume in question from the shelf where she had seen it earlier. Then she marched from the room, head up, chin firm, and a saucy gleam in her eyes.

The soft chuckle that followed her departure brought a grin to her lips. His lordship appreciated her ridicule of Egbert's pompous attitude. Not but what he was right.

Morning saw a light sifting of snow, but Elizabeth believed the weather looked as though it might change for the better later on, and she grew hopeful.

Rose entered bearing a cup of chocolate, full of news of the day.

"His lordship's ever so much better, miss. Purvis will be that puffed up when she learns how effective her tonic is, and that's the truth." Rose set about drawing back the curtains and shaking out the warm kerseymere gown Elizabeth had brought to wear.

"What a relief. You and Filpot managed to come to terms over the night nursing, I gather." Elizabeth downed her chocolate in a rush, then slid from the warmth of her bed with reluctance.

"His lordship said that if it pleased you, he would take you skating after breakfast." Rose looked round-eyed at her mistress. "What do you wear to skate?"

"Something warm and sensible, I gather from what I have heard of it. I shall put on my stout half-boots. And do not forget my fur muff." She exchanged a look with her maid, one that said she doubted the outcome as much as Rose.

When she met Lord Leighton in the large hall, she still held doubts but thought she hid them successfully. In her favorite aquamarine pelisse and bonnet, she braved the day.

"Come, the wind is down and 'tis a fine day for skating, as the temperature looks to rise. I tested the ice, and it seems to be fine."

Tucking her hands inside her muff, Elizabeth walked with him along the path leading down the hill. Below, she could make out a pond, one with little inlets and pretty knolls above upon which to view the scene.

"I believe I ought to stand there to watch you, sir," she said primly.

"And not skate?" he replied, scandalized.

"I shall fall, most likely."

"But I will be at your side to assist you."

She darted a dubious look at him then, wondering if this was some sort of ruse to tease her.

Placed close to the pond was a stone bench, and it was here that Lord Leighton urged Elizabeth to put on her skates. Or rather, to allow him to fit them on her boots.

"Your footwear is most practical for skates. I heartily approve." That he also could not miss a glimpse of her shapely calves while adjusting those skates didn't escape Elizabeth, and she thought him outrageous.

The iron-bladed runners were fixed to sturdy brass plates. He brought the leather straps about her boots to tightly fasten with a knot just over the instep. He screwed the heel peg into the sole of her boot and proclaimed her ready. He affixed his blades to his Hessians, and she thought he appeared smart in his blue tailcoat buttoned up with large brass buttons and a dark round hat set jauntily on his head.

"You are not wearing your sling. Dare you use your arm? I would not have you expose yourself to further injury just to amuse me."

"I am not concerned," he said in a typically masculine disdain for pampering.

When it came time to venture on the ice, Elizabeth put a tentative foot on the slippery stuff, then withdrew.

"What? Are you such a timid creature? Allow me."

The wickedly handsome Lord Leighton proceeded to introduce Elizabeth to the delights of ice skating. Placing his arm firmly about her waist, with a look that told her not to quibble about his closeness, he led her forth. At first hesitant, she began to relax, and soon found herself able to perform simple gliding steps.

"I really believe you ought to permit me to guide you a bit longer," he admonished as Elizabeth sailed past him toward the far end of the pond.

"Nonsense. I cannot see that this is so difficult after all," she sang back gaily, enjoying the crisp air and faint sun that peeked through the clouds.

"It is possible to dance on ice with a partner," he said in an aggravatingly appealing manner.

Absorbing this intriguing notion, Elizabeth returned to his side, tilting her head as she decided whether he was serious or not.

"Willing to try?" he dared her.

"On my headstone you may carve that here lies one who dared anything," she quipped, even as she offered him her hand.

This time one of his strong arms went about her waist in a tantalizing way, and his other hand, of the arm that had been shot, firmly captured hers, letting her know he would not allow her to fall.

Had she paused to consider, she would have thought it most peculiar that he used that wounded limb so well. However, Elizabeth was lost in transports of delight, and far from reality.

With a taunting side glance, reminding her that he well recalled her inability to do the same, he hummed a gay waltz, then slowly guided them away from the bank.

She decided it lovely to be spinning around and around on the ice. Then it occurred to her, "The surface is remarkably smooth, my lord. I had always thought ice to be a bit bumpy when it formed."

He actually looked chagrined at her words. "As to that, I went out last night with three of the men, and we sloshed water over much of it. Not that we covered it all, mind you."

"I see." But she didn't, not really. That he should go

to such lengths to please her seemed unlike him. Tease, yes. Please, no.

"You are a very clever pupil, Miss Elizabeth," he said with approval.

His provoking grin and dancing eyes brought warmth to her cheeks. "I wonder that your cousins do not indulge in this delightful pastime."

"Egbert might, if he ever gets out of bed in time. But Jeremy said he does not care for skating, or ice, for that matter. He insists he has business to attend." He added as an afterthought, "I should like to see his account books."

"Now," she reproved, "do not be putting the poor man in a quake. You are rather good at disconcerting him." And Jeremy was not the only one who found Lord Leighton intimidating at times.

"But not you, I think. Why, I could kiss you here, and you would not bat one of those delightful lashes at me."

She pulled free of him, darting away with surprising speed for a novice. Although she wobbled a bit, she chuckled to herself. Kiss her, indeed.

"Elizabeth, wait!"

"Oh, no, I will not." He had teased her once too often. Foolish man, he must learn that a lady has limits to her tolerance. Elizabeth wished for sensible conversation, not trifling.

"Elizabeth!"

Ignoring his call, she turned again to look ahead of her. Unfamiliar with the pond and skating, she really should have been paying attention to what she did.

An ominous creaking reached her ears, and she came to an uncertain stop. Little lines radiated out from where she stood. Not sure what it meant, she turned, her face serious, to gaze back at Lord Leighton. He approached warily, and even from here she could see his concern.

"I suspect you had best keep your distance."

"Little fool, you could get hurt. All you have to do is say no. And mean it."

"No, and I mean it."

"I am wounded . . . again."

"I do not believe a kiss will make it all better."

"My mother told me that, however. She was a great believer." He offered a cautious hand to draw her away.

"I daresay she was, if you say so," Elizabeth said with a composure she didn't actually feel. He was fast, she decided, and the tattlemongers of London had the right of it.

The creaking increased, and Elizabeth wondered aloud, "Is that something to be worried about, that funny sort of noise?"

When he looked down, a comically dismayed look was quickly replaced by one of concern. "I would have sworn the ice to be more solid here." He took her hand, tugging her to follow him.

But it was far too late for departure. The cracks rapidly spread, and in seconds Elizabeth first, then David, plunged through the surface into the icy water.

She clutched at the pieces of ice, trying to obtain purchase so she might pull herself from the water. Fortunately, the pond seemed shallow at this end, for as she went under the water, she found her toes just touched the bottom. Or something solid.

Heavy clothing and rapidly numbing fingers prevented success, however. David dragged her up, then instructed her, "Hang onto me if you can. I shall get us out."

She had flung her muff across the ice as she fell, and now she longed for its warmth. "I do not see how," she confessed.

"Oh, ye of little faith," he muttered, attempting to pull himself from the pond, then deliberately breaking the ice some more in order to reach a branch that poked up through the ice.

This proved an effective means of leverage, and in short order he crawled from the icy water, inching his way across the cracked ice to firm ground, leaving Elizabeth to cling to the ice. Here, he soon located a stout limb, then extended this to her, pulling her free with a great effort.

She stood with her arms tightly about her, shivering in the slight breeze. "I do believe I prefer a fire at the moment, my lord."

"For once, I cannot help but agree."

She bent over to pick up her muff, then thrust her hands inside, hoping for warmth.

They skirted the edge of the pond, clumping through the snow in their skates even though it meant a longer route. Eventually they made their way up the hill to the house.

A horrified Sidthorp ushered them in, while Lord Leighton barked out orders one after another. "Hot baths for us both, and a posset to warm our insides. The brandy one I think best. Send Hadlow to me, and Rose to Miss Elizabeth. Immediately." He pulled off his boots, then fumbled with the straps that held Elizabeth's skates on her half-boots.

He was seized by a fit of shivering, and Elizabeth realized that the cold plunge augured far worse for him than for her.

She had always been a healthy sort, not prone to colds and megrims. But Lord Leighton was still recovering from that bullet she had shot him with and could be in grave danger.

After a very hot soaking bath, Elizabeth dried her hair by the fire wrapped in a black velvet robe. Her long curls hung down in a chestnut fan of waving silk as she brushed.

A knock at the door gave warning, but barely. She hastily composed herself, withdrawing bare toes beneath the wealth of velvet just in time. As she suspected, Leighton entered, barging in without an apology.

"I sent Hadlow out to inspect the pond. He and one of the stable lads found what we missed. Elizabeth, that was no accident! Someone wished us ill. He hoped we would fall into the frigid water. The ice on the deep end of the pond was thin, so a sign had been posted. That warning sign was found hidden behind a bush."

8

"How TERRIBLE, to endanger your life like that!" Elizabeth cried, rising to commiserate with David as best she could. "How is your arm? Have you had the bandage changed? I hope you do not develop an inflammation of the lungs, or some dreadful infection of your wound." She studied his face for signs of incipient debility. "Oh, *who* could have done such a horrid deed?"

"Your concern is welcome," he said hesitantly. "We must consider that you were with me, and that you were as much the intended victim as I, however." He stuffed the hand of his wounded arm into the pocket of his velvet banyan that he had donned over a blessedly dry cambric shirt, buff pantaloons, and shoes.

"I, a victim?" she said in amazement. Then she smiled at the absurdity of that idea. "Nonsense." She paused a moment, then admitted, "Now, if I truly intended to marry you, there might be an heir who wished me out of the way. Tell me, who is next in line in the event that you fail to marry and produce the required heir to the title?"

Elizabeth drew closer to the fire, still a trifle chilled from their wetting. She played with the hair brush in her hands, while studying the flames that danced, such a contrast to the frozen cold beyond the window.

"Augustus." David watched her, the black velvet clinging to her slender form, so enchanting, so desirable. Her beautiful hair curled delicately about her face, a veil of finest silk. It was unthinkable that someone wish her ill, but he didn't trust anyone at this point, and however silly it might seem, it must be considered.

"I want you to be careful when you go about here,"

he insisted. "Remember, the others believe our betrothal is genuine. You could be wished out of the way."

"Oh, pooh, what a poor honey you must think me. I refuse to jump at every shadow. Although," she admitted, "there is the problem of your father's condition. I still say that whatever ill will abounds is directed toward him, for some obscure reason."

Rose entered with a tray of posset for them. She gave her mistress a bland look as she offered her a steaming cup of the brew, then his lordship.

"Now we shall be warmed on the inside as well as the outer being." David sipped the herbal potion mixed with his favorite brandy. He smiled as Elizabeth took a taste, then made a face at him.

"I hope I am not required to drink this often. I fancy this is an excellent way to keep one well, if for no other reason than to avoid drinking it." She grimaced, then sipped some more.

Rose hovered in the background. David turned abruptly to her. "You may leave us."

When the maid had scurried from the room without a backward glance, Elizabeth gave him a look of reproof. "That was not well done of you, sir."

"I do not like to think of her tittle-tattling to others about our private conversation. Not even accidentally. However good she might be, what she does not hear she cannot repeat. We have much to discuss." He crossed to firmly close the door after first checking the hall to see that no one lingered along the corridor. He was alone with Elizabeth in her room—in the entire wing, for that matter.

He drew up a chair to the fireplace for her, then found one for himself. "These may not appear comfortable, but I have found them tolerable." He gestured to the fashionable chairs with their graceful arms curving under and curved legs. "As to the maid, we are past caring about what she thinks.

She sank down, looking suddenly uncomfortable, as though she had just realized that she entertained him in her private quarters dressed in her velvet robe and with bare feet. An adorable expression of confusion that warred with annoyance sat on her lovely face. He longed to caress her, but knew he must be wary in his dealings with the attractive Elizabeth Dancy.

"I must return to Aunt Bel's as soon as the weather permits," she announced abruptly. Then, meeting his eyes, she added, "It is not because of the ridiculous assumption you have made. Not for a moment do I believe that someone wishes me ill. But," she continued, "your father seems much improved. You have no further need of me."

He cradled his cup of posset in his hand, staring at the flames much as she had done earlier. He needed to find an excuse for her to remain. He said suddenly, "But I need you here. You see, I can trust no one, other than my father, and I would not burden him with all my suspicions. I need a fellow confederate, as it were. Someone I can discuss my problems with and confide in and feel comfortable with, if you follow my thoughts. Also, if you leave, he might take a turn for the worse," he concluded, throwing himself on her mercy and relying on her sense of duty to do as he wished.

"I . . . I do not know quite what to say. I admit I am flattered that you feel able to confide in me, trust me to such a degree. But what about the others? Do you not worry about what they will say? This is a highly irregular plan, you must agree."

She took what he felt to be a resolute sip of the posset, and he prayed she would suffer no ill effects from the wetting she'd had in that freezing water. A cousin of his had died under similar circumstances, succumbing to an inflammation of the lungs.

"I have no regard for what others say," he said. "They have been gossiping over me for years, ever since I went to London to acquire that patina of Town Bronze so desperately wanted by all young sprouts." He watched the play of emotions over her expressive face, but could not figure out what went on in her mind.

"I see. You are a sad rattle, I fear," she replied with a flash of amusement.

"What about you? I place you in an unpardonable position with my request. Your aunt is of the opinion that we will wed, and so it may not be reprehensible to her if you at least spend your days assisting me. My father's condition provides the excuse, if you will.''

"My aunt is inclined to be rather silly, but she is none-theless a formidable lady. Should she take the notion that we must wed immediately, I fear you would find yourself waiting at the altar for a bride you do not wish. I feel you must be warned of the danger you face.''

Her face wore a speculative expression, but her voice reflected serious concern. He would be ill advised to ignore her warning. He reflected on her words, then shook his head. "My need of you, your assistance, is greater than my fear of your aunt.''

Elizabeth rose from her chair before the fire, and walked across the thick carpet to look out the window. "The sun is out, however weak it might appear. The roads ought to be passable before long.''

"Another day, I beg you. Then I shall return you to your Aunt Bel.''

"Could we send a groom to her with a message? Not but what she knows the weather forbids my return just yet.''

He marveled that she should fall in with his wishes so easily, then reminded himself that he must not trespass on her kind nature with the sort of attention he would like to bestow on her, those inviting lips. It was the first time he had ever placed his scruples ahead of his desires for a woman who responded as she did to his advances. Not one of his London acquaintances would believe it possible. His friends knew differently.

"Certainly.'' He had risen when she did, and now followed her to the window. "I want to know who was out there. Everyone knew we planned to skate today after you invited them to join us.''

"I scarcely wished it to be a secret. Now, that *would* have looked odd.'' She picked up a drapery cord, playing with it in seeming nervousness.

"Nevertheless.''

"I expect I ought to make myself respectable, then meet you downstairs.'' She smoothed a hand over her dressing gown. It covered her from neck to toe and concealed her in an enticing manner.

"I am sorry for the ruin of your lovely pelisse. That

aquamarine color well becomes you.'' He decided she had the most attractive blush he had ever seen, a delicate bloom that suffused her cheeks like a lovely peach rose.

''It can be replaced, thank you. I have a great many items of that color in my wardrobe. Vanity, I imagine.''

Her rueful laugh pleased him. 'Not vanity in the least,'' he refuted, ''merely common sense—to wear what is becoming.''

She strolled to the door, drawing him along with her. ''I shall join you below before long. My hair is nearly dry, and I feel much more the thing.'' She held the nearly empty cup of posset up for him to see.

Unable to stop himself, he pulled his hand from the pocket, reaching out to run his fingers through that fall of silken hair. ''You look startled. You must know that your hair is a lovely feature.''

''Sir, you make me feel the temptress. I protest.''

Her blush had deepened and he cursed himself for a fool. ''Later, then.''

She closed the door behind his rapidly disappearing figure, and wondered if she had completely lost her mind. Swallowing the last of the posset, she allowed it to heat her insides while returning to the window again.

Curious how she was so terribly willing to fall in with Lord Leighton's plans. Of course, she knew why in the innermost part of her mind. But she refused to accept that reason, for it was utter folly. No, she had best lay it to her quite reasonable desire to see the solution to this puzzle.

Cup in hand, she paced back to the fireplace, ruefully recalling the state of her feet as she felt the lush thickness of the carpet. How unspeakably foolish to permit his lordship to enter her room, make himself at ease, then listen to him tell her that he needed her! Utter stupidity.

With that thought she briskly rang for Rose, then strode to her dressing room, undoing the velvet robe as she went. In short order, her hair was properly dressed, as was the rest of her.

The corridor appeared deserted as she peeped from her room. Not surprising, she supposed. But one never knew. Unable to contain her curiosity any longer, she peered into each room as she proceeded along the hall. Since no one occupied this wing save herself, she felt quite safe in doing so.

The earl, or whoever had assisted him in the decoration of the house, had excellent taste. A lovely sleigh bed graced one room, a four-poster from an earlier time another. That every room was tastefully arranged, with no thought spared for economy, brought home to her precisely the temptation that might exist for a man who wanted all this, plus the remainder of the estate. If this was merely a small residence, what must the others be like?

On that depressing thought she marched down the stairs, then sought the drawing room.

Lord Augustus turned from his contemplation of the fire to greet her. "Heard about your dip in the pond, dear girl. Really, not quite the thing to do on a February day, what? Now, come July . . ." He subsided a moment, apparently contemplating a lovely summer day. "Shan't leave here today. Roads bound to be nasty. Always are," he reflected gloomily.

"Ah, the intrepid Miss Elizabeth." Young Mr. Percy sauntered into the drawing room, raising his quizzing glass to inspect her person, as though anticipating a drapery of pond weed or some such nonsense.

Elizabeth was hard put not to laugh at his pretensions. "Indeed, sir. Not altogether as intrepid as you might believe. I fear I wholly disliked plunging into that frigid water, then being trapped by my heavy skirts, unable to climb free. It is a good thing that Lord Leighton found it possible to pull himself out, and thus drag me free of the pond's icy grip." Had he used both hands to do so? She worried that he had harmed himself and was too heroic to complain. Oh, if he had reopened his wound, she'd not forgive herself.

"Ah, dear cuz, ever the champion," Egbert said with a sneer.

"My maid informed me that Lord Crompton is improved," Elizabeth said to Lord Augustus rather than reply to his son's graceless remark.

"Good to hear," offered Lord Augustus, shifting about in his chair accompanied by the usual creaking of his corset.

"Pity David couldn't have kept you from ruining that admirable pelisse I saw you wearing earlier," Egbert added in a snide undertone.

She tensed, wondering how Mr. Percy had seen what she wore if he had remained in bed at that hour. "I fear it is a total loss, in spite of Rose's attempt to restore it. I shall wear it home and hope that not a soul sees me."

He affected a look of horror. "My dear Miss Elizabeth, that would indeed be unfortunate."

Firmly repressing a strong desire to laugh, she calmly replied, "At least my fur muff escaped a watery grave. I tossed it toward the shoreline when we plunged into the water."

"Indubitably fortuitous." He raised his quizzing glass to his eye again, offering Elizabeth a highly magnified view of that slightly reddened object.

She turned aside, choking back the laugh that longed to escape. "How true," she managed to say. Then she considered the foppish gentleman. The notion had occurred to her before that he must spend an inordinate amount of money on those elaborate clothes, not to mention the seals and fobs—discreet but of the highest quality.

Shifting about, she attempted to study him without his being unduly aware of her scrutiny. Would he? Could he? Everyone in the house knew that Egbert slept late of a morning, that he detested ice skating. What better cover than to slip from his room when all expected him to be inside? He could have made his way to the pond, removed the warning sign that had been posted, then returned to his bed with none the wiser. If Lord Augustus inherited, Egbert would have access to all the funds he desired, for his parent seemed most indulgent.

"I say, Miss Elizabeth, you are inspecting me as though I was a worm that had turned up in your apple."

"I do beg your pardon, I was deep in reflection." She added, "I hope that Lord Leighton has not taken ill from his immersion in that frigid water. It is not long since he was injured."

"You ought to tell me more about that particular event. I find I am most curious." Egbert strolled closer to where she stood, peering at her with intent curiosity.

She had done the foolish now, Elizabeth decided. Not knowing what Lord Leighton had revealed to his family about his injury, or her part in it, she hadn't the vaguest idea what to say.

"Ought not pry," Lord Augustus growled from his chair by the fire.

"Pry?" queried Lord Leighton as he strode into the room, looking for all the world as though he never heard of such a thing as falling through thin ice or a February wetting. He had exchanged his banyan for an elegant corbeau coat which covered a rose waistcoat of fine marcella. His buff pantaloons blended nicely and created an impression of refinement.

"Questions," Lord Augustus said abruptly, staring at Elizabeth from beneath those shaggy brows as though she were responsible for his son's behavior. He brushed a bit of snuff from his dark brown coat as he happened to catch sight of it.

" 'Tis all very vague, you know," Egbert continued, ignoring his father.

"Did you enjoy the novel by Miss Brunton last evening?" David turned to inquire of Elizabeth, just as though he had not seen her in her sitting room but an hour past.

Guessing that he did not wish to have the subject of his injury brought up for discussion, Elizabeth searched for an intelligent reply.

"Well, she has a charming manner, but I fear I fell asleep before I could get very far into the story."

"I trust that virtue will be rewarded?" he said with a lift of that devilish brow.

"Ought to replace her pelisse," Lord Augustus volunteered, totally ignoring their conversation. "Poor gel. Not the thing to be falling into ponds in the middle of February. Not the thing at all," he scolded.

David tugged at his earlobe while he considered this comment.

Unable to repress a smile at his obvious surprise at this attack from his uncle, Elizabeth picked up a dainty statue from the table, ostensibly to study it.

"No worry, Papa. Once David and the lovely Elizabeth are wed, she'll have no end of pelisses—and other interesting things as well, no doubt.'' Egbert's smile was excessively crafty.

"Forgot,'' Lord Augustus mumbled, studying the fire once again.

Hoping the sound she heard in the hall was that of Sidthorp coming to inform them that it was time to march across to the dining room, she was dumbfounded when the portly butler ushered in her cousin Hyacinthe.

The pretty redhead rushed to Elizabeth's side, then flung her arms about her in a tender show of sensibilities.

"I vow, when his lordship's footman brought news of your catastrophe, I simply had to come. It was not easy to persuade John Coachman to make the trip, for the poor man feared for the horses all the way over, but I knew there would be no peace in my heart until I assured myself that you were safe. You *must* need more of the tonic Purvis made.'' She thrust a basket at Elizabeth, cast a calculating glance at Lord Leighton, then shifted her attention to Mr. Percy.

"I believe I may set your heart at rest, Miss Dancy,'' Lord Leighton quietly replied, his very calm making Hyacinthe seem silly and affected. "Your cousin is quite all right, and there is no cause for alarm in the least.''

He met Sidthorp's inquiring look with a nod, then said to Hyacinthe, "I do hope that you will join us for dinner. Uncle Augustus prefers to keep country hours, and so we dine early here.''

She fluttered her hands in the air, looking fragile, lovely, and frightfully vulnerable. "I should adore it, if it does not discommode you?''

"I should think that anyone who has the temerity to charge into another's home at this hour of the day might expect to find them at the dinner table,'' Elizabeth could not resist saying, her tone as dry as a desert.

Hyacinthe's pretty chin trembled, and from the depths of her reticule she fetched up a scrap of lace and cambric to dab her eyes. A flash of what Elizabeth believed resentment appeared for a moment when Hyacinthe looked at her. It disappeared when she turned her splendid green eyes toward Lord Leighton.

"I merely grew concerned, and I fear I am never practical,'' she added with a helpless shrug of her slim shoul-

ders incased in sheer, buttery velvet. She seemed like a
delicate flame, all red and gold, glowing with her inner
fire on this cold, snowy February day. Elizabeth felt like
a frump in yesterday's gown that was not quite unwrin-
kled, in spite of Rose's valiant attempt to restore it.

Hyacinthe gave the sort of performance, Elizabeth decided, that brought out every chivalrous instinct in any
living, breathing male. Lord Leighton appeared stricken,
Lord Augustus lumbered to his feet, intent upon assuring
the fragile creature of who knew what, while Egbert
sauntered to Hyacinthe's side, offering his arm.

"This is all frightfully tedious. Let us set aside reasons
and all that dreadful nonsense. Join us for dinner, for
you will perk up the dining room no end."

Blinking in surprise at the assertion of the dandy into
what had been a conversation between herself and Lord
Leighton, Hyacinthe nonetheless placed a dainty hand on
Egbert's arm. A triumphant glance at Elizabeth told her
that Hyacinthe had planned and hoped for, well, not precisely this event, but near enough.

"I do apologize for my cousin's sad want of manners,
my lord," Elizabeth whispered as she walked with Lord
Leighton some distance behind Hyacinthe and Percy.

"I dimly recall another young lady who was used to
be thought a bit of a hoyden." Although she could not
see his face, she could hear the laughter in his voice.

"No names, please," begged a chagrined Elizabeth.

When they were seated at the hastily rearranged table,
she considered the order admirable. Hyacinthe perched
between Egbert and Augustus, who took his brother's
place at one end of the table. At the other end, Lord
Leighton bent his attentions on Elizabeth, which seemed
to irk her adorable cousin no end.

Jeremy Vane sat silently between Elizabeth and Lord
Augustus, making no attempt to engage either young
woman in conversation, although he stared frequently at
Hyacinthe.

It was truly amazing, considering the lengths Hyacinthe had gone to be here so she might assure herself
of Elizabeth's health, that not once had she actually inquired about it. Oh, there had been that touching display
when Hyacinthe arrived. But Elizabeth hoped that at least

David would see through her beautiful cousin's machinations.

"I fancy you will find the roast to your liking," David said as he gestured to a laden platter. "Even if the little cabbage is a bit strong."

Elizabeth smiled. He understood, bless him.

The meal had proceeded nicely, she thought later, as Sidthorp offered the sweets—burned pudding and a nut torte.

Hyacinthe eagerly consumed her portion of torte. Elizabeth accepted a dab of the same, but spent her time watching Egbert with a narrow gaze.

When they left the gentlemen to their port, Elizabeth steered her cousin to the drawing room, urging her to take one of the chairs by the fire.

"You seem quite at home here." Hyacinthe pouted, not quite as charming as when the men were around.

"One can quickly accustom oneself to almost anything. It was most unwise of you to come dashing over here. I fear Lord Leighton now considers you a harum-scarum sort of girl. It is not well done to behave so. And I thought better of you. Indeed, Aunt Bel has been constantly reminding me of your propriety ever since I arrived at Montmorcy Hall."

"Truth be known, I felt it incumbent upon me to rescue you from what must be an intolerable situation. Imagine being cooped up in this house with all these men." Hyacinthe gave a dainty wave of a golden-sheathed arm.

Elizabeth wondered if her aunt had ever seen this side of Hyacinthe, then decided that even if she had, she'd not pay the least attention to it. It seemed that once Aunt Bel made up her mind about something, it remained set.

"Well, I will be glad enough for your company on the ride home. It has been a trying day." Hyacinthe had not made it any better. It was clear that now Elizabeth would have to leave. There was no excuse for her to remain.

Any reply she might have made was lost when the men strolled along the hall and into the drawing room. Quite familiar with the leisurely consumption of port, while ladies languished in the drawing room, eagerly awaiting the gentlemen, Elizabeth raised an expressive brow at Lord Leighton.

He immediately sought her side, drawing her away from the others. "We must send your cousin back to your aunt. I shan't allow her to interfere with the progress we have made. Improper little baggage."

Elizabeth struggled to avoid drowning in those hazel eyes, so deep with meaning. "She is curious and a bit willful, but means no harm."

David shook his head, turning his gaze on the young woman.

"As much as I would keep our delightful guest here, I fear her carriage awaits without," he said in a more carrying tone, bestowing a charming, and quite impersonal, smile on Hyacinthe.

As on cue, Sidthorp entered the room, carrying Hyacinthe's lovely purple cloak that had a hood trimmed in ermine. He placed it over her shoulders, then stood waiting to usher her from the room.

Hyacinthe obviously wished to protest, but Lord Leighton inexorably swept her along to the hall, ignoring the complaints from Lord Augustus and Egbert. He ushered Hyacinthe to the coach, fussing over her comfort in a manner that brought pink color to her cheeks. The door clicked shut, and Hyacinthe left long before she intended.

The scene at Montmorcy Hall was as frosty as the weather outside. Aunt Bel proceeded to ring a peal over Hyacinthe.

"I vow that was the strangest dinner I have ever attended," Hyacinthe complained, trying to direct the subject away from herself.

"Actually, you were not invited, so you scarce have cause for grievance," Aunt Bel reminded.

"Well, I think it strange that you permit Elizabeth to remain there." Hyacinthe fussed with her gloves, then her reticule. "I do not see why I shouldn't have gone."

"I suggest you retire for the night, Hyacinthe Dancy. We shall discuss this further in the morning."

9

"I KNEW IT! I knew he had overdone," exclaimed Elizabeth upon learning that Lord Leighton was in bed with a slight fever and not feeling at all the thing. She had spent time with Lord Crompton after breakfasting in her room. When Rose had returned from the kitchen with a light meal for the earl—prepared by Rose and Filpot— Elizabeth had been appraised of Lord Leighton's setback.

Not bothering to check her appearance, she marched down the hall. "I had best give him some of the tonic Purvis sent with me. She must have anticipated such a thing, for she sent an ample supply. I knew he ought not have exerted himself. That stubborn man!" Elizabeth muttered as she made her way along the south wing.

Continuing on to the last room, she stopped, then hesitantly rapped on the door to Lord Leighton's room, unsure of what she ought to do.

Hadlow answered her knock, looking very much the melancholy soul. He immediately ushered her inside, gesturing to the bed across the room.

"How is he?" she whispered. The bedroom was utterly dark, the only light from the fire and one candle. It was stifling.

"I fear for him, and that's a fact," Hadlow intoned in a gloomy, sepulchral voice. He gave Elizabeth the shivers.

"Why do you not join Rose for a moment? Perhaps there is something she needs. You would be just the one to tell her how to go on." It had not escaped Elizabeth that Rose much admired Hadlow, and was not the least reluctant to work with the valet. It was highly doubtful that Filpot had been around, or that he would be willing to assist a mere lady's maid.

"Very good, miss." Hadlow bowed, then reluctantly left on silent feet. His mouth had quirked a moment, and she supposed it passed for a smile.

Once he was out the door, Elizabeth charged across the bedroom and quietly opened the draperies. Soft winter light sifted into the room and over to the great four-poster bed where a man lay in utter stillness.

Sick at heart, Elizabeth cautiously approached the bed, carrying the satchel containing the tonic and potions concocted by Purvis.

She placed a tentative hand on his brow, then nearly jumped out of her skin when a husky voice said, "I am not dead yet, my dear."

"You have a slight fever, however," she replied briskly, once she gathered her wits about her.

"You believe I shall survive, do you not?" One hazel eye peered up at her, followed by the second, wincing at the pale light that now flooded the room.

"Of course. Only the good die young." She prudently avoided meeting that hazel gaze.

"I knew there was a reason for my wicked ways."

"Hush. You ought not say a word, especially those," she admonished. Her heart grew lighter at his silly talk, for she absurdly felt that it meant he was far from hopeless when he could still tease her.

"Truth."

"Rubbish. Now, I shall give you some of the tonic Purvis sent along. I daresay it shall be no more nasty-tasting than that posset you urged on me." She poured out a spoonful, then held it to his mouth. Ignoring all the sensations that came from leaning over his bed, practically falling into his arms once again, she played the proper nurse, poking the spoon into his mouth. "Good," she concluded, backing away from the bed with haste.

"Don't bite," he mumbled, then sneezed.

"Perhaps, but I believe you shall sleep, and well."

"Rubbish," he drowsily replied, closing his eyes once again.

Elizabeth perched anxiously on the chair placed by the side of the great carved bed, a holdover from some other house, for it was not in the current style.

Perhaps he merely had a severe cold, she thought with

hope. His arm lay outside the covers, and once he looked to be soundly asleep, she ever so gently pushed up the sleeve of his nightshirt to examine the bandage. Observing that he did not stir, she deftly cut it loose with the scissors she had tucked into the pocket of her enveloping apron.

A smile wreathed her face as she beheld the wound. A sigh of relief escaped her lips as well, for his injury appeared to be healing nicely. It certainly mitigated her feelings of guilt, although precisely why she ought to feel guilty when *he* was the one who had snuck into her room like a thief was beyond her ken.

"Wait until I tell Purvis," she whispered to herself. "How pleased she will be."

She applied the ointment from the jar Purvis had tucked into the satchel, then put a fresh bandage on his arm, smoothing his sleeve down again and tucking the coverlet nicely about him when finished. If he had a fever, it was best to keep him warm.

Purvis had said she found it helpful to listen to a chest, for it seemed to reveal a good deal about the person's health. Taking a deep breath, Elizabeth cautiously bent over the great bed and placed her ear to David's chest after pulling back the coverlet a little. There appeared to be a bit of a wheeze, but no rattle such as Purvis had warned about. The scent of sandalwood permeated his nightshirt, and she felt an overwhelming desire to place her head against his shoulder, to know again the comfort he might offer—when he wasn't teasing her to death.

She straightened, then smoothed his sheets, studying his face with worried eyes as she worked. Pray his ailment was no worse than a raging cold.

Deciding that since Lord Leighton slept she might as well return to her other patient, she quietly left the bedroom. Out in the corridor Hadlow paced back and forth.

"He is resting nicely, Hadlow. Why do you not catch a bit of sleep? I feel certain you must have been awake half the night, looking after him."

After giving her a grateful nod, the valet ambled off to the little room adjacent to David's, while Elizabeth sped down the hall toward Lord Crompton's room.

"Well, well, if it is not the little angel of mercy," Egbert drawled hatefully.

She looked up, then held the door lever firmly in one hand, guarding the earl against intrusion. "If you like to think so."

"How does my esteemed cousin go? Hadlow refuses to say a word. One might think David at death's door." He minced down the hall toward her, wearing extremely smart Hessians that looked to be too small for him.

"Hardly." She wondered if he wished him there and beyond. "Lord Leighton is sleeping nicely at present, but I believe he has nothing more than a nasty cold. No small wonder when you consider the wetting he took."

"You did as well, yet you appear glowing this morning. How fortunate that David manages to find such a charming attendant to nurse him to health. If I did not detest those nostrums, I might consider it as well." The somewhat oily smile he bestowed on Elizabeth did not appeal to her in the least.

She gave him a furious look. "He is not feigning illness, sirrah. And *I* did not have the affliction of a wound. Excuse me, if you will." She flashed him a quelling look, then entered the earl's rooms.

Rose greeted her with relief. "He wants to speak with you, miss."

Instructing Rose to rest in the earl's dressing room, Elizabeth hurried to his lordship's side, tilting her head as she assessed his condition. He looked much improved.

"Well? I have heard you keep busy today."

"Your son is under the impression he is at death's door, no doubt due to Hadlow and his dreary countenance. Poor man."

"And how did you manage to reassure my son?"

"I told him that only the good die young." Her eyes met his lordships in rueful admission of her absurd conduct.

The earl gave a frail bark of laughter, his eyes twinkling in just the manner she had noticed in his son. "I would sit up, I believe. I feel quite in prime twig today."

"Is that so? We shall see." She touched his forehead, then settled him, nicely fussing over his pillows with womanly touches.

"My son is a shrewd man. I approve his betrothal to you. Sensible girl."

Elizabeth almost laughed, recalling her hoydenish ways while in London. She felt as though she had aged years since coming to live with Aunt Bel—especially the last week.

"I should like to explain a few matters for you, since you are to be David's wife," Lord Crompton declared once settled against his pillows.

"What might that be?" She ought to inform him that she most likely would not wed his son, but that was David's responsibility. Elizabeth drew up a chair to the bedside, looking expectantly at the earl, his knitted nightcap sitting jauntily on his head while he fixed on her that gaze so like his son's.

"I went over my will and the estate papers not long ago. As you may know, much of the estate is entailed and would go to my heir, David, as a matter of course. The settlement is set up in a peculiar way, for ordinarily he could arrange leases. My grandfather did not wish to release a whit of control, and so tied the land to himself and the subsequent earls, reserving even the right to grant leases to himself, and those to follow." He coughed slightly.

"Here, sir," she murmured, offering him a glass of barley water and smiling at his grimace of distaste.

"I gave him the income from this estate, for under the terms of the entail he cannot get any other until he takes my place. At the time of his marriage, I shall settle additional income upon him, and when he has a son, if I still live, that income shall be raised. Since you have no father to bargain on your behalf, rest assured that I shall see to it that you are well guarded, my dear. You need have no concern that you or your children will be unprotected. Your children shall inherit David's land." He reached out and gently patted her hand.

"Oh, dear," she murmured. Elizabeth felt sure that she must be as red as a beet root at these candid words. She didn't know what to say to him, for although David had announced the betrothal and the earl approved, with Aunt Bel pushing things all she could, the two central characters in this farce were not of a mind to wed. Or at least one of them felt that way.

"I like a gel that is modest," the earl said with decided approval. "I trust your brother will be home one of these days. David said he is in Portugal. But rest easy that in the event he is delayed and you two wish to wed beforehand, I shall not let you down."

Elizabeth wished to avoid the subject of a wedding. In her heart she well knew that were the matter of the Valentine's Day visit to her room be widely exposed, she would have no choice. But she also knew she longed for a loving relationship with her husband. And David teased.

"I appreciate your caring more than I can say. I miss my own papa very much, and I should like nothing more than to claim you as my substitute father, if I might." There, she had revealed her affection without actually declaring that she would wed David.

"Do you suppose you might read for a time?" he asked wistfully.

"Certainly." She shared a smile with him before picking up the book again. " 'The next day opened a new scene at Longbourn. Mr. Collins made his declaration in form.' "

"Silly chit," muttered the earl. "She will get into a hobble, mark my words."

Elizabeth nodded, then added, "It is very vexing to have a character in the book with my name who is such a silly widgeon, sir."

"Quite." He shifted, then looked expectantly at Elizabeth, waiting for her to continue.

She returned to the world of Jane Bennet and Mr. Darcy, utterly absorbed in their problems, and annoyed with Elizabeth Bennet as only one can be with a character in a book.

She read until her voice began to fade and he looked as though he would welcome a bit of sleep. Placing the book on the beside table, she gave him a fond smile. She eased him back down in the bed, tucking him in as though he truly were her father.

"Perhaps a little nap after all that reading. I vow the morning has sped by far too quickly."

A willing Rose took her place in the room, while Elizabeth sought a pot of tea and perhaps a small nuncheon.

Out in the corridor, she decided to check on David. Assured that he still slept, she marched down to the ground floor to begin her intensified assault. She was determined to find a clue as to who might be the one who used the poison. Both Augustus and Egbert had strong reasons. Filpot might out of stupid spite, or some peculiar grounds. Only Jeremy Vane was free of suspicion, as he had no motivation. He couldn't inherit, could he? So what would his motive be?

Entering the north wing of the house, she found that here the business of the estate was conducted. In the first of the rooms, Jeremy Vane sat behind a desk piled with ledgers and papers. She glanced at the shelves neatly stacked with books, then smiled at him.

"I haven't seen you in some time. You certainly are a busy man." She casually looked about the room, running a finger along a row of books. She might think Mr. Vane to be as innocent as a lamb, but David detested him. Distrust usually had a foundation, even if it were illogical. Although this was one time she had to ignore an intuition.

"Good day, Miss Elizabeth. I trust you are well. That your dip in the icy water left you none the worse? May I say you look in radiant good health?" His face reddened, and he fiddled with the pen in his hands like a schoolboy.

Elizabeth smiled kindly. "I fare well, thank you. And I believe both Lord Leighton and his father improve daily."

Mr. Vane bowed his head. "I hope that is the case. Poor Lord Crompton has had a time of it, what with his wife dying at the birth of their daughter, and then the child as well. The Percy family is not a prolific one, I fear."

"Witness Lord Augustus and his only son." She glanced at the shelves, then added, "Is there a family tree about?"

"I believe there is, but not quite up to date," he replied dryly. "There will need to be changes once you wed David."

Not knowing quite how to evade that subject, for she

was beginning to tire of the matter, Elizabeth murmured a vague reply, then drifted from the room. If she wanted to investigate this wing, she would have to do so when Jeremy Vane was elsewhere. Whereas Mr. Vane seemed to her eyes all that was amiable, appearances could be deceiving.

Back in the central hall, she studied the elaborate fireplace surround while pondering motives for murder. She absently straightened a picture, then adjusted the placement of a chair too close to the wall.

"Out and about again, Miss Elizabeth? I trust that David appreciates your devotion to the family," Egbert said in a somewhat acid voice. "Of course, I expect there is a bit of self-interest lurking in your deeds, if truth be known."

Remarking the contrast between biting language Egbert used and the gentle speech employed by Jeremy Vane, Elizabeth wondered how the two could manage to survive in the same house. Perhaps that was why Mr. Vane retreated to the estate offices in the north wing.

"I am well, sir," she gently replied, ignoring his insulting remarks about her interest in family affairs. "And your father? He does satisfactorily?"

"You are wandering about the house this morning," Egbert said, ignoring her inquiry. "Inspecting your future home, are you?"

"I understand that Lord Crompton requested that you remove yourself to London, or wherever you chose to live. Yet you choose to remain. How decidedly odd. One would think a gentleman would wish to take himself elsewhere were he not wanted." She'd had enough of his vitriolic words. Time to let him know that she was not the milk and water miss he might think her. "Unless he is at point non plus and has no alternative but throw himself upon the mercy of a relative. In which case, one would also think he would conduct himself with amiability."

He bowed, as one hit. "True. When illness struck my uncle, I could not leave. Such callous disregard for the head of the family would be ill received."

"Ah, yes," she agreed, "Society esteems a *respect* for family ties."

His mocking inspection served to bring a blush to her cheeks, one she considered slight, thankfully. "If you will excuse me," she said pointedly, wishing him gone, preferably to the ends of the earth.

"Ah, it would be most ill bred of me to permit a guest in the house to be at loose ends. Allow me to be your guide, as it were."

There was no David to rescue her from his attentions, unwelcome as they were. Elizabeth bowed to the inevitable, acquiescing to his company. He led her past the library toward the front of the house.

"And this is the study, a small room you've not yet seen, I feel sure."

"Charming." Elizabeth paused in the door to the lovely little room. It would be an ideal place for the woman of the house to keep her accounts. From the desk she could gaze across her beautiful gardens to the forested hills beyond. She also would have an excellent view of the drive that approached the house, thus appraised of company long before the estimable Sidthorp could find her.

"You actually feel you might be able to settle in this house, so far from the delights of the city?" Egbert gave a faint shudder, picking an imaginary piece of lint from his coat sleeve with exaggerated care.

"*You* are here, are you not? And you appear to be surviving nicely. Besides, one could arrange picnics at Box Hill, and Brighton is not all that far away—nor is London, for that matter. It is not the ends of the earth, sirrah." Her derisory glance pinned him in his place for a moment before she swept past him along the hall back to the central portion of the house. He followed close behind her.

"My, my, the little angel has a forked tongue," he whispered in that sarcastic way he had.

"I do not speak with such. However, I cannot say the same for others."

At that moment Lord Augustus ambled toward them, corsets creaking louder than usual. "Ah, Miss Elizabeth. How goes my brother this day?"

She opened her mouth to suggest that he visit his brother, when the realization that Lord Augustus might well have a motive for wishing his brother in the grave. It could no be agreeable for him to be a charity guest at his brother's home. Aunt Bel had breezily informed Elizabeth that Lord Augustus Percy had not a feather to fly with. How Egbert managed to finance his foppish attire on such meager expectations provided additional suspicion.

"I assure you that your brother improves daily," Elizabeth managed to say at last.

"Good, good. Tolerates me now, you know. Were once the best of friends," he reminded. He sighed gustily, his corset sounding perilously like it neared the breaking point.

Not wishing to become involved in family wrangling and intrigues, she merely nodded, looking about her for a means of escape.

"Would you excuse me, gentlemen? Mr. Vane promised to find some papers for me." With that vague pretext, and pleasant murmurs of regret, she slipped away from them, drifting down the hall to where she suspected Mr. Vane still lurked in his little den, much like a spider spinning his plans for the estate.

" 'Tis time for nuncheon, Mr. Vane. Do you not join us? I vow, I shall be quite displeased if I must bear the company of Lord Augustus and Mr. Percy alone." She grinned at him, feeling quite in charity with the unassuming young gentleman.

He turned a pleased pink, nodding. "I shall be there." When she lingered, he went on, "Is there anything else?"

"That family tree. I should like to see it, if I may." She hoped her voice sounded sufficiently wistful to prod him to action. How provoking if he again kept her from seeing so simple a thing. Although what it would accomplish, she was not sure.

He said nothing about not knowing where it was this time, but went directly to a drawer from which he extracted a large, much folded sheet of paper. It almost seemed as though he had anticipated her return and had hunted it up for her.

"The details are written in those books up there on the shelf. This is the illustrative drawing representing the various lines of the family. The Percys may lay claim to an extraordinary and illustrious background.'' He smiled, but she noted that it did not reach his eyes.

He lovingly unfolded the paper, then began to point out the diverse lines of the family, how they were linked by marriage to many of the great houses in the land. It made her very aware that a Dancy, not withstanding she was the daughter of a baron, had scarcely the noble background to become the wife of the future Earl of Crompton. Not when one studied the lineage of past Percys.

Elizabeth stood at Jeremy Vane's side, studying the paper while beginning to appreciate all that had gone into creating her rake. Small wonder he carried himself like a lord of the land. He was one.

''I am exceedingly impressed, Mr. Vane. Most of the Percys did produce large families—until the present generation, that is,'' she said, reminding him of his earlier words regarding the dearth of Percys and heirs.

''I should think that both David and Egbert would be starting their nurseries instead of dashing about London and worrying about the cut of their coats.''

Surprised at his bitterness, she spoke without due thought. ''You sound as though you resent them, or at least their behavior. Is it the costs involved? Your concern for the estate?'' From what Aunt Bel had said, Elizabeth believed the estate to be in fine shape, which made Mr. Vane's antagonism all the more confusing.

''Yes,'' he finally said. ''I have a deep concern for the estates, its future. However, if *you* are to come here, I fancy that might ease my worries some. From what I have seen, you appear to be a woman of uncommon good sense.''

''What a charming thing of you to say, sir. I am flattered, indeed.'' She beamed a smile of goodwill at him, backing toward the door with the family tree still in her hands. The sound of a monstrous sneeze halted her retreat. Spinning about, she clutched the paper to her breast, exclaiming with dismay, ''Lord Leighton! You ought not be down here.''

''I suspect I had better not be in bed, at least not alone.'' Giving Jeremy Vane a wrathful glare, David availed himself of Elizabeth's arm. Leaning upon her just enough so she could not scold him for an impropriety, he guided her from the office.

"What are you doing out of your bed?" she hissed at him in an angry undertone.

"Good thing I came down," he declared righteously after blowing his nose. "Found you most improperly closeted with that blasted cousin of mine."

"When I left your room, you were sleeping like an angel." She stopped at the end of the corridor as it opened onto the central hall. In the distance she could hear the querulous voice of Lord Augustus railing at his son.

"Pity I had to miss your presence. I am almost reconciled to this notion of marriage, if it means having you in my bed," he teased.

Elizabeth could feel the heat that flamed in her face. Without doubt it spread down her entire body, most likely making her look like a giant strawberry. Those wicked eyes of his danced with glee when he saw her discomfort. Oh, how she would love to put him in his place, just for once. And to get the better of him in one of their contests of wits suddenly became her utmost ambition.

"Sirrah, I protest," she snapped.

He blew his nose again, then surprisingly agreed. "As do I. You are too lovely a girl to be involved in this mess. However," he added as he appropriated her arm again and began to walk toward the dining room, "I have need of your intelligence at the moment."

Irritation fought with another, deeper emotion. "I have not uncovered a clue. Have you thought of anything? Even though your father improves daily, you must be on your guard lest you become a victim. After all, as his heir, would you not be the next target?"

David paused just inside the dining room, glancing back to make sure they were alone. "I had considered that gruesome thought. I appreciate your concern. I believe you have actually come to care for me a trifle?"

Elizabeth blushed, to her annoyance, and refused to respond to that sally. Rather, she veered to another matter.

"I suggest we study your family tree. Your father has been threatened, you as well. Who is to say but what your Uncle Augustus and Cousin Egbert might not be future victims too? Who would be the next in line for the title?''

Elizabeth spread out the paper on the dining table for him to peruse, pointing out how meticulous additions to the various families had been made.

"I do not know. It would take a clever investigation by one trained in that sort of thing. It would involve a third cousin and the like, you know." He studied the large paper again, looking at the names printed so neatly.

"There are a lot of us, are there not? Would you mind joining such a motley crew?''

"Motley, indeed," she said, seizing on that word as a means of evasion. "You well know that you are anything but.''

The timely arrival of Lord Augustus, Egbert and Jeremy prevented the exploration of that dangerous subject. She hastily folded up the family tree, tucking it under her arm as the others moved into the room.

"Hear, hear! Out of your bed? Think that wise?'' Lord Augustus plodded over to peer at his nephew.

"I am flattered, cuz. I rightly suspect that dearest David did not trust me with his betrothed.''

"What utter nonsense," Elizabeth roundly declared, not wishing to hear David say the same. "Why do we not sit down so Sidthorp may get on with the serving?''

At Aunt Bel's home, nuncheon was a casual affair. Late sleepers might stray into the dining room to pick at the spread of food as they pleased. It seemed that at Penhurst Place the gentlemen met at the table for a repast, perhaps to discuss the day's plans.

Feeling that she inhibited this, Elizabeth nonetheless was loath to depart to her room. How dreary to contemplate eating from a tray all by herself.

Once the meal drew to a tedious close, for the men spent their time conversing about masculine interests, Elizabeth escaped to the library.

She was followed closely by Lord Leighton. Curiously enough, Mr. Percy watched without making an effort to join them. Instead he agreed to a game of billiards with his father.

David closed the door snugly behind them, surveying

Elizabeth as she sauntered about the room nervously, still hoping to find a copy of a good herbal. "Why are you here?"

"Why, indeed. Because, my little temptress, I cannot stay away."

Then he sneezed, and Elizabeth rang for Sidthorp.

"I have just the thing for you, my lord."

"I was afraid of that," David muttered.

10

WATER DRIPPED FROM the eaves. Beyond the house the snow dwindled into little splotches of white in the heavy shade under the hedges. The late February sun filtered through the bare branches of the trees about Penhurst Place, touching on swelling buds with a gentle caress. The cold spell had broken.

Off across the meadow a plump duck paddled its solitary way along the shore of the once frozen pond, although pieces of ice still lingered near the center of the shallow water. A slight breeze ruffled budding shrubs and last summer's grasses. In sheltered meadows crocus sent forth hesitant blooms, and clusters of snowdrops boldly sought the sun.

Elizabeth ignored the beginnings of spring.

In the library she wandered about, wondering why the herbal Lord Crompton had said ought to be on the shelf was not there. Did the same person who had hidden the book on poisons in the middle of a library shelf remove the herbal for nefarious purposes? She shivered at the thought that such a person might be beneath this roof.

"Ka-choo."

Without turning about, she absently said, "God bless you."

"I am feeling neglected," Lord Leighton said from the doorway, sounding a bit like a petulant schoolboy. "Everyone avoids me today. The least you might do is talk to me."

"You persist in teasing me, sir. I vow I become tired of it." She gave him a cross look, for she was indeed tired of everything this morning. The previous evening had been tedious in the extreme. Lord Augustus and Egbert had persisted in claiming her company until she went up to bed. They perpetually wrangled, until she decided she ought to take up billiards, for then they remained silent.

"You're blue-deviled," David announced with gentle derision. He strolled to the French window that looked out on the rolling expanse of green across to the woods on the far side. "That warm wind and brighter sun may have banished the snow, but it has done nothing to better your mood. We need to get out of the house."

"Your father improves, but you, sir, have a wretched cold." Elizabeth was suddenly reminded of Victoria's attempt to solve the difficult cipher, and how she had said it was imperative to get away from the problem at times, else she would go mad.

"On the other hand, perhaps you are right," Elizabeth said slowly. "I could see if I might persuade the coachman to take me back to Aunt Bel's."

"I need you here to keep your eyes open," he said hastily. "With you at my side, I may be less inclined to succumb to poison." He assumed a vulnerable look and gazed at her with the saddest expression she had ever seen.

"You accept you are in danger?" With a worried flash of turquoise eyes at the gentleman who lounged against the window surround, Elizabeth said, "I had not expected to find hunting for missing, er, books to be so trying."

"Ah, yes, discretion," he whispered, glancing at the open door. "Very wise. Now, where shall we go?" he mused, quite ignoring her statement in regard to the coachman and returning to Aunt Bel's.

"You may stick your head in a bucket for all I care," Elizabeth muttered, gathering her reticule and shawl in her hands.

"Now, now, mustn't get tetchy. Sign of old age," he teased.

"I am beginning to feel a hundred, what with catering to you, worrying about your father, and wondering if there is anything to be salvaged from my poor reputation."

"Fine time to begin fretting about that." His eyes seemed to dance with amusement at her belated show of discretion. "Besides, your respectable Aunt Bel is agreeable, most likely to ensnare me good and proper."

In fairness, she nodded regretfully. "I daresay you have the right of it." Elizabeth had no desire to ensnare anybody. She ought to have had more concern before, but her wits appeared to have gone begging.

He straightened, leaving the window to walk to her side. Elizabeth paused on her way to the door, wondering what was up his sleeve now.

"You are not to brood over that. I have a plan to take care of the matter." He reached out to gently touch her cheek, which quite undid her.

Blinking back a threatening tear, she said in a constricted voice, "Filpot would not allow me in to see your father this morning. I just know something is amiss. Tell me that he is not worse."

"I am not a doctor, Elizabeth. I cannot say. I confess he is not the same as yesterday, however."

"I knew it. The dear man. And he had so enjoyed my reading *Pride and Prejudice* to him." She hunted in her reticule for a handkerchief, then dabbed the moisture in her eyes. "I believe I shall return to Montmorcy Hall to persuade Purvis to attend your father." She blew her nose, a dainty sound compared to the great noise when Leighton followed suit.

"We, sir, are a pair of watering pots." Her giggle was distinctly quavery.

"Precisely. I suggest we take ourselves out of here for the nonce." He gallantly offered his arm.

Suddenly wanting to be away from the house, the problems that seemed so threatening, Elizabeth nodded her agreement. Placing her hand on his proffered arm, she gave him a tentative smile. "Where?"

He urged her along the corridor toward the front hall. "Have you ever been to the grotto? My father had it constructed for my mother before I was born. It was her great delight—after me, of course."

"Naturally," Elizabeth replied, chuckling at the mischievous lilt to his grin. "What a pity your mama could not have seen what a scamp you have become."

The look he gave her was most peculiar, unfathomable, and Elizabeth feared she had overstepped that line betwixt friendly banter and polite social chitchat. However, he did not say anything more, which left her totally at sea.

When they reached the hall, he spoke again, relieving her of the worry she had somehow offended him.

"Put on a warm pelisse and stout half-boots, for the caves can be chilly this time of year, and the ground may be quite damp in patches."

"Ought you go there with such a nasty cold?"

"I have a friend who firmly believes that the best way to cure a cold is to take a plunge in an icy pond, then go to bed with a bottle of gin."

"That sounds like a feather-brained notion, if you ask me," Elizabeth said, shaking her head at the image it provoked of a thoroughly soaked Lord Leighton, both inside and out.

"Go," he urged, then stood watching as Elizabeth walked lightly up the stairs.

She wondered what thoughts went skimming through his head. How did the rakish gentleman perceive her now? Then the very idea that she might even care about such brought her to her senses, and she scolded herself all the way to her room.

When she rejoined Lord Leighton, he was also dressed with more care than customary. Even though the day appeared mild, he had wound a scarf about his throat, and his coat was neatly buttoned over his vest. He extended a gloved hand to her, and Elizabeth hesitantly accepted it.

"The grotto?" she sought to confirm.

"Never say you are off to that hideous creation," Egbert sneered from the entry to the hall. "With all due respect to your mama, David, that is a ghastly place, dripping moss and decorated with bizarre statues. Gives me the chills just thinking about it."

"I had not thought you such a poor-spirited creature, cousin." David edged Elizabeth toward the door.

She was relieved that David did not appear angered by his cousin's nasty little barb. Rather, it seemed to her that he sought to avoid conflict with this odious relative. She caught sight of Jeremy Vane hovering in the background, coming from the other wing of the house.

"And do you share Mr. Percy's lack of enthusiasm for the grotto, Mr. Vane?"

The flicker of alarm on his face really was nothing to be concerned about, Elizabeth assured herself.

"Curious spot. I daresay you shall like it. Some might think it romantic." His eyes darted from Elizabeth to David, then back to her again. Suddenly she wondered if she was doing the right thing.

Once outside the house, she turned to Lord Leighton, saying, "I ought to bring Rose along with us. Really, sir, you have drawn me into the most scrambling ways."

"Unquestionably," he smoothly replied. "But then, you must be accustomed to unorthodox conduct, living with your sisters."

"If you mean that we were ostensibly alone after Geoffrey went off to the Peninsula, that is true. But Julia is a highly respectable widow, you know. We were not ever *that* out of bounds, I assure you, and never uncouth, I believe."

"Are you working on a commission at present?" he queried, apparently wishing to change the subject. He assisted her along the rough path, guiding her over a fallen log and around the end of the pond.

"A series of country scenes for Mr. Ackermann. There was but one left to complete when you so precipitously entered my room. I daresay he will accept them, figuring to publish them for next winter. I ought to finish that final one before I forget what winter looks like. Things change so quickly." She gestured to the scene about them, green buds where light snow had blankered shrubs not long before.

Elizabeth thought the grounds near the house sadly neglected, something Jeremy Vane ought to have tended and obviously had not. Reeds marched thickly along the edge of the water, and pond weed looked to be rampant. Good for the ducks perhaps, but not proper management to her way of thinking. She revised her opinion of the young man as she glanced about her. The gardens ought to have been groomed as carefully as the house or fields, not forgotten.

"Why the frown? Are you having second thoughts about the grotto?"

"Nothing like that." She was loath to reveal her new opinion of the steward and sought a different direction.

"I confess I wonder about this clever person who wishes you and your father ill. We have not inspected the kitchens. If you believe the food suspect, might not the poison be found there?"

He stopped, turning to face Elizabeth, quite serious for once. "I expect you are right. Cannot think why it did not occur to me before this. Perhaps you could snoop about down there, for I dare not consider such—the cook would sense something odd immediately."

"I shall try," she replied, wondering how the cook would accept her presence.

They had reached a cavernous opening some distance from the pond. Large stones buttressed the front and into the entranceway. A forlorn statue of Hera stood guard nearby.

Elizabeth decided that David appeared even more handsome when he became solemn. She matched his mood, standing quietly, waiting for him to conclude his remarks.

"Actually, I suspect that Jeremy Vane is the one we seek." His stark revelation shocked Elizabeth.

"Preposterous," she scoffed. "It seems to me that Egbert takes a far greater dislike of you than poor Mr. Vane. Your own father took him in, trained him," she reminded. "How could Mr. Vane possibly wish his benefactor dead? I think you are wrong. Where does he appear in the line of succession?"

"I confess I had not considered him in that light. He would need to do in the lot of us. Jeremy always presents his best face to others, no one would suspect him but I."

"You are absurd. He is always agreeable to you. Certainly, he has been nothing if not helpful to me." She stepped from David's side, her confusion causing her to withdraw from him in every way.

"Does that mean you shan't help me? Remember, you *are* betrothed to me, and you did shoot me in the arm. You owe me something." That mischievous look had returned to his eyes. Elizabeth did not trust it in the least. She fingered the ring he had given her, presumably for appearances.

"We shall see," she temporized, not wishing to be forced into a decision she might regret later. She looked about her, observing the unusual entrance. "I gather we have arrived at the grotto. I should like to see it now that we are actually here."

He smiled, then took her arm, guiding her along a rugged path that broadened out as they entered a fantastic cavern. It was studded with seashells of every size, shape, and color. Delighted with the beauty concealed beyond the rather grim entrance, Elizabeth clapped her hands with pleasure.

"I gather that you like it?" He stood not far away, watching her as she stared about her, wide-eyed at the unusual scene.

"Yes, indeed. You sent someone ahead to light the torches. How thoughtful of you." Her antagonism began to melt as she slowly turned around to study everything. She observed how the lighting brought out interesting shapes, accenting the beauty of the shells and their delicate colors. From here and there shy cupids and dainty fawns peeped at them, their subtle colorings blending in with the shells rather nicely.

"There originally were small apertures to admit light. Over the years they have become clogged with dirt and debris."

"Mr. Vane ought to have better attended to the care of this charming place," she murmured as she wandered away from David's side to study a particularly lovely shell.

"There are a lot of things Mr. Vane ought to have tended and has not. He has hoodwinked my father, but not me. I see through that mealy-mouthed talk. He is an earwig who tattles tales to my father about me. Fortunately, my father is not about to believe those stories."

"He carries malicious tales? About you?" Elizabeth was shaken. She had believed Jeremy Vane to be a just and righteous man, and had worried that David was not all that was honorable. Could she have been so mistaken? About both of them?

Not wanting to probe further at this moment, she turned to inspect another shell. "Where did these come from?"

"My father had an arrangement with a number of sea captains to bring boxes of shells back from their journeys."

They began to stroll along the irregular wall. The gentle sound of water cascading over rock grew louder until they turned a corner, and the breathtaking view of a dainty waterfall came into sight. Elizabeth stopped short, altogether entranced with the sight.

"This idea is not all that unusual. I have learned of several others who have achieved similar results with their grottos and so-called 'sublime' gardens."

"Well, and I think it very fine. So I shall tell your father when I see him again. If I see him again. I rather suspect there is something you are hiding from me."

He failed to meet her eyes, glancing off to where the icy water tumbled and foamed over the rocks, then bubbled on its way to the pond, not far removed. He began to lead her away from the falls, to where she could hear what he said more clearly. He stepped close to her, tilting up her face so he might search her eyes. "Elizabeth . . ."

She held her breath, looking at David to see if he also heard the click of footsteps on the stone.

"Someone is in here," she whispered, uneasy, suspecting that the grotto had but one entrance, that if another chose to do them harm it would be a simple matter.

A sharp report and a chunk of the ceiling fell next to where David and Elizabeth stood. They stared with shock at the debris near their feet.

Flashing her a warning glance, David cautiously edged forward around the bend. He motioned for Elizabeth to follow him. Inch by inch they made their way along the rough path. Elizabeth stubbed her toe on a rock, and pressed her lips together to keep from crying out in pain.

When they came to the central portion of the grotto, they found it empty. The trickle of water down the walls and around and over the stones was all that could be heard. Elizabeth placed a shaky hand on the head of one of the cupids, feeling stupidly weak.

"Whoever it was has disappeared. I wonder what he planned for us?" David wandered about, studying the floor. He bent over to pick up a small object, dropping it into his pocket without comment.

"I believe I should like to return to the house." She shivered, suddenly aware that she felt very chilled.

David quietly agreed. Outside, they discovered the sun had retreated behind clouds. The wind had picked up and bit cruelly through their coats, tugging at Elizabeth's snug-fitting velvet bonnet with frigid fingers. Many times she found herself stumbling on the path, and was exceedingly grateful for the helping hand extended her. But she remained silent for the most part.

Elizabeth worried over David, although she'd not give him the satisfaction of knowing it. He had insisted upon leaving his bed, and seemed bent on destruction, what with ice skating and now the walk to the grotto. She was sure he ought to have remained quiet, warm, and safe by the fireside, if not in bed.

When they entered the house, she spoke quietly to Sidthorp while he assisted her with her pelisse. Then hesitantly she turned to face David, very much Lord Leighton at the moment, looking down that nose of his at her as though she were no more than his serf.

"I have requested Sidthorp to order you a hot bath. May I suggest you take that bottle of gin along, for surely you are as cold as when you were in the pond."

"What an amazingly selective memory you have."

"Do not sneer at me."

"I can't do it half as well as Egbert, anyway."

Not able to argue this point, Elizabeth walked beside David to the top of the stairs, where she paused. "I believe I shall investigate the kitchen and send for Purvis as well. I should like her to have a look at your father, not to mention tend your ague, which you are sure to develop. She has a way of making a person remain in bed, which is where you ought to stay," she scolded.

"I think you might persuade me," he said with a roguish grin. "I like the way you soothe my fevered brow."

Elizabeth digested this suggestive taunt, vividly recalling the kiss that had followed, then decided to prudently ignore it. "Perhaps Filpot will allow her into your father's bedroom. She does have a way about her." Elizabeth still felt hurt at being excluded from the room where she had spent most of the past days.

"That has a grim sound." He spoiled his frown by a magnificent sneeze.

"Off with you. Now," insisted Elizabeth with a shooing motion as she backed away from him, then turned to hurry along the north corridor to her room.

Rose greeted her with a look of dismay as she saw the wind-tossed appearance of her usually neat mistress.

"Help me tidy up some. I have no desire to have anyone else see me so disheveled." She gave a horrified glance in the looking glass at her rumpled self, then hurriedly divested herself of her pelisse and bonnet.

Elizabeth allowed Rose to straighten her gown and then repair the damage to the arrangement of her curls.

"Filpot will not permit you in the earl's room?" she inquired as Rose brushed Elizabeth's hair.

"No, miss. Said I was not needed. Hadlow, he thinks that Filpot a smarmy sort of fellow." Rose threaded an aqua ribbon through Elizabeth's curls, then stood back to survey her work. "I suspect something havey-cavey is going on."

"Indeed." But then, Rose was given to seeing ghosts and all manner of spectral creatures. "It may be that the earl caught Lord Leighton's cold and has truly taken a turn for the worse." She shared a worried look with her maid.

"I do hope 'tis nothing serious, miss."

Elizabeth did too. Over the days she had grown exceedingly fond of the old gentleman, and did not wish anything to happen to him.

"The food has been handled only by you and Hadlow?" she said with sudden concern, wondering if something had managed to slip past them.

"Yes, miss. The cook don't like it by half, she don't. Muttering something about her special herbs for the earl and the like. I fancy my own cooking to hers, and I'm no cook." She grinned at her mistress.

Once she was restored to a respectable appearance, Elizabeth turned to her maid, studying her open face. "I want to send off a request for Purvis. Could you see that one of the footmen takes it to Montmorcy Hall for me? Then I intend to visit the kitchens."

"Oh, miss, be that wise?" Rose wore a horrified expression on her face at the mere thought of her dear mistress going into such a place.

"I have been in the still room at my aunt's home, and the kitchen as well. Come now," Elizabeth chided.

She wrote a careful note for her aunt, explaining why she needed Purvis to come. Then she gathered a shawl and bravely marched down the stairs to the hall. Sidthorp was nowhere to be seen. The house was as quiet as a tomb.

"Peagoose," she muttered to herself, "you shall be as bad as Rose if you keep this up."

At the door to the kitchen she paused, watching the preparations for the evening meal. Across the stone-flagged floor the kitchen maid bustled about. A high dresser was loaded with platters of all sizes. Several Windsor chairs stood along the wall, and in the center of the room a wide wooden table was littered with vegetables ready for the pot.

A closed range stood on the far wall. The open fire was covered by a hot plate, waiting for the pots and sauce pans. The ovens sent out a welcome heat which would undoubtedly become oppressive by the time dinner rolled around. The pot of soup on the back of the stove smelled dreadful, and Elizabeth did not look forward to dinner if that was the beginning of the meal.

A rusty tin hastener was set in front of the fire, a joint of beef suspended from the dangle spit. One look revealed why the meat was often underdone on one side and overcooked on the other. The bottle jack by which the roast was to revolve worked only sporadically, if at all.

Elizabeth wondered why Mrs. Sidthorp as housekeeper didn't insist that the cook maintain a higher standard of cleanliness—seeing to it that the pots and utensils were polished and things worked properly—when the cook entered from the scullery room.

She was an enormous woman. Her grimy mob cap perched atop frizzled gray hair, her many chins rested on a massive bosom, while a none-too-clean apron was tied around her girth. And she was undoubtedly the meanest, most foul-tempered-looking woman Elizabeth had ever set eyes upon. Little raisin-dark eyes peered

suspiciously at Elizabeth, making her hard pressed not
to shudder.

Small wonder that meek little Mrs. Sidthorp daren't
chastise the cook. Cook would most likely pop her in a
pot and be done with it.

"Who be you, and what do you in my kitchen?" Cook
demanded, arms akimbo.

Elizabeth stood her ground. "I wished to make a tisane for Lord Leighton. His cold bothers him dreadfully.
Where is the still room?" This should have been the
province of the housekeeper, and Elizabeth could only
hope it proved in better condition than the kitchen.

Before the cook bothered to answer, the scared little
kitchen maid tugged at Elizabeth's sleeve. "Please, miss,
it be this way."

Ignoring the glare from Cook, Elizabeth gratefully followed the maid into a small room where the smell of
herbs and spices scented the air. The herb chest drew
Elizabeth's gaze. "Thank you," she murmured to the
maid, dismissing the girl.

An inspection of the chest revealed the usual assortment of herbs, from what Elizabeth knew of the matter.
Purvis would have a better idea if something was missing, or if there was a substance that ought not be here.
The spice chest was locked up, a not unusual occurrence,
for spices were expensive and easily purloined. Sugar
was kept out and available, a sign of an affluent household, for Elizabeth knew many kept it under lock and
key as well.

Up on a shelf, Elizabeth spotted the missing book—
the *Family Herbal* by Thornton. She walked back to the
kitchen door, watching the cook for several minutes before she observed that there were no cookery books to
be seen on the two small shelves next to the dresser. Most
households had at least one cookery book, along with
the Bible and a few other works for the staff to read, if
they were able. All Elizabeth could make out was a dusty
copy of the Bible and another book, presumably ser-
mons, from the look of it.

"You cook by memory?" Elizabeth inquired in a gentle voice.

"Cain't read, I cain't," Cook replied in a huff and a

wheeze. It was clear that a cook who could not read
would not bother to take a book, conceal it in the scullery, with the intent of using the knowledge therein to
poison someone. For that matter, the woman could not
read the other book.

"Howere, I can cook with the best of 'em," she asserted, and Elizabeth warranted that there was not a soul
who would argue with the intimidating woman, even if
the meat was overdone and the soup utterly dreadful.

"But I don't take kindly to people snooping in my
kitchen," the cook said, picking up a meat cleaver. "That
Hadlow, sneaking about here, says he fixes somethin' fer
the earl. Hmpf. I's sp'osed to use my special herbs for
him, I am." The cleaver was plunked down with a thump,
and the woman began to plop vegetables into a pot.

"Special herbs?" Elizabeth inquired in what she hoped
was an encouraging manner. The peculiar taste of much
of the food might be discovered if those herbs could be
identified—and tossed away.

Cook, seeing the strange miss getting overly curious
about the doings of her kitchen, clammed up and turned
her back on the guest.

Deciding it was unlikely that she would learn anything
more, Elizabeth left the room and proceeded back to her
room. She had the foresight to bring a pot of tea with
her, along with two cups. She and Rose often shared a
pot of tea while at Penhurst Place, for Elizabeth found a
household of gentlemen not always to her liking.

"Rose," Elizabeth said with a half laugh as she entered her room, "I quite see why you looked so horrified
when I spoke of going to the kitchen. What a dreadful
woman. How do you suppose she ever came to be here
in the first place?"

Rose poured the tea and they each sipped for a moment
before Rose timidly said, "I think she crawled out of the
wall one night and has been here ever since."

Elizabeth chuckled at the unlikely tale, then fell silent.
If Cook was not involved in poisoning the food, who
was?

11

"I DECLARE, this rain has been more tiresome than the snow," Hyacinthe said, an adorable pout on her pretty mouth.

"I believe it looks to clear this morning. John Coachman said his rheumatism is better, which he insists is a reliable sign," Lady Chloe offered in hope of soothing her impetuous cousin. Hyacinthe had paced about the house like a caged animal. No doubt the lack of gentleman callers had something to do with her restlessness.

Aunt Bel ignored them, consulting her collection of superstitions to discover if there was anything to be found regarding rain, other than references to building an ark. "Do you know," she said to no one in particular, "that the superstition regarding red hair goes back for centuries?"

With this she captured Hyacinthe's attention, for she insisted her hair was not the least red, although she did admit her hair might be a bright chestnut.

" 'Twas said that the red-haired Danes who wrought such havoc in our land brought about the feeling that a red head covered a violent disposition."

"Pooh," Hyacinthe snapped, "that was hundreds of years ago. I fail to see what the Danes might have to do with anything." She idly picked at the keys of the pianoforte, playing the same melody she had heard on Elizabeth's music box.

Since Lady Chloe thought the notion about red hair was a deal of nonsense, she said nothing, merely stood by the window and stared at the avenue leading up to the house as though by that means she might conjure up news.

"Well, I will admit," Hyacinthe continued, "if we do

not find something different to amuse us, I might contemplate violence of a kind." Her fingers crashed in a discordant sound to reflect her mood.

In her position by the window, Lady Chloe tensed, catching sight of a coach making its careful way up the avenue.

"I believe you are to have your wish, cousin. Visitors are coming."

Hyacinthe bounced up from the bench, dashing to Chloe's side. "Who? Can you tell? Oh, I do hope it is Lord Norwood."

A little smile curved Chloe's lips. While she sympathized with her cousin, she also thought it no bad thing that the exquisite Hyacinthe discover there were men impervious to her charms. She had known far too much success for her tender years. It would do her good to experience a bit of neglect, especially from the man Hyacinthe had made such a dead set at. It seemed to Chloe that her cousin had exhibited a want of good conduct in dealing with the marquess. Norwood was no youth to be dazzled by a lovely face. Hyacinthe needed a lesson.

"I do not think it to be Norwood's coach. There is no crest on the panel." Hyacinthe drooped against the window surrounds, then perked up. "At least it is someone. I wonder who."

"We shan't troop down to the entry hall to find out," cautioned Chloe. "Even I know that to be bad form."

"Hyacinthe has such a lovely voice. Why do you not sing up a song while Chloe plays for you? I shall listen, for I am very accomplished at that, you know," Aunt Bel suggested with a twinkle in her eyes.

Hyacinthe hastily selected, then began to sing a pretty country tune suited to her light soprano.

Gibbons presented himself in the doorway and announced, "The Viscount Leighton and Miss Elizabeth, my lady."

Elizabeth entered the drawing room at David's side. She had removed her outer things, wishing to change while here. David looked complete to a shade in a dark blue coat, white marcella waistcoat, and gray pantaloons tucked into his boots.

"How is everything at Penhurst Place?" Aunt Bel

begged to know. "Your father? Is he any better? I have prayed he would improve with Purvis to attend him."

"About the same," he replied. "She says even less than Filpot, and that is precious little."

"Odd, that," Aunt Bel declared. "I felt certain that Purvis wold have your father on his feet in a trice."

"She is a treasure, make no mistake. My arm is as good as new, and that ague that threatened me completely gone," he politely assured Lady Montmorcy. He turned his attention back to the girls.

"We have come with a proposition. After all this dreadful weather, you must be as anxious for diversion as we are. Why do we not venture down to Dorking? I feel sure there is something one of you ladies must desire from the shops, and it would be a nice change."

Hyacinthe whirled about in delight, facing her aunt with a pleading look. "Please, dearest Aunt Bel?"

Not to be ignored, Lady Chloe added her appeal. "Oh, do say we may go, Mama."

While they discussed the things that might be purchased on such an expedition, David waited at Elizabeth's side.

" 'Tis very kind of you to offer amusement for us," Aunt Bel said most properly. "It has been dreadfully dreary for everyone, especially the girls."

He chuckled. "With Uncle Augustus demanding everyone play billiards with him, and Jeremy quibbling with Egbert over scoring, it is a welcome change for me and Elizabeth as well. I'll wager she is about to take up billiards just to challenge my uncle."

As she had considered that very thing, she chuckled in response. "Indeed. It is either billiards or something quite drastic. Although I have been greatly worried about the earl, they allow me to do nothing and that becomes tedious."

An elusive expression crossed David's handsome face before he replied. "Yes, well, he did seem better, and then he changed. I fear I cannot give you details."

To her utter distraction he captured her hands and tenderly kissed the inner wrist of each. "I shall look forward to a day spent away from all the troubles at Penhurst Place and in your lovely company."

Uncomfortable, Elizabeth tugged her hands free, putting them behind her in an effort of striving for calm.

His lips twitched, almost breaking into a smile, then he said, "What a blessing it is that I possess unlimited patience." With that, he turned away from Elizabeth. He walked to where Aunt Bel perched on a striped satin sofa, fingering her locket watch.

"I have said the gels may go along with you, although I suspect Elizabeth would have gone regardless." Lady Montmorcy glanced at her niece, still standing by the door with a bemused expression on her face. "Mind you, take umbrellas. I shall have Cook send along a packet of food in case there is trouble on the road. I trust your coachman has the sense to bring a spare wheel in the event of disaster? 'Tis wise in such abominable spring weather."

"All is in order, dear lady. Shall I chat with you while the young ladies fetch pelisses and reticules?"

"Do not forget your pattens, girls. The streets of Dorking arc sure to be wretched after this rain," Aunt Bel admonished the girls, who were well on their way out of the room.

Elizabeth paused by the door. "Is there anything you wish, Aunt Bel? Perhaps some thread I may buy for you?"

"Considerate child," her aunt replied. "I do need another packet of needles for my embroidery. I declare, I cannot fathom how they disappear, when I am certain I have them carefully inserted in the fabric."

"Very well, a packet of needles it shall be," Elizabeth said, smiling at her aunt's dismay. The dear lady might be as punctual as a well-sprung clock, but she often forgot where she put things, particularly needles. Elizabeth had lost count of the number of packets she had bought since coming to the Hall.

In her room, Elizabeth slipped into her best turquoise pelisse, then donned a cottage bonnet that was lined with the same fabric and tied with matching riband. Drawing on her gloves, she again studied the diamond ring on her finger before covering it up with turquoise silk.

What to make of David and his puzzling attentions? Why did she have the uncomfortable sensation he was concealing something from her? When she asked questions, he kissed her wrists most intimately. And gave no reply.

Normally a woman did not expose her hands to a man unless he was someone close to her. Elizabeth was pleased with her hands at the moment. There were no stains or scratches from etching to mar them, and they were as soft as even she might wish. But his kisses presented a mystery. Why had he acted so in Aunt Bel's presence? Did he not realize it would show him as the lover? And make it more difficult to break their betrothal?

In the hallway she could hear the excited voices of her cousins as they made their way down the stairs to the entryway. She hastened to join them, unwilling to think about the riddle posed by David any longer. He had been too particular in his attentions, and if he continued to display such an attachment to her, Aunt Bel would be justified in believing the betrothal would lead to matrimony. He used her Christian name as though given that right, which, of course, betrothal offered him. But they were not really betrothed. In spite of the magnificent diamond on her finger.

Whether or not this was desired by Elizabeth was an entirely different matter. That she had been using David's first name for days remained forgotten, or perhaps ignored by her, in her wish to delude herself into thinking that she truly did not long for marriage with him.

David ushered the three young women to his traveling coach. "I daresay you shall not think the trip too tedious when it permits an escape from the house," he said with that twinkle restored to his eyes.

Not voicing an agreement, Elizabeth merely smiled as she entered the coach. Hyacinthe looked about the inside, a pleased expression on her face.

It was most attractive, with an interior of rich brown leather and plush velvet on the seats in a particularly lovely shade of dark blue. In addition to wood blinds that could be let down if one wished, there were pockets in the door panels to hold articles, or books, in the event one wished to attempt reading.

"I shall leave those odious pattens in the coach," Hyacinthe declared. "If a bit of water lingers in the streets, I feel certain someone will assist me." She did not look at Lord Leighton, but rather gazed dreamily off into space.

Lady Chloe followed suit, tucking her despised pattens away in the corner, hoping her mother would not know she had ignored the horrid things, with their rings of steel that clanged on the stone like dull bells.

"And what do you contemplate purchasing on your foray to the shops, Elizabeth?" David inquired in deceptively dulcet tones.

"I, sir, shall make my way to the best bookshop. Having read everything of interest to be found on your shelves, I desire something else." She spoke quietly, hoping to avoid being heard by her cousins. This might be possible, for they prattled away, discussing what they hoped to find.

"You left Miss Brunton's book unfinished? Or perhaps you have had you fill of *Self-Control?*"

She knew that note of teasing far too well to be surprised at his words. Self-control, indeed. Ignoring his taunt, she said, "I left my copy of *Pride and Prejudice* in London. It is a delightful book, and I believe I shall buy a copy to leave here, for my aunt has never read it. Your father seemed to enjoy it very much."

She darted a look that told him she clearly understood he was trying to discompose her. She'd not have that. She clasped her gloved hands in her lap and gazed from the window, allowing Lady Chloe and Hyacinthe to chatter away, inquiring about the shops, wondering if they might see anyone they knew, and in general monopolizing Lord Leighton.

It was to his credit that he exhibited great patience with the two girls, for away from Lady Montmorcy they forgot to be prim and proper.

"I shall arrange for a repast at the White Horse. Should we somehow become separated, meet there," David suggested.

Elizabeth exclaimed in delight as a deer bounded along the road, then darted off into the woods of beech and oak, soon disappearing from view. After they were gone from her sight, she turned to David. "That is kind of you, but we do have Aunt's packet of food."

Hyacinthe sniffed in disgust. "As if it would compare to the White Horse. All due apologies to your mama, Chloe," she added, not wishing to hurt her cousin's feelings.

The road wound down into the town west of Box Hill. Lady Chloe leaned forward to tap Elizabeth on her knee. "Later on there are simply masses and masses of bluebells along this road. Quite lovely, actually."

"Decidedly," Elizabeth replied, sitting straighter as they neared the center of town. She intended to separate herself from the others, find the needles for her aunt, then enjoy some time in the bookshop without Hyacinthe and Lady Chloe driving her mad with their chatter.

"Do you know," Hyacinthe whispered, although why, Elizabeth couldn't see, "that 'tis said Lord Nelson took leave of Lady Hamilton at the Hare and Hounds before he went off to the Battle of Trafalgar?" She peered out of the window at the building as they passed, quite as though she expected one of the people involved to step from the doorway.

Elizabeth couldn't resist a glance at David, nearly laughing when she met his amused grimace. It was lovely to have someone to share a bit of humor with on occasion.

Lady Chloe and Hyacinthe were enchanted when they discovered that others they knew had also decided to enjoy the respite from the rain. Lady Chloe spotted John Harlowe, dimpling a smile at him when he strode to her side.

Hyacinthe displayed more subtlety when she espied Lord Norwood across the busy street from the inn where they had stopped. She simply allowed her scarf to wave in the breeze, as though unable to capture it. The flutter of ivory silk caught his eye, and he sauntered to the party, bringing along his friends, Peregrine Forsythe and George Barr.

"My, what a lovely day," trilled Hyacinthe, sure of her charms, not to mention looks in a periwinkle pelisse trimmed in cream velvet. She tilted her head, becomingly demure in her smart bonnet cap of cream satin and double borders of scalloped lace. With a dainty hand she coyly toyed with the cream ribands that firmly anchored the bonnet beneath her chin. 'Sirs, what a pleasant surprise. Do you come to shop?''

"Like you," the elegantly attired Norwood said, looking down his aristocratic nose as he spoke, "we are come to town for diversion."

John Harlowe, not appreciating the other tonnish gentlemen in the least, drew Lady Chloe apart, persuading her, with frequent glances at the others, to permit him to escort her to the shops. When they drifted away along the street, Hyacinthe seized the opportunity to snare Lord Norwood, Mr. Forsythe, and Mr. Barr as her escorts.

Elizabeth thought her cousin in fine fettle, and barely suppressed a grin. Lady Chloe ought to have had a maid along, but in this small town it was unlikely to be remarked upon if she was escorted by a neighbor boy, especially one as well liked as John Harlowe.

"And now for you, Elizabeth," David murmured from a point shockingly close to her ear. "What was it you desired?"

She turned her head, finding him close, indeed. Although he was exceptionally tall, he had inclined his head so that his eyes were near the level of her own, and for a moment she found herself lost in those hazel depths. The golden lights in his eyes sparkled with humor, and Elizabeth found herself shaken to her core when she took a step away from him, saying, "Sir?"

"Your desires, Elizabeth. What are they?" That rich voice stroked her senses, teased her with yearning.

Heavens, she knew she must be blushing, for at that moment the notion of a kiss appealed to her more than anything in the world, much less the Dorking shops.

He chuckled, seeming satisfied, even though she had not answered him. He tucked her hand close to his side, guiding her across the cobbled street to the far side, then along the walk. "It is here somewhere, I recall."

Quite stupidly, she said, "What is?"

"Why, the bookshop, to be sure."

Elizabeth wished the ground would open up and swallow her. Never had she felt such a silly miss, not even at the Fenwick ball, where he had teased her with that first kiss. She had never told him that he was the first and only man to kiss her, but perhaps he had known, for she was indeed an innocent and inexperienced in things like kisses.

"Ah, here we are." He ushered her into the bookshop with great polish.

Elizabeth found she rather liked being escorted as though she were fragile china. In the past she had dashed about, not caring in the least for such. Memory of her previous confrontations with Lord Leighton while in London burned in her memory. What he must have thought of her.

"You hunt for that copy of *Pride and Prejudice* you want while I look over their stock of other books. I've a notion to see if they have something on landscaping. Father said my mother wished to have a white garden and formal landscaping out to the grotto. He expressed a desire to fix things up as she would have liked. What do you think about such a thing? Do you agree?" He appeared touchingly eager for her reply.

"It seems most admirable to me. I trust your father will be able to oversee the work himself." If she had hoped for further revelations about his father's health, she was to be disappointed, for David said nothing.

He evaded her searching look, turning to inspect the little penciled markers that gave one a clue as to what books were where.

Elizabeth paused a few moments before slowly wandering off to find the novels. Her mind seethed with the strangest notions. He was being less than truthful with her. No, not that precisely, but secretive. Still, it was none of her affair. With that reminder she persisted until she found what she wished. Knowing her aunt did not possess either of the books, she also bought a copy of *Sense and Sensibility,* and picked up a Minerva novel in the hope that it might prove diverting.

When she returned to the front of the shop, she found David waiting with a stack of books he had purchased. A quick glance at the titles revealed that he had found not only a work on landscaping by Repton, but a number of other volumes as well. A novel, a new history of

Greece, and several other works were being wrapped by the flustered clerk.

She paid for her books, then allowed David to lead her from the shop. Although she wondered, there was no proper way she could question him about his choices. Hyacinthe would have. But Elizabeth had achieved more dignity, unfortunately. It was not deemed fitting for a young woman to ask too many questions.

From the top of the street it was easy to discover where the others were. Hyacinthe waltzed along the way, peeking into the shops, disappearing into one that stocked pretty ribands and lace.

"Have you ever replaced that becoming pelisse that was ruined in the pond?"

"I've not had time, more's the pity," Elizabeth replied, vividly recalling that dreadful accident.

"I feel I ought to buy you a new one. It was most attractive."

"That would be highly improper," she said primly.

He laughed at her. "But I am your betrothed. I am allowed to do things like that. Come, I see a mantua maker up ahead. Permit me my whim."

Distressed, but somehow finding herself swept along to the shop, Elizabeth discovered that when David wanted his way, he attained it. In surprisingly short order the pleasant woman who kept the shop had Elizabeth measured, the fabric selected—by David, to match Elizabeth's eyes—and paid for. Arrangements were made for delivery of the fine wool garment, and they departed, no doubt leaving the mantua maker thinking she had taken a very quick order.

Once again outside the shop, Elizabeth turned to remonstrate with him. "You ought not have done that, sir."

"I am David, my dear girl. And, actually, I cannot lay claim to the idea as my own. My father was distressed to find you had suffered such a loss. He requested I replace your garment."

Surprised, Elizabeth could say no more, other than to issue a proper thank-you. She walked close to him, for he persisted in bringing her arm to his side in a highly familiar way. When she gave him a questioning look, he merely smiled.

"This walkway is narrow, and I would not lose you."

With that, Elizabeth had to be content. Indeed, the proximity of David, Lord Leighton, would have been quite enough to send her into transports if she had been a silly girl, which she wasn't. Not in the least.

It was a gay, almost frivolous group that met at the White Horse for the satisfying repast David has ordered.

Lord Norwood unbent sufficiently to talk to David most knowingly about planning gardens. It seemed that Norwood had rather grandiose plans for his own estate, not far from Oxford. He had consulted several landscape specialists, and brought forth a piece of paper upon which he sketched the final design that would be implemented once the weather proved more amenable.

While the two gentlemen had their heads together over the gardening discussion, Lady Chloe and John Harlowe, Hyacinthe and Peregrine Forsythe—George Barr having found it necessary to take his leave—chattered away with great amiability. Although, as Hyacinthe confided to Elizabeth when they retired to wash their hands and check their hair and bonnets, she could never be serious about Peregrine.

"Fancy being Hyacinthe Forsythe, if you please!"

Elizabeth chuckled, seeing how amusing it would sound. She wished she could share the silly whimsy with David, but when they joined the gentlemen, he still discussed gardening with Lord Norwood.

Oddly enough, Lord Norwood became quite animated when he found something that deeply interested him. He lost that rather stuffy mien, and his eyes crinkled up in a pleasant way. He really was attractive, with his hair tousled by a distracted hand that he thrust through it while pointing out the importance of proper fertilizer.

Hyacinthe was in a miff. "I vow," she whispered, "he is excessively tedious." There was little doubt as to whom she referred.

Only the entrance of the serving maids and the innkeeper with the platters of food prevented Hyacinthe from making a cake of herself. She darted annoyed glances at Norwood, then bent her attentions on Mr. Forsythe with devastating results. The poor man was overwhelmed.

Elizabeth could have swatted her cousin with very little encouragement.

"I beg your forgiveness, Elizabeth," David said quietly while the others began eating the excellent meal. "I do not usually neglect my lady when I can have the pleasure of her company."

"Fertilizer is by far the more important, I suspect."

"What, are you piqued too?"

"Not really," she replied, grinning when he glanced at Hyacinthe. "I wonder that I was ever that young, although we are only a year apart in age."

"May I say the time sits well on your shoulders?"

"You may say anything, sir. Whether I shall believe it is another matter."

"We ought to find a bonnet to go with that pelisse," he said, throwing Elizabeth completely into a dither.

"I'll have you know that it is bad enough for you to order that pelisse for me. To buy a bonnet would be totally beyond the pale."

"At least you did not call me sir," he grumbled.

Elizabeth thought it quite good that he failed to get his way. To her thinking, any gentleman who got his way too often became so spoiled as to be hopeless. Not that she wouldn't pamper a husband with loving care. Thankful the talk was loud and that no one seemed the least noticing of her, she nibbled her food. Finding it surprisingly delicious, she ate a disgustingly hearty meal. So much for the theory that lovelorn maidens wasted away on sighs. Not but what she couldn't sigh. That she might do very well without any doubt.

The happy party broke up shortly after that. Lord Norwood and Mr. Forsythe promised to join them for a small party at Montmorcy Hall two evenings hence.

Once in the coach, Hyacinthe bubbled and bounced until Elizabeth longed to tie her in the corner.

"I trust you have found the trip to your liking, Miss Hyacinthe," David inquired.

"Oh, yes," she replied, batting her lashes at him in her delight. With Hyacinthe flirting seemed to come as naturally as breathing.

Lady Chloe giggled, as young girls do when encountering something vastly amusing.

"What a good thing we left those horrid pattens in the carriage. We had not the least need for them," Hyacinthe declared as they entered the avenue to the Hall.

When the coach pulled up before the Montmorcy house, Lady Chloe and Hyacinthe got out, then bobbed proper curtsies and expressed their pleasure as well-reared girls ought.

Elizabeth was detained by the simple expedient of being kept in the coach awaiting David's help. At last he turned to assist her down the steps.

At her cool look he gave her an amused grin. "I want to see you at Penhurst Place on the morrow. Shall I send my carriage for you?"

"Odious man, to take it for granted I shall come at your bidding. I planned to stay here and not return."

"But you will," he replied with confidence.

"Very well, but only because I care about your father and wish to see how he goes on," she added truthfully.

He smiled a wry acceptance of her words, entered the coach, then waved farewell to her.

She stood by the front door, watching as his coach disappeared down the avenue. Something was up. She could feel it in her bones. But what?

12

"OH, DRAT AND BOTHERATION!" Elizabeth exclaimed.

A wheel of the coach slid into a particularly deep rut, and she found herself tossed about, nearly landing on the floor. She wondered if she had been wise to attempt the trip to Penhurst Place. Righting herself, she glanced at Rose, who sat in wide-eyed silence as they jounced along the country road.

"It looks to rain again," Elizabeth commented.

"Yes, miss," Rose replied dutifully.

Deciding that she preferred peace to attempting a conversation with the taciturn maid, Elizabeth fell to contemplation of her trip to Dorking. David had been all that was amiable, seeing to their every need, especially hers. She had enjoyed their time in the bookshop. Aunt Bel had exclaimed with delight over the novels, declaring they were just the thing to ward off the green melancholy in this dismal spring weather. She had not found a superstition to cover the rain, but she still searched.

Elizabeth ought not have permitted him to buy her the pelisse. Yet when confronting Aunt Bel with the matter, that most proper lady shrugged it off, reminding Elizabeth that not only was it a very nice gesture from Lord Crompton to replace the ruined garment, but that since Elizabeth was practically married to Lord Leighton, there was nothing inappropriate in the purchase.

Chloe and Hyacinthe were no better. Of course, their interest was captured by the coming party to be held at Montmorcy Hall. Elizabeth could not truly be surprised at their dismissal of her concerns.

So she was essentially alone, with no one in whom she might confide her fears. For every instinct in her body told her that danger lurked somewhere nearby. Bizarre,

but there it was. Something in David's face had given her
the clue. That and an intuitive sense within. Logic as
well. For if there was someone who wanted the earldom
badly enough to find a way to poison the present earl—
supposing that to be true—surely that same person would
do away with any other who stood in his way? A man
had to be utterly mad to think he might get away with
such a scheme. Yet it was terribly difficult to detect a
smidgen of poison artfully concealed.

If Lord Crompton was intended for elimination, would
his son not be next? Why could they not figure out what
substance was being used? And from where it came? She
knew that poison was extremely difficult to detect. Even
doctors found it difficult. But still . . . It had to be someone in the house.

But Jeremy Vane? That mild-mannered, unassuming
man who was politeness itself to Elizabeth? She couldn't
accept him as a reasonable suspect. Egbert Percy was the
likely one.

Actually, no part of the situation made sense, real
sense, to her in the least. But then, murder was a frightening, stupid act and poisoning the grimmest. Victoria
had dealt with murder, but Elizabeth had been more sheltered, as had most young women her age.

Further speculation ceased when the coach drew to a
halt before Penhurst Place. Even on a cloudy day, the
house wore a welcoming look. What a pity that strange
circumstances brought her here, for she found the house,
and its occupants—excepting Egbert Percy—charming.

The door opened wide and Sidthorp watched her walk
up the steps, waiting to usher her inside. "Good day,
Miss Elizabeth."

"Where shall I find Lord Leighton, please?" She removed her gray cloak, handing it to the butler, but left
her bonnet on, as was proper. It was a small, rather neat
bonnet of warm gray velvet, its narrow brim trimmed
with a bunch of coquelicot feathers. Her gloved hands
nervously played with the cords of her reticule.

"Come to hold my cousin's hand?" Egbert sauntered
from the drawing room wing into the central hall, a superior sneer on his face as he observed her start.

"Not really. I do wish to see how your uncle goes on."

"Ha! They won't let you see him. Not even m'father sees him. I think the old chap is dead, and they are keeping it a secret until whatever my dear cousin seeks is found."

At her look of alarm he smiled, a particularly snide smirk, then continued, "I am not deaf or blind, you know." His gesture encompassed the library and drawing room wing, for he had drawn her along with him down the corridor, out of Sidthorp's hearing.

"You had best ask David," Elizabeth said discreetly.

"Do you really think you have truly captured him? He shows no inclination to marry, in spite of the ring you wear for the moment. I expect you are merely a ruse to help hunt for whatever it is he seeks. Recall, my dear girl, that David is a king among rakes. Whatever would he do with an innocent like you?" He drew back to peer at her with an exaggerated leer. "Do not tell me you really believe him to be in love with you? That is too, too amusing. Remember, David adores being amused, dear girl."

"People change," she said, her voice stiff with anger.

"I doubt that he will. But I daresay you have provided him with no end of *amusement*. Country life can be so deadly dull. A chap needs a bit of excitement to liven things up. I shouldn't be surprised if the betrothal is all a hum just to have you here." He strolled away from her side, down the hall, turning partly to add, "But then, some women think they can reform a rake. I say, once a rake, always a rake. He could have his pick of the cream in London. Do you really think you could satisfy him?"

Elizabeth watched Egbert disappear around the corner toward the billiards room. Most likely he would meet Lord Augustus there to commence their tedious rounds of play.

She turned in the opposite direction to walk slowly into the library. A look out of the window revealed that the rain had begun again. If it kept up, they most definitely would need that ark. Or a boat of some sort. Water stood along the roads, fields looked more like ponds.

And she was avoiding her dilemma. David.

How lowering to have to face the truth.

"Elizabeth. Sidthorp sent word you had arrived. Good to see you, my dear." David entered the room, then stopped. Something in her expression must have warned him that all was not as it should be.

She studied his face. Did Egbert have a basis for his words? Would David honor Aunt Bel's insistence the he and Elizabeth marry? Or did he merely toy with her affections?

"David? Kiss me."

She had clearly startled him, not to mention herself. Whatever she intended to say to him, it was not these words. But she did want to discover his real feelings for her. The words hung in the air between them. They had been spoken.

He took a step toward her, then halted, looking exceedingly uncomfortable. "Elizabeth, be serious. You know full well I dare not kiss you."

It hadn't stopped him before, she reminded herself. Her inner mind had been correct, as had Egbert. David had his own reasons for involving her in his scheme, but it did not include love. Perhaps not even regard.

She thought she saw regret on his face, a hint of something else as well. Whatever it was, it was an emotion she didn't recognize.

Pride rushing to her rescue, Elizabeth pinned a polite smile on her face. This was the prime rake of London. She had best remember that. He was not to be *her* rake after all.

"Good morning, my lord. Forget those silly words. I cannot think why I said them." Her laugh was a trifle forced, but she managed it. "Now, what do you hope to do today?"

She crossed to the desk, studying the house floor plan that lay spread out there. "Is there a room we have forgotten, some attic or cellar?" She glanced back over her shoulder to give him a bland, politely inquiring look.

"Elizabeth, for pity's sake, what is going on?"

"Nothing, my lord. Not one thing." She turned to face him, noting the confused look on his handsome face. He was no more bewildered than she. "How long do you wish me to wear this ring? I worry about it. I shall not feel easy until it is safely returned to you.''

She extended her hand toward him after slipping off her glove. ''As it is, I am very careful always to wear my gloves. Chloe laughed when I came to breakfast with them on. I shall take no chances, my lord.''

He approached her with a wary look on his face, as though expecting her to do something extraordinary. Like bite. He took her slim hand in his strong, capable one, glancing at the beautiful diamond, then turning that remarkable hazel gaze on her face.

She stiffened her spine, and her resolve as well. There was only one phrase he could say that would alter matters now, and she strongly doubted he would utter those words.

He didn't.

Elizabeth found herself in his arms, with his lips seeking hers in a hungry, searching kiss. Did he think to uncover her very soul this way? For one mad moment she yielded, for she knew this would be the last of his kisses for her. Then she tensed.

His hands were not idle. From cradling her head just so, they had slipped over her body in a most familiar way, and now compelled her intimately close to him.

She broke free. Somehow her arms had found their own way around him, and the fingers of her ungloved hand had thrust up into those tumbled brown locks, twining possessively in them as though she had that right. ''Forgive me. I feel quite foolish,'' she said in a strangled voice most unlike her normal tone.

Her hands slid down to his shoulders, but neither of them moved away from the embrace.

He shook his head, as though to clear it. ''I ought to be asking your forgiveness. Elizabeth—''

''Well, well,'' Egbert said from the doorway in his most insinuating voice, ''what have we here? The rogue's seduction? The rake's ravishment? Dalliance with an innocent is so sweet.''

Elizabeth stepped away, in her mind echoing the soft swearing Lord Leighton made under his breath. She might have learned something, perhaps heard those words she longed to hear, had Egbert not made his unwelcome entry.

Then again, perhaps his intrusion kept her from facing the truth again. That she would not have heard the words she longed to hear, rather the teasing of a seasoned rake, that dashing man about London who captivated more hearts than could be numbered.

What a silly little fool she was, to think she actually had seized his interest.

"I had something in my eye, and Lord Leighton was merely getting it out for me. The roads are so utterly dreadful in these rains." Elizabeth fumbled in her reticule for a handkerchief, finding it in the very bottom. Dabbing her eye, she turned away so neither man could see the very real tears that now fell.

"Dusty too," Egbert observed in malicious tones.

David assumed an amused look, then strolled across the room to confront his cousin. "I say, old boy, can you not think of something else to do but spoil my fun? May I remind you that my father strongly suggested you take off for London, or anywhere but here. I repeat his request."

"I would not dream of leaving here with my uncle so seriously ill that no one, not even your soon-to-be-bride, can see him. What is it, David? Why the secrecy? Perhaps you grow tired of waiting for the earldom?"

"Egbert, that is quite enough," David insisted in a firm but quiet tone.

"Really?" With his familiar contemptuous sneer tilting his mouth, Egbert sauntered from the room, leaving the door open behind him.

By the time David had collected himself, Elizabeth had dried her tears and composed her emotions.

"That was unforgivable," he declared angrily.

"He is a very bitter man. Do you see now why I feel he might be responsible for the threat?" That David had called that precious kiss mere fun cut her deeply.

She might be inexperienced, but she knew better than to believe a rascal like David could change. No, she would finish what she had promised to do, then go away, with fond memories of the dashing Corinthian, her very own rake, even if but for a brief time.

A loose shutter banged against the house as the wind picked up. Rain slashed against the window panes of the French doors, and they began to rattle and shake as though an angry giant wreaked vengeance upon the house.

Elizabeth looked out in alarm. Once she might have been willing, even eager, to remain in this house overnight. Now she knew she must return to Montmorcy Hall, come what may.

"Surely you do not believe his spiteful words?"

She swung her gaze back to him, then dropped it to study the elegant carpet. "I scarcely know what to think, do I? As he said, I am a little innocent. Hardly the sort to appeal to a rogue like you. It is intelligent to face reality, my lord. And I believe I am quite sensible."

A stir at the door brought her gaze up again. Filpot stood there, an apologetic expression on his thin face.

"Excuse me, milord. Your father requests your presence." He bowed most properly, then left the room.

"You had best go. And I as well. This was a harebrained scheme to have me here today. Ask Sidthorp to summon a carriage, please."

"Elizabeth, nothing is as you believe. Nothing."

He gave her a frustrated look quite as though he wished to say more, then tore himself from the room, marching down the hall, then up the stairs with impatient steps.

She glanced about the room, wondering if she would see it again. She noted a patch of damp beside the fireplace, and her thoughts turned to Jeremy Vane. At first she had believed him to be a fine steward. But now she wondered.

She had heard of dishonest stewards, men who lined their pockets with vast amounts of money while their masters, absent in London or the continent, believed them tending their jobs. Indeed, Victoria had worried about the management of their father's estate once he was gone. The girls knew nothing of estate administration, and Victoria had done her best. But who knew if the steward was honest, or if he embezzled sums here and there, difficult to detect.

Elizabeth resolved to ask her sister's new husband to look into the matter, if Victoria had not already done so.

She walked over to the fireplace to touch the spot of damp plaster. Odd.

"Miss Elizabeth, your coach awaits you."

She turned away, then swiftly joined Rose, walking along the corridor as though she could not leave fast enough.

Sidthorp looked puzzled, but naturally said not a word. He held an umbrella over her while she entered the carriage, then he disappeared into the house before the coach had gone a few yards.

"A fool's errand, that's what it was, Rose. I ought to have stayed at home." Elizabeth pulled the handkerchief from her reticule, blew her nose, then resolutely faced the wretched trip back to Montmorcy Hall.

Gibbons met her with the large red umbrella kept for such inclement weather.

Once inside the house, Elizabeth ignored questioning looks from her cousins. Instead she threw herself into planning the party.

"Do you think the rain will stop long enough for our guests to come?" Chloe asked with a dismayed look out the window.

"If I could travel on these roads, anyone could. Especially if they are as tired of being confined indoors as we have been. Mark my words, they shall be here."

Hyacinthe had not missed the grim inflection Elizabeth had not been able to keep from her voice.

"And what about Lord Leighton? Will he join us?"

"When I left the house, he had been called to his father's room. I cannot say whether he will be able to come or not."

"I would think if he had any tender sensibilities, he would stay home," Chloe said. She inspected a vase she had filled with blooms from the greenhouse, turning it this way and that to see which angle proved the best.

"He is different," snapped Elizabeth. "Do not expect the more tender sentiments from Lord Leighton. Recall that he is among the premier rakes of London."

"I detect a bitter note in your voice, cousin," Hyacinthe said thoughtfully. "Am I to gather that the course of true love does not flow smoothly?"

Elizabeth gave a wavery chuckle, then plumped herself

down on the sofa, proceeding to mangle a pillow while she spoke. "I believe that might be an accurate assessment of the situation. Except there has been no love from the beginning. It all stemmed from that silly superstition of Aunt Bel's that I must marry the first man I saw on Valentine's Day."

Hyacinthe sank onto a chair not far away from Elizabeth, looking at her with concern. "But if he was in your bedchamber in the middle of the night, what other conclusion can there be? 'Tis not your fault the silly man climbed in your window because he knew you'd not see him otherwise."

Chloe drifted over to join them, leaving her bouquet on a low table. "You had been in that room earlier, Hyacinthe. Perhaps he intended to see you!"

Elizabeth shook her head. "No, he claimed he knew I occupied the room, for he heard me singing, and you all know what a frightful voice I have."

"How did he know?" Chloe demanded, her eyes wide and pretty mouth ajar.

"He had heard me sing whilst on our way back from target practice while in London. With that nasty spy sneaking into the house, Victoria decided we had better prepare for the worst. That is when I got in the habit of sleeping with my pistol beneath my pillow. I heartily wish I had never thought of the notion. If I had not shot the blasted man on Valentine's night, I'd not be in this pickle now."

"Are you in a pickle?" Chloe blurted out, fascinated by this glimpse of the older, most sophisticated girls' lives. "What sort?"

"Ninny," scolded Hyacinthe. "Elizabeth is disappointed in Lord Leighton and being compelled to wed him." She turned to look at Elizabeth, adding, "Although I should think it not so bad. He is most attentive to you whenever I have seen you together. If Lord Norwood paid me that much consideration, I should be in alt, not crying in my soup. I fear all is lost with that man, for he is more concerned with his gardens."

"Who says I cry in my soup!" Elizabeth jumped to her feet and marched to the door. "I intend to do what I can to make the party an enormous success."

"I wonder if John Harlowe will manage to come," Chloe said as Elizabeth strode away.

Far from her cousins and their comments, Elizabeth paused by a window that just happened to face in the direction of Penhurst Place. What went on over there? She thought she could see smoke spiraling up from the chimneys.

Lord Augustus would have his fireplace in a roar, if he wasn't nagging Egbert to play billiards with him. And David? Oh, she did hope that his father was all right.

A carriage appeared on the avenue, but rather than stop in the front of the house, clip-clopped around to the back. Curious, Elizabeth slipped down the servants' stairs and out to the back hall.

Purvis stamped into the hall, shaking her umbrella with care, then setting it aside to remove her patterns.

"What happened? Why are you back home?"

Purvis straightened, giving Elizabeth a narrow look. "So you listened to the earwig, eh? I came back because there was nothing more I could do."

She snapped her mouth closed and Elizabeth suspected that she would not say another word on the subject, come what may.

However, Elizabeth tried. "Is Lord Crompton dead?"

"What's it to you if he is, missy?" the abigail snapped pertly. Then seeing the distress in Elizabeth's eyes, she added, "No, not at this point, he isn't."

Once Purvis had returned to her quarters next to Aunt Bel's room, Elizabeth wandered about, adding finishing touches to the rooms when she remembered where she was and what needed to be done.

By the following evening, the house stood in readiness. Chloe was all flutters and giggles, as might be expected in a young girl barely out of the schoolroom. Hyacinthe worried about her looks, sure her gown was not quite right. Elizabeth was a bundle of sensibilities.

Acceptances had been received from all invited. Aunt Bel had expanded the original group to include the Harlowe family, Emma Fenwick and her family, plus a goodly number of other local notables. As far as Hyacinthe was concerned, the only notable of importance

was her marquess, Lord Norwood. All looked forward
to a break in the tedium caused by miserable weather.

Elizabeth wondered if Lord Leighton would dare show
his face.

"Your betrothed accepted, but I expect you knew he
would be here," her aunt informed her.

"Actually, I had no idea," Elizabeth replied, tugging
the neckline of her gown. She looked like a frump. The
dress was dreadfully proper. Insipid French gauze over a
turquoise silk slip decorated with a row of dainty silk
roses about the hem looked horridly prim, what with the
little puffed sleeves above her gloves. She tapped her san-
daled foot impatiently, anxious for the evening to be over.

Since they were in the country, country hours would
be observed. Dinner was to be at five of the clock, and
all knew Lady Montmorcy's insistence regarding time.
None would dare to be late to one of her parties.

Hence, the carriages began to roll up before the house,
laughing, chattering guests hurrying in to escape the light
drizzle. Gibbons ushered each party inside with remarkable speed, then returned for the next group, holding his
huge red umbrella aloft like a torch.

Only Lord Leighton was late.

Aunt Bel was very annoyed. "Ain't like the boy to be
late. He is usually most considerate. Cannot think what
has happened," she fretted softly to Elizabeth.

"I fear I know nothing about his plans, Aunt. The last
I saw him we were not precisely in good footing with
each other."

"I did not realize you quarreled."

Disregarding her aunt's exasperated look, Elizabeth
calmly, for she had practiced for hours at this, shook her
head.

"Not quarreled, precisely. A mere difference of opinion." How could she confess that she had been such a
goosecap as to fall head over toes for a polished Corinthian from London who saw her as a delightful girl to
tease?

"Well, that is all right, then," Aunt Bel said, relieved.

They proceeded to dinner, Lady Montmorcy unable to
tolerate lateness even in her dear Lord Leighton. Midway
through the meal, a disturbance in the front hall brought

Aunt Bel's gaze to Elizabeth. A faint nod of her head, and Elizabeth excused herself from the table, hurrying out of the dining room.

Lord Leighton stood in the process of being brushed off by a horrified Gibbons.

"What on earth happened to you? You look as though you crawled through a hedge backward, my lord." Elizabeth added the words of respect as an afterthought, being dumbfounded at David's less than perfect appearance.

"Carriage overturned. Road's a damn quagmire. Ought to know better than to have a party in miserable weather," he grumbled.

"None of the others assembled seemed to have any difficulty."

"None?" He gave her an arrested look, then turned to Gibbons with a softly spoken request. The butler nodded, then bustled off in the direction of the kitchen.

"I suppose your aunt will never forgive me for being late."

Elizabeth allowed a prim smile. "You are a favorite of hers. Like Lady Jersey, she has a soft spot for rascals. Given the circumstances, I would wager you can slip into your place without any difficulty. Come."

Why she was being so nice to the blasted man was beyond her. Yet he winced as he moved, and limped slightly as he walked along with her to the dining room.

Aunt Bel was properly horrified at the accident. At Elizabeth's side, Lord Leighton managed a wicked grin under the cover of his napkin.

She ignored him the best she could, given the fact he sat next to her and frequently brushed up against her, thanks to Aunt Bel cramming so many people at the table.

Before long Lady Montmorcy gave the signal for the ladies to withdraw. Elizabeth gratefully left the table, aware that a speculative gaze followed her all the way to the door.

Rather than join the other women in the drawing room, she went directly to the rooms Aunt Bel had ordered prepared for dancing. The musicians were tuning up, the chairs in place, flowers arranged perfectly, and all in readiness.

How would she manage to survive the evening? Just seeing the dratted man tied her insides in double knots.

"Elizabeth? Here you are. Somehow I suspected you would sneak away from the others."

"David! That is, Lord Leighton. What may I do for you?"

He pulled her along with him until they were safely concealed from any chance view. Then he kissed her with all the expertise at his command.

All those exhilarating sensations charged through her like bolts of lightning in a summer storm. Elizabeth forgot to push him away, much to her disgust when he at last released her. She desperately tried her "serene" look that she had practiced so diligently. "That was not well done of you, my lord." The set-down proved difficult when he still clasped her in his arms, clinging to her as though she were a haven in a storm.

"You will never know how much I needed you." At her raised and skeptical brows, he went on. "I just learned the accident was deliberate. The coach had been tampered with before we left."

"Then someone does wish you ill!" she cried softly. "I suspected it was but a matter of time. After all, if a madman plans to murder your father, would he not also want to do away with you?"

"Dear god," he whispered. "I cannot risk you coming back to the house, even if I could manage to convince Egbert to leave. Yet I want you there."

"So you agree with me that he is the more likely one!"

"Although he is not precisely penniless, for his father does well enough, Egbert has exceedingly expensive tastes, else he could manage nicely on the allowance he receives. He may well wish to step into my shoes," David concluded with a grim twist of his mouth.

People began filtering into the rooms, and Elizabeth saw David and she must end their earnest discussion. Placing her gloved hand most properly on his arm, her earlier resolutions evaporated, she guided him from the room and down the hall. With the strains of music in the background, she turned to him for further talk.

"It is a good thing we are officially betrothed. Otherwise I should put paid to a respectable marriage. As it is, I most likely will have to take myself off to a far corner of the country where they have never heard of me before. I wonder if I have a relative there."

"Elizabeth, cease this nonsense at once," he muttered in her hair.

"It is all very well for you, my lord, but I have a life after this, I should hope. And you as well. Think of London." She had sought to tease him, but he ignored her efforts.

"It might not be Egbert. He may be taking advantage of the situation to be his nasty self."

"Surely you do not hark back to poor Jeremy Vane," Elizabeth scoffed.

"Promise me that you will not listen to the evil words from either of them, or my uncle, for that matter. Just return to the house. I do need you, Elizabeth."

What was a girl to do when the most handsome man she had ever known, or seen in her life, pleaded with her to help him? Begged her to join him? Implored her to lend her intelligence to solve his mystery, looking at her with those melting hazel eyes? Violate propriety and invite possible kisses . . . or worse?

"Of course. I shall come tomorrow."

13

IT WAS A GREAT PITY that Elizabeth had so much time to think. Upon reflection, she could find more holes in David's highly persuasive talk than in a yard of lace netting.

For one thing, why had he refused to kiss her when she had asked him—most foolishly, she admitted—and then when he wished to turn her up sweet, kissed her, and most thoroughly? Devious creature. If she didn't love the dratted man so dearly, she would most assuredly plot some cunning means of revenge.

It must be the nature of men, she decided. They—at least the handsome, charming ones—used their attractiveness as a means of securing what they wanted. She ignored the basic truth that women had been doing the same thing for centuries.

"You will be careful, will you not?" Aunt Bel quietly demanded. "I have an odd notion that things are not what they seem at Penhurst Place in spite of your reassurances. I suspect you have been less than forthcoming with me, my dear niece." Her eyes held a hint of speculation.

"Oh, I think it positively thrilling that you are going to Penhurst Place to help Lord Leighton," Chloe cried, clasping her hands before her.

Elizabeth paused in the act of drawing on her aqua gloves that matched her ensemble, wondering if Lady Chloe could possibly be as naive as she appeared. Another look, and Elizabeth decided that dear Lady Chloe had a goodly amount of growing up to do before she was ready to cope with the gentlemen of this world. John Harlowe might be good enough for a beginning, but she had better forego Lord Norwood until she had learned a thing or two, and practiced her feminine wiles a bit more.

Elizabeth could testify to the need for a great deal of exposure to the flirtations offered by Society gentlemen to be able to tell the genuine from the false.

"Indeed," she murmured. She turned to check the portmanteaus Rose carried out of the door, to ascertain all she wished was along. Gibbons bustled about, chatting with Rose, admonishing the coachman from Penhurst Place to take good care of Miss Elizabeth.

The door swung shut. Elizabeth found herself once again alone in the entry with her relatives. Odd, how Montmorcy Hall was a mostly female residence, while Penhurst Place remained essentially male—other than a few maids and that utterly dreadful cook, who rarely presented a decent meal. With a well-equipped kitchen, it must be the cook's face that curdled the puddings. A great deal of food at Penhurst Place was ruined, causing Elizabeth to wonder if perhaps the cook embraced a pagan religion that required burnt offerings three times a day.

"Mind you, send me a message regarding Lord Crompton," Aunt Bel urged. "I would come myself, only the dratted man would most likely bar me from his room." Her feeling of ill usage was most likely mitigated by the knowledge that she really did not do well at nursing the ill. A woman of her sensibilities left that sort of thing to a servant.

"Remember, before I left, I was banished as well," Elizabeth said in reply. That was another point that Lord Leighton had failed to address. Why, after caring for his father for days and days, was she suddenly not allowed to enter his room? It seemed to her that something dashed havey-cavey was going on at Penhurst Place. But what?

Aunt Bel checked her locket watch. "You must leave us now. We will keep you in our thoughts, dear girl." She enfolded Elizabeth in a scented hug, then stepped back to study her face, as though searching for something.

Elizabeth tried to conceal the exhilaration that welled up within her when she considered being close to Lord Leighton. Her aunt had that foxy, I-know-something-you-don't-know gleam in her eyes again. It would almost be worth the coming separation to puncture that balloon of

Aunt's when Elizabeth rejected the connection with Lord Leighton. For the break most assuredly would happen, the betrothal must be ended. After all, who would countenance a marriage based on a silly Valentine's Day superstition?

"We shall entertain Lord Norwood, Forsythe, and the others in your absence the best we may." At a nudge from Lady Chloe, Hyacinthe added, "and John Harlowe as well. I *do* wish you were going to be here, for although you are a quiet girl, we always seem to have a far better time when you are around. You always know just the game to play, or the entertainment sure to please." Hyacinthe wore a puzzled expression for a few moments as she reflected on that curious reality. "I only hope that they will take to a game of cranbo when you are not here to lead us. You think of the silliest words to use." She chuckled, as though remembering a particularly absurd word.

"Well, I feel certain you shall do very nicely. You are both lovely girls and should manage very well, indeed." Elizabeth gave them a bland smile, then marched out of the door to the coach sent from Penhurst Place. It seemed that Lord Leighton wished to take no chances that she might back out of her promise to him.

The road had not improved in the last few days. The coachman tried to avoid the worst of the ruts. Although it did seem, as they drew closer to Penhurst Place, that his lordship or Jeremy Vane had dispatched a number of men to fill up the deepest holes.

Yet she suffered a jouncing drive. Rose looked likely to cast up her accounts if they did not arrive shortly. When the coach drew to a halt before the Penhurst Place entry, Elizabeth exited the coach with a feeling of profound relief. Even Rose was heard to give a great sigh.

"Sidthorp, how is everyone? Does Lord Crompton improve?" Elizabeth inquired upon entering the house. The entry hall was deserted but for the butler. She heard voices coming from the south wing of the house. Evidently Lord Augustus had induced the others into a game of billiards, for the talk was loud and argumentative.

"His lordship passed a tolerable night, I am told,"

Sidthorp replied. He took her warm cloak, then joined
Rose to remove Elizabeth's things to her room.

It left Elizabeth alone in the entry hall, looking about
her while wondering what she was supposed to do.

Jeremy Vane came from the north wing, papers in
hand, reminding her of a rabbit on a serious errand. She
half expected his nose to twitch. "Good morning, Mr.
Vane," she said, speaking up a trifle to catch his ear. He
looked as though he might be hunting Lord Leighton, and
if he was, she wanted to make her presence known.

He gave her a startled glance. "Ah, good morning,
Miss Elizabeth. I trust you are well?"

His timid remark and obvious desire to be gone amused
her. How could David suspect this person of treachery?

"Are you off to find Lord Leighton? Would you be so
kind as to tell him I am here?" Her cordial smile became
fixed as she observed him. Had she not been watching
him carefully, she might had missed that flash of resentment that crossed his face so briefly. She was taken
somewhat aback by this reaction, for if he was the steward here, he must be accustomed to carrying a message
now and again.

"Of course." He bowed just enough to be respectful,
then hurried off as though Elizabeth carried the plague.
Something elusive niggled at the back of her mind.

Sidthorp came down the stairs from supervising the
disposal of her belongings, and Rose as well. It seemed
that quiet Rose was a favorite among the staffs of both
houses, for they all fussed over her. She was one of those
rare treasures, a maid who did her job well, never gos-
siped, and liked everyone, particularly Hadlow.

"When you see him, please inform Lord Leighton that
I shall wait for him in the library." She gave Sidthorp
her warm, gracious smile, earning her a look of devotion
from the butler.

Then Elizabeth drifted off across the hall and along the
corridor to the library.

Across the courtyard, the gentlemen could be glimpsed
through the windows as they moved about in the billiards
room, for that door was wide open. She stopped, watching as Lord Augustus stood waiting to play, cue in hand.

There was something about his stance, his attitude. He stared at David.

Drat the glass. If it were not for a bit of reflection, she might see more clearly. But it seemed to her that the genial Lord Augustus eyed his nephew with less than cordiality. More like hatred.

She retreated to the shadows of the corridor. It must be a distortion. Why, after all these years, would Lord Augustus turn against his brother? Or his brother's son? But she knew stranger things had happened.

Pity, that, for she rather liked the old gentleman with his creaking corset and brusque speech. His indulgent attitude toward his son could be excused on the grounds that Egbert was an only son. Yet . . . what would Lord Augustus be willing to do to insure that his heir inherited more than was his rightful lot? More than one man had murdered for money, and this involved far more than that.

Rain began to fall again, obscuring her view of the billiards room, with streaks of water cascading down the panes. The scene became a blur of black and cream, shadow and light.

Realizing that anyone could stumble across her in the corridor, she continued on her way to the library, mulling over the twist in the mystery of who might be behind the poisoning attempt. Lord Augustus joined Jeremy Vane as somewhat plausible suspects. Her money was on Egbert Percy, the cousin who stood to gain the most.

The curious snippet of knowledge that had teased her memory returned, and she eagerly awaited David's arrival so she might share it with him. He would undoubtedly tell her it was not significant, and she was not all that certain, but it was curious. Most curious.

Then her eyes focused on what she was looking at, and she walked to the fireplace. No fire warmed the hearth or the chilly room. And just above, slightly to the left of where she stood, was a patch of damp plaster above the surround.

"Really," she muttered, "Mr. Vane is most careless."

"What are you nattering about, my dear Elizabeth?" David silently entered the library, strolling over to join her. He was dressed for his day at home in his usual

impeccable style: fawn pantaloons under a cream waistcoat and corbeau coat. Hadlow must have used champagne in the blacking, for those Hessians had a shine to
rival the sun.

David was about to ring for a footman to arrange a fire
when Elizabeth stopped him.

"Do you not think this odd, my lord?" She pointed
to the suspicious spot inches from the mantel. Then she
frowned. "Although I do remember seeing it the other
day, come to think of it. It slipped my mind."

" 'Tis this blasted rain. And Vane is not quite the
wonderful manager you think him," David said sourly.

"I confess," she said slowly, "I begin to believe you.
At first when we came, I thought everything so noteworthy. It seemed to me that he did a fine job of it." She
turned to meet David's gaze with troubled eyes.

"I suspect you were rather seeing the results of my
father's management, teaching Jeremy, as it were." David returned her concerned look with one of his own.
"As long as Father was out and about, things were well
done around here, at least that is what Sidthorp reported
to me when I came."

"I just recalled something curious. When I studied
your family tree, I noticed Jeremy's name was *not* to be
found anywhere. I searched very carefully. Is that not
peculiar? For he has claimed to be a cousin."

David rubbed his jaw while she spoke, nodding
thoughtfully. "I would think so, but it is not conclusive.
Some of our relatives are frightful correspondents. Yet,
as you say, it is peculiar. You would think he'd have corrected the omission once he came here."

"David." She reached out a tentative finger to touch
the sizable patch, and her nerves tensed as they did when
she was working on something critical. "I have this feeling." Her eyes flashed when she caught sight of his handsome face alight with amusement. "You may well laugh
at me. I do not mind. Be so good as to fetch me that
knife you use for sharpening your quill." She gestured
to the desk, then resumed picking at the patch of damp
plaster. "I feel a point of something here."

"Your obedient servant, ma'am," he said, mincing
over to his desk in a parody of the perfect footman. He

returned with the small tray upon which rested the long silver knife, a pot of sand, a stick of red sealing wax, a gray feathered quill pen, and in a chamber at the end of the tray, a full bottle of black ink.

"Foolish man," she chided indulgently, unable to be annoyed with him. "I merely needed the knife."

"I thought you intended to write a reminder to my dear cousin that he ought to tidy the place up a bit, or at the very least manage some repairs to the roof, or chimney, or whatever is the problem."

He proffered the contents of the tray with a slight bow, his eyes brimming with mischief.

Elizabeth ignored that tantalizing face, picking up the knife instead. She commenced to scrape the plaster.

"Here now, what *are* you doing?"

"I have a hunch, a feeling if you like, about this plaster. True, it has rained, but not that much. The roof at Montmorcy Hall is old, and perhaps not in the best repair, but if there is seepage, it comes out around the ceiling, especially in the attics. Not in a patch near a mantel on the ground floor. There is something concealed within. Do you not want to know what it is? It could be jewels or secret documents or something exciting."

"I suppose it is possible, love."

She tossed him a confused glance, then turned her concentration to the patch. "I suspect the plaster is much newer than that surrounding it. Of course, it is possible that it is wet due to all the moisture about, and the chill in the room. Have you never noticed how an unheated room seems much damper than others where there is a fire?" she murmured, concentrating on the curious patch.

"True," he murmured, coming closer to watch what she was doing, after setting the tray on a nearby table.

"However, I believe that in this case there is a different cause." She dug some more with interesting results.

A chunk of plaster fell to the hearth, then another. Elizabeth tried to catch them but failed. At any rate, she did observe there was a peculiar lump protruding. Her heart accelerating its beat, she dug more deeply, ignoring the bits and pieces that flew in every direction.

"Do you see what I see?" she whispered. "A wad of

papers wrapped up in oiled silk. What a peculiar place to put papers, my lord. At least it appears to be a pack of papers. One would think that whoever placed them there was trying to conceal them. If *I* had papers I wished not to be seen, I'd burn them.''

"Indeed. May I?'' He pried out the packet with the knife, also ignoring the pieces of plaster that bombarded his fine corbeau coat. Once he had the packet free, he walked to the desk, Elizabeth at his side.

"Best keep this to ourselves.'' She darted a glance at the door, then stole softly over to close it. She felt it better they would be warned if someone intended to enter the room. The rattle of the door lever ought to be sufficient to alert them.

David had the oiled silk unfolded and spread open on the desk when she rejoined him.

"Well?'' She was simply dying of curiosity. Was he not going to say a word to her?

He studied the first of the papers, then the second. There was a third letter in the packet, and this too he scrutinized. He was absorbed in his thoughts. At last he seemed to realize she had asked a question and said, "What did you say?''

"What did you find?'' She generously ignored the fact she had made the discovery and he had but pried it out.

"Will you excuse me, Elizabeth? I must take these upstairs immediately.'' Then he glanced at the ragged hole in the wall and grimaced. "Would you take care of that mess?''

With that request, he hurried from the room. Elizabeth stared at the empty door with exasperation. How like a man to dump the mundane details in a woman's lap. *He* was to have the satisfaction of presenting the intriguing papers to his father, while *she* mended the wall. She sighed with acceptance of a situation that was not likely to change.

The room must not be left unattended. Anyone might stroll in here. The gaping hole to one side of the mantel could scarce be missed. Then she caught sight of the key dangling on the inside of the door, as though it was locked on occasion. While it might excite curiosity, she would secure the room while she sought help. It was the only way.

She locked the library door, then dropped the key into her reticule. In the entry hall she found Sidthorp crossing from the dining room to the stairs.

"Please, a moment of your time, Sidthorp. I need someone who can patch a bit of damage to the library wall, and be discreet about it. It *must* be someone who can be as mute as a fish." She gave him an expectant look, but offered no explanation as to the cause for the hole in the wall. She hoped he might think it due to the excessive rain, which in a way it was. He paused in thought, then nodded. "I believe I have just the man for the job." Never would the butler satisfy his curiosity to inquire how the damage came about. That would not be proper.

"I shall await him in there. Tell him to knock, for the door will be locked."

Even then the stately butler did not stoop to question. He nodded in his dignified way, then started for the office wing of the house. Elizabeth did not bother to tell him to remain silent, for she knew that no one would have torn that information from him, given her secretive attitude when she'd made the request.

She paced about the library after securing the door once again, pausing to stare out of the window from time to time, then resuming her restless walk. What kept the workman, anyway? And what was David discussing with his father upstairs all this time? And why was she not allowed to poke her head into Lord Crompton's room? Was he better or worse? Questions she had asked herself ran through her mind over and over, with not a solution being offered.

A soft, hesitant rap on the door brought her dashing over to grasp the key. "Who is it?" she asked in the softest voice that would still carry to whoever might be on the other side.

" 'Tis Ben, miss. To patch . . ."

She used the key, opening the door just enough to permit the workman to enter, then quickly locked it again.

Ben hardly needed her to point out what needed repair. He had mixed up some plaster, bringing it along in a small bucket. With surprising speed he had filled the hole and smoothed the place over so it looked much as it had before.

While he worked, Elizabeth set about building a fire that would help dry the plaster. Once she had it lit, she stepped back to study the restoration. The workman busied himself cleaning up the hearth.

"That looks very good, Ben. You did a fine job. Lord Leighton will be ever so pleased."

The man was overcome at this high praise, and bobbed his head on his way to the door. Here he paused, waiting.

Elizabeth swiftly walked to free the man, whispering her thanks. She knew she need not remind Ben to keep silent. The very manner in which this all had been done might arouse his curiosity, but if his job depended upon his being as silent as the grave, he would never say a word.

She relocked the door, then returned to tend the fire. Since it was such a dreary day, she found a book to read. With nothing to do, her mind became far too active, dancing off in too many directions. It was a novel she'd read before, but no matter. Her other choices appeared less appealing.

Some time later, after she had replenished the fire several times and read a good deal of the book, another rap came on the door. Placing her book carefully on the table, she glanced at the plaster, noting it still showed a bit of dampness. Shrugging her shoulders, she went to turn the key.

"Oh, David, I am ever so glad it is you. Hurry." She tugged him inside the room, then turned the key again.

He chuckled, causing her to frown at him.

"It is very well for you to be amused. I have been in here tending the fire, watching over this dratted plaster, while you have been doing far more interesting things."

"True." He sobered at once. "I took the papers to my father. They are important documents. And they throw a new light on the threat to Father. Dashed spot for concealment, if you ask me." As to what that threat constituted, he didn't say.

"Perhaps whoever wants to become the next earl is the one who hid the papers. But it seems to me that Egbert

would be more creative than this." Elizabeth gestured to
the still damp patch on the wall. "As I said before, I
should think the papers would have been burned rather
than holed up in the wall. What a curious thing to do.
Why, do you suppose? And who?"

"I am not convinced that it is my odious Cousin Egbert." David wandered back and forth before the fireplace, while Elizabeth quietly tossed on another scoop of
coal over the flames.

"I saw your uncle watching you while you were playing billiards," she said. "It was when I first arrived today, before the rains began. I realize I was seeing him
through two pieces of glass, but he gave you a most peculiar look, as though he hated you." Elizabeth was loath
to tell David about what she had seen. It surely would
distress him.

"Well, I was trouncing him rather roundly, which
might have accounted for that look you saw. But hate?
That seems a bit strong."

"Not if he wants to lay his hands on the money and
the estates, secure it all for his son," she argued.

"Somehow old Uncle Augustus does not seem the sort
of man to want to poison his brother, or do in his nephew.
If you follow my thoughts." David put his hands behind
his back, tapping his foot on the hearth before the fireplace. Elizabeth knelt before the flames, trying to remove the chill that had settled over her at this discussion
of premeditated death.

"What do you intend to do?"

She watched as he walked over to the bookshelves,
where he commenced to hunt for a book. Upon finding
it, he tucked it beneath his arm, then gave her an absent
smile. "I shall take this upstairs, then discuss the problem with Father. Unless," he added suddenly, "he is not
feeling up to it."

"I fancy I ought to return to Montmorcy Hall. You
appear to have solved your mystery." And wouldn't tell
her. Elizabeth rose from the hearth and waited for him
to tell her to depart from his life.

"What! On no account. It has been pouring rain for
hours. Can you imagine what that stretch of road will be
like now? No, far too dangerous. Besides,"—he gave her

a curious, unreadable look—"do you not want to see how this all turns out?"

"You believe it will be resolved so quickly?" She walked across to join him by the door. Closer up, his face revealed no more to her searching eyes.

"I should say within the week at the outside."

"You are very confident, my lord."

"I thought you agreed to call me David," he complained, leaning against the frame of the door to give her what she considered a highly flirtatious leer.

"That was for the benefit for the others. We have no need to dissemble, do we? I was under the impression that you were eager to conclude this sham betrothal."

He drew himself away from the door, a frown briefly crossing his face. "There is nothing sham about that ring on your finger. Just because I did not get down on bended knee to make some flowery declaration of undying love does not mean I am reluctant to do the proper."

"How vastly condescending of you, my lord," she snapped at him, her temper flaring beyond control. "What makes you think I wish to wed a reluctant man?"

He glanced at his pocket watch, then tucked it back into place. Giving her a hasty kiss, he hurried off down the hall, tossing a few words behind him. "We shall discuss this later, my love."

His love, indeed! Elizabeth spun about, her hands clenching into fists that would have enjoyed pounding the arrogant Lord Leighton.

Unfortunately, he was correct in one thing. With the roads truly horrid, she could not, dare not leave now. Perhaps by tomorrow, if the rains ceased, she might leave this house of torment.

When she joined the gentlemen for dinner, it was to be presented with the same dreary food. How could they tolerate it?

"I see Cook is in a bad mood again," Lord Augustus muttered.

"Is she ever in a good mood?" Egbert snapped.

"I trust you might find a replacement," Elizabeth ventured to offer.

"Father feels sorry for the woman, no one would hire

her without a recommendation, and he could not in good conscience give her one.''

Elizabeth flashed him a look of disbelief. What he said was inconsistent with the concept of good management of an estate. One rewarded a good servant, punished an unsatisfactory one. She nibbled her food, trying to find something edible.

When it came time for the men to have their port, she rose promptly. Never had she left a table with such gratitude for release.

The evening passed very slowly. Egbert begged her to play or sing.

It was the one moment of humor in a dreary evening. Elizabeth chuckled. ''I could not carry a tune in a bucket, I am sorry to say. And I have no skill at the pianoforte, either.'' She held up her hands in mock dismay, and Egbert smiled in return.

''She has other, more fascinating talents,'' David added with a curve of his mouth.

''I shan't be so rude as to inquire what they might be,'' Egbert began, a devilish look on his face.

Elizabeth inserted, ''I believe he means my etchings, Mr. Percy.'' With that little comment, she added, rising as she spoke, ''I believe I shall retire for the night.''

Alone in her room in the unoccupied north wing of the house, she reflected that David had deliberately led Egbert to think ill of her. What a wretched thing of him to do . . . unless he was trying to make her angry with him.

The house was oddly still come morning. Even Rose tiptoed about, although there seemed no need for her to do so.

Elizabeth dressed rather than eat in her room, and quietly went down to the dining room. There was an array of food on the sideboard. Wonder of wonders, the toast was not burnt, nor the eggs cooked to a crusted lump. The ham looked succulent and tender. Had the cook changed her religion?

Egbert entered the room, glanced at the food, then helped himself to a small portion. He sat down without greeting her or saying a word, just sipped a cup of coffee, deep in thought.

Accustomed to a home where everyone chattered with one another, Elizabeth politely said, "Good morning."

"Not so good, I fear. The earl took a turn for the worse in the night."

Her plate clattered on the table. "Oh, I am so sorry."

"David is up there now. He's been with the old man most nights, and last night he slept in his own room. Wouldn't you know it was the night when my uncle elected to get worse?"

"He must feel utterly wretched. Poor David."

"Yes," Egbert murmured, with none of his usual nastiness.

At that moment David entered the room, dressed in somber black. His face looked gravely strained.

Fearing the worst, Elizabeth rose from where she had so abruptly sat down. "Your father . . . ?"

"I am sorry to say he has gone aloft."

14

"DEAD!" Elizabeth exclaimed in horror. She leaned back against the table, thankful for its support. "But he cannot be."

Egbert rose from his chair. "Sorry, old chap. Your father was a fine man." His normally caustic tongue refrained from any nasty barb. Rather, he walked around the table and placed a hand on David's shoulder in sympathy before leaving the room.

Had it not been for the suspicions Elizabeth harbored regarding Egbert, she'd have thought his sorrow genuine. She stared after his retreating figure, then went to David's side. "Is it really true? I would have sworn he was getting better."

"True." His reply was excessively strained, and he turned his head away from her to stare out of the window.

"So you are now the earl."

"And with all the more reason to marry and produce an heir," he said without intonation. "Father wished that Egbert not be permitted to inherit the title." He gave her a curious look, one that confused her. "So it would seem that our accidental Valentine's Day betrothal is most fortunate."

Elizabeth kept a firm clamp on her reactions. "So it would seem," she replied, hoping her voice was as colorless as his.

"I shall need a wife, and as I said once before, I could do far worse than marry you. You'll not hand me the mitten, will you, Elizabeth?" At her startled denial, he went on, "You have been denied a courtship. I shall try to make that up to you." The earnest look on his face surprised her for some reason. It was as though he truly wished that things could be otherwise, and that their betrothal might be as any normal one.

Surprised by his concern over something like a courtship in the midst of what must be a painful time for him, Elizabeth placed her slim hand on his arm, turning his face toward her with her other. "Do not trouble yourself over such a trivial matter now." She lightly touched his arm, then dropped her hand to her side.

"Oh, Elizabeth," he murmured, enfolding her in his arms, as though to draw strength from her slender form. He leaned his head on hers and stood quietly, just holding her.

After a few minutes he withdrew, then began to slowly pace back and forth. "There are a great many details to work out. I have sent for our solicitor. Dr. Dibble was here during the night, thank goodness. He has supervised the laying out. Poor Mrs. Sidthorp was not up to the task, for she had served my father since girlhood."

"The house was so silent this morning. It seems the very wood and brick knew your loss." She waited a moment, then offered, "Is there anything I may do for you?"

This restless ambling about the room was unlike David, she thought. Somehow she had expected him to be more resolute. But people handled grief in so many ways. She recalled how devastated she had been when news of her parents' death had reached her and her sisters. Each of them had shown their heartache in a different way.

David paused by the fireplace. "Pour me some coffee, would you?"

Taken aback, she obeyed his request, handing him a steaming cup while watching his expression carefully.

He continued to deliberate a few moments, then gestured to the table. "Sit with me. Perhaps together we could plan the next few days. Please," he added politely as he moved toward the table.

The absurd thought crossed her mind that she was glad she had donned her coffee-colored mull this morning. Although it had a soft cream lace collar, it was near enough to the acceptable mourning color so as to not be objectionable. Odd, how a little thing like that could bother a person.

"When do you wish to have the funeral?" It was a

sensitive subject that must be dealt with. Notice must be sent out immediately to those in the surrounding area. London was too far away, even though it was sufficiently cold enough to preserve the body for longer than several days. It would take time to send the announcement to London—too long for people to be able to journey to Penhurst Place for the funeral service.

He turned his head to look out of the window at the falling rain. "The heavens mourn the passing of a good man," he said in a soft voice.

"David," she reminded gently. "We must notify the vicar, send notices to the papers in London, and what about the family?"

"I have a list in the study. There is paper in there, everything you could need. If you will take the trouble, I would rather you write them out than Jeremy."

She quailed at the black look that settled on David's face. "Surely you do not cling to *his* having something to do with your father's death?"

"I cannot reveal all yet, even to you." The sadness in David's eyes tore at her heart. How bleak, how utterly grim his countenance had become.

"Of course, I shall do whatever I can."

He rose, then paused, standing over her. While he stared at her with that unreadable expression on his face, he said, "You will not leave me here alone, will you? You *will* stay, will you not, Elizabeth?"

Confused by his words, and the stress he had placed on her remaining in the house when he had his uncle and cousin to keep him company, she reluctantly nodded. Her reputation was likely in tiny shreds by this point. What did it matter? She wanted nothing more than to help her dear rake at his time of sadness. How she missed that teasing look in his eyes, which now were dark with grief and a sort of anger.

"I shall stay. When is the funeral to be?" she repeated, reminding him of the necessary details to be worked out.

"The day after tomorrow." He glanced at the window again, then added, "With this never ending rain, his interment may be postponed. There is a family mausoleum on our principal estate, Crompton Vale, but that is some miles away to the north. I shall have to consider what will be best.''

Confused, but not wishing to pester him for explanations at the moment, Elizabeth rose from her chair, then walked to the door, where she encountered Lord Augustus.

Corset creaking more than usual, the older man paused in the doorway, then studied his nephew with a shake of the head. ''I'd not expected Crompton to go before me. Thought he'd live to a ripe old age. Who'd have believed it? I'm sorry, my boy.'' Tears brimmed in his light brown eyes. He walked over to join his nephew with ponderous steps.

To Elizabeth it seemed as though Lord Augustus had aged ten years overnight. She murmured words of sympathy, then slipped from the room, leaving the two to discuss the matter of the former earl's passing in privacy.

Once in the study, she discovered a neat stack of stiff cream paper, bordered in black. The thought crossed her mind that it was odd David should be prepared to the extent of having the proper paper at hand. Perhaps he'd had a premonition it would be needed. But he had fought the idea so strongly, she was surprised that he'd willingly admit the approaching death to that extent.

Her first task was to write a note to Aunt Bel. It would be a shock for her; Elizabeth suspected that her aunt had nursed a fondness for the earl. Elizabeth also requested that her aunt send over a suitable black gown. Even though Elizabeth was not an actual member of the family, she had been fond of the old earl.

If David was to be believed, she would in six months time—providing they observed proper mourning—be his wife. That she found difficult to accept. In fact, there was something about this entire arrangement of his wishing to marry her that seemed distinctly unreal.

She chalked it up to her shattered sensibilities, and wrote out a note to be taken to the vicar, requesting his presence.

She rang for a footman to deliver the first two notes, the ones she considered most urgent. He assured her that he would ride immediately to deliver them, pointing out that the rain had dwindled to a mere mist. He then took himself off in a rush to be gone, looking gratified to be the bearer of such important missives.

All of the servants wore black armbands, and the maids wore their most somber dresses beneath their aprons. Already a lozenge-shaped hatchment had been hung on the front of the house near the door. The late earl's armorial bearings were beautifully carved in bold relief.

Elizabeth returned to the list on the desk, a surprisingly short one in view of the earl's age and station in life. Perhaps David felt that the information would be obtainable in the newspapers.

But still, it seemed decidedly peculiar. When she completed her task, she stacked the letters in a neat pile to be franked by David.

Around noon she drifted to the dining room. She hadn't expected to see any formal, set meal, and there was none. Rather, the sideboard had an arrangement of dishes. There were beef and vegetable soup in the *bane-marie,* cold meats, rolls, pickles alongside it, and a dish of fruit in the center of the table.

Elizabeth picked a few things, selecting fruit and a roll, for although far from hungry, she knew she needed to keep her strength if only for David's sake.

"Good afternoon, Miss Elizabeth," Jeremy Vane said as he entered the dining room. Gone was his habitual rabbity demeanor. Rather, he stood taller, looked more assured. Could it be that he felt the responsibility of his office more keenly with Lord Crompton gone and a new earl stepping into his shoes, as it were?

She made note of the alteration of character in the back of her mind, then turned to her slight meal.

Lord Augustus joined them, his jowls drooping more than usual in his unhappy state.

"Shall miss him, y'know. Quarreled often, but never really meant it. Suppose everyone thinks he would like to do things differently if given the chance. I do." Lord Augustus dipped out a bowl of soup, then took a crusty roll. With a sigh he joined them at the table.

"Too late, I fear," Mr. Vane inserted, his voice polite.

He appeared somewhat hostile to Elizabeth's eyes. She

had watched him rather than Lord Augustus, recalling David's unreasonable antagonism toward the steward.

"M'brother was always good to you, you scamp," Lord Augustus grumbled, throwing Jeremy a look of dislike.

"I fancy you will be moving along now, sir. With your brother gone and a new earl taking his place, you shall wish to be elsewhere, I daresay," Jeremy replied with a thinly veiled note of contempt in his voice.

Elizabeth barely stifled a gasp of dismay. How bold the steward had become suddenly. It was scarcely his place to suggest anything of the sort to the late earl's brother.

"Eh? Getting above yourself, are you not?" Lord Augustus bristled with anger at the presumptions of the lowly steward, even if he was a relative.

Mr. Vane shrugged, then said, "It is true nonetheless."

A silence fell over the room which none of them cared to break, it seemed. When Egbert entered to seek a bit of nourishment, he was disinclined to disturb the quiet. He ate his food without saying a word, other than softly worded comments that didn't reach beyond his father.

As soon as she could escape the dreadful atmosphere of the dining room, Elizabeth hurried across the central hall to the corridor leading to the study. Halfway there she heard a rap on the door.

Sidthorp bustled to open it, while Elizabeth paused, wondering if it was the vicar, or if the solicitor would appear. Nothing would surprise her now, not even the arrival of a man who would not receive word of the earl's death until tomorrow.

"Oh, Sidthorp, where is my dear niece? I must see her at once."

Aunt Bel caught sight of Elizabeth across the entry hall and walked to her, arms outstretched. "My dear girl, what a tragedy to occur. But then, I knew something was to come, for the cock crowed three times last night, and you know that means a death to follow."

Tears rushed to Elizabeth's eyes as she greeted her aunt. In spite of her eccentricities and superstitions, she was the closest person to being a mother to Elizabeth, and the truth of one's mortality had been brought home to her in the past hours.

"Now, explain to me what has happened, and what has been done. I have come to help you, for you were too young when your mother and father were killed to remember the details and what the proper order of things must be."

Elizabeth led her along to the study, all the while explaining what David had requested.

Behind them, the knocker sounded again, and the gruff voice of the vicar could be heard in conversation with Sidthorp.

"Funerals are such sad occasions," Aunt Bel remarked. "You must prepare for the expenses. There will be the sums for the mourners in the village. Will the late earl be buried here, or is Lord Leighton removing his body to Crompton Vale in the north?"

"David had not decided when I last spoke with him." Elizabeth debated a few moments, then seated her aunt on one of the armchairs, while seating herself at the desk. "There is something decidedly odd in all of this."

Her aunt looked up in surprise. She had been surveying the stack of paper on the desk, absently glancing at the list of people to be notified.

"Do you think it singular that David had the black-bordered paper to hand this morning? He had the list of names all drawn up for me as well."

"I doubt that anything unusual is going on," her aunt replied thoughtfully. "It may be that he suspected that his father would not live long and anticipated the need."

"Aunt Bel, it takes time to get that paper, although I know most stationery shops carry such all the time. Yet I do not recall a recent trip to the village, or any servant being sent off on such an errand."

"But then, you are not privy to everything his lordship does, are you?" her aunt reminded.

"True," Elizabeth admitted. Of course Aunt Bel was right. Elizabeth was being foolish about the entire matter. Pushing her feeling of unease aside—for after all, why would David behave in such a bizarre manner when *he* had not murdered his father?—she set to work on the remainder of the letters.

To say that dinner was subdued was to say that a funeral is a jolly occasion. Lord Augustus mumbled morosely all through the meal. Egbert, oddly enough, had great patience with his father, rather than arguing as was his wont.

Jeremy Vane sat quietly at his place, watching the others with that strange look on his face that Elizabeth had observed earlier. No one else seemed to question his behavior, so she said nothing, deciding that David had enough on his plate without her silly observations.

When Elizabeth and her aunt elected to go upstairs to their rooms in the north wing, the men left the table, each for their own unstated destination.

At the top of the stairs, Lady Montgomery paused, catching sight of Filpot.

"My good man, we would like to pay our respects. Would you please show us to his late lordship's room?"

The valet looked stunned, and hemmed and hawed without giving her an answer. Finally he replied, "I cannot do that, ma'am, until I 'ave a talk with Lord Leighton."

Aunt Bel sniffed and marched down the corridor to her room with her nose tilted in the air.

A thoughtful Elizabeth followed her.

"I believe I shall take to my bed at once. This has been a shocking day," Aunt Bel announced in aggrieved tones.

Purvis waited for her inside the bedroom, which was immediately next to Elizabeth's room. Across the bed lay three black gowns.

"Ah, Elizabeth, I found these in the attic," Aunt Bel declared, perking up when she saw the work to be done, which she intended to supervise. "They are relatively recent, for I had them made only last year. One never knows when one will require mourning. Hold them up to her, Purvis. See which can be made to fit."

The following hour saw two of the gowns made presentable, and one which could do only after considerable taking in. Elizabeth declined this, suggesting that her Aunt had rather keep the dress for her own use.

Aunt Bel fussed about, urging Elizabeth to take a sleeping potion, for that was what she intended to do.

"Sleeping with a dead person in a house is so depressing, you know," she said with a sigh. "But then, few have my tender sensibilities."

Elizabeth escaped to her room before she gave way to the ridiculous urge to laugh. Aunt hadn't meant it to sound as though she actually slept *with* the deceased, but it had sounded frightfully like that. Elizabeth decided she was on the verge of hysteria, and accepted the hot milk from Rose as an aid to sleep.

Tomorrow would be another hectic day.

But as she drifted off to sleep, she recalled Filpot. Now, she might not like the man in the least, but even taking this into account, she thought his behavior was most peculiar. Her intuition told her that something was distinctly havey-cavey. The problem was to figure out what it might be.

In the morning, Elizabeth rose with a feeling of apprehension hanging over her. A look at the black gown that Rose held out for her to put on brought everything back in force.

David now held the title of Earl of Crompton, with a second title of Viscount Leighton, and head of the Percy family. Such an awesome responsibility for one so young.

And curiously he insisted that she marry him. Elizabeth took comfort that in the six months required for mourning, anything might happen. He might even learn to love her, she thought, as Rose adjusted the black gown of lightweight bombazine. Turning about before the looking glass, Elizabeth could see that the judicious tucks and stitches that Purvis had taken proved rather nice.

While a depressing color, the gown strangely enough flattered Elizabeth to a surprising degree. The bodice was very low in the front and back, but there was a sheer scarf to wear around her neck, so she needn't feel indecent. The short sleeves were quite full, and a pretty little bow tied in the front, directly below the bodice.

With that comforting thought hugged to her ample bosom, she went down the stairs to the dining room.

The only occupant turned out to be David. Elizabeth paused on the threshold, wondering what she ought to say. He wore the deepest black, and the thought crossed her mind that it was fortunate he possessed the proper clothes. But then, men as dashing and restrained in their dress as he would be apt to own a black tailcoat and breeches. Black hose and shoes, the black waistcoat, all could be found in his wardrobe, couldn't they? She suspected they could, yet was she being overly suspicious again because she wondered about it? Foolish, silly, addlepated, that was what she was.

He glanced up from his plate to meet her concerned gaze. ''I understand your aunt wished to see my father last evening. Inform her, unless I chance to see her first, that she may see him today if she likes. She flustered Filpot, for he wasn't prepared for such a request.''

Elizabeth wondered why not. It was a common occasion after a death for friends and relatives to view the deceased. While this was normally confined to the funeral service, it was not that unusual.

She said nothing of her feelings, for they were so absurd as to be outrageous. ''I shall, my lord.''

''There is another matter I wish to speak to you about. My father declared he wished that we be married as soon as possible. I have sent off an express to Doctor's Commons for a special license. When the vicar was here yesterday, he indicated he would respect my father's wishes. No one will think a thing about our marriage if we do not wait for six months, for we have been betrothed for weeks.''

Elizabeth groped for a chair, then sank down upon it, feeling as though she had stepped into a fantasy world where wishes came true in the most unlikely fashion. What could she say? She had promised only the day before that she would not hand David the mitten. Actually, she had provocation to jilt him, for he certainly had displayed none of the loverlike manners one expected. Perhaps rakes did things differently? She certainly did not know.

''I, er, this is indeed a surprise,'' she said shortly.

He relaxed a trifle, she noted. Had he expected her to reject him?

''I suppose your aunt will feel it unseemly, such haste. But since she caused the betrothal in the beginning, it is only fitting she see it through.''

Whatever he meant by those words, Elizabeth had no chance to ask, for Egbert wandered into the room.

"Elizabeth and I have decided to marry immediately, as soon as the special license arrives from London." David studied his cousin as he made this statement. Elizabeth also watched keenly.

"That makes sense, I suppose. Best fill the nursery as soon as possible." He walked to the sideboard to select buttered eggs, ham, toast, and coffee.

Elizabeth would have blushed had it not been for his prosaic attitude, as though their action was logical and proper under the circumstances.

The nursery had to be filled. That was the reason for their marriage. And was that not common? No profession of love was required, just a willing body, she thought bitterly. Oh, that her aunt had never moved her to the pink bedchamber on Valentine's eve. She would not be in this predicament now. Hyacinthe would. At that thought, Elizabeth realized she did not like the notion of Hyacinthe being married to David in the least.

When her heart was engaged and David was indifferent to her—or whatever he was feeling—marriage became a less than joyous future. But she was not about to let anyone else have the chance.

Then Uncle Augustus entered, corsets creaking. He grumbled a "good morning" to them all, then selected an amazingly hearty meal to begin the day. "Need sustenance, y'know. Dashed hard to get through the day otherwise."

Before Elizabeth could think of a reply, Jeremy Vane walked in, neatly garbed in black, a superior look on his face that she found revolting under the circumstances.

What had happened to the rabbity, meek, and mild man she had first known when coming here? He had been such a delight. This man was a stranger.

"Good morning, all. Pity the rain must continue. However, it does fit the occasion." Jeremy strolled to the sideboard to survey the offerings.

"David and Elizabeth are getting married as soon as the special license arrives from London," Egbert announced somewhat baldly. His words fell into a silence that Jeremy did not immediately break.

He had tensed upon hearing the news. Elizabeth could see his shoulders stiffen as though receiving a blow. Then he relaxed a trifle and assumed a polite mask—for that is what it appeared to her.

"Fine, fine," he declared slowly with patently false enthusiasm, then compressed his lips a moment before continuing. "Understandable, considering the circumstances. How fortunate for David that he found a willing partner in the wilds of Surrey."

"We knew each other while in London, you know," Elizabeth said in excuse of she knew not what. She did not care for Jeremy's insinuation that David had to snatch at just anyone, or that she was willing to participate in something faintly underhanded, for that is what he made it seem.

"Oh, so you did. How providential for you, David. Things just seem to fall into your lap." With that snide observation he took his plate with him from the room, along with a large cup of coffee.

Elizabeth surmised that Jeremy found their company not to his liking, and she decided those remaining felt the same about him.

"Dashed loose screw, if you ask me," Egbert commented.

"No one did, but for once I agree with you," David replied. He finished his meal, then rose from the table. "There are a few things to discuss, Elizabeth. I shall wait for you in the study."

She dawdled a bit, wondering what it was he wanted to talk to her about. Perhaps he would tell her what was really going on. No, she dare not hint at anything like that, for he'd think her bird-witted for sure.

Deciding the best way to find out what he wanted was to go to the study, she left the remains of her breakfast behind and walked across the entry hall. As had happened the day before, a rap at the door brought a guest, a stranger this time. Elizabeth paused, curious to see who had come.

"Ah, Sidthorp. I am sorry to learn things have come to this pass, indeed. I need to speak with the new earl at once."

Elizabeth spoke up then. "I am on my way to him

now, sir. I trust you are the solicitor, Mr. Fynes?'' He must have immediately surmised the death from the hatchments. He was a pleasantly rotund man, slightly balding, and possessed of a pair of snapping blue eyes.

"I have that pleasure. I need not ask if you are Miss Elizabeth Dancy, for you match the description I was given to a tee.'' He gave her a cordial look.

"Come with me.'' She wondered what had been said about her, like any vain young creature, then scolded herself for being foolish. She escorted Mr. Fynes to the study.

"David, I am sorry this day had to come so soon.'' The solicitor reached out to clasp David's hand.

"Indeed. I am pleased you could arrive with such speed.'' To Elizabeth he said, "Does Jeremy know he has come?''

"I chanced to cross the entry hall when Mr. Fynes arrived. Jeremy had removed himself with his breakfast to the office wing before that. I doubt if he knows aught, unless Sidthorp reveals it, and that is unlikely.''

David exchanged a look with the solicitor. "Now to business. Have you drawn up the marriage settlement? My father particularly wished to see a goodly jointure arranged for Elizabeth. You contacted her family solicitor?''

Mr. Fynes nodded. "By chance he is a friend of mine and was able and willing to reveal such provision for a dowry as has been made for Miss Elizabeth.''

She reeled with shock at the revelations being made, one after another. All this talk of marriage settlement and jointure and arrangements that took a great amount of time to make was almost more than she could absorb.

David's suggestion that they marry immediately had not been precipitous. Their coming marriage had been carefully planned and for some time. Why?

The amount of her pin money, her future jointure, the arrangement for their first son, was discussed and settled. From time to time David glanced to where she sat, but did not ask her to comment. Indeed, she couldn't have said a word, so great was her surprise. A woman did not normally take part on these discussions, anyway.

Since Elizabeth had no father and her brother was on the continent, Mr. Fynes appeared to act on her behalf.

When they concluded the settlement, they turned to other matters, Jeremy Vane, for one.

"What shall you do about him?" Mr. Fynes inquired.

David glanced at Elizabeth, then said, "One moment. Will you inform Mrs. Sidthorp that Mr. Fynes will remain several nights with us?"

"Of course." She rose in a flurry of black bombazine and left the room. Her bosom rose and fell in great agitation as she marched to the rear of the house. He had sent her from the room because he did not wish her to learn what he planned for Jeremy. Just what was going on?

15

"THEY ALL BELIEVE you to be dead."

"Do they, by Jove?" The earl turned from the window, where he had been staring out across the gentle vale to the woods in the distance. The scene presented a misty view at best, but it appeared to offer goodly satisfaction to him.

"You look well enough, I must say," replied a disgruntled son. David dropped onto a chair not far from where his father stood. "I have had to go about with a hangdog face and test my acting abilities to the limit."

"Yes, well, when one ceases to imbibe poison, it does have a beneficial effect on one." The earl joined his son, taking a chair that faced him, and smiled wryly. "Tell me, how do my dear relatives accept the news of my demise?" He gestured toward the bed, where a bust of the earl was placed on the pillow, sheets and a cover arranged so it bore an uncanny resemblance to the real person, what with a few pillows strategically placed to form a body.

"Your brother looks to have aged ten years, expresses sorrow that you quarreled. Whatever did you argue about all those years ago, if I may ask?" David picked at the arms of his chair while watching his dear father grope for words.

"A woman. Suffice it to say that neither of us really cared a scrap for the gel. Egbert?"

"I was surprised there. He has actually been rather civil to Elizabeth and I, conveying words of deep sympathy—for Egbert. However, Jeremy has turned into a toad of the first water. He is cocksure, impertinent, almost patronizing, especially to Elizabeth, as though he pitied her in her betrothal to me."

"Hmm. Of course, that does not mean what we think it might, for whoever it is must be a dissembler of considerable ability. Why the gloomy face?" The earl steepled his fingers while resting his elbows on the arms of his chair, studying his son with a shrewd gaze.

"I cannot like deceiving Elizabeth in all this. You do not know how many times I have come close to confiding in her." David shifted, as though uncomfortable.

"I can see where that might present a difficulty. You are reconciled to the match?" His lordship permitted a smile to hover over his mouth.

"More than reconciled, sir. I have grown to love that aggravating young woman very much. She is such a delight. However, I am not certain if she feels the same about me."

"You arranged the settlements as I suggested?" The earl tilted his head to listen carefully to what was said, and perhaps to what was unspoken.

"She appears quite satisfied with them. And you were exceedingly generous. I thank you for that." David flashed his endearing grin at his father.

"Nonsense. It will all come to you one day, eventually. Although not for some time, I hope. I shall be glad to have this thing over and done with, for I grow restless being cooped in this room. I have read all these books you brought up. Perhaps you will be so good as to exchange them for another selection?"

David chuckled. "Elizabeth saw me with books in my arms. I feel sure she wondered about my wishing to read at a time like this."

"Quite so." The two men exchanged amused glances. Filpot entered the room on tiptoe, carrying a tray he had prepared for the earl while the cook was absent from the kitchen.

"Difficult, milord. Very tricky, indeed. But I find it curious that the quality of the food has improved so greatly since your supposed death." The valet fussed over the tray, placing it on a table close to his master, seeing to it that the dishes and cutlery were just so, the food to his lordship's liking.

Again the earl's eyes sought David, and this time the looks they exchanged were not amused in the least.

* * *

Several hours later, Elizabeth found her aunt relaxing on a chaise lounge in her bedchamber. "The settlement is complete. I daresay my jointure is excessively generous, Aunt Bel," Elizabeth said, referring to the monetary provision for a widow. She paced back and forth in the charming room while her aunt look on in shrewd assessment.

"I was not aware that so many factors had to be considered," Elizabeth continued. "Our first son, should we be blessed with one, is well settled, and the amount of pin money I am to have is wildly handsome." She gestured expansively, while pausing in her walk to look at her aunt.

"The dowry my parents arranged for me is more than I expected. The solicitor was vastly pleased with it, and murmured something about the marriage being a good contract and highly advantageous, as my dowry was so substantial. It appears to me that women are sold into marriage, much like slaves."

"Rubbish," Aunt Bel denied. "It is the way of our society, my love. Without our families to watch over our interests, we could be left without a roof over our heads, utterly penniless. Our children might be denied their rightful share of an inheritance by unscrupulous relatives and conniving solicitors." She paused to reflect, as though she recalled instances where this had occurred. "Whether or not you love the man you wed is immaterial in the long run. Through the settlement, your future is assured by careful planning. Lord Crompton is being extremely considerate, and you are a very fortunate girl," her ladyship gently scolded.

Elizabeth considered this information at length, then paused by the fireplace, exchanging a puzzled look with her aunt.

"I do not reject marriage, not even to a man who has never said he cares for me. I am a silly, romantic girl and would dearly like to have my future husband say other than he could do worse than marry me." She flounced into a chair, propped her chin on her fist, and glared at an inoffensive vase full of snowdrops.

"He said no such thing. Or did he?" Aunt Bel inquired in faintly horrified tones.

Elizabeth nodded, then roundly declared, "When it came to the discussion about Jeremy, I was requested—ever so politely—to inform Mrs. Sidthorp that Mr. Fynes will be staying several nights. As though Sidthorp had not already done that. It was merely a ruse to remove me from the room. David might have saved himself the trouble of inventing an excuse and just told me to run along, like a child of six."

"My, my, such a feeling of ill usage," Aunt Bel said dryly.

Elizabeth smiled acknowledgment of her infantile anger. "I know. I am being a peagoose. I suppose I long for a chivalrous knight to sweep me into his arms, rather than a prosaic melding of my dowry to David's estate, with a ceremony to mark the event. He said something about his not having courted me, almost sounding sorry about it. Do you suppose he intends to woo me properly later on?" Elizabeth gave her aunt a wistful look.

Aunt Bel smiled at her romantic niece. "Stranger things have happened."

"There is a funeral service tomorrow morning. I thought he would wait until he took his father by hearse to the main estate up north. Apparently he has decided to hold two services, with the interment up there where the family vault is located. That will be an enormous undertaking. I recall seeing a procession once. With six horses for the hearse and six for the mourning coach, plus all the outriders, it was an impressive sight. When they come to the town near the home estate, a great many people assemble along the road. The mourners require such an outlay. Funerals are expensive." Elizabeth sighed, lost in reflection.

"I believe I shall venture forth to the other wing and pay my respects to the deceased. That valet, Filpot, has said we might." Lady Montmorcy rose from her chair, then walked to the door. Here she paused, turning to study her niece. "Will you join me?"

Reluctant to admit how depressing she found the entire viewing, Elizabeth obediently rose to join her aunt, knowing this was expected of her as David's future wife.

Her coming wedding seemed unreal, like a fantasy, or something she read about as happening to another. She well knew it was inevitable, and she truly did not hate the idea. She longed for it to be a love match, however. And it seemed to her that David was not very loverlike for a rake.

As the two ladies walked across the central area to the south wing, she glanced down at the hall below. Sidthorp could be seen crossing on some errand. Egbert entered, obviously having come from a ride in the morning mist. He shook his hat and coat to shed the moisture from it.

Would it ever turn warm and sunshiny again? This was undoubtedly the longest winter she could ever recall.

Filpot met them at the door when they knocked. At the sight of Lady Montmorcy, he opened the door a little wider, enough to permit them to enter. He coughed discreetly, then said, "My Lady Montmorcy and Miss Elizabeth," as though announcing them to the body on the bed.

Elizabeth did not quite believe her ears and followed her aunt into the room with considerable reluctance.

The room was as dark as night, with but two flickering candles some distance from the bed. Draperies were drawn tightly over the windows. Filpot muttered something about it being like Lord Nelson's viewing, when there were but two candles lit.

The earl's face looked handsome, carved in high relief as though in stone. Although she had to admit it was difficult to see very much, for he was in deep shadow. Not having been at a similar scene, for she had never viewed her parents after they died, Elizabeth couldn't say if the sight was typical. Burning incense produced a heavy, spicy odor, not unpleasant but slightly overwhelming after a time. Had it been any other situation, she would have sworn she smelled food as well, but surely Filpot would not eat in this room!

"Hmph," Aunt Bel murmured to Elizabeth. "One would think there was a heavy tax on candles, as dark as it is in here."

"It presents a mood, Aunt." Elizabeth agreed that the room possessed an odd appearance, but what did she know?

"I shall miss him. I thought I might have a chance to renew our acquaintance, for he was always a darling boy to me. Oh pride, how foolish it can be. I loved him deeply before my parents compelled me to wed Giles. I could not even tell Herold that I cared, for I was whisked to London to be married there. Years later, when I returned after Giles had died, Herold did not call on me. I trust he had forgotten all about our youthful attachment. And now it is too late for me to tell him. I am merely a silly old woman," Aunt Bel concluded softly, mindless of Filpot and Elizabeth. She accepted the sprig of rosemary from Filpot to place on the bed, then stepped away, a handkerchief to her eyes, her head bowed.

Elizabeth felt her aunt's murmured words were more to herself than to her niece, and so remained silent. But she was filled with sadness at what she had heard. How tragic to allow foolish pride to come between two people who had once loved each other.

When they at last returned to Elizabeth's sitting room, her aunt rang for tea, declaring she needed restoration. She blew her nose a number of times, but had composed herself when the maid entered bearing the tea tray.

Elizabeth drifted over to the window, wondering what was going on in the study, where David again was meeting with his solicitor after a break. Did she dare intrude? She had taken his request to Mrs. Sidthorp, who had indeed known all about the solicitor's visit.

Something simply did not feel right. Was she becoming as superstitious as her aunt? To rely on hunches, feelings?

"Join me, my dear. We shall drink to a fine man with a good cup of Bohea."

"Better that than port, I suppose." Elizabeth left the window, after noting that the mist continued to fall outside. She returned to the chair she had occupied earlier and accepted a steaming cup of Bohea from her aunt.

"What shall you do, my girl? If David proceeds with the wedding?"

"What can I do but agree? Everyone around knows we have been betrothed ever since Valentine's Day. I did not write of it to Victoria and Julia, thinking it useless, for I had intended to hand him the mitten long before this."

"Did you, now?" Aunt Bel peered at Elizabeth over the rim of her teacup, her brows rising.

"I feel it wrong to compel two people to marry merely because of a superstition. But somewhere along the line things got out of hand. I should like to let my sisters know. Victoria has returned from the continent, and is in the family way, according to her latest letter. Julia is off up north, and I doubt if she can be here, either. I am excessively glad I have you, Aunt Bel," Elizabeth added with a fond look at her slightly eccentric but much loved aunt. "Chloe and Hyacinthe shall stand up for me in place of my sisters."

"Sensible, for you do not know precisely when the wedding is to be, do you?" Aunt Bel took another dainty sip of tea.

"He keeps remarkably quiet about that," Elizabeth replied thoughtfully. "I believe I shall approach the matter now. A girl likes to plan for things. Especially a wedding. Although I realize that many people do not make a great fuss. When the sixth Duchess of Devonshire married, only her parents, her grandmother, and the duke's sister were present. And Lady Harriet Cavendish had no one but her father and stepmother and Lord Granville's sister attend her wedding. David said he had written for a special license, and I suspect he wants no fuss, particularly so close to his father's death. It would be unseemly."

With her aunt's permission to discuss the matter with David, Elizabeth left her rooms, walking down the corridor with an anxious heart.

A hush hung over the house when she ran lightly down the stairs. Sidthorp was not to be seen. Egbert could be heard chatting with his father in the billiards room. She could see them standing near the billiards table, cues in hand while they discussed something.

Her footsteps lagged. There had been a distant alteration of the attitude of both of them since the earl's death. She stopped, watching the two, who carried on as though nothing had occurred. Surely that was not the way to behave? While she did not actually know, not having been around a house where there was a death for years—and then being quite young, it seemed callous to just go on as usual, playing game after game of billiards.

As she neared the study, she discovered the door stood ajar. Not wishing to intrude, she slowed her steps again. Mr. Fynes's deep voice could be clearly heard. In spite of her resolve not to listen in to another's conversation, she could not help herself.

"Marrying her is the best way out, my boy. You may rest assured, that is one area settled. Her dowry is respectable, and even if she is a trifle young, that is not so very bad. She is a lovely girl. Remember, a wife cannot testify against her husband." He chuckled at this bit of wit.

Elizabeth froze, waiting to hear David's reply.

"It was not what I had wanted."

"Is anything in this life?"

Not wishing to hear another word—for she had certainly heard no good of herself, as she supposed was only just—she fled. A silent skimming across the hall brought her to the stairs, then up to her room. Fortunately, Aunt Bel had returned to her own quarters, and Elizabeth was quite alone.

Now she knew why David insisted they wed. The only feeling he possessed toward her was gratitude that she was so conveniently at hand. Confused and hurt, she paced about the room, threading a hand through her curls.

What a pity her parents had left such an acceptable dowry. Mr. Fynes might have counseled David to look elsewhere for a more eligible wife.

She wouldn't do it. She would run away. Somewhere there must be a place she could hide. Perhaps Victoria and Edward would allow her sanctuary?

Then her common sense returned. She had shared lovely kisses with David, they had laughed together, and he did possess a sense of humor—something she felt important. Could she not take the risk of marriage with him, and try to build on the shaky foundation to achieve something more solid?

Then another thought occurred to her. Since she cared so deeply for David, could she not do this for him? Marry him to protect him from whatever he and his solicitor feared? She did not know what circumstances might be that she could testify against David. She did know she would never do anything to harm him. Not willingly.

"That is what I shall do. I shan't say a word about what I have heard," she declared to the vase of snow-drops. "I will proceed with the wedding just as he wishes, when he wishes. It will be my gift to him."

Chin up, resolve quite firmed, she slowly strolled back downstairs, as though she had not just stormed back to her room in hurt anger minutes past.

"Elizabeth, there you are," David exclaimed as he strode across the hall to her side.

She gave him a wary look, wondering what he would say. "Yes?"

"I have finished with the solicitor. I thought perhaps you and I could discuss the details of the wedding."

She forced a brave smile to her lips. "That is precisely what I hoped to do now, why I was coming to look for you."

Was that a sigh of relief from David? she wondered.

At the entrance to the office wing, Jeremy Vane watched the two lovers stroll arm in arm toward the drawing room. They ought not be alone, even though betrothed. But then, propriety had not been strictly observed in this house for a long time.

If he had the running of the place, things would be different.

On the other side of the courtyard, Egbert also watched David and Elizabeth walk to the drawing room, deep in discussion. Did his cousin know how lucky he was? What a treasure Elizabeth Dancy had proved to be. Egbert felt that his dear cousin did not fully appreciate his good fortune.

If he were in charge of affairs, things would be different.

"What are you doing, lad?" Lord Augustus spoke with unusual sharpness to his only son.

"Watching the betrothed couple head for the privacy of the drawing room. I fancy they want to plan the wedding. Shall we join them?" He gave a faintly malicious smile at the thought of disrupting a lover's tryst.

"Someone ought to be there. Can't think what that totty-headed Isobel is thinking of, to leave her niece alone with a rake like Leighton. Even if they are to wed. Were I in charge of things around here, they would be a good deal different, I can tell you that.''

With a nod to his son, the two men set off to the drawing room, virtuous condescension in their faces.

Elizabeth looked up in startled alarm when Lord Augustus entered the room, followed by Egbert, who wore a distinctly gleeful look on his face. She stood by the fireplace, David not far away. They had been about to set the time and place of the marriage when so rudely interrupted.

''Ho, what have we here?'' Lord Augustus said with false jollity.

''The lovers, no less. Cannot have this, you know.'' Egbert wagged a finger at the pair across the room. ''Not at all proper. Would never want the servants to spread it about that the new Lord Crompton was less than honorable in his attentions to his future wife, now would we?''

Elizabeth cast about for some means of changing the subject. A glance at Lord Augustus gave her the idea. ''Would anyone care for tea?'' She had scarce touched the food set out at noon, and would welcome something to nibble.

''Allow me to ring for the footman. I trust a slight repast will be an acceptable way of passing the time?'' she begged, hoping that Egbert would not be nasty about it.

''Ain't proper, my boy. Dallying with a young lady don't show respect befitting your station as the new earl,'' Lord Augustus declared with more than a hint of pomposity.

David raised his brows at this bit of reproach. His uncle had lived a life anything but decorous, according to what Elizabeth had heard.

''Begin as you mean to go on, perhaps?'' David reached out to draw a reluctant Elizabeth to his side, for she stood not all that far from him.

''Do not mock, David,'' Egbert scolded in a serious voice all of a sudden.

''I wasn't.''

Not understanding what was afoot, Elizabeth was about to walk away when she found herself firmly held. It was impossible for her to leave without an unseemly struggle. She remained, deciding to add her bit to the scene by snuggling up to David. If he wanted to make a particular impression, it behooved her to cooperate. Besides, she rather enjoyed it. Oh, what a wicked girl she was, to even think of her desires when the poor earl lay dead upstairs.

The footman who answered the summons could not fail to take note of the proximity of the betrothed couple. She was all but enfolded in David's arms, for pity's sake.

Feeling distinctly at a disadvantage, Elizabeth requested a tea tray, with a substantial repast included. She was curious to see if the cook repeated the accident of unburnt food.

With Lord Augustus and Egbert playing chaperone, it was impossible to discuss the coming wedding in a way they would like. When Aunt Bel strolled into the drawing room, it made the group complete, for immediately behind her came Jeremy Vane.

"The funeral is tomorrow morning," observed Aunt Bel. "Do you intend to have your wedding before you go to Crompton Vale?" she added with a delicate reference to the trip north with the corpse.

"That would be the following day, I believe. How do you feel about it, Elizabeth?"

"Sooner you wed, the better, in my opinion," Lord Augustus inserted, his corsets creaking as he leaned over to select something from the tea tray just delivered by the young footman.

"You ought to know," David replied with dangerous quiet.

Aunt Bel glanced up sharply at this note, and with a horrified look at the footman, who seemed to have turned into stone, she said, "I do hope the rain stops. It would be nice to have sunshine on your wedding day."

Elizabeth settled against David, knowing that somehow her aunt would take matters in hand, and that tempers would not be permitted to flare out of control.

Trapped by the look David sent him, Lord Augustus harrumphed twice, then nodded, as he accepted a cup of tea from Lady Montmorcy. "Dratted stuff," he murmured before taking a tentative sip.

"Well, it seems to me," Egbert said sometime later,

"that one should be prepared for the past to return to haunt him." He was looking at David when he spoke, rather than his father.

Elizabeth suspected what was in his mind, and she said, before David might utter something he'd regret later on, "If you refer to anything my future husband may have done in his past, imagined or real, I daresay there is little I do not know, or have heard about. And if there is something I do not know of, I do not wish to be told." She gave Egbert a cold stare, aware that he could ultimately cause a great deal of unhappiness if she did not make this point crystal clear at the outset.

"Well, well," David murmured at her side. "My little valentine has claws."

"That's not all," she whispered back quite daringly.

The following morning the family, along with Aunt Bel and Elizabeth, assembled in the entry hall. The servants, given the morning to attend the modest service in the village church, joined the procession.

There was a hearse of sorts, more of a dray pressed into service, given the lack of proper notification to the undertaker from the nearest town. This was followed by carriages bearing the relatives, then Aunt Bel and Elizabeth, and last, the vehicle containing Filpot, Hadlow, Rose, and the Sidthorps. The remaining servants drove along in a somewhat antique coach.

The service was blessedly short, and the casket remained closed, much to Elizabeth's surprise, for her aunt had informed her it usually stayed open so that others could pay their respects.

However, she had little time to dwell on this, for the procession was reversed, and they all trouped back to Penhurst Place.

"Most peculiar, I say," Aunt Bel pronounced when she and Elizabeth were once again in Elizabeth's room.

"What does it matter? I must look to the wedding now. I do hope that people will not look too askance at our haste." Elizabeth stared at her aunt from her comfortable chair by the fire. She uneasily twisted the diamond that David had placed on her finger.

"No, no. If there is gossip, something else will come

along to catch their ears. It usually does. I must send a note to Chloe and Hyacinthe. They will think themselves sadly neglected. Poor Hyacinthe has declared Lord Norwood too stuffy. She announced that he can take himself off to his landscaping and fertilizing for all she cares. Not only that. Some fool told her that he is a shocking rake when in London. She is totally undone.''

Elizabeth smiled at that, then said, ''Surely they understand the circumstances?''

''True. I would wish them to find suitable gowns to wear to your wedding. Which brings me to another matter. What shall you wear?'' Aunt Bel leaned against her chair, studying her niece with a careful gaze.

''I detest wearing black, for it is so gloomy, but I expect I must.'' Elizabeth sighed, then turned her gaze to meet that of her aunt, who frowned.

''Perhaps not. Pale lavender might be acceptable, or dove gray. I fail to see the haste, my dear. I cannot think why David does not wish to wait the proper six months of mourning before marriage.''

''I do not know, but I have my suspicions.''

Beyond that, Elizabeth refused to confide. There were some things a woman did not share with anyone, not even a favorite aunt. There was something decidedly smoky going on at Penhurst Place. She didn't know what it was, but she would support David in any way she could. It was the least she could do for the man she loved.

''I wonder what will happen at the reading of the will. Mr. Fynes said something about meeting in the library this afternoon. I suppose he is anxious to return to his office.''

Elizabeth also wondered. Would they learn at last who had poisoned the earl? She had the feeling that it was not a stranger, but one known to them all. Which one? Jeremy Vane, Lord Augustus, or the dreadful Egbert Percy? Or could there be another?

16

HE HAD TO BE the most provoking man alive. Elizabeth glanced at the man who nearly drove her mad, one way or the other, and sighed with discouragement. He had not sought her out for further discussion regarding their wedding, even though they'd had a bit of time to themselves. Perhaps all he had truly wished to know was that she did not plan to jilt him.

Then Mr. Fynes cleared his throat, gesturing to those assembled in the library to be seated. He had taken a place behind the large desk at the far end of the room. Behind him was the fireplace, the damp patch now reasonably dried out, thanks to Elizabeth's diligent efforts.

Lord Augustus settled on a high-backed chair to the right, amid the usual corset-creaking accompaniment, with Egbert lounging immediately behind him and to the side.

Ranged on the other side were David and Elizabeth, with Aunt Bel sitting discreetly behind them, although neither of the women actually needed to be present. David had requested them to come. Elizabeth wouldn't have missed it for anything, and she suspected that Aunt Bel had itching ears as well.

By the time everyone had gathered, the afternoon was nearly past and the room was dim. Sidthorp supervised the lighting of a good many candles, plus an Argand lamp for Mr. Fynes. This delay was tolerated by all, for each appeared to want to see the others.

Jeremy entered late, taking a chair near the far end of the room, not far from where the Sidthorps and other servants clustered.

While Mr. Fynes shuffled papers on the desk, Elizabeth spent her waiting moments studying the faces of the three men she suspected. Lord Augustus looked uncomfortable, and she wondered if his corset was too tight today, or if he felt guilty. Egbert wore his usual expression of boredom, tinged with curiosity. Knowing more of his relationship with his uncle, she surmised that he really did not have great expectations.

By turning her head a bit, as though to listen to something Aunt Bel might be saying, Elizabeth could see Jeremy Vane. He puzzled her. That newly acquired demeanor of his could not be liked in the least. Whereas he had been so kind and polite before, he now wore a sort of sneer on his face and held himself aloof from the others. Well, she hadn't liked that sort of timid-rabbit expression he'd worn in the past. But surely he should have been able to figure out something halfway between?

Mr. Fynes coughed, then commenced his reading of the will. David, quite naturally, took over the entailed estates, as well as the bulk of the fortune. Elizabeth was impressed at the number of estates that the family owned. In addition to Crompton Vale and Penhurst Place, there was a hunting box in Scotland, a manor house in Oxfordshire, and a house in London that possessed an excellent location.

His brother, Lord Augustus, was to receive a handsome bequest. This would go to his son in the event his father was no longer living at the time of the earl's death. Then Egbert also received a tidy sum in his own right. Not the vast estate that David received, naturally. But nothing to scoff at. She noted that he sat in his chair with a nonplussed expression on his face, from which she reckoned that he had not expected to be remembered quite so generously.

A suitable amount had been designated for the distant relative and steward, Jeremy Vane. An ample amount to permit Sidthorp and his wife to retire was also included, plus other random amounts for various others. The servants filed from the room at a word of dismissal from Mr. Fynes.

Elizabeth sat on her chair, tensed, waiting. What next?

Mr. Fynes cleared his throat once again, then took a sip of water. This was followed by a long look at David.

"There is an unexpected complication. A challenge to

David Percy, Lord Leighton and now Earl of Crompton, has been issued by one claiming to be the rightful earl.'' There were a number of gasps at this news. Elizabeth glanced at David, suspecting he had been warned in advance, for he looked not the least surprised. ''I have had lengthy communications with his solicitor recently. This young man asserts that he is the legal son of the now deceased sixth earl's elder brother, Edward. As such he would have legal claim to the title.''

There was a rustling of fabric as everyone looked about them. Elizabeth could not see that any new figure had entered the room.

''Mr. Vane, would you please come forward?''

Aunt Bel gasped. ''Of all the . . .''

Lord Augustus mumbled something that sounded like ''Presumptuous puppy.''

Jeremy Vane strode to where Mr. Fynes considered him with an unsmiling face.

''I have carefully studied the letters from your solicitor. I confess that I do not know why you have waited so long to make your history known.'' Here he paused to look up at Jeremy from beneath his brows. ''Surely, if you felt the title rightfully yours, you would have been most anxious to lay claim to your birthright. Do you have any additional papers to offer? For I must tell you that what has been proffered so far falls considerably short of convincing me. I doubt the House of Lords will accept the claim, either.'' Mr. Fynes clasped his hands neatly before him on the desk, staring at Jeremy with a hard expression.

Elizabeth decided she would not like to challenge Mr. Fynes at any time, in a court of law or elsewhere.

Jeremy extracted several papers from a folder, then presented them with a flourish to the solicitor. ''These bear the signature of my father. I also include papers which prove the validity of his marriage to my mother.''

With this done, Jeremy tossed a confident smile at David, then stepped away from the desk. He waited for a moment, then continued. ''I daresay that you will wish to study them further, but I assure you that the signature is legitimate. If referred to Committee in the House of Lords, I believe they must support my claim.''

"Lord Augustus, will you have a look at this?"

With the customary creaking of his corset, Lord Augustus rose to his feet, then ambled to the desk. He perused the various documents, frequently raising his eyes to look at Jeremy, then David. "I cannot say, in truth. But I am not a one to remember signatures. It appears like it, but I could not swear one way or the other in a court of law." His final look at David was one of apology.

Elizabeth reached out to cover David's hand with her own, trying to offer comfort during what must be a dreadful ordeal. That Jeremy should wait to present his case immediately after the earl died was highly suspicious to her. He must be responsible for the earl's death. But . . . how could they prove such a thing? She would like to institute an inspection of his room. It might be well to check the estate books, come to think on it. Anyone who guilty of murder could be guilty of embezzlement as well.

"Pity you did not think to demand a hearing before my brother died," Lord Augustus mused. "He was the one who knew Edward best, y'know. There ought to be a number of letters with his writing on them. He was not much to correspond. Like me, there. Hated to put pen to paper. But Herold kept what few he sent. Where are they? We can compare the writing on them."

"Papers?" Jeremy queried with seeming innocence. "I have seen no papers as you describe among the late Lord Crompton's correspondence."

"What did you see, cousin Jeremy? Or more to the point, what did you do?" David had risen to face his defiant relative with a surprisingly cool demeanor. He stood with crossed arms, looking rakishly handsome but most assuredly determined.

Elizabeth watched the two intently, a worried frown pleating her brow. How could David be so cool? He said those papers she'd found had been important. If so, how?

"I did all the tedious little jobs no one else wanted to do," Jeremy snapped, glaring at David. "And I learned far more about this estate, as well as the other places, than you will ever have a chance to know."

"Dashed odd, seems to me," grumbled Lord Augustus. "I smell a rat."

Egbert rose from his chair, then sauntered between David and Jeremy. He looked at one, then the other. To Mr. Fynes he said, "Choose David, please. I could not bear to think of the family being represented by this rabbit."

Jeremy tensed, clenching his fists. "Should I be declared the new earl, you will be out of here in a flea's leap."

Egbert shrugged. "Ta-lol. With you in residence as the earl, I scarce believe I should want to stay, old chap." After this shot Egbert strolled back to stand behind his father. Although his bequest had been read, he was not about to leave the field of battle, as it were.

"I fancy you have done your job well enough," David inserted smoothly. "I am told you even took to doing minor repairs. Like plastering?"

At this thrust Jeremy paled, but stood firm.

David strolled to the desk, picked up the quill knife, examining it as he walked to the fireplace. He glanced at Jeremy, then began scraping the wall where the recent plaster had been applied. As might be expected, it had not hardened to match the old, but was still somewhat fresh, although not moist.

Jeremy strode to the fireplace, his face mottled with anger. "Here, what are you doing? I demand you stop at once!" He reached out a hand to wrest the knife from David's hand, only to be pushed away while David easily kept the knife out of his reach.

"Problems, Jeremy? What difference could it make to you if I dig at this plaster?" David's eyes flashed with menace as he stared at his cousin.

"I do not want my property damaged," Jeremy declared in a shaking voice. "And why do you want to dig there, anyway? Seems a dashed fool thing to do." He shrugged off David's detaining hand, but did not make another attempt to take the knife away from him.

"Almost as foolish as concealing papers in the wall, eh?" Another chunk of plaster fell to the floor. David raised the knife again. It glittered in the light from the Argand lamp.

The former steward winced when the piece clicked on the hearth. He stared at it, then looked back to David.

"What do you mean?" Jeremy said, looking distinctly taken aback and not a little worried.

"What he means is that you hid some papers in the wall." Elizabeth rose, crossing the room to join the two by the fireplace. "During that dreadful rain the new plaster stood out, for it was not quite dry. I saw it and wondered. You did not do a very good job of it, or so Ben tells me. With David's help I dug until the packet of papers came to light. I should like to know how you thought you could get away with the deception," she demanded, standing between the two men.

She faced Jeremy, hands on hips, wishing she had the gun that now reposed beneath her pillow at Montmorcy Hall. How she would like to wave it beneath this scoundrel's nose and threaten him for daring to challenge so fine a man as David Percy.

"I should like to know that as well, Jeremy," came a raspy voice from the shadows in the back of the room. The supposedly dead earl stood erect; one hand rested on a chair, the other clasped a cane. At his side the dour Filpot hovered like a sentry on guard.

"Dear heaven! Herold!" Aunt Bel exclaimed, then fainted dead away against her high-backed chair, a heap of black bombazine.

Made of sterner stuff, Elizabeth whispered, "Oh, Lord have mercy," and groped for the nearest chair. Ignoring her aunt, who would regain consciousness eventually anyway, Elizabeth concentrated on the old earl. She slowly sank to the seat, while she watched him come nearer and nearer.

Jeremy froze, looking as though he saw a ghost. "But you can't be . . ."

"Why? Because you poisoned me? The potion was tested, first by Purvis, then the local apothecary, so we know what it was. Opium." The earl drew closer, one step at a time, making his way with determination. "You believed me safely out of the way so you could stake your illegal claim to my title once I was no longer about to refute your dastardly attempt." He waved several papers in the air with his free hand. "I was the only person alive who could identify my late brother's signature, the only one who stood between you and your claim on the title. Or what you hoped to claim."

Elizabeth recognized the papers the earl carried as the ones that had been concealed. She glanced to see if Jeremy also grasped their import. He had.

"Where did you get those?" he said, his confidence rapidly seeping away.

"My future daughter-in-law discovered them. David found himself a treasure in that girl. None of your namby-pamby sort, she. A true partner in the best sense."

Jeremy darted a look at the plaster, now deeply gouged, then back to the earl. "You cannot prove a thing."

"No? Mr. Fynes is taking the estate books to have them gone over. After checking a number of pages, David and I both suspect that you have diddled the estate, my lad. I have been remiss there, trusting you too much." The earl exchanged a firm look with his solicitor, then continued, "I am reluctant to take you to court for that out of respect for Edward's memory, but I daresay I can convince the cook to reveal that you paid her to put certain herbs in my food. Only it was to poison me, was it not? You kept feeding me doses of opium. Then, when I became too weak for regular food, you convinced her to put the poison in the potions my valet brought me. Everyone seemed to suspect Filpot. It was he, however, who discovered the part that Cook played in the entire affair."

"I refuse to listen to such rubbish," Jeremy exclaimed, while looking as though he would dearly like to flee. He took several steps in the direction of the door before Egbert casually moved between Jeremy and his objective.

"Rubbish?" The earl queried. "I think not. You see, I have those missing papers in my hand, and it will take but minutes to compare them with the ones you have offered to support your claim."

The earl suddenly sank onto a chair that Filpot had brought forth. "I expect, with the tender care of my new daughter, to be as fit as ever." With this, he turned to Augustus. "I apologize for the deception. But do not worry, I shan't turn you out." Then his eyes shifted to Egbert, and he added, "As yet."

Mr. Fynes walked around the table, accepting the papers from the earl. He examined them, then compared them with the ones Jeremy had set forth. Giving Jeremy a narrow look, he then turned to David.

"I believe you have no cause to worry for your future, my lord. Your father is safe as the present earl, and you certainly have your title assured."

"I would wager, although I could not say for certain, that you are indeed my brother's son, for you have the look of him," the earl said to Jeremy. "But your mother was never married to him, of that I am certain. You know, had you made known the whole of your tale, I might have been more generous with you. A good education, good marriage, you might have had so much, although you could never have had the title."

"It is not fair," Jeremy cried, his face blotched red with anger and frustration. "He intended to wed her, she told me so after he died. The title should be mine. Mine, I tell you!"

David exchanged glances with Elizabeth. She stepped closer to him, wishing to be near his protection. She said to the pretender, "You wanted David out of the way so that there would be no chance that he could fight your claim to the title and estate. He would have made a compelling defense before the House of Lords Committee, one they'd not have rejected." She narrowed her gaze. "I rather fancy Egbert would have been next to die. But as for me—I suppose I merely got in your path, an annoyance to you, someone to eliminate. You sir, are no better than a murderer even if the Earl survived, for you had intent to kill."

Mr. Fynes moved to Jeremy's side, taking a firm hold of his arm. "I believe we shall handle you and your false claim immediately. I trust a new life in Canada will be to your liking? Or perhaps transportation to Botany Bay would please you?" He offered the choice in a wry voice, for he, and everyone in the room, knew there actually was not a chance that Jeremy would refuse the ticket to Canada.

"This is outrageous," Jeremy sputtered, but walked

along with the solicitor. His words were brave, but his shoulders drooped in defeat. He knew he had little choice in the matter, for if the earl chose to prosecute, who would take his part against a peer of the realm?

"There is a ship sailing this week. If you are to be a passenger on it, we had best get you on your way immediately." The solicitor turned to Sidthorp, who ushered Jeremy away to his room at once. Packing would commence instantly, and by the following day Jeremy Vane would be an unpleasant memory.

Elizabeth hoped that the former steward would not be allowed to escape with his filched money. Concerned, she spoke up. "The funds he took? Can they be recovered?"

"I shan't take any chances, my dear," the earl replied. "I shall have Fynes check everything, you may be sure. I hope it is not too late for that. Perhaps Filpot will discover useful information when he goes through Jeremy's things. Possibly the money?"

From behind them Aunt Bel spoke up. "Let that be a lesson to all of us, not to put off what needs doing." She moved closer to the earl, fiddling with the scrap of black-bordered cambric in her hands before adding in a hesitant voice, "Herold, I would have a word with you at your earliest convenience." She glanced at the locket watch she always wore.

"Ah, yes, my dear," the earl said, turning in his chair to look at Isobel. "There is a bit of unfinished business between us. It is not too late, my lady," he said with a smile. He rose, offered her his arm, and they began to walk to the door.

Sidthorp returned just then, appearing somewhat flustered. "Sir, if I may have a word?"

"What is it? What is it? I am in a hurry. So much to be done. No time to waste." The earl paused in his walk to stare at his usually calm butler.

"The cook has disappeared, milord. Decamped."

Lord Crompton glanced at Lady Montmorcy, then at his son. "Not surprising, I imagine. It merely proves, in a way, the charge I made regarding her. Had she nothing to fear, she would be here yet."

"I think not," muttered David. "We'd all had enough

of her scorched meals. If you had not sent her packing, I daresay the entire household would have risen in revolt.''

The earl looked chagrined, but said nothing in defense of the cook. He turned to Sidthorp. ''Who prepared the food today, for it seemed good enough to me?''

''Cook had sent word she was indisposed, so the kitchen maid stepped in to do what she could, with Mrs. Sidthorp's supervision. It was not until the kitchen maid sought instructions for the evening meal that the absence was discovered.''

''Gave Cook time to get clean away, eh? Well, carry on, Sidthorp. The kitchen maid is doing fine, until you locate a new cook.''

''Very good, milord.''

''I wondered about breakfast, for the eggs were not crisp, nor the toast burned,'' Egbert said as he passed the others on his way to the drawing room.

Lord Augustus lumbered toward the door, intent on convincing his son to join him in a game of billiards rather than settle for a dull round of cards in the drawing room.

Mr. Fynes gathered his papers, then removed himself to the study to complete his task. If he was put out at having to make the trip under false pretenses, he didn't show it. As it was, he had the problem of the estate books to handle, and that would occupy much time.

The earl and Aunt Bel strolled toward the corridor before glancing back to where David hovered at Elizabeth's side. ''We shall see you later, I trust. David, I cannot begin to tell you how much it has meant to have you at my side for support during this ordeal. I suspect that had it not been for the intrepid Miss Elizabeth, I should be dead by now.'' He gave them a benign smile.

He turned to Aunt Bel and added, ''Your Purvis is indeed a treasure. I hope that she comes with you?''

''Why, whatever do you mean, sirrah?'' Aunt Bel said in a fluttery voice, tapping the earl lightly on his arm.

''Why do we not find some privacy so I may explain it to you in greater detail?'' He chuckled, the twinkle in his eyes matched by her sparkling smile.

''Well, I shall never forgive you for that business of

the body. Dreadful thing it was,'' Aunt Bel declared as
they continued their walk to the other side of the house.

The earl was last heard explaining how they had managed the deception, and why he and David had felt it
necessary to conceal the truth from everyone, even his
dearest Bel.

Alone in the library, Elizabeth turned to face David,
her beloved rake. She wanted everything settled as soon
as possible, for in the event she lost him, she wanted to
be out of this house as soon as she could.

"I suppose you realize that it is no longer required
that you marry me?" Elizabeth began. "With all that has
gone on, the announcement that we are not to marry will
be virtually ignored. I should think your father's resur-
rection from the dead, as it were, will have tongues
wagging for some time to come."

"You wish to hand me the mitten?" He sounded outraged, or at the very least deeply wounded.

"Well," she blustered, unable to lie outright to him,
"not jilt you, precisely. More like a mutual agreement.
I would set you free, for I have no wish to marry a gentleman who treats me like a sister"—she ignored the
several kisses that had been most decidedly unbrotherly—
"and may long to marry someone he truly cares for.
Unless . . . you must marry me for some vital reason?"
Not waiting for his response, she rushed ahead. "I overheard Mr. Fynes tell you to marry me, for a wife could
not testify against her husband. And you"—she cleared
a sudden obstruction from her throat—"said that it wasn't
what you wanted."

"Go on." He leaned against the desk, arms crossed,
staring at Elizabeth with a look that did not make her
words any easier.

"If there is trouble afoot, I shall marry you," she
declared resolutely, "for I do care about you, David, and
I would never wish anything bad to happen to you." She
clasped her hands in front of her, willing him to reveal
what it was that she could do for him. She had decided
that if he wished her to wed him in order to protect him
for some strange reason, she would, and gladly. As Rose
often said, half a loaf was better than none. And besides,

if given time, she might learn to entice him, so as to progress from teasing to something better.

"As to what precipitated the comment from Mr. Fynes. I had told him that there were moments when I could easily throttle Cousin Egbert. That prompted his reply, the one you unfortunately overheard."

"Then you do not *need* to marry me?" She thought she well concealed her disappointment from her voice. "Well, I hope that you will forgive me for shooting you, sir. But," she hastened to add, "you did ask for it, by coming into my room in the middle of the night." She reflected a moment while twisting the handkerchief in her clasp to mangled shreds. "Pity that Aunt Bel dashed in so quickly, or that you were foxed. Else you might have gone back out through the window, and no one would have been the wiser."

"I might have died without your care," he suggested, leaving the desk and walking to her.

"Oh, pooh. You would have found help," she replied, but did not sound convincing, even to her own ears. Then, determined to allow him freedom should he desire it, she said, "It is silly for Aunt Bel to say that we must marry merely because you were in my room on Valentine's Day. I believe that for two people to wed because of a superstition is not at all the thing."

Her resolution slipped when he reached out to bring her closer to him. She could feel the strength of his body as she was slowly drawn up against him.

He drew her closer yet, removing the shreds of cambric from her hands. He tossed the pathetic remains aside, then studied her face. "You care for me?"

She chewed her lower lip, uncertain what to admit. If she confessed her love for him, he might feel constrained to marry her out of pity. If she lied, and said she cared not a jot, he would be free, and she would be forever lost.

Deciding she would acknowledge something, she at last said, "I care for you."

"It is not like you to hedge, Elizabeth. One of the things I love about you is your fearlessness."

She heard only one word of what he said. "Love?" She snuggled closer to him, wondering if what she heard was true. Searching those beautiful hazel eyes, Elizabeth was at a loss on what to do next. What a pity David was merely a tease, not her splendid knight. Chivalry was indeed dead.

"I do *not* think of you as a sister, you know. Haven't for a long, long time." He feathered a finger along the sweet curve of her face, ending up in threading his hand through her curls.

Fascinated by this turn in their conversation, Elizabeth took another tiny step closer to him and said a breathless "Oh?"

"Indeed. I love you, my little one, and I suspect you love me as well, only are too wary to reveal it. Perhaps a bit of persuasion will help?"

With that, any gap between the two was closed completely.

Elizabeth cherished the feel of his strong arms about her, not to mention his powerful physique as she nestled in his embrace. If she had believed his previous kisses teasing, taunting, and quite provoking, this was not. This kiss was all any girl might wish for.

At last he released her, but just enough for her to look up at his face. There was no denying the expression she saw there. He loved her, plain as that aristocratic nose on his face.

"Ah, that look in your lovely aquamarine eyes tells me you do love me. Why is it so difficult to say?"

Honest as ever, Elizabeth said, "I did not wish you to feel compelled to marry me, as you might if I declared myself to you as you seemed to wish. I do love you, very much," she affirmed.

"My Valentine bride may come to me in March, but come she will. Since all in is readiness, I believe we should marry at once. I fear I cannot wait much longer for you, my little love."

As he captured her lips again in another kiss, Elizabeth decided that Aunt Bel's Valentine's Day superstition was not quite as foolish as she had first thought. In fact, it appeared to have considerable merit. Chivalrous knights might be well enough in books; she would happily settle for the man in whose arms she snuggled.

CUPID'S
MISTAKE

Prologue

March 4, 1810

Paul Templeton, Marquess of Blytheland, stared at the fire before him but did not see it. He sat, his fists clenched on his knees, and saw only the face of his wife as she was when he first met her. He remembered her as she was long before this night, not as she was now, lying in her room next to his, giving birth to the child of another man.

A loud groan came from the other room, and he raised his head briefly, listening. But it was only a groan and not her voice calling out for him. He turned his head away from the connecting door, despising himself for listening, for even being here, waiting. His love for Chloe had not quite died yet—he could tell by the persistent ache in his chest as he listened to her laboring to bring forth the child. He had given up too much of himself when he married her and even now it was hard to pull away, hard to admit that all the love he had invested in her had brought such bitter returns.

He looked into the grate again, and saw in the flickering red flames the color of her hair and the bright laughter she had always brought when she entered a room. He had fallen in love with her for that, and for her superior intellect; stupid women had always bored him. Chloe had excited his mind with her radical ideas and wide-ranging thoughts, and the wildness of her passion had excited him in the marriage bed.

He had been mad for her, though his friends had told him he was mad for marrying her. He should have listened. He should have heeded Lord Eldon, his best friend, when the man had shaken his head and said Chloe Fenwick was not a woman to marry but to bed. Blytheland had almost called Eldon out for that. Was she not a well-chaperoned and therefore innocent young lady, after all?

A high scream sounded from the other room, and then there was silence. The marquess tightened his fists, closed his eyes, straining to hear more. There was no other sound. Even now he wished to go to her, but he would not. He would wait for the news to come to him. He was tired of being a lapdog, running when called. He had been a fool, and he would be so no longer.

He had felt quite vindicated on their wedding night three years ago, for she had indeed been a virgin. She'd not repulsed his advances either after that, not until last year. He had not known what had changed . . . she had continued to hold her salons, writing her papers and discussing her ideas with her guests. Chloe had been well occupied, he had thought. He should have known better, once she had started to espouse the ideas from that Wollstonecraft woman's books. He'd seen too many people copy the style of life of the philosophers and teachers they'd admired, but he had thought Chloe more clear-minded than that. But she was as unoriginal as the others . . . Wollstonecraft had taken lovers, and Chloe had adopted that philosophy as well.

He could not, in the end, reason it away. He had enjoyed philosophical discussions himself, had enjoyed the talks he had had with Chloe. But when she had cheerfully come home one day, telling him she had taken a lover, he had felt as if he had received a blow to the gut. She could not even understand why he had grown so angry—did he not understand the principle of it?

He had not, and could not, though there was a space of time where he had actually tried. And yet . . . and yet, here he was, waiting for another man's child to be born, despising himself for a fool.

There was still no sound from the next room. A distant clock tolled the hour—it was two in the morning. He almost rose to go to the next room, but forced himself to sit where he was. At last a knock sounded on the door to his chamber, and he stood up at last and opened it.

It was Dr. Jenkins. The man's gray hair was tousled, his eyes tired and sad. He glanced at Lord Blytheland then looked away, clearing his throat.

"My lord . . . It is not good—"

"Chloe?"

"Her ladyship did not—she is—" The doctor straightened himself and looked Blytheland in the eyes. "She is dead, my lord."

Blytheland closed his eyes briefly and swallowed down the hot rage and sorrow that filled his throat. "The child?" he asked after a moment.

"It, also."

"I see." Blytheland turned and gazed into the fire again and tried not to see the image of his dead wife in the flames.

"My lord, what do you wish me to do?"

"What you usually do in these cases, I suppose. If you need anything, you may speak with my solicitors and tell them you have my approval." He glanced over his shoulder at Dr. Jenkins. "You may go." He heard the doctor step away from him.

He could not help himself and turned swiftly, impulsively holding out his hand. "Stop! I would like to know . . ." The doctor looked at him in inquiry. "Did she—did she ask for me at all? Say my name?"

A look of profound pity entered the doctor's eyes, and the marquess hated himself for being so weak as to ask. "No, my lord," the doctor said. "No, I am afraid she did not."

"I see," Blytheland said again, and turned away.

"I am sorry . . . she was a lovely lady."

"Yes."

There was only silence, then he heard the doctor's footsteps go away from him and the door close, and for a few minutes he did not move. The long sigh that came from him echoed in the room, and he rose at last. He wandered around his room and randomly picked up different items in it, looking at them and putting them down again. An odd blankness was in him, an aimlessness—he did not know what to do. Moving about seemed better somehow than simply sitting.

He came around at last to the trunk at the foot of his bed, and hesitated. Slowly he kneeled and opened it and took a leather violin case from it. He ran his hands over it slowly, feeling the smoothness of the leather. His hands hesitated for a moment, then he unlatched the case and brought out the instrument.

It was a beautiful thing, still polished and shining; he had not touched it in years. His music was another thing he had given up when he married Chloe. She had, for all her intelligence and education, not liked music much—he knew now it was because she did not have an ear for it. Anything in which she was not accomplished, she generally despised, but it was not something he realized until much, much later. But her reason for being against his playing had seemed so sensible—gentlemen did not take playing instruments with much seriousness; that was a thing for hired musicians only. Other people had thought the same thing—it had been his father's opinion, too. It was one more thing he had given up, a thing he had once thought had been an inseparable part of himself.

Could he still play it? He took the violin from its case, settled it against his chest, and drew the bow across the strings. A long wail came from the instrument—it needed tuning, of course.

His hands shook, and the violin dropped into the trunk. Not even this. He had given Chloe everything he could think of to keep her with him, had given up his music, too. Now it was all gone from him—he had no wife, no child, no music—and he had lost himself, somehow. Blytheland sank to his knees against his bed and pushed his palms against his eyes, pushing back the weeping he knew would come if he let it.

He took in a long, shuddering breath and rose to his feet. When he put out his hand to close the lid of the trunk, however, he hesitated. He still had the violin, and he remembered all the music he had ever played—it had been his special talent. Could a talent disappear if one did not practice it? He was not sure.

Blytheland brought out the violin again and carefully placed it back in its case. He would find out if he could still play, and if he got his music back, he would never let it go. He would never lose that part of him again, not to anyone.

The latches clicked in place, and the violin was protected once again inside its leather case. Blytheland pressed his lips together tightly. He would do as *he* wished from now on, and surround himself with people with whom *he* wished to associate, and do things that *he* pleased. Did he not still have his estates, his title, his fortune, things most men would envy? Was he not still young—only four-and-twenty years old—? Chloe was gone now, and she had been unfaithful to him. All his giving had been for nothing.

It would not happen again. He would make sure of it.

A sudden shuffling, fluttering noise made him look up, then he shrugged. It was no doubt the doctor in the next room attending to . . . his duties. A rising nausea filled Blytheland's throat and he closed his eyes tightly. He could not stay here, not tonight. He would go out—there were gaming hells enough where he could occupy his mind with either wagers or drink.

The marquess gazed around his room once again. It

seemed dark and empty and cold. Quickly he stood and pulled on the coat he had discarded earlier. He strode to the door of his chamber and for one moment his steps faltered as the grief and anger threatened to surface again.

No!

He shut the door firmly behind him.

There was no noise now except the ticking of the clock on the mantelpiece . . . and then a flutter, as if a bird had settled itself into the room. A slight glow moved from one corner of the marquess's chamber, and slowly, cautiously, the glow took shape: a face, shoulders, hands, torso, legs, and feet. And then, with another flutter, wings.

The boy who materialized gazed at the closed door with a slightly guilty look on his face. He had made a terrible mistake. He was usually very accurate with his arrows and his darts, and his timing had always been impeccable, but this time he had erred badly. He had meant to shoot Lord Blytheland when he was looking at another young lady, but the marquess had suddenly shifted his gaze at the last moment and had looked at Chloe Fenwick instead, falling desperately in love with her. The boy had hoped that it would work out anyway—often it did; for being loved to distraction was often irresistible to men and women alike and softened their hearts to love in return. But Chloe Fenwick had not been like that—she had been all mind and little heart.

The boy took in a breath and let it out again in a resolute burst of air. Well, there was nothing for it but for him to remedy the mistake. Now that the woman had died, the marquess was free once more to follow his heart. The boy suddenly felt uncertain. Lord Blytheland's face had looked as if he had decided to encase his heart in a steel cage, rather than let it free to love again. The boy hoped it was not too late. He frowned. He had never made a mistake before, except perhaps once; it was nonsense to think he might not remedy this situation. In all the millennia of his existence, his arrows had always shot with purpose and extreme accuracy, moving his victims—that is, targets—to love, to revulsion, or indifference, depending on if they needed a lesson in love or humility. He was Eros, the God of Love, and took whatever shape he needed to accomplish his goals—successfully. There was no reason to think he would make another mistake again.

The frown turned into a considering expression, and Eros reached over his shoulder to the quiver between the wings on his back and pulled out an arrow. He ran his thumb against the edge of the arrowhead in a contemplative manner. A slow, mischievous smile grew on his lips and a silent laugh shook his shoulders. The young lady he had first intended for Lord Blytheland would be in town the next year or two for her first Season. She was a little different now than she was when she and Lord Blytheland had passed in a crowd at a country fair, but not much; the two would still suit very well. Neither one remembered the other. He could start fresh: it would be as if the whole incident with Chloe had never happened, he was sure.

The boy turned to look out the window of the room, down at the tall figure walking purposefully down the street beneath the light of the full moon. Eros sighed, then slowly his form faded to a faint glow again. The windows of the room opened, and a breeze stirred the bed curtains. Then the windows closed, as if an invisible hand had moved them, and the room was silent and still once more.

Chapter 1

"Heavens, Cassandra, could you not have held your tongue?" cried Lady Hathaway. She pulled her shawl fretfully about her shoulders and eyed her oldest daughter with deep discontent. "I devoutly pray that you do not speak so—so unbecomingly when we go to the musicale tonight as you did just now!"

"But, Mama, I could not let people speak so harshly of Miss Matchett. Granted, Miss Matchett's style of dress is slightly dowdy, but she cannot help that. She does the best she can on the income she receives." Miss Cassandra Hathaway moved gracefully into the parlor with her mother and draped her own shawl upon the back of a chair before she sat down.

"I do not know how I shall show my face at Lady Amberley's ball next week," replied Lady Hathaway mournfully. She gazed at her daughter and sighed. At three-and-twenty, Cassandra was all that a mother could want in a daughter: accomplished, modest, good-hearted, and lovely to look upon. But she was also painfully blunt, and it was already bruited about that she was a bluestocking. It wanted but a week to the Season, and already Cassandra had attracted some male attention—from afar. Lady Hathaway greatly feared that Cassandra's impetuous speech and lack of dissembling would keep them there.

A concerned look crossed Cassandra's face and she leaned over and patted her mother on the arm in a comforting manner. "Never fear, Mama. I shall apologize for speaking so forwardly, and you may hold up your head with the best of them."

"And say you were much mistaken, too?" Lady Hathaway asked tentatively.

Her daughter looked at her, and a crease formed between her brows. "Whatever for? I believe I am not mistaken at all, and to say so would be a lie."

"Yes, well, my dear, sometimes one must make allowances—"

Cassandra's gaze turned reproachful. "Must I make allowances for cruelty? Have you and Papa not said many times that lying is wrong and cruelty worse?"

"Yes, of course, Cassandra, but, but . . ." Lady Hathaway drew to a faltering stop in the face of her daughter's attentive and inquiring expression. She sighed. How did one explain the need for discretion in society? It was not something her daughter had learned in the country or in all the lessons taught at her father's knee. "Well, I suppose I should be grateful that you remembered not to talk of your climbing boys."

Her daughter shifted in her seat and looked away.

"Oh, Cassandra! You have not taken in yet another one?"

Cassandra rose and her hands twisted together anxiously. "But, Mama, he was so little, and so hurt! He had sores on his feet and could hardly walk!" Tears formed in her eyes and she swallowed. "I have only sent four to the Dower house at home. Only four! And it does not take a great deal to feed and clothe them, I am sure."

Lady Hathaway gazed at her daughter, exasperated. "You have no idea how much it takes to feed children, especially boys! Why, I often feared your brother would eat us out of house and home when he was a child!" She pulled her shawl closer around her and sighed. "I suppose you are completely out of your pin money this quarter, too?"

Cassandra looked up at her mother and smiled. "Oh, no!

I have thought of a famous scheme! I wrote to our vicar last month and enlisted his aid. He was very approving of it, and so has got up a collection for the boys. So I only spent what it took to send little Tommy home."

Lady Hathaway groaned and sank into a chair.

"Is there something the matter, Mama?" Cassandra asked, a worried frown creasing her brow.

"No, of course not," Lady Hathaway replied, and she could not help the irony that crept into her voice. "Only that Vicar Thomason is one of the worst gossips in our county. I can depend upon him to spread the news of your generosity all over the village, and everyone will think you more of an eccentric than before. Heavens, why *do* you do these things, girl?"

Cassandra looked at her mother earnestly. "But if you had only seen little Tommy, Mama! He was so thin, and shaking with cold and pain. And that monster of a chimney sweep! He asked the most exorbitant price for him, and then he *hit* Tommy when the child did not come to me straightaway!"

Lady Hathaway's heart melted, though she kept her face stern. "Well . . . well, I suppose in this instance it would have been difficult to ignore. But, Cassandra, do try not to be so impulsive! And *don't* mention your activities to anyone in the *ton*, if you please!"

"But I do not see—"

The door opened, and Sir John wandered in, spectacles at the end of his nose, brandishing a dry quill. He looked vaguely about, and then his gaze sharpened as he spied his quarry. "Ah! Thucydides! Now how did it come to be in the parlor, and on this table? I know I had the book in my study yesterday." He gazed severely at his wife and daughter, as if somehow they had stolen into his inner sanctum and taken it for some nefarious purpose.

Lady Hathaway felt bewildered, but Cassandra smiled fondly at her father. "Papa, you know you brought it down this morning. You were looking for Euripides, and exchanged Thucydides for it."

"Oh, is that how it was?" Sir John's brow cleared, and his smile encompassed both Lady Hathaway and Cassandra in its beam. "Well, then, I shall be more careful, and not leave my books laying about." He put down his quill on the table, and picking up the book, he opened it. "Yes. Here it is . . ." he mused, and walked in the direction of the parlor door, leaving his quill behind.

"Oh, my love!" Lady Hathaway called to him.

"Eh?"

"I wish you would speak to your daughter!"

Sir John looked at his wife over his spectacles. "But I just did speak to her, my dear," he said reasonably.

"No, no! About her forwardness! Her lack of discretion!"

"What is this, my girl? Have you been seeing some man clandestinely?" He turned to Cassandra, his voice stern.

"Heavens, John!"

"Oh, no, Papa!"

"Well, what is it, then?" Sir John said impatiently.

"She is so . . . so impetuous in her speech!" Lady Hathaway said.

"And—?"

"Papa, I have taken in another climbing boy," Cassandra confessed. She looked at him earnestly and told him of her encounter with the chimney sweep. "Truly, I could not ignore his plight!"

Sir John's brow creased as he bent his powerful brain to the question. "Of course, you could not!" he said at last, and smiled proudly at his daughter. "That's my good girl!"

"But what of her reputation? Do you really think a well-connected gentleman would wish to marry a young woman who spends all her money on such things? It is not as if Cassandra's dowry were a fortune, after all!" Lady Hathaway protested.

Both husband and daughter looked at her with clear incomprehension.

Lady Hathaway let loose a sigh that was almost a moan of despair. How was she to tame Cassandra's impulses when Sir John agreed with her? There were a number of reformers amongst the *ton,* but they were people with a great deal of money and could afford such things. If it came to anyone's ears that Cassandra spent her allowance on climbing boys as if she considered them her sole responsibility, she would not only be seen as an eccentric but possibly a liability. Who would wish to marry a girl who would no doubt insist on bringing her charity cases along with her? Face, figure, and a good dowry would be as nothing compared with the burden of the climbing boys. It would be worse than marrying a young woman with a poverty-stricken family. Certainly it would be seen as a drain on the estate and the future of one's own family.

"Oh, heavens!" Lady Hathaway said, irritated. "You may do as you like, Cassandra, with your charity cases. But *don't* speak of them, if you please. It is not considered . . . polite conversation." Inspiration suddenly struck her and she smiled triumphantly. "Indeed, it would seem much like boasting of one's virtues, and you cannot think that would be at all becoming!"

Cassandra blushed and stared at her mother in consternation. "Oh, no! I would never, never wish to puff myself off in that manner!"

"See that you do not, then," Lady Hathaway said sternly. She sighed in relief. Thank goodness! It was one less thing to worry about in company. She glanced at the clock on the mantelpiece and rose from her chair. "We will need to be at the musicale in the next hour. Do go up and ready yourselves for it—hurry! And don't forget your quill, husband, for you will come wandering down again and lose yourself for at least a half hour looking for it."

An hour later her irritation faded completely when she gazed at her eldest child. Cassandra's green eyes sparkled, her cheeks glowed, and her lips were parted with eagerness. And nothing could have been more demure or ladylike than her demeanor upon entering Mrs. Bostitch's house. Lady Hathaway bit her lower lip anxiously. Perhaps this time all would go well. Cassandra's bluntness and scholarship were only known at home, around and about Tunbridge Wells, and not yet in London. Surely, she had talked stringently enough with Cassandra so that she would guard her tongue and not speak with such alarming forthrightness. But Lady Hathaway remembered how her daughter had reprimanded Lady Amberly and could not dismiss her uneasiness. Well, Cassandra had not precisely reprimanded—perhaps "corrected" was the more accurate word. Lady Hathaway winced. "Corrected" was no better.

But there had been sympathetic looks from some of the other ladies. Perhaps the display of Cassandra's warmth of heart and sense of Christian charity for Miss Matchett had found favor with a few of the ladies who were Lady Amberley's equals. Who, after all, could fault a generous impulse?

Lady Hathaway sighed and could not help the uneasiness that lodged itself in her heart. She knew London society far better than either her husband or her daughter, and well knew that diplomacy often took one farther than honesty and good-heartedness.

The first faint sounds of the musicians tuning their instruments floated down the hall as the Bostitchs' butler led her, Sir John, and Cassandra to the conservatory. Cassandra looked up at her mother, anticipation clearly in her smile, and Lady Hathaway smiled in return. Perhaps it would not be so bad, she thought. Perhaps Cassandra would occupy her mind with the music and keep her comments to musical appreciation and away from any other subject.

Lady Hathaway sighed again. One could always hope.

Paul, Marquess of Blytheland, brushed the air in front of him with his hand, as if brushing away an annoying fly. He

frowned. This had happened before. It was as if a warm
draft of air briefly blew upon his face. Sometimes it was accompanied by a soft sound, like the fluttering of wings. He
would not have thought much of it had it occurred out of
doors, but it had lately happened indoors, at night, and now
mostly just before a performance. Perhaps someone had
opened a window. He shrugged and bent his attention upon
his violin again.

An odd, sharp ache suddenly struck his chest, a sudden
weeping agony, and the image of Chloe flashed before him.
He drew in a long, slow breath, and then it disappeared.
This was another thing that had happened before. He knew
what this was, however. Every once in a while, when he
was preparing to play his violin, the anticipated emotion of
the music opened the wounds of the past, and painful memories of his wife would try to surface once again. He had always been successful in suppressing them—better now, for
she had died more than two years ago. But that was the
danger of playing music, was it not? Music was an emotional thing, after all. In fact, he had lately been very successful at using that emotion and putting it into his
performances. That was the secret of an artist, a great musician once told him: using one's own pain and making it
sing in one's music. Lord Blytheland smiled and raised his
eyes to the guests waiting in front of him.

And his fingers failed on the strings of his violin. The instrument let out a small moan at being so mishandled, but
the marquess ignored it.

She was not the most beautiful lady he had ever seen, but
she was, indeed, very lovely. The lady caught him staring,
blushed, then looked away. Blytheland recovered himself.
He concentrated on tuning his violin, and accidentally
twisted a pin too far. He cursed under his breath and
glanced toward the lady again. She walked into the room
with a slightly familiar, graying gentleman and a middle-
aged lady who bore a strong resemblance to the young

woman—her parents, no doubt. He would recall the name
of the gentleman if he gave himself time to think of it. He
twisted the pin again, and now it was too loose.

"May I be of assistance, my lord?" asked one of the musicians politely.

"What? Oh, no, my good man, just a little nervous."

The musician smiled as he bowed in assent. Blytheland
at last tuned his violin correctly and tried not to look at the
young woman in the audience.

He failed. She seemed almost to float within her dress,
like a fairy woman walking through a mist of rose silk and
silver net. She glanced at him from across the room, and
there was something at once innocent and frank in her gaze.
He wondered who she was.

He smiled to himself. It was often thus just before and
during a performance. He had often thought the anticipation and sizzling energy he always felt as he prepared to
play and when he was in the midst of a performance was
similar to that of seduction. Music was a sensual thing that
made the heart beat faster and made the mind fly in wild
imaginings. It was easy to be influenced by the sight of a
lovely woman when in such a state.

His smile turned bitter. Still, after two years, after his experience with Chloe, he was susceptible. How contemptible
and weak he was! But he had learned to be discriminating,
at least. All he needed was to find some fault with the
woman and concentrate on that, and he would grow bored
or contemptuous. There was nothing better than boredom
or contempt to obliterate the beginnings of any interest he
might feel. If his attention was still tied to the young
woman by the end of the piece, he would be sure to obliterate it quite thoroughly.

I will be on my best behavior, Cassandra thought to herself, and will not worry Mama again. She sat down with her
parents, fairly close to the musicians, feeling slightly em-

barrassed at her own behavior, but could not help glancing from time to time at the violinist who had stared at her so when she first came in. She gave herself a pinch. There! You will *not* stare, because you know it is rude, and heaven help you if Mama catches you doing it. She smiled, satisfied. She *could* be vigilant of her own behavior.

She rewarded herself with another glance at the violinist—it was just a glance, after all, not a stare. Of course, he was not one of the professional musicians, for his clothes were too fine for that. He affected a slightly more colorful raiment than most other gentlemen she'd seen so far, but it suited him. His golden hair was swept back and he wore a coat of Bath superfine. His waistcoat was blue-and-silver chased, and in the intricate folds of his neckcloth sparkled a sapphire pin. If his collar was not so high as some she had seen, perhaps it was because it would interfere with the playing of his violin. Was he a dandy, perhaps? She saw none of the padding to broaden the shoulders that so many dandies used, however, and his knee breeches outlined his legs—Cassandra looked away, blushing, and gave herself another admonishing pinch. She was not merely glancing, but *staring* again, and she must not do so, for she had promised her mother to pay strict attention to her manners.

A tapping of the baton brought Cassandra's attention to the musicians again. She felt irritated at herself. She had been so intent on not looking at the man that she had missed hearing who he was, and what the musicians would play. Perhaps it was a piece she had heard before—she had a good memory for music, and she would know the title as soon as she heard the first few notes.

It was a Mozart divertimento. Cassandra sighed and lifted her eyes to the violinist again; surely it was proper to look at him while he was playing.

He was looking at her, and she could feel her face become warm. Once again she looked away, but not before she noticed that he had blue eyes. The music! That is why you came to the musicale, Cassandra told herself sternly. Do pay attention!

The music flowed around her, and the high, sweet notes pulsed an alluring andante beat. Once again she looked up, and to her relief she saw the violinist was not looking at her. Cassandra allowed herself to be pulled into the music, as she always had in the past. And yet she could not feel comfortable. The music seemed different somehow—that was why she was feeling so strange. The rhythm became slow, but at the end of the movement she felt breathless, as if she had been running, and that had never happened to her before. The violinist was a virtuoso, it was clear; it was the skill and intensity of his performance that made her feel so.

And yet, the divertimento finished before she was quite aware it had come near the end. Cassandra applauded politely, again annoyed at herself. She had not listened closely as she had always done, but had been partly caught up in watching the violinist. How stupid she was being! One came to a musicale to listen to music, not to stare at the company or the musicians.

The violinist bowed very elegantly to the crowd, and then once again in her direction. Cassandra blushed and looked down at her lap. Did he mean to do that?

"Quite excellent," Lady Hathaway commented. "It is almost a pity young Blytheland is a marquess. His talent outshines most professionals."

So, he is the Marquess of Blytheland, thought Cassandra. And it seems Mama knows him—or knows of him. She shook herself mentally. Really! Her thoughts were quite wayward this evening. She looked up again and saw that the marquess was no longer with the musicians. She firmly tamped down a spark of disappointment. She was here to listen to music, not think of possible beaux. Cassandra smiled wryly to herself. As if someone as talented and handsome as the marquess could be one of hers! She understood by now that she could not rate her attractions high at all; to think that Lord Blytheland would—Sheer foolishness!

"Ah, Sir John! I hope I find you well?" said a soft baritone voice next to her. Cassandra looked up. It was the marquess.

"Eh? Oh, yes, Blytheland!" Sir John wiped his spectacles with the end of his neckcloth and put them on his nose again. "Quite well, quite well! And how does the duke, your father? I understand he has found a manuscript of great antiquity—an Arabic translation of *De Res Medicos*. I am not at all proficient in Arabic, however—Eh, what was that, my love?"

Lady Hathaway smiled sweetly at her husband. "My dear, I am sure Lord Blytheland would like to discuss his father's discovery at length—*later*."

Sir John's eyes focused at last upon his wife and daughter. "Ah, of course! Not enough time at a musicale."

"But perhaps at supper?" said the marquess. His gaze went to Cassandra, and he smiled at her. Cassandra could feel her face grow warm, but she could not help responding with one of her own. His smile was truly charming—it lifted up on one side of his mouth more than the other and gave him a slightly boyish look.

At his wife's nudge, Sir John looked at the marquess and his daughter. "Ah, yes! If you would permit me to introduce my wife and daughter . . ."

The marquess bowed most elegantly over Lady Hathaway's hand and Cassandra's. Perhaps it was her imagination, but did he linger just a little more over her hand than her mother's? His lips hovered just a few inches above her fingers before he rose from his bow. She could feel the warmth of his hand through her gloves, and when he released her hand she felt, almost, as if the warmth remained.

"I am most pleased to meet you, my lord," said Cassandra.

"And I, also. But I would be further pleased if you accompanied me to the supper later—if you would do me the honor?" He looked to Sir John and Lady Hathaway for permission. Lady Hathaway smiled and nodded.

"Oh, yes!" Cassandra said, then blushed. "That is, I am flattered that you ask me, sir. I would be happy to accompany you."

The marquess smiled at her again, bowed to Sir John and Lady Hathaway, and left. Cassandra watched his passage through the crowd. Could it be that he found her attractive? It seemed that some men had found her so, since her arrival in London. However, they never did call again after the first couple of meetings. It was a surface, transitory thing then, this apparent attraction, and not to be taken seriously, she was sure.

She had never considered her looks before—it never seemed important, and Papa had always taught her that true beauty came from the mind and heart. But since they'd come to town, the notion that one's physical appearance had more than ordinary significance—aside from sheer aesthetic appreciation—to the world at large, kept intruding upon her attention. Indeed, she was nigh infected with the idea. Certainly, the marquess's appearance seemed to have affected her in more than a purely aesthetic way. She shook her head. How odd it was!

She felt a touch on her arm and found her mother gazing sternly at her. "Now, Cassandra, when Lord Blytheland comes to take you into supper, you must be all that is amiable and pleasant. And please do not blurt out every thought that comes to your mind. Gentlemen do not find that way of speaking at all attractive."

"Yes, Mama," Cassandra said.

A look of deep misgiving came over Lady Hathaway's face.

"I will *try,* Mama!" Cassandra exclaimed. "Truly! Have I not tried these past weeks?"

Lady Hathaway's expression softened. "I know you have

tried, my dear, and you have improved. But really, do be careful."

The sound of tuning instruments made Cassandra glance eagerly at the musicians again, and she gave her mother a hasty yes in reply. This time she heard the name of the piece—a violin sonata by Herr von Beethoven.

For the first time in her life, Cassandra could not keep her mind on the music playing before her. It was as if each sweet note conspired to make her think of Lord Blytheland and the way he looked, and smiled, and held her hand. It did not help at all when it was time for him to play the solo. His manner was cool and polite as he stood by the orchestra. But once he put the violin against his chest it seemed as if some otherworldly spirit seized him, for his bow and fingers attacked and caressed the strings and brought forth music that sang from heaven or cried up from hell—she knew not which.

Finally, after what seemed an age, the music stopped. Cassandra found she could breathe again in a normal fashion. She still looked at him, and it appeared as if his smile was just a little warmer in her direction when he bowed to the audience. She looked away, irritated at herself for blushing. How silly she was being! She was acting no differently than the shallow schoolgirls she'd known at the Bath girl's school she had stayed in—until, thankfully, Papa had rescued her. There was no education to gain there, Papa had said, and he was in the right of it.

She would speak honestly when they went into supper, she thought, determined to rid herself of the silliness that threatened to overcome her. If the marquess did not like it, why then she was certain Papa would say the man was unworthy of a man's—or woman's—esteem.

Cassandra felt a moment's unease when she remembered her mother's dictum. It was true she tended to speak before she thought. But this time, she would be careful of that. She would think through her responses before she spoke and make certain she spoke as carefully—as truly—as she could. There could be no offense in that.

Perhaps it was a slight noise or a little breeze stirred by his movement toward her, but Cassandra was suddenly aware of the marquess's presence. She looked up and found him smiling down at her.

"Shall we go in to supper, Miss Hathaway?"

Cassandra looked uncertainly at her mother, for her father had left her side to talk with an acquaintance, but Lady Hathaway merely smiled and nodded. "Of course, my dear, do go. Your father and I will follow you, as soon as I can tear him away from discussing his musical theories."

"Thank you, my lord, I shall be pleased to accompany you." Cassandra glanced at him. The marquess was still smiling at her, and she could not help smiling back. He took her hand in his own—gently, caressingly, as if it were some rare treasure. She rose, and he led her to the supper room.

Mrs. Bostitch had set up an informal supper, with little tables in the middle of the room and sideboards filled with delicacies next to the walls. The marquess led Cassandra to a small table set behind some palm fronds. Though the table was otherwise not secluded in any way, Cassandra felt as if the plants lent the table a certain intimacy. She smiled at herself. How fanciful she was becoming! Her parents were clearly in sight—she could see her mother standing patiently next to her father as he talked with his friend. Yet when she looked up at Lord Blytheland, she felt almost as if she were alone in a small room with him. There was something about his deep blue eyes, whose penetrating look seemed to read her heart as well as he surely read music. He said nothing, but seemed content for the while to look at her. His gaze seemed almost assessing—then he glanced away briefly, and she was sure she fancied the whole of it.

"You play beautifully, my lord," Cassandra said. She felt

she must say something, for his gaze and the silence had stretched out to an uncomfortable length. "I think the second movement of the sonata was especially well done."

"You are musical, then, Miss Hathaway?"

"Oh, I play the pianoforte, but I am in no way the virtuoso you are."

"You flatter me, ma'am."

Cassandra raised her eyes to his. "Oh, no, I never flatter. You must be quite an acclaimed musician, for I have heard many violinists, but you are far better than any I have heard so far."

Blytheland began to feel a touch of boredom. He had heard these words before, from other quite insipid misses. That was why he generally kept himself to older, much more sophisticated women—fast widows preferably. He wondered if Miss Hathaway was going to gush out further tedious little phrases. It was just as well if she did—that would be the flaw he would concentrate upon, and thus banish any incipient interest he might have. He let his gaze wander away from her.

"However, I did think you could have added a little more forte in the middle phrases of the first movement."

Blytheland returned his gaze swiftly to Miss Hathaway's face. Her expression was open and clear of guile or coquetry. Indeed, her brow creased in thought, and her eyes seemed to consider the subject seriously.

"How so?" He wondered how much of music Miss Hathaway really knew.

"Well, I have always believed that Herr Beethoven favored the pianoforte above any other instrument, and it is clear even in this sonata. However, it *is* a piano and *violin* sonata, and the composer gave the violin the opportunity to express itself in the middle phrases of the first movement by having the pianoforte play a less complex melody than the violin there. It was your opportunity to establish that this, indeed, was the violin's place. I felt you did not take complete advantage of the opportunity."

The marquess did not know whether to feel delighted or annoyed. He looked at her large green eyes, her soft pink lips, and delicate skin. She dressed in good taste and becomingly—not daringly—but well enough to enhance her charms and hint at more intriguing assets.

For now it could not hurt to be delighted, he decided.

"You are quite right, Miss Hathaway. That passage has always been a difficult one for me, and I tend to take it with more caution and less spirit than I should."

Miss Hathaway looked at him in a considering manner. "But you are clearly a most excellent musician. I would think you could easily overcome any difficulty and play it with ease."

He now saw she said this with no intention to flatter. She furrowed her brow as if she were working out a puzzle, and she stated her opinion simply, as if she expected her reasoning would be taken seriously.

Blytheland smiled. "I fear you vastly overrate my abilities."

She gazed at him, her eyes earnest. "Oh, no, my lord. I fear *you* vastly *underrate* your abilities. I am excessively fond of music, and I have never heard anyone quite as proficient as you are." She reached over in an impulsive gesture and pressed his hand. "You really should have more confidence in yourself, Lord Blytheland," she said kindly. "How else can you continue to improve?"

The marquess opened his mouth and then shut it, suddenly bereft of words. He wondered if she was aware that she praised and insulted in the same breath. And yet, he felt he could not take offense, for clearly she spoke nothing but what she perceived to be the truth, and clearly she meant well. A mischievous part of his mind wondered how other people took her blunt statements. It would be very, very amusing to see.

"Improve?" he said. "and I thought you said I was of virtuoso status! I am sorely cast down, Miss Hathaway." He put on a look of extreme dejection.

He noticed she blushed wonderfully. "I did not mean— That is to say—" She stopped, looked at him straightly, and lifted her chin. "You, my lord, are a terrible tease."

"I?" He put on a wounded expression and spread his hand over his heart. "My dear Miss Hathaway, how can you say so?"

"Very easily! Do you have sisters?"

"Yes, I do."

"Then I daresay you were a menace to them."

"Not I! Rather the opposite. Never was a poor, helpless boy so besieged by his termagant sisters."

"With reason, I am sure!" But her lips quivered upward.

"Ah, there you are!"

Blytheland turned to find that Lady Hathaway had arrived with Sir John in tow. Sir John had an abstracted air about him, as if he were in profound thought. The lady smiled benevolently at her daughter and the marquess.

"I am terribly sorry we were delayed," she said. "I hope Cassandra has been keeping you entertained." Blytheland noted wryly that she did not look sorry in the least. No doubt she considered him a good "catch" for her daughter. He would put an end to that notion, and soon . . . although it could not hurt to linger in Miss Hathaway's presence for just a little longer.

"Quite," he replied. "Miss Hathaway, I find, is a music connoisseur." He turned to Miss Hathaway. "Do you play your pianoforte often, ma'am?"

"Oh, I try, but it is nothing—not with the skill you have at the violin, my lord." Miss Hathaway blushed, but the marquess felt perhaps this was not false modesty. There were very few ladies who played with much skill or talent, after all.

"Perhaps I may ask that you play for me at some time,

Miss Hathaway?" Blytheland surprised himself. He did not intend to say that at all. But as he looked into her beautiful eyes, he could not help but continue. "Tomorrow, if it is not inconvenient?"

Lord Blytheland cursed himself roundly as he put away his violin and made ready to leave Mrs. Bostitch's house. If he had any sense at all, he'd quit society and become a monk. He'd only meant to seek out some flaw in Miss Hathaway when he had introduced himself to her and her family. Well, he'd found one, but had he concentrated upon it and politely detached himself from her and his attraction to her? No, he had not. Instead, he had asked to call upon the Hathaways and asked to listen to Miss Hathaway play the piano.

An image of Lady Hathaway's smug smile and eager agreement that Miss Hathaway should play for him came before him. He grimaced. Not only had he allowed himself to be drawn into the Miss Hathaway's company, he had raised Lady Hathaway's matrimonial hopes for her daughter. He sincerely hoped Miss Cassandra Hathaway was a wretched pianist and he could depress any pretensions in that quarter, and in her mother. He closed and latched his violin case with a decided snap.

"Hit a sour note, old man?" said a familiar voice.

Blytheland looked up to see his friend Lord Eldon, and he grinned. "No. Not that you'd notice if I did—which makes me wonder why you are here, El."

"Oh, you know how it is with m'sister and the mater. It isn't enough to have my younger brother caught in the parson's mousetrap—although I must say Susan is quite a pretty little thing—they must have me caught, too." Lord Eldon held up a hand. "And before you accuse me of being led around by the nose by the females in my family, I came only because St. Vire's here—damnably fond of music

these days, it seems—he told me he'd reveal the trick to
trying a perfect Mathematical."

Blytheland eyed the impeccably tied neckcloth around
his friend's collar. "Seems like you already know the trick,
El."

Eldon looked pained. "One may always improve. A man
of fashion does not rest on his laurels."

"Nor does he ignore the ladies when his mother tells him
he needs to produce heirs."

Eldon gave a disappointed sigh. "How you malign me—"
But a grin broke out on his face. "Well, there it is. If I don't
see what's available in the marriage market this year, I'll
never hear the last of it from the mater, and will have to
leave town just to get out of earshot. Damned awkward,
that, especially when I need to replenish my supply of
waistcoats." He shrugged. "I'll just cast a glance at the
usual gaggle at Almack's, tell the mater they're not worthy
of the Eldon name, then spend the rest of my time at
White's." He lifted an eyebrow at Blytheland. "Although I
must say, the lady to whom you were so attentive was
above the usual run of misses one sees in London these
days. Thinking of giving another try at a nursery, Blythe?"

The marquess turned a sardonic eye to his friend. "Misery loves company, is that it? A nursery—hardly. Why you
should think so is beyond me. Just because a man speaks
with a young woman, it does not mean he's thinking of
matrimony."

"True, true. But it seems she was accompanied by her
parents . . . and I've not seen you go near a marriageable
young thing in a while."

Blytheland shrugged. "Sir John Hathaway is a classical
scholar, as is my father, and they are acquainted. Sir John
wished to ask after an ancient manuscript, that is all."

"Of course." Lord Eldon grinned widely.

"Stubble it, El." The marquess picked up his violin case

and gave his friend an irritated glance before stalking from the room.

"Anything you say, Blythe," Eldon called after him and chuckled.

Eros kept himself fairly insubstantial and hovered near the ceiling so that his glow would blend with that of the chandelier's candlelight. Well, he had done it, and he was quite satisfied. He had known for a long time that Miss Cassandra Hathaway would be the right mate for Lord Blytheland, although it had taken him three tries to do it. He had hit the marquess each time, but for some reason, the man had seemed unmoved, as if he had not seen Cassandra at all. Instead, he had had a brief affair with some other woman, over in less than a month.

The thought that something was quite wrong with the marquess had definitely occurred to Eros, and even now made him feel a little uneasy. He shook his head and grinned. Well, it was of no matter now; Lord Blytheland had seen Cassandra at last, and certainly must have fallen in love with her.

Chapter 2

"Cassandra," said Psyche, "do listen to me."

Cassandra turned slowly toward her younger sister as if pulled unwillingly from a delightful dream. She looked at the girl blankly.

"I am sorry, Psyche. Did you say something?"

"Only that you have knotted your fringe in a terrible tangle."

"Oh, have I?" Cassandra looked down in her lap at the fringe she was trying to make. Her face suddenly lost its dreamlike expression and she let out an exasperated sigh. "Oh, good heavens! So I have." She turned a rueful smile to her sister. "Dear Psyche, do be a good child and unknot this for me. You know how terrible I am at fringing, and you are so good at disentangling things."

"I don't know why you even try fringing at all, Cassandra," Psyche said, taking the piecework from her sister and curling up in an armchair by the parlor fire. She carefully started picking it apart. "I thought you had given it up long ago."

"Well, I thought it might be good for me. Mama says that fine work helps keep one even-tempered."

"I do not see how she can say that," Psyche replied, cocking her head to one side in a considering manner. "I have always been good at needlework, but Mama always says I am too unruly for words." She gazed assessingly at Cassandra. "And why do you need to be even-tempered?"

Psyche had always thought that Cassandra must be the best-behaved young lady ever, for she never got into trouble like she herself did.

"Oh, goodness, I don't know! I truly do not know what came over me—I detest fringing." Cassandra rose from her chair and poked at the fire in the grate.

"Harry says it's the marquess." Psyche nodded her head wisely.

"Really, Psyche, how can you say so?" She turned around and faced her sister. Psyche smiled privately to herself. She'd be willing to wager that the pink in Cassandra's cheeks was *not* caused by the heat of the fire alone.

"Well, Cassandra, I don't. That's what *Harry* says."

"You know very well that your Harry is purely imaginary. And you also know Mama does not like you to speak about him—it! You are all of twelve, Psyche, and should have outgrown your pretend playmate long ago."

"He isn't pretend. Besides, Papa believes me."

"Oh, I daresay Papa thinks you are speaking in metaphors." Cassandra walked to the pianoforte and absently toyed with a melody.

"No he doesn't, and Papa does believe me—he told me so!" Psyche retorted. "Not only that, but Harry is here right this minute, turning the pages of—what is it? Oh, it's Aristophanes."

Cassandra turned to look at the open book Psyche pointed to across the room. It sat on a table close to the window. As she watched, a page flipped over. She started, but then recovered.

"Oh, nonsense, Psyche! It is only that this house is dreadfully drafty. It is merely a breeze—and yes, look here—someone's left the window open." Cassandra closed it with a snap.

"Window or no, Cassandra, you must admit that some things have come about that you couldn't account for."

"Such as—?"

"Our butler and housekeeper. They used to have dreadful rows belowstairs, and now the maids say the Thrimbles act like a new-wed pair. Harry told me he detested their noise and so he shot his arrows at them."

Cassandra smiled kindly. "I think it was more the books on marriage Vicar Thomason asked me to give them, Psyche, than any of Harry's arrows." She let out an exasperated breath. "Oh, now you have me talking of him—it!—as if Harry were real!" Her eyes settled on the clock upon the mantelpiece. "Oh, heavens! I must change my dress! I think the mar—That is, we will be having callers soon." Gathering up her skirts, Cassandra rushed out the door.

"I told you."

Psyche put down the fringe and looked at the boy sitting on the table near the window. She made a face at him. "So you did. But I really wish you would let another one of my family see you, too!"

Harry leaned back, clasping one knee in his hands, and his wings waved lazily. He grinned. "You needn't talk about me, you know. Then there would be nothing for them to disbelieve."

"How can I stop when you pinch housemaids, for instance? And Kenneth was unjustly accused of it, too!"

"I do not pinch housemaids," Harry replied loftily. "It was only *one* housemaid. Besides, it is not as if your brother hasn't pinched housemaids himself—and got away with it."

"Well, I think it's beastly of you—whatever did that poor maid do to you?"

"Oh, nothing—more's the pity," Harry said. He looked up at the ceiling, folded his wings, and looked quite angelic.

Psyche put her hands on her waist. "Don't come the innocent with me, Harry! I know you must have been up to mischief!"

"Not I! I was only seeing that justice was done."

"What, by pinching the maid?"

"No, by seeing that your brother was accused of it. I find it unfair that any number of housemaids have fallen head-over-tails in love with Kenneth, and all he does is steal a kiss and pinch them."

"I should hope that is all he does with them! Mama and Papa would be quite angry if he fell in love and ran off with one of them!"

Harry smiled in a superior manner. "You are such an innocent, Psyche. But never fear. I will make sure he will do nothing scandalous."

She looked at him suspiciously, then sighed. "Well, at least Papa likes to hear of you."

"He likes to hear *stories* of me, you mean."

"Do you think, then, that he does not believe me, either?" Psyche felt a little bereft at that. It was a lonesome sort of thing to have a dear friend and not be able to introduce him to anyone else.

"Oh, he would like to, but he believes you have a fine imagination and would make a good writer of improving tales for children someday." Harry grinned mischievously. Psyche looked reprovingly at him. He had been eavesdropping again, she was certain, and she never did feel quite right about it—although she had to admit it did have its uses.

"Well, I cannot see why he should think that," Psyche replied, wrinkling her nose. "I detest improving tales." She sighed. "But Papa does like to believe the best of us, and so perhaps he has forgotten that I do not like such stories." Psyche gazed at Harry questioningly, hoping that he might enlighten her as to her father's state of mind.

Harry shrugged his shoulders and looked bored. He opened the window that Cassandra had just closed and looked out at the street. A small breeze lifted one lock of his golden hair and a ray of sun suddenly broke through the clouds to shine upon his face. He glanced at her and smiled.

Psyche smiled back. She was glad he had decided to come with her to London, for otherwise she'd be bored to tears. Sometimes she would accompany Mama and Cassandra on a shopping expedition or drive to one of the parks. But aside from these activities and her discovery of many delightful Minerva Press novels, as well as attending to Cassandra giving her lessons in geography and the Italian language, there was little for Psyche to do. So she was thankful that Harry was here. There is nothing like a change in one's circumstances, she thought, to make one appreciate one's friends. And Harry was her very best friend, for she had known him ever since she was a very little girl.

She'd been about seven years old at the time—really not much more than a baby. She'd been with her older brother Kenneth near the lake at their country home. Awaking from a doze in the sun, she had found that Kenneth had either hidden himself or had left her alone, and it was growing quite dark. Crying because she could not find her way back home, she stumbled into the woods that circled part of the lake and grew more frightened.

And then there he was. Psyche had thought he was one of those angels her nurse had told her about, for he had white wings and wore white clothing. But he had laughed at her and shook his head when she asked him this, and he told her his name. Well, it was hard to get her tongue around it then, so she had called him Harry instead, and never bothered to change it.

He grew up, as she did, although he seemed always to be a few years older than she was—he looked to be twelve or thirteen years of age now, although he would never tell her how old he actually was. She had learned more about him, however, not so much from Harry, for he found such things tedious to relate—but from her father's books. He looked a little like the pictures in those books, although his nose didn't come down straight from his forehead like the people depicted in them had, but it looked like her own quite normal one.

She wished the rest of her resembled Harry, for she was short rather than tall, and instead of blue eyes and blond hair, she had a mop of unruly red curls and large, undistinguished gray eyes. She'd learned that his dress—for it looked like a very short dress, indeed—was called a chiton. Psyche thought that perhaps she should have been embarrassed that his bare legs showed, or when he'd unpin one shoulder of his chiton when he shot his arrows, but he was Harry, and she'd known him for so long that it did not matter. But his arrows! Those were another thing altogether.

In fact, Harry was pulling one from his ever-present quiver right now, his gaze intent on something in the street below. A wide, crooked grin was forming on his lips. Psyche knew that grin, and alarm flashed through her.

"Harry, what *are* you doing? Get away from that window!"

It was too late. He drew back his bow and loosed the arrow before she could rush to his side.

"A hit!" he crowed. "Two with one shot!"

"Oh, Harry!" Psyche cried.

She leaned out the window to see whom he had struck. There! A tall young man held a fainting lady in his arms. The arrow had apparently hit the young man through the arm and scratched the lady as well. Psyche could see the arrow fading from sight as she watched.

"*Ma chère* Stephanie!"

"Oh, Phillipe, Phillipe!"

They kissed passionately while onlookers made a wide berth around them. Some people cheered. Psyche blushed and covered her eyes.

"Oh, Harry, how could you? In broad daylight and in the middle of the street as well!" She looked at him reproachfully through her fingers.

"*They* don't seem to mind," Harry said carelessly. He

twirled another arrow between his fingers in a negligent manner, a lazy smile on his face.

Psyche peeked between her fingers at the entwined couple again, this time with more interest. She had rarely seen Harry shoot people or the immediate after-effects of one of his arrows; it had been very embarrassing to watch usually well-behaved people kiss and act in a very silly manner. She'd mostly only seen Harry's complacent reaction after he'd made a successful hit. She had become a little curious lately, however, for she had once caught her parents kissing—briefly—and she supposed it was something adults did from time to time. "Did it hurt them? Your arrows do look sharp, you know."

"Mortals are too dense to feel much. They felt nothing—not the arrows, that is."

"My, it did act quickly, didn't it?"

"I've told you it does."

"Well, you are wont to boast, Harry, you know you are!"

"Not I! I am in general very truthful."

She made a face at him, then leaned against the windowsill next to him to get a better look at the pair outside. "Do they breathe much when they do that, Harry?"

"Very much. They usually gasp like fish."

"Good heavens, Psyche! Stop acting like a hoyden and remove yourself from that window!"

Psyche jerked upright immediately at her mother's voice and bumped her head on the casement handle. She rubbed her temple gingerly. "Yes, Mama," she said and stepped quickly away from the window. She could not help casting a glance at Harry, who was still watching the scene below.

"What *were* you looking at?" Lady Hathaway said, going to where Psyche had stood. She leaned over and peered out the window, then straightened herself suddenly. "Scandalous! In broad daylight! I do believe it is—My word. Mademoiselle Lavoisin and the Comte de la Fer. I never would have thought it, although they do make a handsome couple. The last I heard, they were at daggers drawn with each other! One would think that well-born emigrés would comport themselves with more discretion! However, they *are* French." Lady Hathaway turned, a small smile of triumph on her lips. "And Hetty Chatwick is out of town today! Well, I shall have something to tell *her* for a change!"

Lady Hathaway's gaze encountered her youngest daughter, and her smile abruptly disappeared. Her eyes became stern. "And what, may I ask, were you doing staring—yes, staring!—at such shocking behavior?"

"Well, Har—" began Psyche, but Harry shook his head at her. "That is, I heard a scream, and I thought someone was injured! So naturally, I looked to see if someone was indeed hurt, so I could call for help if it were needed."

Her mother's eyes narrowed in a considering manner. Psyche held her breath.

Lady Hathaway smiled then, though her eyes still held a bit of sternness. "I shall let it go this time, child, for I know you are a good girl at heart. But please! You *must* try to comport yourself with more decorum, and *not* stare or lean out of the window no matter what may be occurring in the streets! Although, I must say," Lady Hathaway mused, "that such shocking behavior would make anyone stare, to be sure! The Comte de la Fer, of all things! And I had thought him very ancient regime in his manners."

"Oh, Mama, I am so sorry!" cried Psyche, feeling tears come to her eyes. She ran to her mother and put her arms around her. She felt terrible that she had lied, for she never liked to do so. She cast Harry a burning look, and he had the grace to look ashamed.

"Now, now, my dear girl, there is nothing to cry about. You take these things too much to heart, Psyche." Lady Hathaway smiled and smoothed her daughter's hair back fondly. "My, your hair does go every which way, does it not? Do go up and get it brushed properly, love. The Mar-

quess of Blytheland is calling on Cassandra! Can you believe it? I shall allow you to come for a short while, but you
must only speak when spoken to! He has come to see Cassandra, and I do hope she minds her tongue for once."

"I am very glad Cassandra has an admirer, Mama. She is
a very good girl, isn't she? So she deserves someone who
will love her as we do," Psyche said loyally.

Lady Hathaway sighed. "I certainly hope so. Now do go,
Psyche and tidy yourself."

Psyche went out of the parlor, with Harry trailing behind.
She did not look at him.

"Psyche."

Silence.

"Psyche, don't be angry with me."

The girl turned and looked at her friend. "You made me
lie to Mama."

"You know it was for the best, Psyche! You would have
received a terrible scold about making up stories, and you
would have been sent up to your room."

Harry's face looked solemn and sad. Psyche's heart
melted. She could never stay angry with him for long.
"Well, I suppose it wasn't so horrid. Let's go up, then."

"May I come to see this marquess of Cassandra's?"

Psyche looked warily at him.

"It's only to see what sort of man he is—if he truly deserves to be Cassandra's suitor."

"Oh . . . very well, then. But no tricks! And promise you
will leave your arrows behind."

"I? Tricks?"

"Harry!"

Harry sighed. "I promise."

Chapter 3

When Thrimble, the butler, announced the marquess, my lord saw no one in the parlor except a young, mop-haired girl. He felt slightly put out, even though he was only a little earlier than usual for the *ton's* afternoon calling hours. Then he remembered that Sir John was considered rather provincial in his habits and perhaps kept different hours. Annoying, that, but understandable.

He looked at the girl, who had stood up from her chair at his entrance. He thought she must be Miss Hathaway's sister, for though her hair was a decided red, her eyes and nose had the same shape as the elder Miss Hathaway's. She looked at him, her expression uncertain and shy. He wondered if she was mute, for she simply stared at him, and as the minutes ticked by on the mantelpiece clock, her face grew anxious and urgent. She wriggled her nose and grimaced, as if she had something to say but could not. Well, the least he could do was introduce himself and see if she responded.

"The younger Miss Hathaway, I presume?" Lord Blytheland said, smiling, and bowed. "I am Paul Templeton, Marquess of Blytheland, here to call upon your mother and sister."

An expression of profound relief crossed the girl's face, and she sketched a competent curtsy. "Yes, sir—that is, my lord. I am Psyche Hathaway. Please be seated. Mama and Cassandra should be here shortly."

His smile turned into a wide grin. "I see your father is truly the complete classicist." He sat down in a comfortable chair by the window.

The girl rolled her eyes toward the ceiling. "Yes, my lord."

Blytheland chuckled. "Fathers can be a burden, can they not? My father is also fond of the classics."

"But *you* do not have to suffer under a name like mine!"

"Ah, but here's something I do not tell everyone: my middle name is Xanthus."

"Oh, dear." Psyche made a face, then looked contrite. "It is not a terrible name, about as bad as my own, really. But at least it's not your *first* name," she said consolingly.

"Certainly, I may be thankful for that!" Blytheland laughed, reflecting that the elder Miss Hathaway was not the only blunt one in the family. A slight noise made him look up and he rose immediately, for the door opened and Cassandra entered, Lady Hathaway following her. He caught his breath.

He had thought perhaps his perception of Miss Hathaway's charms might have been partly due to his imagination. Blytheland had known times when, caught up in the afterglow of a successful violin piece, he'd overestimate the attractions of a woman. He had not done so this time. Indeed, the sun that had finally broken through the clouds shone through the windows and showed all that the dim lights of candles might have hidden—but there was nothing to hide. The soft curve of her cheek, the large and dark-fringed eyes, the pink lips, and the long, smooth column of her throat seemed to glow as she moved gracefully through the sunlight toward him.

"Your servant, Miss Hathaway," the marquess breathed, and raised her hand to his lips.

She blushed and glanced at her mother, who raised her brows but smiled nevertheless. Blytheland felt annoyed at himself for going so far as to kiss her hand, and was glad at

his annoyance. It gave him a measure of control over his reactions, and he vowed he'd not give Lady Hathaway reason
to raise her brows or smile in that matchmaking way again.
He would keep in mind that Miss Hathaway was a bluestocking, perhaps even as extreme in her views as Chloe
had been. He'd finish calling upon the Hathaways, and
never come near Miss Cassandra Hathaway again.

Bowing to Lady Hathaway, he said, "I find you and your
family well, ma'am?"

"Quite well, thank you, my lord. I see you have been
talking with Psyche. I hope she has not prattled on too
long." She gave an inquiring look at her youngest daughter.

"Oh, no, Mama. I did just as you said. I did not say a
word when Lord Blytheland came in until I was spoken to,"
Psyche said earnestly.

"Oh, for goodness sakes, child!" Lady Hathaway exclaimed, flustered. "Did you not even greet him? I certainly
did not mean—Oh, heavens!"

The marquess grinned. "She was not to speak until spoken to, eh? So that was what all your silent grimacing was
about. You looked as if you were about to burst, Miss Psyche!"

A choking sound caught his ear, and he looked at Cassandra. Her shoulders were shaking, and she had her hand
over her mouth to stifle her giggles. Her laughing eyes met
his, and there was no self-consciousness there, but an invitation to laugh along with her at her sister's literal interpre-
tation of Lady Hathaway's dictum.

"Well, I *felt* I was about to burst, my lord," Psyche
replied. "I wished so badly to make you welcome, but
Mama said not to speak until—"

"Yes, yes, I do remember what I said," her mother said
hastily. "My word, child, must you take me so literally?"

"But I—"

"Perhaps you should go upstairs now. I am sure there are
some lessons for which you need to study."

"But I thought Cassandra was going to play the pianoforte. Could I not stay for that—just for a little while?" Psyche looked hopefully at Lord Blytheland and Cassandra, obviously abandoning any hope of support from her mother.

"Of course," Lord Blytheland said, earning a grateful smile from Psyche.

"Oh, do let her stay, Mama," Cassandra entreated. "You know how quiet she is when there is any music. I know she will behave quite properly."

"Very well, then. But mind, Psyche, no fidgeting or interruptions!" Lady Hathaway settled herself in a chair and bade her guest to choose a comfortable seat.

"Oh, no, Mama!" Psyche said, all smiles.

The conversation before the music would normally have been tedious for Psyche, for it was all about people she did not know. She glanced at Harry, glad for his presence, for she would have been hard put to keep her promise not to fidget otherwise.

"Harry," she murmured almost under her breath, even though she was at quite a distance from her mother, "what do you think of him?"

Harry looked at her admiringly. "You become better and better at not moving your lips at all when you speak."

"Do I?" Psyche said, pleased.

"Yes. I remember a man once who could do that. He could even make his voice seem to come from objects at a distance from him."

"No, really? I should like to do that someday."

"What was interesting," Harry continued, "was that he had two heads and traveled about in a raree show." He gave her a wicked smile.

"You are the most detestable boy imaginable! I do not have two heads!"

"I never said you did!"

"Did you say something, Psyche?" Lady Hathaway called.

Harry shot Psyche a warning look.

"No, Mama." Psyche made herself look as innocent as possible. She sighed and sipped the tea the butler had brought in. Telling lies was becoming quite easy lately. Her mother smiled at her and returned to the conversation.

"Really, Harry, you are provoking!" Psyche whispered. He opened his mouth to retort, but she shook her head slightly. "Now enough! What do you think of Lord Blytheland?"

Her friend, wings motionless from concentration, stared at the marquess, then frowned. "I can't have made another mistake . . . no, there must be something wrong with him."

"Whatever can you mean?"

"Only look at him. He is obviously attracted to your sister, but he resists it. It is not something I like at all."

Psyche felt uneasy. Harry could be the most amiable boy imaginable, but he took certain things quite personally, especially when it came to the way gentlemen and ladies behaved toward one another. He was staring at both Cassandra and Lord Blytheland in a most intent way, as if trying to solve a puzzle. His frown deepened.

"Perhaps we should tell Mama that he is not really a good match for Cassandra," Psyche said. She felt a little uneasy. Harry could be very persistent if things did not go the way he wished.

Harry shook his head. "He *is* a good match. I never make a mistake about such things." A brief, uncomfortable look flashed across his face, but he continued. "He is arrogant, Psyche. It's hubris, and *that* is always offensive to me."

Psyche was not entirely sure what hubris was, but it was not something one did or had without getting Harry and his relatives irritated. Her uneasiness grew. She remembered the stories her father had told her about Harry's relatives, and began to wonder if the marquess would end up turned

into a tree, or chained to a rock and eaten by vultures. However, she was certain there were no vultures in England, so
perhaps his punishment would not be so very severe. There
were ducks, though. She tried to envision death by duck,
but it did not seem very much the same as death by vulture,
somehow.

Harry made a short, angry sound, so startling Psyche out
of her thoughts that she almost upset her tea. She looked at
him and watched his expression grow more stormy as he
gazed at Lord Blytheland.

"He believes he is invulnerable when he truly is not. In a
way, he is a little like your brother Kenneth, who pinches
maids and kisses them, but never does anything else.
Blytheland tells himself he does not need a wife, is not in
love with your sister, and that he is looking for more than
what she has to offer as either wife or lover." He looked
solemnly at her.

"Are you saying he will pinch Cassandra?" Psyche
gnawed her lower lip. She had thought the marquess a very
amiable sort of gentleman. She could not imagine him
pinching anyone, much less her sister.

Harry suddenly grinned. "If only he would! Then I
would not need to give him the punishment he deserves for
his arrogance. Your sister would give him such a set-down
that he would need a shovel to dig himself out of the
ground."

"Then where is the trouble?"

"Look at Cassandra."

Psyche turned in her chair. Her sister's gaze was intent
on Lord Blytheland's face, drinking up his words as if they
were some life-sustaining elixir.

"Is she in love with him?"

"Of course, though she does not know it quite yet."

"Of course? Why is that?" Psyche looked suspiciously at
him. "You didn't!"

"No, I did not shoot any of my arrows at her!" Harry said

indignantly. "Your sister doesn't need any. I shot my arrows at *him*. And he has such arrogance that he refuses to give in to them."

Psyche looked at him, horrified. "You *didn't*!"

"Yes I did." Harry smiled in a satisfied way. "It was when your sister and your parents went to the musicale. I'm certain he fell instantly in love with your sister, but he is a stubborn case. He has overcome my arrows before, but this time I'll make certain he does not."

"You *always* think people are arrogant when they resist you, Harry! You *shall* change him back!"

Harry frowned. "Why should I? He's eligible enough, and Cassandra is not opposed to his attentions at all. Only look at him! Would he not make a perfect husband for her? He is handsome, plays exquisite music, and is quite intelligent. Also, he is wealthy and has a title. Few females can resist that."

"Cassandra is *not* mercenary!"

"But you cannot deny his other assets would influence her."

Psyche looked at the marquess again. She had to admit he was quite handsome, and Cassandra was excessively fond of music. She creased her brow in thought. "He *is* amiable, even if he is rather old. He must be all of thirty. Hmm. It is not as if she would know the difference, after all." She shook her head. "No, I cannot like it, Harry. You must change him back. I am quite right about such things."

"He is six-and-twenty. *That* is not old, Psyche," Harry replied, smiling. "At least, not for your sister."

"No. Mama thinks that Cassandra is nearly on the shelf, so she must be getting a bit on, don't you think?"

Harry's smile widened into a grin. "Not really. You will understand when you are turned three-and-twenty."

Psyche made a face. "I do wish you wouldn't talk to me as if you were so much older than I am. *You* can't be any more than fourteen, if that."

"But I am much—"

"And I still think you should change him back." Psyche stared at him sternly. Harry was very good at distracting her from her purpose, and she knew he was doing it now, but she knew better than to let it go too far.

"No." He stared back at her, his chin thrust out stubbornly.

"Then I will tell Cassandra what you have done."

Harry smiled sweetly at her. "She won't believe you."

Psyche stared at him again, but he only stared back defiantly. She could try not talking to him again, but sooner or later he'd say something and she'd forget about it. Perhaps she could think of a way of persuading him later. She sighed and shrugged her shoulders.

"Well, for now, let us listen to the music. Cassandra has learned a new piece by Herr von Beethoven. She told me it is called 'Sonata in F minor,' " she said, proud that she had remembered it.

When the first notes broke the parlor's silence, Blytheland sat up abruptly, recognizing the music at once: the "Appassionata." It was not at all a feminine piece to play, and when he glanced at Lady Hathaway's disapproving face, he saw that she thought so, too. And yet, gazing at Miss Hathaway, he felt not disapproval but despair that he had come to listen to her play, and that she had chosen this music.

Cassandra's eyes had widened, absorbed and intent upon the keyboard. Blytheland watched her fingers fly over the keyboard, sure and practiced. Her technique was excellent, her talent superior to any young lady's he had heard so far. He had hoped that she would play poorly, that her apparent knowledge of music was false.

But it was not so. For she was clearly caught up in the music, as he often was himself when he bowed his violin. And passion! Her hands pounded it from the keyboard, and her fingers coaxed it out to shimmer hotly in the air. A single curl fell forward onto her brow, and Blytheland closed his hands against the feeling that he must brush it back. He made his body still and forced himself to sit in a negligent manner on his chair. But his mind was not still and he envisioned himself brushing back the curl, his fingers feathering across her cheek and tracing the outline of her lips before his own lips followed. Her mouth would open under his, and she'd respond with, yes, passion. Her slender fingers that now slipped amongst the keys would slip downward from his chest and—

With a last flourish, Miss Hathaway was done, and the pianoforte fell silent. Blytheland blinked, suddenly released from his imaginings, and drew in a deep breath. He saw Cassandra cast an uncertain glance at Lady Hathaway, and at her mother's meaningful look, she bit her lip and looked worried. He stood up abruptly.

"Truly masterful, Miss Hathaway! An excellent rendition of the sonata." Before Lord Blytheland could stop himself, he strode to her and lifted her fingers to his lips. He did not need to look up to see Lady Hathaway's smug look—he could well imagine it was there. He mentally cursed himself, but put a smile on his face. "It is not what I would expect a young lady to play, but it was very well done."

Instantly, Miss Hathaway's look of pleasure at his words faded, and he regretted his words. After she gave another apologetic glance at her mother, she smiled briefly and murmured, "You are too kind, my lord."

An odd, twisting sensation went through his chest for a moment as he looked into her eyes. "No, I am far too moderate. In truth, you are an excellent musician, and I would welcome a chance to play a duet with you." The words came from his mouth before he could stop himself. It does not matter, he told himself, gazing at Miss Hathaway's now sparkling eyes and softly smiling mouth. Besides, it was not as if he were declaring himself by wishing to play a duet with the chit. It was merely that she was an excellent musician. He would want to play a duet with any musician of her caliber.

Miss Hathaway blushed and pulled her hand from his, and he mentally cursed himself again for holding her hand for so long. "Oh, to be sure I—that is to say—you flatter me. I would be pleased to join you in—in practicing music."

He raised his eyes and caught Lady Hathaway's not-quite-concealed look of triumph. However, it would not do to seem too eager. He smiled coolly at them both and bowed to Lady Hathaway.

"I hope I do not impose, ma'am."

"Oh, heavens, no, Lord Blytheland. Why, you need only say when you wish to practice with Cassandra, and I shall set aside the time." Lady Hathaway's face was wreathed in smiles.

Of course you will, he thought wryly, and ignored her expectant look. Really, it seemed he was digging a deeper hole for himself than he had thought he would. Well, it was not as if he hadn't got himself out of worse situations. He turned to Miss Hathaway.

"Do you go to Lady Marchmont's ball, Miss Hathaway?"

"Why yes, I believe we do." Cassandra smiled shyly up at him. "Shall we see you there, my lord?"

He picked up his hat, bowed over Lady Hathaway's hand, and then Cassandra's. "Perhaps," he said, and smiled. There. He had promised nothing, and when he did not appear at the Marchmonts' ball, both the Hathaway ladies would have no one to blame but their own expectations for any disappointment they might feel.

If he had thought Miss Hathaway beautiful before, he was mistaken. The smile that parted her lips also delicately blushed her cheeks and seemed to light her eyes from within, and he could not help staring at her again.

"Oh, Lord Blytheland, I do hope I—we shall see you there."

Her voice made him blink and he hastily released her hand. He really should try not to be so influenced by music. He smiled once more and bowed before he left.

Chapter 4

"Oh, heavens, Cassandra, do hurry and change your dress!" cried Lady Hathaway two days after, waving a calling card at her daughter. Cassandra looked at her mother, startled. "He has come to ask you for a drive in the park—Blytheland!"

"Oh!" Cassandra's heart beat a little faster and an odd confused feeling came over her.

Lady Hathaway turned to the butler. "And, Thrimble, take Lord Blytheland to the drawing room and offer him refreshment while he waits. I shall be down as soon as I tidy myself." The butler left and Lady Hathaway glanced at Cassandra. "What, are you still here? Silly girl! Go up, quickly! I will be with you directly to see that you dress as you ought."

"But, Mama, my errand—"

"Never mind, Psyche and I will attend to it. Just *go!*"

Cassandra hurried up the stairs, wondering why her mother seemed so impatient of late. Her mother rarely dictated what she wore, for she trusted that Cassandra would choose her clothes carefully, and with an eye to modesty. Well, she would be careful to do just that; surely Mama would be pleased.

But she was quite wrong. She had chosen a simple walking dress with a light woolen pelisse, which covered her from chin to toe, very pretty, too. But the moment Lady

Hathaway caught sight of Cassandra's clothes, she frowned.

"No, no, Cassandra, not that one! You must wear your new walking dress, the one with the frill at the collar."

Cassandra glanced out the window at the partly cloudy sky and looked at her mother doubtfully. "But, Mama, I thought that one might be a little light for this weather."

"Nonsense!" Lady Hathaway said firmly. "You can see the clouds disappearing. And if you think you will feel a chill, you may wear this black velvet spencer on top of it."

"But it buttons only underneath the bosom! What if a wind should come up?"

"If a wind comes up, you may wrap yourself with your shawl."

"Mama, I do not think the dress quite matches the spencer," Cassandra replied, gazing at her mother and feeling very puzzled. How odd! She could not account for it. Mama had told her all her life to wrap herself up warmly in case a chill breeze should arise, but now she was insisting on a dress and spencer that was not as appropriate as what she had been wearing.

"Well, then, you shall start a fashion," Lady Hathaway said firmly.

Cassandra cast her mother another puzzled look, then sighed and turned to her maid to change her dress.

At last she was done dressing, and Cassandra could not help glancing at her mother a little suspiciously. The green walking dress was well enough; it had a large white frill that draped around the back collar of the dress and outlined the low neckline in front. But the spencer was a little smaller than she remembered it to be and felt tight about her chest. There must be a reason she was told to wear these clothes, but Cassandra could not tell what it could be from Lady Hathaway's proud and satisfied gaze. She smiled at her mother. Surely it was nothing, and surely she must appear quite well; her mother would not look so proud, else.

But then they entered the parlor, and after Lord Blytheland smiled, stood, and bowed over Lady Hathaway's hand, he bowed over Cassandra's as she curtsied . . . and he seemed to stop breathing for a moment before he rose, slowly. Then he met her eyes.

His eyes should not be blue, Cassandra thought as she looked into them. Blue was a cold color, and the emotion that showed in his eyes was hot, and caused heat to rise from the pit of her stomach to her face. It frightened her a little, for she did not want to turn away; she wanted to stare and stare at him, and it was a strange, unfamiliar feeling. His smile faded, and his gaze traveled slowly down from her face and up again.

Cassandra looked down as well, and her face heated even more. He was still holding her hand and—oh, heavens! Her spencer, which had seemed perfectly respectable when she had first put it on, had shifted her dress about during her descent to the parlor, and now gaped open more than it ever used to. She shot an agonized glance at her mother, but all she received in return was a smile and a nod, as if Lady Hathaway was oblivious to her state of dress.

"Please . . ." she whispered and tugged at her hand. A startled look crossed the marquess's face and he hastily released her. Lord Blytheland smiled again, but his mouth looked a little strained at the corners. He took a step back, putting his hands behind him.

He cleared his throat. "I am happy, Miss Hathaway, that you were able to accept my invitation on such short notice."

Cassandra made herself smile. "Yes, I was going to run an errand, but Mama told me she and Psyche could just as well do it, and that I was free to go with you if I wished."

She heard an exasperated breath from her mother, and wondered if she had said something she should not have.

Cassandra swallowed. She was not doing as she ought, that was clear, but she did not know quite how to remedy it. However, the marquess smiled at her again, and this time it was wide enough to be a grin. Cassandra almost sighed in relief. At least *he* was not displeased with her, and perhaps he did not mind her spencer fitting improperly.

"And did you wish it?" he asked.

Cassandra smiled, relieved. "Why, of course! I have never been in a high-perch phaeton before, and should like to try it. I used to think it a frightening thing to be up so high, but I am sure you are a competent driver and will not overturn us."

"Really, Cassandra!" Lady Hathaway's voice was reproving. "You must know that Lord Blytheland belongs to the Four-in-Hand Club!"

"Does he?" replied Cassandra, not entirely sure of the significance of this. She had heard it mentioned from time to time, but since she was not particularly interested in driving carriages she had not paid much attention to what was said about the club. "I suppose that must be a good thing, then." Her mother gave her an exasperated look, and Cassandra bit her lip. How she wished she had listened! But she had always gone to balls to dance and to musicales to listen to music—that was what they were for, after all—and so had never thought she ought to do more than that.

She saw Lord Blytheland's smile turn wry. "It *is* a good thing," he said. "It is almost a guarantee that I will not overturn us." He moved forward and bowed to Lady Hathaway, then turned to Cassandra. "Shall we go?"

"Yes, please," Cassandra said. She glanced at her mother and an embarrassed irritation grew in her. Mama was looking positively smug, and Cassandra was sure now that Mama meant to try to push her and the marquess together as much as possible. It was clear now why her mother acted strangely, and not as dignified as Cassandra was used to seeing her act. It disturbed her, and the idea that her mother was being mercenary on her behalf suddenly came to her. Perhaps she was wrong. . . . But even though she tried not to listen to gossip, she could not help hearing of estates and dowries, of incomes and titles when sitting amongst other ladies. It did not sit well with her; how her mother could wish for a monied marriage when she herself had married for love, Cassandra did not know.

Lord Blytheland took her hand and placed it on his arm and drew her to the parlor door. His arm felt firm underneath her hand, and she felt, somehow, more confident. *She* would not be swayed by monetary considerations. No, when—*if* she fell in love with Lord Blytheland, or any other man, for that matter—it would be a true meeting of minds, for how could anyone live one's whole life with someone who did not enter into one's interests or beliefs?

She would be sensible, and not let her mother's efforts on her behalf—and she was certain her mother meant well, for did she not love all her children dearly?—blind her to a man's true virtue. All she needed was to find out if the man was truly compatible in mind and spirit. She thought of the philosophies she had discussed with her father, and her spirits lightened. She would be scientific about it—did not her father say that logic would someday solve all questions? She would think of it as a scientific experiment, and then she would know to whom she'd give her heart.

Lord Blytheland was almost certain he would overturn the carriage. For all that Miss Hathaway's dress was modest in its basic lines, the tantalizing glimpse of her bosom revealed between the frills whenever she turned to speak with him distracted him. Twice he had to rein in his horses sharply before he ran into a pedestrian or passed too close to a cart.

"Is my mother right, saying you belong to the Four-in-Hand Club?" Cassandra asked after he had missed the cart.

"Yes."

"Are only the best carriage drivers allowed in it?"

Lord Blytheland glanced down at her and saw she had pulled her shawl close to her chin. "Yes," he said again and breathed a sigh of relief.

She gave him a quizzical smile. "I would not have known it just now."

"I am, however," he said stiffly.

"Oh, you need not poker up, my lord! I can see you are quite a good whip." Cassandra smiled kindly at him. "I was only teasing you."

"Really." He stared straight ahead at the traffic, concentrating on squeezing his phaeton between a curricle and a barouche. A good whip. He was, actually, known as one of the best. Irritation twisted within him, and then he felt relieved. There, that was another flaw in Miss Hathaway. She was ignorant of society ways, and therefore not at all the sort of woman he admired. She had no finesse whatsoever. Oddly, a sinking feeling went through him at the thought.

"Ah, I see!" Miss Hathaway's voice was contrite. "You are offended, are you not? I am sorry, but I did not realize you could not take a joke," she said.

Blytheland stared at her, but she had turned away and her bonnet obscured her face. How did she do it? She apologized, apparently sincere, but in the same breath strongly implied she found him humorless.

"Miss Hathaway, I can indeed take a joke."

"Really."

He shot her a keen glance and glimpsed her smile and the mischievous sparkle in her eyes before she turned away again. He burst out laughing. "You are a minx, Miss Hathaway! How is it that you have escaped strangulation at the hands of your siblings?"

"Oh, we have a rule at home, my lord, that speaking the truth does not constitute grounds for execution." This time she smiled widely.

Blytheland laughed again and caught up her hand and kissed it. "Why *is* it that I have not met you until now?"

Miss Hathaway blushed. "Well, I—This is my first Season, my lord."

He watched how the blush fired her cheeks and then descended to her neck—and then a shout caught his attention. He quickly reined in his horses before he touched wheels with another carriage, and was glad he could concentrate on something that needed his immediate attention. He grimaced. Miss Hathaway was right; no one could tell by his driving today that he belonged to the Four-in-Hand Club.

He glanced at her still-pink face and knew he had gone too far—he had kissed her hand again, perhaps raising her expectations. Or did she have expectations? Certainly, she seemed not to employ any of the tricks young ladies did when trying to attract a man. He took in a deep breath and let it out again.

"You astonish me," he said, making his voice more cool than before. "Since we are trading frank words, I would guess you to be at least one-and-twenty."

"I am three-and-twenty and more," Cassandra said primly. "Practically on the shelf, or so my mother says."

"And your parents did not want you to leave their home so early?"

"No . . ." For one moment she hesitated, and then smiled at him. "I did not want to leave at first. My life has always been comfortable and useful at home; why should I wish to change it? Why should anyone?"

Blytheland felt much in charity with this attitude, and nodded. He, too, had a pleasant life now, and did as he wished; why *should* he want to change? But she had hesitated. . . .

"But what of marriage and children?" he asked. That was not an unusual question to ask, surely, especially since she had revealed a reluctance to change her life.

Cassandra blushed again, but looked at him. "I think I

could be just as happy caring for my parents in their old age, if I cannot find love as they have. Then, too, I can easily occupy myself in such pursuits as my—in my charitable pursuits."

Blytheland gazed at Miss Hathaway for a moment and smiled slightly. He was certain she had just caught herself before blurting something she shouldn't. Should he try to find out what had changed her mind? A brief, anxious look crossed her face, and he decided he would not pry. If she wished to talk of charities, so be it. It was a safe enough topic, after all.

"And to what charities do you contribute?" He watched her as she looked even more anxious.

"I . . . the usual ones, my lord."

He smiled. "I am afraid I will sound like a selfish fellow if I say I do not know what the 'usual' charities are. But I do contribute to a few as well."

Cassandra cast him a glance that was clearly relieved. "I am so glad you do!" she said, then looked worried. "Oh dear. I did not mean to imply that I thought you uncharitable! It is just that talking of one's charities is akin to talking of one's virtues, and *that* is a prideful thing. I don't wish to seem prideful."

What knots she seemed to tie herself into! Blytheland could not help feeling a little sorry for her. Her bluntness was clearly often at war with her wish to be virtuous, and it was just as clear she knew she blundered—after the fact, unfortunately. He smiled widely at her.

"I promise I will not think you prideful, Miss Hathaway." He turned the carriage on to Hyde Park, then glanced down at her.

Her lips were slightly parted in a smile of gratitude and the sun chose just then to peep from behind the clouds and shine upon her hair, making her curls seem like the waves of the sea at night. The light kissed her cheek and chin and brushed her lips with the color of coral. Suddenly he wanted to plunge his hands into her hair and kiss those lips as the sun had kissed them, to see if they were as warm as they looked.

And then the sun hid behind the clouds again. He grew conscious of the silence between them, how her eyes seemed at once confused and lost, and how he held the reins so tightly that the horses stopped. *She must not fall in love with me, for her own sake. I do not have what she needs for me to give.* He looked away from her and concentrated on his horses.

What nonsense! He took a deep breath, and it cleared his mind. He did not know the state of her heart and would prefer not to think of it. He smiled wryly to himself. Indeed, what arrogance it was for him to think she might love him! No woman really had before, or not that he could tell, not even Chloe. And truly, it was better that way. He'd best tend to his own unruly passions instead of pondering the doubtless nonexistent ones of Miss Hathaway, and think in a more rational vein than he had lately.

"Did I say something amiss, my lord?" Cassandra's voice was uncertain.

He smiled at her. "No. Or rather, because you have not yet told me what charities you sponsor, I was left to my own imaginings. For all I know, you are devoted to the reclamation of abused coal scuttles." Cassandra laughed. "One never knows what charity will be in fashion next," he said.

She frowned for a moment, then said, "I suppose there are many who contribute because it is fashionable to do so. And though it is not the best reason to do so, one must be practical about these things."

"You, of course, have chosen a far more practical one than coal scuttles, I imagine?"

Cassandra smiled briefly, then pressed her lips together for a moment. "Yes. I . . . there are various parishes that need help. Food, clothing, blankets—I try to provide them."

She seemed to watch him for some reaction, and her voice was hesitant, as if expecting a reprimand. He wondered for a moment who it was had told her it was not a thing to mention in society. Her mother, probably. Perhaps it was not something most young ladies indulged in, but it was not a socially damning thing after all. He felt a slight touch on his sleeve and looked down at Cassandra's earnest face.

"It is a terrible thing, the way the poor ch—people live, Lord Blytheland—often abused and starved. No one who has seen one can help but be moved to one's very heart."

He raised his brows. "You have seen them?" he was accustomed to people who gave to charities and spared themselves the sight of the recipient.

Cassandra bit her lip. "I . . . I have seen some at the meetings I go to."

Shown off like a freak at a raree-show, Blytheland thought with distaste. But he supposed it was an effective way of eliciting sympathy for one's cause. He nodded.

"A worthy cause, Miss Hathaway. I commend you."

Her smile lit up her face, and it was as if the sun had come out from the clouds again. Again, he nearly touched wheels with another carriage, and exasperated, gave it up.

He turned to Cassandra. "Would you like to walk a little? I believe the ground is not damp."

"Yes, please," Cassandra said.

"Tim, take the reins," he said to the tiger sitting behind them as he slowed, then stopped the phaeton. They descended the carriage and walked next to the line of trees next to the roadway.

He took Miss Hathaway's hand and put it on his arm, and they walked in silence for a moment. He heard her sigh and he looked down at her. She had a speculative look on her face as she gazed at him, and at once he felt wary. He'd seen that look before on women's faces, and it usually meant they wished to entrap him in some manner. Was she, after all, like other young ladies with an eye toward marriage? He felt some disappointment, though, really, he should be pleased she was not above the ordinary.

"Is there something you wish to say, Miss Hathaway?" he said. He thought of a number of set-downs he could use if she decided to flirt with him after all.

"I was wondering . . . if, well . . ." She hesitated, and a slight blush appeared on her cheeks.

If she asked him if he would attend some social function or other, he would definitely say no. He had too many commitments as it was. "Yes, Miss Hathaway?"

"I was wondering if perhaps you might be interested in contributing to our charity," she said all in a rush, and her cheeks grew even more pink.

Lord Blytheland could not help feeling some chagrin. She was not, apparently, interested in his presence anywhere at all. He felt quite the fool, thinking that she might. He wondered if perhaps he was becoming arrogant, and if it showed.

"The poor ch—people,they are so hungry!" Cassandra looked at him pleadingly. "You don't know how horribly they've been treated, and some of them so very young, only babies!" He saw her swallow, and turn away, taking a deep breath before she continued. "Some of them fear even the kindest of approaches, thinking we come to cause them harm." She gazed at him, and he could see her eyes, wide and with a hint of tears. She touched his sleeve. "Please . . . it is a terrible thing, and should happen to no child—no one in England."

"But of course, Miss Hathaway," he said, before he could stop himself.

She gave him another smile of clear gratitude, and pressed his arm. A speculative look entered her eyes, and she said tentatively, "And do you think perhaps you can persuade your father to speak on the matter when he goes to Parliament?"

Blytheland gave her a sharp look. She immediately hung

her head as if in chagrin, then peeped up at him from beneath her lashes. She looked very much like a puppy who wanted to play but had gone beyond the line, Blytheland thought. And then she grinned and shrugged her shoulders.

Blytheland burst into laughter. "You are incorrigible, Miss Hathaway!"

"Ah, well. I thought I ought to try."

Blytheland opened his mouth to speak, but hesitated. He wondered what her reaction would be if he did as she asked. She would smile at him again. He realized suddenly that he liked to see her smile; her mouth curved in at the corners in a slight curl and made him want to kiss her. It was pleasant to have such an attractive companion, of course, but it was a trying thing to walk beside her and not give in to his impulse to—He let out a slow breath and tried not to think of his impulses.

Well, it would not hurt to approach his father about the poverty in the parishes about town . . . and it was not as if the duke was opposed to such things, after all. "You are very devoted to your cause, I see," he said.

Cassandra's expression sobered. "One cannot help being so, after seeing the poverty."

"I suppose I could speak to my father upon the matter . . ."

A tiny shriek made him look down at her, and he found his hands seized in hers and squeezed tightly. Cassandra's face was alight with joy, and she gave a little jump, almost seeming about to dance. But she bit her lip instead, clearly restraining herself, then raised his hand to her cheek. "How good you are!" she exclaimed.

Blytheland stared at her, feeling the warmth of her cheek against his hand. If she moved her head but a fraction of an inch, he'd feel her lips against his hand, and he could not help imagining what it would feel like. Warm, of course, but nothing compared to what it would probably feel like if it were his lips instead of his hand. He looked into her eyes and found she was staring at him. A blush rose in her cheeks and she hastily released him, and he was able to look away at last. He sighed. In a way, he wished she would not smile at him. It was her best feature, and it distracted him.

"I am not as good as you think, Miss Hathaway," he said. "Besides, I cannot guarantee my father will agree to speak on the matter at all."

"It is enough that you ask him—and I know I was impertinent to ask it of you, so I think you are indeed very good to agree." She gave a happy sigh. "It is more than anyone else has agreed to do."

Blytheland grinned at her. "Do you always go about impertinently demanding support for your charities?"

"No, because I have learned that it puts off a great many people when I do. But you looked as if you understood about the—parishes, and then your eyes were smiling in *such* a way that I thought you would not mind."

"Do my thoughts show that much, then?" He did not like the idea that they might.

Cassandra pursed her lips in a thoughtful manner and swung her reticule to and fro as she walked beside him. "No . . . no, not really. I doubt most would be able to discern your state of mind. But I have had to watch people carefully—I suppose you have noticed that I sometimes say things I ought not?"

Blytheland could not help laughing. "Yes, I am afraid I have."

"You should not laugh at me, my lord," Cassandra said, her voice solemn, but then she sighed. "Well, I suppose it is something I must become used to, for I forget, you know, and cannot keep from saying what I think, though I do try! And it is certainly better than being angry at me. But one good thing I have learned is to watch people carefully, so that I may discern whether they are angry or not. I think I have become fairly good at reading countenances."

He nodded, thinking that perhaps it was necessary for someone as defenseless as Miss Hathaway to find some way of dealing with others. He hadn't thought of it before, but he supposed she was rather defenseless, since she seemed to have very little notion as to how to navigate through the *ton*. It was an uncomfortable thought and nothing he should be concerned about, certainly.

The wind picked up and blew against Miss Hathaway's bonnet, and Lord Blytheland looked up to see that heavier clouds were forming above them. "I think we should return to the carriage," he said.

They hurried their steps and found Blytheland's tiger bringing up the carriage. Hastily they ascended and seated themselves.

"But all of this—your charitable pursuits—should be no barrier to marriage, Miss Hathaway," Blytheland said, taking up the reins again. "You could just as easily do them if you married." The horses moved forward.

She hesitated, looking oddly . . . bereft, was the closest he could come to a description, then said, "I have no guarantee that my husband would be a good man. Why should I risk possible unhappiness when I can logically, sensibly choose the happy life I already know?"

"And where did you get such ideas, Miss Hathaway?"

"Oh, from a book I read by Mrs. Wollstonecraft." Her voice faltered slightly at the end.

A hard, hot anger seized Blytheland's gut, and his hands clenched, bringing the horses to a stop.

"Lord Blytheland?" Cassandra's voice sounded tentative.

His fingers were digging into his gloved palms. He loosened them, and the horses went forward again.

"Your father allowed you to read such nonsense?" He could not help the sneer that came to his voice.

An angry light entered Cassandra's eyes. "It is *not* nonsense—not all of it. You need only look about you to see that there are people who are not happy in their marriages."

"It is not necessary that people be happy or unhappy in their marriages. It is a thing one does to continue the family."

Cassandra felt as if a chill had come over her, and she pulled her shawl tighter around her. "I daresay many people think that. But I believe it is best that a marriage be a loving one. If one cannot have one such, it is better to remain unwed, and even better, find a useful occupation so as not to be a burden on anyone."

For one moment an uncertain expression crossed Lord Blytheland's face. Then he smiled coolly.

"You are an idealist, Miss Hathaway. As you said, there are no guarantees about one's husband or wife. The best anyone can do is to rub along amiably."

Cassandra gazed at him doubtfully. Before the uncertainty, anger had marred his expression. Something she had said had caused him to be angry, but she did not know what it was.

"And how would you know, Lord Blytheland?" she asked. She supposed he must base his opinion upon his own family, but she had heard nothing scandalous of either his father the Duke of Beaumont, or his mother the duchess. The reports were that they were always amiably disposed toward each other, at least in company. Although, this was not saying much, to be sure, for she rarely listened to gossip and probably would not have remembered if she had heard it.

He smiled coolly, then looked past her. "Ah, I see Lady Amberley waving to me, and her most charming daughter is with her." He nodded to a carriage coming toward them.

Cassandra smiled to herself. So, that was one of his setdowns. It comforted her in a way, for it was one more puzzle piece she had gathered for a better picture of his nature. Lord Blytheland was not the sort of person she was used to . . . there was a part of him that seemed hidden somehow. She was used to being able to assess easily those she met and pin down the pattern of their behavior. Once she understood, it was a little easier to refrain from saying things that would offend them. She sighed. But oh, people did become offended at the most innocent things! And the fact that the marquess was not so easily assessed, disconcerted her. How was she to know what would offend him or not? The only way was to speak what she thought and see how he responded. If he became offended, then she would know enough not to speak of things that offended him.

Cassandra made herself smile in a friendly manner at Lady Amberley and her daughter Sophia when Lord Blytheland introduced them, though she felt rather abstracted. She was still puzzling over the marquess. For one moment she felt a little guilty. Perhaps it was not a very well-mannered thing to do, making people reveal themselves. She sighed. But what else was she to do? Men, she found, were the most contrary sort of people of all. One could not always use much logic with them, for all their claim to be the more logical sex. They tended to become quite emotional when one reasoned with them—and how logical was that? Not at all, to be sure.

But it did seem, at least, that in such things as discussions, Lord Blytheland was as other men. As a result, she was that much closer to knowing more of him. And she did so wish to know more of Lord Blytheland. Not, of course, because she wished . . . well, what she wished, she was not certain.

"Do you stay in London long, Miss Hathaway?"

Cassandra turned her attention to the young woman in the barouche next to her. Miss Sophia Amberley was beautiful and had large blue eyes. Cassandra would almost have thought they were innocent eyes, but the sharp, speculative look Miss Amberley gave her and the marquess was not innocent at all. Cassandra's face became warm. Surely Miss Amberley was not thinking that Lord Blytheland could be very much interested in her, Cassandra? No other gentleman had this Season, and there was no reason why he should either.

Stop it! Cassandra scolded herself, and made herself smile at Miss Amberley. "Oh, only until the end of the Season, for there is not much more left to do after that."

A satisfied expression came to Miss Amberley's face. "That is too bad. There are dozens of diversions in London after the Season is over, you know. We often stay into the summer."

Cassandra nodded, pleased that there was something upon which she could converse. "Oh, yes! But it gets terribly warm here in the city by then, and I cannot think the miasma that rises from the river at that time is at all healthy. It could make one look quite sickly."

"That is to say," Cassandra said hurriedly into the silence that ensued, "the fresh country air in the summer is bound to bring a healthy glow to one's complexion—not that *you* do not have a healthy complexion, Miss Amberley! Or you, Lady Amberley!"

"I am glad to know you think our complexions quite . . . healthy, Miss Hathaway," Lady Amberley said, her voice chilly. "Well, Sophia. I do believe I see Lady Stonebaugh a little farther along the road." She nodded her head to the marquess and barely glanced at Cassandra. "My lord, Miss . . . Hathaway. Good day to you both." She signaled to the coachman, and the barouche went forward.

Cassandra's heart sank. She looked down at her tightly closed hands, then flattened them on her lap. She must have insulted Lady Amberley and her daughter. She glanced at Lord Blytheland. He was not looking at her, but ahead as he slackened the reins, moving the horses forward. For a moment, a small smile played about his mouth and relief flowed into her. Perhaps she had not totally ruined this afternoon carriage ride, for he could not smile and be displeased at the same time.

She felt half regretful and half relieved when they drove

up to her family's house once again. They had not spoken of much else except of the weather on the way back, and for this Cassandra was thankful. She had experimented a little by teasing him, to see how he would respond to it, and she felt she had done it quite successfully. But she had also blundered and was just as glad they had started talking of the weather, for she did not want to blunder again. The weather, at least, was a safe subject.

When the carriage stopped, Lord Blytheland handed his reins to his tiger and stepped down to help her from her seat. This time, his eyes were cool as blue eyes were supposed to be, though his smile seemed just as wide as before. She wished, suddenly, that he looked warmly upon her as he had before the carriage ride, and despondency rose in her. It was, no doubt, because she had been so gauche during their carriage ride that he looked so coolly at her now. She was not at all sure now he'd wish to see her again. Why should he? But how she wished he would!

"Shall I see you at the Marchmont's ball, tomorrow?" Cassandra blurted. Lord Blytheland's brows rose, and her face grew warm. "That is I—never mind—I should not have—" She swallowed and looked away, then summoned up a smile. "I am very foolish, am I not? I never know what to say to people. Please excuse me." She stepped down from the carriage and gave him as cheery a smile as she could. "Thank you very much for a most delightful ride, my lord. Our conversation was quite delightful, and the weather was delight . . ." Her voice faltered. She gazed down at her hands clasped tight together, then turned quickly to the door of the house.

"Miss Hathaway."

Cassandra stopped, her hand on the doorknob.

"I shall be at Lady Marchmont's ball."

She turned to look at him and found he had followed her up the steps. This time she could not help the hope and joy that rose in her heart and made her smile. "I am glad," she said.

Lord Blytheland stared at her for one moment, his expression serious. "Will you save a dance for me?" he asked. There was an intent air about him, as if he were holding his breath.

It was a ridiculous thing to be so happy over such a small thing as a dance, Cassandra thought. But she *was* happy, and she felt sure she looked like an idiot, grinning so widely as she was. "Oh yes!" she said, then firmly reined in her feelings. "Yes, thank you, my lord."

The marquess took her hand and kissed it. "I shall definitely look forward to it, then." He gave a brief smile, bowed, and went down the steps to his carriage again. Cassandra watched him as he touched his hat to her in another bow and drove off.

Cassandra turned and stared at the door of the house as she went up the stairs. She missed the doorknob at first when trying to open it, then shook her head at herself for being in such a daze. How silly she was!

She sighed and went up to her room to change her dress. Silly indeed. There was no depending upon a man's interest, really. No man had been all that interested in her before, and there was no reason why Lord Blytheland should, either.

But he has paid more attention to you than any other man, whispered a little voice that crept into her mind.

Cassandra pressed her lips together and took the little voice to task. Well, there! she told herself firmly. She was becoming foolish over a thing that was wholly insignificant. So what of Lord Blytheland's attentions? That he had paid her more attention than any other man was an insignificant thing. He could very well stop at any time, as did the others. Besides, he had only been with her one or two times.

It could be three or four or five . . . said the little voice.

And what was the use of "could be" in such matters? she argued. One was best served by placing one's reliance on what was and what *should* be.

A clock tolled the hour and Cassandra hurried up the rest of the stairs. It was almost time for the meeting of the Society for the Rescue of Climbing Boys. She had done very well, she thought, in speaking in general terms about her charitable pursuits. Mama would be quite pleased that she had not mentioned climbing boys at all during the ride with Lord Blytheland.

She hastened into her room; she would have to change her clothes quickly. Most certainly she could not wear this spencer and dress to the meeting! She glanced down at the dress and blushed—it had become disarrayed even more than before. Heavens! She would give the spencer away to Psyche, for whom it would be a little large and certainly not as indecent. What could her mother have been thinking?

The little voice began to speak up, but Cassandra quashed it as firmly as she shut the door to her room.

Chapter 5

Miss Hathaway was definitely not the sort of woman he usually liked. Lord Blytheland smiled at his reflection in his chamber's mirror as he adjusted his neckcloth. Slowly he let down his chin upon the folds of cloth. Satisfied, he turned to his valet and put on his coat.

No, Miss Cassandra Hathaway was too blunt for him, too impetuous in her speech, and she blurted out whatever happened to be in her mind. She had little finesse, though in general her manners were good, and she was inept in company. Further, it was clear she was a bluestocking, and worse, a believer in that Wollstonecraft woman's ideas.

Like Chloe.

A hard, hot anger surged in his chest, and for one moment his hand stilled before he drew his jacket together. He took in a deep breath.

No, to be fair, not like Chloe. He let out his breath and frowned slightly. Chloe had had a great deal of charm, and a sparkling wit. She would never inadvertently insult anyone. He remembered suddenly a smiling remark his wife had once uttered, and how he had thought her clever for giving a set-down to an encroaching guest with such finesse. She had done this often, he realized.

Miss Hathaway was not like this. There was something about her. . . . He grinned. She often seemed to have a bewildered, worried air, as if she were some small wild creature suddenly uncovered from under a sheaf of bracken.

Somehow he could not imagine her giving a deliberate set-down to anyone.

Which was why, despite all her awkwardness, her gaucherie, and her definite bluestocking interests, he'd asked her for a dance at the Marchmonts' ball. Blytheland pulled on his greatcoat—the Marchmonts' house was a good half hour from town, and the night was cool—then sighed as he took his hat from his valet. He had attempted to depress her pretensions, and when she had looked at him with her wide, hurt eyes, he had felt like a cad.

Chloe had never been like that. She had made fine play with her eyes, had coaxed and cajoled, she had tossed her fiery hair or smiled and reasoned with one in such a way that her desires seemed altogether sensible. He would not be so trapped again.

Yet, he was not imperceptive, either. It was clear to him that Miss Hathaway was not at all like Chloe in nature. Miss Hathaway did not cajole or coax and he wondered if she knew how to flirt with her eyes. When she looked at him, it was as if she searched for something beneath his words, down to his very heart.

Perhaps her interest in radical ideas was not deep and perhaps she could be persuaded away from them. And who would do the persuading? The thought made him pause one moment before ascending the steps to his coach.

"Thinking of setting up a nursery?" Eldon had said. Blytheland leaned back onto the squabs of the carriage and carefully let the thought settle into his mind. He was six-and-twenty years old, the only heir of his father, the Duke of Beaumont. Though his father had not pressured him into a second marriage, Blytheland was quite aware of his obligation to continue the line.

It had been two years . . . two years since Chloe had lain with another man and died of the result. An anger still burned in him from time to time, and sometimes he felt an odd ache of emptiness. No one could fill Chloe's place, for she had played a role he thought he had loved and now knew he hated.

But was he not older now, and wiser? And he was not so much of a fool as to think that all women were like Chloe. Was not his own mother a devoted wife? And his sisters were certainly faithful also, and no scandal had ever touched them.

He smiled and felt the tension fall away from his shoulders. Eldon may have been teasing, but he was quite right. It was time to think of marrying a suitable young lady of good morals and good birth. Indeed it did not matter if he loved the lady or not, it was an heir he needed and a respectable, honest young woman who would neither play him nor the title false. He would go about it in a reasonable manner this time and would select his new wife with careful reason, and pay strict attention to all that he required in a wife.

Indeed, his preoccupation with Miss Hathaway—and he admitted his thoughts had been a little too filled with her image of late—was a clear indication of one thing: it was time he was married again. He needed to continue the Templeton line after all. Marriage would certainly help assuage whatever passions he'd been experiencing lately, and he was growing tired of flitting from one brief liaison to another.

The coach rumbled to a halt in front of the Marchmonts' house, and the image of Miss Hathaway rose in his mind. Blytheland smiled to himself. Oh, she was eligible, for her breeding was good, however socially inept she was, but he could do better than Cassandra Hathaway, a baronet's daughter of moderate fortune. He was heir to a dukedom, and owed the title a lady worthy of it. One who was elegant and beautiful, preferably, and certainly one who had much better address than Miss Hathaway.

The Marchmonts' ball would be just the place to start his search. There should be many eligible ladies attending, because the Marchmonts were of good *ton* and had many connections with the best families in England. There should be no question that he had no more interest—perhaps even less—in Miss Hathaway than in any other young lady. Once he looked over the unwedded female portion of the guests, he could have his mother handle the rest . . . or perhaps not. His mother tended to have strong opinions about who was suitable and who was not, and she had objected mightily to his choice of Chloe. He grimaced. Well, she was right in that case. Perhaps it would be good to have her handle the whole, winnow out the objectionable ones, so to speak, so he could pick the one he liked best. Yes, he would do that.

He smiled as he descended the coach and stepped up to the Marchmonts' door. All he needed was a young lady of good family, comely enough for him to wish to bed, intelligent enough not to bore him, appreciative enough of music so as not to deplore his interest in it, and her family wealthy enough not to be a drain on his estate and the future of his family. Once more the image of Cassandra Hathaway rose in front of him, but he pushed it firmly aside. She was one possible candidate only, and perhaps he'd dance only the one dance he had requested of her. There would be many other eligible ladies at the ball. With such opportunities, how difficult could it be to find a wife, after all?

Bright candlelight shimmered through the windows of the Marchmonts' house. Cassandra's hands clutched her ivory-handled fan tightly. For the first time since she'd come to London with her family, she felt agitated about going to a ball. To be sure, her first one had made her a little nervous, but she'd found since then that though she was not popular as were some other ladies, she always danced at least a few dances, talked with at least a few people, and generally enjoyed the music. It became an expected thing, a weekly routine.

But this time *he* would be there—Lord Blytheland. Please, dear God, she prayed silently, keep me from acting like a ninny. Cassandra sighed as she descended the coach with her mother and father. Heaven knows she had not been herself since meeting the marquess. Stammering and blushing like a girl of thirteen instead of a lady of three-and-twenty! Indeed, worse, for even Psyche did not falter and stumble over her speech when in his presence. *Really, Cassandra*, she mentally scolded herself, *Lord Blytheland is just a man—not any different from, say, your father or your brother!*

Oh, but he was *different!* whispered what she believed was her baser side. She could not deny that. How could he not be? He looked nothing like her father, and as for any comparison of character with her younger brother—! Ridiculous! How kind the marquess was to call on her and listen to her play the sonata. Cassandra bit her lip. She should not have played the "Appassionata"; she knew her mother preferred her to play more feminine music—a ballad, or a dainty divertimento. But she'd found the music for Herr Beethoven's work at the bookseller's and could not resist playing such a moving piece for the marquess. Not that she wanted him to be moved, of course! It was merely that she thought Lord Blytheland might appreciate the sonata's beauty and power as she did, since he was such a talented musician. It seemed he thought the music unlady-like as well, but he so kindly praised her on it, and even asked to play a duet with her at a future date. Perhaps he did appreciate it. She hoped so.

As Cassandra and her parents entered the Marchmonts' ballroom, she could not help looking about her for the marquess. She did not see him. Her shoulders went up in a small, involuntary shrug, warding off disappointment. Well, it was as she thought. He was merely being kind when he had asked for a dance. Whatever the case, she would enjoy the ball. She had dressed with care in a royal blue round gown with a silver-net overdress—a trifle more low-cut than she was accustomed, but which her mother said looked very becoming on her. What did it matter that Lord Blytheland was not here to see her? She was not, after all, an ornament to be displayed.

They sat to one side of the room, close to the refreshments. "Dashed thirsty work, this dancing," Sir John said, although Cassandra did not know how her father could say this since he would dance only with her and her mother, and perhaps one other lady—if forced. She noticed that he found a seat next to an old acquaintance, and was soon deep in a discussion of Greek plays. Cassandra smiled and allowed herself to relax, watching the people begin to gather for the first set of the dance.

"Miss Hathaway, would you grant me the honor of this dance?"

The marquess's soft voice startled her, and she jerked her head around to look at him.

She'd thought Lord Blytheland handsome before, but she had rated him low. He was dressed in a blue coat so dark as to seem black, his knee breeches were of the palest yellow, his shirt points were high, and a sapphire pin glistened within the folds of his neckcloth. The close-fitting coat displayed his wide shoulders to perfection, and the breeches clung to his long and well-muscled legs. His gold embroidered cream waistcoat declared him one of the dandy set, and on any other man the effect would have been overdone. Instead, it set off Lord Blytheland's tall and elegant form, and he looked magnificent.

Cassandra felt herself blushing, but she was determined not to be missish. Drawing in a deep breath to calm herself, she put her hand in his outstretched one and said, "I would be delighted to dance with you, Lord Blytheland."

She smiled at him, for she had succeeded in controlling her voice so that it did not shake or stutter—but then she was glad she'd said her piece before she looked into his face. He was gazing at her intently, and a smile slowly warmed his expression. It reached his eyes and there something seemed to glow as if a stronger emotion than kindness existed for her.

She must be imagining it! Looking hurriedly away, Cassandra concentrated on getting to the dance set before her. It was a simple country dance, and there would be little chance for them to talk. She sighed with relief.

"A sad crush, is it not? Lady Marchmont should be happy." The marquess tapped a guest's shoulder, smiled, and passed through a small gap in the crowd.

"Yes, although why anyone should be happy that their guests cannot move an inch except on the dance floor, I do not know," Cassandra replied. He laughed. She glanced at him again. He was still smiling, but the emotion she thought she saw in his eyes was gone.

"Nor do I. But it seems to be every hostess's ambition."

"Ambition is not a virtue, my lord. It is very like to greed."

"Just so."

Cassandra cast a suspicious look at him. "Are you laughing at me, sir?"

The marquess put on an innocent look. "I? My dear Miss Hathaway, why should I laugh at you?"

A chuckle bubbled up behind her lips, and she failed to suppress it. "But you are! Odious man! Indeed, I do believe you meant to give me a set-down!"

"Not at all," replied Blytheland. "Were I to give you one, you would definitely know it."

"Now *that* is a set-down, if ever I heard one."

The marquess laughed again. She smiled but looked at him thoughtfully, and though he grinned down at her she wondered how blistering his set-downs could be. He could be quite unpleasant about it, she felt. There was that intensity about him, despite his meticulous clothing and easy address. It seemed to come out only when he played his music, but she imagined it must always be there, beneath the calm.

"Oh, Lord Blytheland! Is that you?" cried a female voice. Cassandra turned to look and stared. The lady coming toward them must have been the most—"decorated" was the only word Cassandra could think of—person she had ever seen. Her voluptuous form was draped in jewels and necklaces that covered a bosom barely contained within her bodice. Cassandra looked at the marquess. A fleeting, irritated expression seemed to cross his face, then a cool smile took its place. He bowed politely.

"*Is* it me, Mrs. Bradstead? I thought it was my twin." His smile turned more cool than before.

Mrs. Bradstead seemed not to notice. "Naughty man!" she said, lightly tapping her fan on his arm. "I know you do not have a twin, so you *cannot* hoax *me*! Now, tell me, where *have* you been? It has been an age since I saw you last!"

"An age, ma'am? I thought I saw you just a few days ago."

Her fan traced a line down his lapel. "It seemed an age to me," she said, her voice caressing.

Blytheland's finger halted the fan's progress, and he pushed it away from him. "And here I thought time passed slowly only for the young—or young in mind." He smiled charmingly at Mrs. Bradstead.

The woman looked nonplussed, as if she could not think of a reply. She looked at Cassandra. "And who is your charming—young—companion, my lord?"

The marquess's smile grew wider. "Miss Cassandra Hathaway, ma'am. Miss Hathaway, Mrs. Aurelia Bradstead."

Cassandra curtsied, feeling a little sorry for Mrs. Bradstead. The woman was clearly not good at understanding allusions or metaphor. Lord Blytheland must see this; he should not tease her so! But then, Cassandra had already

experienced his teasing earlier; he was not much different
in this respect from her brother. *She* could tolerate it, but it
was clear this poor lady could not. Perhaps she should turn
the conversation, to spare Mrs. Bradstead discomfort.

"I am pleased to meet you, Mrs. Bradstead. I hope you
do not mind, but I cannot help but admire your beautiful
necklaces. You do have such a lovely display of them, do
you not?" Cassandra smiled kindly at her.

"Why, why, I—I have never—!" Mrs. Bradstead sputtered.

Cassandra nodded and smiled comfortingly. "You need
not explain. I know how it is! When one is fond of a certain
thing one tends to wear it to excess, does one not? I myself
was surprised one day to find that most of my dresses are in
varying shades of blue—and how tedious that could be!
But there it is! One cannot help wearing what one favors."

Mrs. Bradstead shot her one burning look, then stalked
away as fast as the crowded room would allow. Cassandra
suddenly felt uncertain. It seemed Mrs. Bradstead had taken
offense at something she had said; but how could that be?
She had only complimented her on her selection of jewelry.

She glanced at Lord Blytheland, hoping he was not displeased at her. She was surprised to find a wide grin on his
face. "I . . . I did not mean to offend your friend, my lord,"
she said tentatively.

"It does not matter," the marquess replied. He looked
down at her, and it seemed that a mischievous light danced
in his eyes. Was he laughing at her? Cassandra put up her
chin defensively.

"If you must know, I thought you were teasing her, so I
tried to turn the conversation." She gazed at him sternly.

"And very successfully, too, Miss Hathaway."

"*I* cannot see that. Why, she acted as if I offended her
terribly."

"Of course you were successful. You turned the conversation so well that *she* turned and left."

"So I *did* offend her!" Cassandra looked down at her clenched hands, then gazed at Lord Blytheland earnestly. "I must go after her and apologize!" She turned to go.

She felt a firm hand on her arm. "No, don't," he said. "If you must know, I was trying to give her a set-down myself."

"That was not well done of you, my lord," Cassandra replied gravely.

"Was it? She is an encroaching creature, and malicious. I did not know it when I first—met her. It is just as well she left us." The look he gave her was as cool as the one he had given Mrs. Bradstead.

Cassandra's heart sank. She had offended *him,* now. But it was not wrong to speak the truth. She gave him a firm look. "And *that* set-down was meant for *me,* was it not?"

"Yes, but it was not very effective, was it?"

"No," Cassandra replied baldly. "I spoke nothing but the truth, after all."

Lord Blytheland's eyes lightened, and he laughed. "I see it was not at all effective."

She looked at him uncertainly. How unpredictable he was, to be sure!

They came to where the dance set had formed, but their conversation with Mrs. Bradstead had delayed them and the dance had already started. "Alas, we are too late. Would you mind taking a stroll along the terrace instead, Miss Hathaway?"

A little disappointed that she was not to dance with him, Cassandra nodded. Feeling a little diffident, she cast a glance at her mother across the room.

Apparently catching her look, Lord Blytheland said, "I will ask your parents for permission, of course." Cassandra nodded and watched him maneuver through the crowd, then bow before her mother and father. She saw them talk, and then saw her mother look in her direction. Lady Hathaway merely smiled at her, and Cassandra felt more at ease.

The marquess gave one more bow before he turned back toward Cassandra. He was carrying something, and as he came closer she could see it was her shawl. How thoughtful of him! A glowing warmth crept into her heart, and Cassandra smiled at him. She had not thought that she might be chilled in the night air, but he had.

As they stepped through the threshold onto the terrace, Cassandra felt suddenly uncertain. She thought there might be others on the terrace as well, but she could see only the vague shapes of a low stone wall and shrubbery beyond that, for the curtains kept much of the candlelight from escaping the ballroom. She did not see any people, but there must have been, for she thought she heard the murmur of voices some distance away. Well, it was not, certainly, as if they were totally alone.

The night air was cool and a light breeze brushed the curls around her face. Something else intimately brushed her neck and shoulder, but it was not a breeze, for it was warmer. Her heart beat faster. She looked up to find the marquess smiling down at her, and then her small spark of alarm faded, for she felt him drape her delicate woolen shawl across her shoulders. Really, Cassandra! she scolded herself. As if Lord Blytheland would do anything improper! She let out her breath in a long sigh.

"I thank you, my lord. This *is* pleasant, is it not? I am glad you suggested it." She looked up at the stars sparkling like tiny candles in the sky and gave a little chuckle. "When I was a girl, I used to think each star was an angel that played an instrument, and that someday I would hear a symphony if I listened hard enough."

"Ah, but they are angels, don't you know."

His voice was closer to her than she expected, and she quickly glanced at him to see him gazing reflectively at her. I will *not* be missish, she told herself, and looked steadily out at the night.

"It is best on a clear night like this; you need only concentrate, and listen," the marquess said softly. She could feel his breath upon her ear as he spoke, and then felt his fingers brush against her shoulder. He lifted a curl that lay against her neck and let it drop. She looked up at him, wondering what he was thinking, but felt she dare not ask.

"I—I am afraid the noise of the guests from the ballroom drowns them out."

"Pretend the guests are not there." He put his fingers under her chin, lifting it so that she looked him in the eye. He was gazing at her with a serious, considering expression. Cassandra held her breath. Was he . . . was he going to kiss her? And if so, would she let him?

She closed her eyes briefly, and felt a touch upon her mouth—but it was not a kiss. His fingers still held her chin, but his thumb slowly, gently outlined the contours of her lips. It seemed he watched his thumb's movement, then looked at her as if searching for something. He sighed.

"You should not go out walking alone with me on terraces."

"There . . . there are others walking out here as well." Cassandra felt breathless and oddly dissatisfied, though she should be glad, indeed, that he did not do something so improper as to kiss her.

A wide grin spread across his face. "Others who have invisibility amongst their talents, of course."

"I thought I heard some voices . . ." Cassandra could feel a blush rising in her cheeks.

"Perhaps. However, they are not anywhere in sight. We are quite private here."

"Are we?" But she knew it was so, even as she spoke. They stood just past the windowed doors that let out to the terrace, near the low stone wall that curved into the mansion itself. The curtains obscured the light from the ballroom, and only dimly illuminated Blytheland's countenance. She was glad she was in shadow, for then the marquess could not see her blushes—and then realized the reason she was in shadow was because she stood in a corner, and he blocked her way out.

From within the ballroom the orchestra struck up, and Cassandra knew that another dance set had begun. The music had a hypnotic beat, and she felt her own heart beat faster to its rhythm. Blytheland's hand came up, and she could feel his thumb trace circles along the line of her jaw, in rhythm to the music. She closed her eyes.

"Will you kiss me, Cassandra?" His voice was low and soft.

"I—I have not given you permission to use my—my Christian name, sir."

"Then give it to me now."

"I—"

"Please."

A deep sigh escaped her, and perhaps there was a yes in it somewhere. Cassandra did not have time to consider which question she might have answered, for the marquess's lips came down upon hers, swiftly, firmly, gently. She did not know what to do at first, for she had never been kissed—at least not as Lord Blytheland kissed her. There was something insistent beneath the softness of his caress, and she was half afraid of it, for she felt it was related to that intensity she'd glimpsed within his eyes before. But it seemed as if some natural force within her knew the right response and cared not for any fears she might have: a small gasp opened her mouth and she leaned forward, matching his intensity with passion.

"My God," she heard him murmur as he parted from her only a hairbreadth and for a heartbeat's time.

The music from the ballroom swirled through the open windows and around them, and made Cassandra's perceptions rise to an acute sensitivity. Blytheland's fingers moved from her cheek to her neck and left a scintillating trail, like champagne trickling across her skin. She shivered and pressed closer to him, savoring his warmth in the cool night. His lips shifted from her lips to her cheek, and then down to her throat.

Then he stilled, and stopped, and moved away. Bewildered, Cassandra gazed at his solemn face, but he looked toward the open doors. Voices, louder than she'd heard before.

Reality doused her like ice water across the face, and she drew in a swift breath. Oh, merciful heavens, someone was coming! What *had* she been doing? How could she be so stupid? It was obvious what she'd been doing. She hoped that it would not be obvious to anyone who might see her. She blushed hotly at the thought.

"I think we need to walk, Miss Hathaway," the marquess said.

"Y-yes, of course."

He bent and picked up her shawl, which had fallen to the ground, shook it, and put it around her shoulders. She pulled it tightly around her.

"Thank you."

Blytheland shot a surprised look at her.

"I *meant* for my *shawl!*"

"Of course." A small smile crossed his lips. He tucked her hand upon his arm, and they moved out from the shadows.

Cassandra was glad they strolled about the terrace. The night breeze had picked up and had become chill, and cooled her too-warm cheeks. Another couple did indeed come upon them, but they barely acknowledged Cassandra's and Blytheland's presence, for the couple were too absorbed looking into each other's eyes. Cassandra looked away, embarrassed. Is that how she had looked at Lord Blytheland? She groaned mentally. She was only thankful the couple barely noticed her.

Before they entered the ballroom, the marquess stopped and turned to her gravely. "I have little excuse to have . . . done what I did. I only hope you will forgive me any unpleasantness I might have inflicted on you."

"It wasn't," Cassandra blurted.

"Excuse me?"

"Unpleasant. It wasn't—Oh heavens! What am I saying?" She pressed her hand to her cheek, trying to suppress another blush.

"The ever-truthful Miss Hathaway." Blytheland chuckled. They stepped into the ballroom, and Cassandra saw that a set was just forming. "Perhaps we should dance this time—if you are agreeable?"

Nodding, she laid her shawl across a vacant chair and prepared herself for the dance. She was relieved the music started quickly, for then any high color in her cheeks could easily be attributed to the exertions of the dance. The marquess was no more than polite and as kind as he had been earlier before their . . . kiss. She was glad of that—glad that his behavior was no more or less than normal now—for it allowed her to gain her composure again. When he brought her back to her parents, he bowed over her hand and with a last smile merged into the ballroom crowd.

But Cassandra was not to sit quietly by her mother and father at all, as she was used to after a dance. Immediately upon the heels of Blytheland's departure, three young men came up to her parents, claiming some acquaintance through friends or relations. Lady Hathaway, beaming, introduced them all to her daughter.

"May I have the honor of this dance, Miss Hathaway?" a stocky, dark-haired gentleman asked. Sir Ellery Heysmith, Cassandra remembered.

"Oh, no, Miss Hathaway," Mr. Rowland cut in, grinning at Sir Ellery. "You must know that my friend Heysmith here is the merest caper merchant. He'll stomp your feet to splinters. You'd be much better off with me as your dance partner."

His friend gave him a wry grin. "And you, Rolly, are a

rattle, and would deafen her by the end of the dance with all your tittle-tattle."

"Here's your answer, then, ma'am," said Lord Eldon, smiling at her. "It is I with whom you must dance. Between a caper merchant, a rattle, and myself—is there any question?" He gave an elegant bow, and his friends rolled their eyes in disgust at him.

Cassandra broke out laughing. "Oh, heavens! What am I to do if I am to be fair? Let us see . . . ah! I have it. I shall choose alphabetically: Lord Eldon first, Sir Ellery second, and Mr. Rowland third."

Mr. Rowland put on a dejected look, and put his hand over his heart. "Alas, put off by an accident of birth!"

Cassandra laughed again, and Lord Eldon grinned. "Sorry, old friend. Better luck next time!"

She enjoyed a vigorous dance with him. Suddenly, it seemed she found an astonishing number of other gentlemen who had at least a passing acquaintance with some relative or friend of her parents; between them all there was not one dance in which she did not participate.

Later at home, when Cassandra finally reached her bed in the wee hours of the morning, her feet ached, and she was exhausted. Never had she had so many dance partners in her life! Her thoughts settled briefly on why she was so suddenly popular, but floated away from sheer fatigue.

"At least," she murmured to herself before slipping into sleep, "I did *not* think of Lord Blytheland's kisses all the while. Not while I was dancing . . ."

Lord Blytheland, however, did think of kisses. He could not avoid it. They were there before him—her pink and delectable lips—every time he closed his eyes to sleep. He could even feel them, soft and sweet, then opening and moving upon his with all the passion he'd imagined when she had played the piano but a few weeks ago. He groaned aloud and rolled over, pressing his face into his pillow.

After a moment, he drove his fist into its goose-down depths. The mattress beneath him only made it worse. It reminded him of the press of her form against him—firm yet supple and warm.

He sat up in his bed and pressed the heels of his hands upon his eyes. Good God, he must have been mad. How *could* he have taken Cassandra out on the terrace and made what amounted to passionate love to her? He had only meant to dance one dance with her—which he did, for all the good it did him. Thank God he was able to collect himself afterward and retain the cool exterior he so carefully cultivated. He sighed. What the devil possessed him to take her out somewhere so damned private it was as good as a bedroom?

She was lovely, but he had been around beautiful women before, both experienced and innocent. But he'd never allowed himself to imply, either by word or gesture, that he was anything more than interested in a light flirtation with any dewy-eyed damsel. Indeed, he had always kept himself to more mature and experienced women who liked their independence and would most likely not marry him if he asked—which he never did, of course, just in case. But Cassand—no, Miss Hathaway—now. He had been within an inch of letting his lips follow the smooth curve of her shoulder down to her soft and delightful—

With another groan, Blytheland fell back upon his bed and pulled his now badly mauled pillow over his face, half wishing he'd suffocate so he could be put out of his misery. Never had he meant to succumb to Miss Hathaway's charms—of face and form only, for she lacked the skills of refined flirtation he usually found so enjoyable, and was so blunt as to be—almost—vulgar.

That was it. Vulgar. Blytheland sighed with relief, removed the pillow from atop him, and settled himself down to sleep. He smiled in relief. Lord, the look on Aurelia's face when Miss Hathaway "complimented" her on her jewels! He regretted that he had had a brief liaison with Aurelia two years ago; it was a passion of the moment, but she had obviously wanted something more. She still schemed to get him—between diversions with other men—and he was glad he was out of the liaison. Certainly Miss Hathaway had put an end to any attempt on Aurelia's part to regain her old status. Cassandra had sent her to *point-non-plus* in less than a minute.

And there her upbringing was revealed—Miss Hathaway apparently did not understand that it was vulgar to comment unfavorably about one's person. A small, niggling voice reminded him that Miss Hathaway no doubt truly thought her comments were complimentary, but he dismissed it.

There now. If he concentrated on it enough, he was sure he could convince himself that she was, in some manner, too unrefined for his taste. Indeed, had he not met and danced with a number of other ladies at the ball? Many of them were far more refined than Miss Hathaway, and a few were more beautiful and higher born as well.

Relief flowed into him. Miss Hathaway was nothing much above the ordinary, not in looks nor in refinement. He had begun his search for a wife and had seen women far superior to her in birth and fortune. Now that he had seen some of what the *ton* had to offer in prospective brides, it should be easy to keep these ladies in mind; Miss Hathaway's assets paled in comparison, and whatever attraction he might feel for her would be easy to resist.

Blytheland settled himself into his pillows and closed his eyes at last. He sighed. Yes, he could resist Miss Hathaway now that he'd seen what the marriage mart had to offer. In fact, he would call upon her tomorrow, just to prove it to himself.

Harry watched Cassandra and Lord Blytheland leave the Marchmonts' ball. He smiled, satisfied. He was certain the marquess would propose at any time now, and it would be as if his mistake had never happened. Well, he hadn't *precisely* made a mistake at the time, for it was not his fault that the man had moved at the last moment and fallen in love with the wrong woman the first time. Harry moved away from the Marchmonts' house and flew toward London, to the street where the Hathaway family lived.

Psyche was quite wrong; she'd soon see that his decision to shoot Lord Blytheland was the right one. Did he not kiss Cassandra—and very passionately, too—for more than five minutes? In this day and age, it was considered a significant thing, and the rules seemed to be that a man could not signal his desires in such a way without submitting an offer of marriage eventually.

Harry spied the house at last and descended to the open window of Psyche's room. She was a kindly child and left it open for him at night so that he could come out of cold weather if he wished. Quietly, he moved to the side of her bed where she was sleeping, and pushed away a small red curl from her forehead. He did not know why he had come to her rescue those years ago when she was lost in the woods . . . perhaps there was something that reminded him of his own Psyche long ago, and who was lost to him.

He had taken on the form of a boy, not much older than herself, for he thought it would be less frightening to her to see another child in the dark, than any other shape he could take. He grimaced. The problem with that was one tended to take on the characteristics of whatever form one assumed, and the longer he used mortal form and the longer he stayed away from the realm of the gods, the more mortal he felt and acted. And it was necessary, for he knew his own Psyche was somewhere on earth, and he would take whatever form he needed to find her.

He grinned suddenly. It was, meanwhile, immensely entertaining to be a young adolescent boy, and even more so to linger around the Hathaway family and see how their fortunes went. He had grown quite fond of Psyche Hathaway—all of the Hathaways, for that matter—no doubt because of her namesake, and also because he never knew quite what she would say next. He gazed out the windows at the lights of London . . . the *ton* was still out and about. His grin grew wider. It was also very entertaining to see what came of his target practice here in and about London. He moved away from Psyche and went to the window.

Harry pulled an arrow from his quiver and twirled it around between his fingers. He chuckled quietly. The night was still young for the high and mighty, and it would be very amusing to see how far they could fall.

Chapter 6

"You must be in excellent spirits, my dear," Sir John said, looking at his wife over his spectacles. "You have been humming a tune for the last quarter of an hour."

"Have I? Well, it is not at all surprising if I am." Lady Hathaway put down her embroidery. She was making a pretty counterpane with pink hearts and blue flowers, just the thing for a newlywed's chambers. *She* could see the significance of Lord Blytheland's walk with Cassandra two weeks ago at the Marchmont ball. She sighed happily. "Oh, husband, I do think Lord Blytheland will declare himself soon! Only think! He has gone to every function at which Cassandra has appeared, and has danced at least once with her at each one. And at Lady Harley's, he even danced twice with her!"

"Well, well, our Cassandra a marchioness. But . . . perhaps he is overly fond of dancing?"

Lady Hathaway sat up stiffly in her chair. "It is *not* dancing he is fond of—" She broke off, for she caught the twinkle in her husband's eye. She let out an exasperated breath. "Oh, John, you are such a provoking man!"

He grinned at her. "But you rise so easily to bait, my dear." He sobered and looked at her keenly. "Are you sure his affections are engaged?"

His wife looked affronted. "Of course I am! The man almost haunts our house! If he is not calling on her to practice music, he is taking her out in his curricle, or inviting us to the theater. Last night Hetty Chatwick actually asked me if we had any interesting announcements to make in the near future—so I know Blytheland's attentions have come to people's notice. Well, of course I said that we certainly did not, but I am afraid I could not help feeling a little conscious."

Sir John rolled his eyes and pushed his fingers through his thick, graying hair, messing it terribly. "Amelia, now all of London will believe it is a promised thing. Hetty Chatwick! Good Lord, what a gossip! You must know now that the supposed betrothal of Blytheland and our daughter will be all over town by tomorrow."

"But I denied it!"

"Yes. and 'feeling a little conscious,' you no doubt looked it!"

"Not at all! Indeed, I looked most stern and forbade her to speak of it."

"Of course that will make her say nothing of the subject at all," Sir John replied, his voice ironic.

Lady Hathaway could not reply. She glanced at her husband resentfully and worked with great concentration on her needlework. She well knew that Mrs. Chatwick would spread it about that Cassandra was as good as promised to the marquess. But how could she help it? Any good mother would want an eligible connection for her children, and she did not exaggerate when she said Blytheland practically haunted the house. Well, so did other gentlemen, now that it seemed Cassandra had become so popular of late.

And there! That was another thing. It was clear to her that the marquess brought Cassandra into fashion. He was a much sought-after man, and any lady to whom he paid attention became just as sought-after. And if—although she could not think it at all likely—*if* Blytheland should *not* declare himself to Cassandra, why then her daughter need only choose one of her other admirers. But of course, *that* would not be the case, for the marquess must be in love with her.

To be sure, it had been only two months since he had been first introduced to Cassandra. But then Lady Hathaway had known of affections that had been animated to the point of a marriage proposal in less than a month's time. The little courtesies, the minute-too-long holding of her hand, the way Blytheland looked at her daughter—*those* had not escaped her notice. Then, too, there were the kisses on the hand—not unknown coming from her own, Lady Hathaway's, contemporaries, but unusual from the younger generation.

The door opened and Sir John and Lady Hathaway looked up.

"Mama, Papa." Cassandra smiled at them, but there was a tense air about her.

"Is there something you wished to see us about, my dear?" Sir John asked. He gestured to a chair near his, and his daughter sat down upon it, arranging her skirts neatly about her.

"I . . . I do not want to seem vain, but perhaps you have noticed that I have more . . . gentlemen callers than before." She glanced uncertainly at her mother.

Lady Hathaway smiled encouragingly. "Well, of course. And a most fortunate girl you are, Cassandra! Now, you see what comes of listening to me, and holding your peace in polite company."

"But that is just it, Mama! I speak as I always have—oh, it is not as if I have not tried to heed your words and hold my tongue, but I know I have not been very successful. And then, too, when I go about to these social functions—more than I ever have before—I find an increasing number of people who say the most cutting things about others! I cannot stay silent, Mama, truly I cannot!"

"Well, well, you must have improved somewhat, for you do have a good number of admirers," Lady Hathaway said.

"No. I think something else has changed. I say what I think, and it seems everyone believes I have uttered a witticism! I cannot understand it!" Cassandra rose from her chair, her hands clasping tightly together.

Sir John chuckled. "Ah, my dear, you have become fashionable. Once you are claimed a diamond of the first water—by those who would know and whose words have weight with the frivolous—you may say anything you like, and it will be considered manna from heaven."

"John, really!" cried his wife, scandalized.

Cassandra turned troubled eyes to her mother. "Mama, is this true?"

"Well, it is more likely—in general—that people will view one in a more favorable light than if one were *not* fashionable . . ."

"Oh, how—how detestable! As if—as if I could want them to listen to me for such a reason, and not because I spoke the truth!"

"Oh, for heaven's sake, Cassandra! Try not to be such a ninny!" cried her mother impatiently. "Be glad they listen to you now at all, for you must know they never did before!" Immediately she wished the words back, for her daughter paled and looked stricken. Lady Hathaway opened her mouth to say a few consoling words, but then closed it firmly. No. For all that she was sad for Cassandra's disillusionment, the girl simply had to accommodate herself to the ways of society and human nature. Better she bear a setdown from her mother who loves her, Lady Hathaway thought, than end up living a lonely spinster's life, shunned by those who could make her life so much more comfortable.

"I am afraid your mother is right, Cassandra," Sir John said, glancing sternly at his wife, nevertheless. "Consider which is preferable: the truth ignored, or the truth at least accepted, though lightly?"

Lady Hathaway cast a surprised look at her husband for his support. It was a different approach than she would have taken herself, but perhaps it would work.

"The truth accepted, of course," Cassandra replied reluctantly.

"Very good," her father said and smiled approvingly.

"Then, too, my dear, you must know that it is Lord Blytheland who has so kindly brought you into fashion," Lady Hathaway interjected. "You cannot wish to be so ungrateful as to repel his efforts on your behalf."

A glow effused Cassandra's face, and her eyes shone. "Oh, no, no! Of course I could not! I am sure he meant well by it, even though it is not what I could like. He is so very kind, is he not, Mama?"

My lady was not quite certain how to reply to this, for Lord Blytheland was not as kind to everyone, from what she had heard of him. She looked up at her husband and found him watching her. "I am sure, my dear, that his attentions to you have been all that is amiable and pleasing," Lady Hathaway said. She threw a challenging look at him. There! He could not say that she said anything not remarked upon by anyone else.

Sir John merely smiled, turned to his daughter, and gave his wife another shock by saying, "Your mother is quite right, and I am pleased, Cassandra, that you understand his actions were meant for your benefit, and that you are properly grateful."

Lady Hathaway stared at her husband. Could it be that he approved of Blytheland? Of course, any man would be a fool to pass over such an eligible prospect for his daughter! But Sir John was not just any man. He had little respect for titles or wealth, and he associated with any manner of people who she had to admit were of great intelligence, but some of whom were decidedly odd. She dared let hope rise in her heart: her husband favorable to the match, Blytheland sure to propose soon, and her daughter . . . She sighed. Now if only Cassandra would be so inclined as to go along with it all! But there was no depending on that. Although . . .

Lady Hathaway gazed at her daughter's face and saw a

dreamy smile hovering about her lips. Could it be . . . ? She had not really watched her daughter's behavior in the marquess's presence; she well knew that Cassandra had more than enough modesty to keep her from doing anything scandalous. She had concentrated on *his* manners instead, watching for any signs of a *tendre* for the girl.

"You *have* found Lord Blytheland's attentions . . . pleasant, have you not, Cassandra?" she said tentatively.

"Oh, yes!" And then to her surprise, Cassandra's face turned beet red. "Th-that is to say, his attentions have been very—He has been most—Not that he has been—" She stopped, looked with confused eyes at her parents, and rushed out the library door.

"Well, well! I do believe our daughter finds Lord Blytheland's attentions most pleasant indeed." Sir John chuckled.

"For heaven's sake, John, have you no sense of propriety?" cried Lady Hathaway. "For all we know he might have—have *importuned* her in an improper manner!"

"Kissed her, do you mean, Amelia?"

"John!"

"Oh, come now, my dear. I think you remember a few kisses before we were married . . . ?" He sat next to her on the sofa, slipped his arm around her ample waist, and kissed her ear.

It was Lady Hathaway's turn to blush, now. She slapped lightly at his hand, although a small smile lingered about her mouth. "*That* is neither here nor there! I must go to her and find out the extent of Blytheland's, ah, attentions."

"My dear wife, you would do best to leave it alone. The marquess is a gentleman. Though he is clearly fond of the ladies, I have not heard of any profoundly libertine tendencies about him. I have no doubt he behaved as any gentleman might around our daughter."

"That is precisely what I am afraid of!" Lady Hathaway said. She caught Sir John's quizzical look and sighed. "Oh, I do not know! Before Cassandra's coming into fashion, any gentleman could be counted to keep their distance. Now I do not know what to think! I wish Blytheland *had* kissed her!"

He smiled. "Never mind, my dear. No doubt he has. Why else should our daughter look so conscious?"

Lady Hathaway looked at her husband, aghast. "John! Do you mean to sit there, sure that Blytheland has kissed Cassandra, and do nothing?"

"No. Not at all. I plan to wait, and see how things come about."

"But that is as good as doing nothing at all!" cried his lady, despairing.

"And what do you wish me to do? Challenge him to a duel unless he marries Cassandra?" Sir John took off his spectacles and polished them thoughtfully with the end of his neckcloth. "Nonsense, Amelia. The truth will be revealed of itself, you know. What falls out will be for the best."

"Well, that is precisely what I fear! That it *will* all fall out!" said Lady Hathaway testily.

"Have faith, my dear," Sir John said. "All will be well."

His lady sighed. Her husband was the dearest man, but not at all practical. She herself would have to see what could be done. "Yes, John," she said, resigned.

Cassandra sat on her bed, pressing her hands to her face. "Oh, how could I be so stupid?" she cried. "I should have told them he kissed me—but I couldn't."

She rose, wet a cloth with the water that was left at the washstand, and pressed the cloth to her cheeks. She felt warm and knew she was blushing just thinking of kisses. It would be much better to resolve to herself that she would not allow it—if, that is, Lord Blytheland tried it again. Which he would not, of course, because he was after all a gentleman, and not an adolescent like her brother, Kenneth, who kissed maids indiscriminately.

A knock sounded on her door. "Come in!"

"Cassandra . . ." Lady Hathaway entered, taking what seemed to be tentative steps into the chamber. Cassandra looked at her mother in surprise. She looked at once hesitant and concerned—and oddly, a little guilty.

"Is—is there something the matter, Mama?"

"Oh, no, no. That is to say—Actually, Cassandra, I was wondering if you had anything to say to *me*."

"I? I cannot think what you might mean." Cassandra went to a stool by the fire and sat down upon it, staring into the flames.

"Come now, my dear, this is unlike you! Why it was obvious to your father and me that something overset you." Her mother's voice sounded so very comfortable and warm, as it always had whenever Cassandra had been in a scrape or needed to confide in her.

"I . . ."

"Is it Lord Blytheland? Has he . . . importuned you in any distasteful manner?"

Cassandra jumped up from her seat, feeling her face grow hot again. "Oh, no, Mama! How can you think it? He has always been very much the gentleman."

Lady Hathaway smiled comfortingly at her. "Then what is it? You cannot be blushing as red as a beet root and there be nothing the matter!"

"He—I—we kissed. At the Marchmonts' ball." There was silence for one moment, and Cassandra swallowed nervously.

"How deligh—Ah! And you found it disgusting and shameful, did you?"

"Oh, no, no! It was the most won—It was most pleasant, Mama! What I mean is—" Cassandra could hear her own voice quaver, and she detested herself for it. "Am I sunk in depravity for liking it so? I know I should not have allowed it."

"Oh, heavens, girl!" Lady Hathaway laughed. "Certainly

it was not proper of you—or him—to have done it. But you
were not seen, were you?"

"I am sure we were not."

"Good. Your reputation would have been in tatters if you
were! Although it would not have been a terrible thing if
you *had* been seen, for he would have offered for you
and—"

"No! Mama, I could not marry him if that were so!" Cassandra paced agitatedly in front of the fireplace, then
stopped, clasping her hands tightly together.

"Why, I thought you were not . . . averse to his company,
Cassandra!"

"Averse—! No, never! I—I—"

"Are you *fond* of him, then?"

"Fond! No. That is, yes, but—I have not thought—Oh,
Mama, I do not *know*!" cried Cassandra, sinking down upon
the footstool again next to her mother. "I have known him
but two months! How can I know, truly?"

Lady Hathaway smiled and patted her on the shoulder.
"Well, well, you are right. It is only past the middle of the
Season, and there is plenty of time to come to know each
other better."

"Yes, of course, Mama," Cassandra said, still feeling confused. Mama had told her long ago about not submitting to a
gentleman's attempts at an embrace, but now she seemed
positively merry about the prospect. Lady Hathaway had
maintained a delighted smile throughout their conversation.
She could not understand it. Perhaps . . . perhaps kisses were
not so reprehensible as she had believed?

"You are looking concerned," her mother said. Cassandra
looked up at her with a grateful smile at her quick perception. "Is it that you are worried about kissing?"

Cassandra nodded.

"Well, it was only one kiss, after all! It is not as if it never
happens. I will even confess your father and I shared a few
before we were married. Not that my mother would have

approved, mind you!" Lady Hathaway smiled reminiscently and looked almost young.

Cassandra stared at Lady Hathaway. She tried envisioning her mother's plump form and father's lean one in the same embrace as she and the marquess had shared and failed miserably. But it must have been so, if her mother said it. Well, it was obvious she had refined too much on the matter, and she felt relieved.

"Oh, Mama! I am so glad you came to talk to me about it. I have felt so confused!"

"Of course, my dear. Am I not your mother? You are a good girl, and I know you try your best to behave with propriety." With one more affectionate pat on Cassandra's shoulder, Lady Hathaway rose from her chair and left the room.

Married. Cassandra had not thought of it—or at least, not dared think of it in connection with Lord Blytheland. Of course, she knew the purpose of having a Season in London was to find an amiable husband, and she knew her parents were kind enough to let her follow her own heart. But never, never would she allow the marquess to propose to her under such circumstances in which he would feel forced to do so! If he ever did propose, that is. Certainly she could not expect that he would. He could look far, far higher than herself for a wife.

Or . . . could she? Could he possibly want to marry her? Cassandra shook her head fiercely. No. If so, he would not have so kindly brought her to fashion, would he? For then he would have rivals for her favor. She dismissed the thought that his kiss would have meant anything. After all, kisses did not mean to gentlemen what they did to ladies. Why, she need only think of her brother Kenneth to know that! She had caught him kissing a parlor maid once, and then a week later she found him with a chambermaid. Of course her brother could not seriously intend to marry a servant, and certainly Lord Blytheland did not think she, Cassandra, was a servant, but it just showed how little men treasured kisses or embraces.

Well, then! She would just keep that in mind and make sure they were never caught in any sort of embrace—not that they *would* kiss again, of course! With that firm resolve, she readied herself for the duet she would have with the marquess.

Lady Hathaway leaned against the chamber door she had just closed, and shut her eyes. "Thank you, God," she murmured under her breath. Lord Blytheland *had* kissed Cassandra! He would not have done it if he had not been enamored of her. Never, never had she heard that the marquess trifled with the affections of a young unmarried lady. And, miracle of miracles, Cassandra was not so much of a bluestocking that she found his embrace objectionable. Further, Lady Hathaway was certain her husband would not object—for whatever eccentric reason—to the match.

Ah, what a success it would be! And Lady Chartley thought *she* had done well marrying her girl to an earl's son. Well, perhaps she had, at that, for the chit was but a sallow little thing! Cassandra, now! *She* would not only be a marchioness, but eventually a duchess! Lady Hathaway's heart felt full to bursting with joy, and her step was light as she walked down the stairs to the parlor.

"So . . . I understand you might be looking for a marchioness, Blythe, old man?" Lord Eldon leaned against the marquess's wardrobe and negligently twirled his quizzing glass on its ribbon. He watched as his friend carefully wound his neckcloth around his neck while the valet hovered anxiously next to him.

"Who told you that?" Blytheland pulled one end of the cloth through a loop he had made with the other end.

"You haven't been to White's lately, I see. It's in all the town's betting books."

"What are the odds?"

"Ten to one you'll be in the parson's mousetrap before the end of the Season."

"Good odds for you—if you are betting *against*."

"Should I be?"

Blytheland, holding a twist of neckcloth firmly to his neck, turned to look at his friend. "Why not?"

"Well, I might lose, Blythe-my-old." Eldon grinned at him. "Seems to me you've been seen much more than once at Hathaway's house."

"Miss Hathaway is a superb pianist. It is rare that I can play against a performer who is more than competent."

"Oh, and let's see—you danced with her twice at the Amberleys' ball, you escorted her to supper at the Bramhursts' rout, and I think I saw you at the theater with her last week," Lord Eldon continued, ticking off each item on his fingers. "And then of course there was that stunning beginning where you disappeared with her on the Marchmonts' terrace—" He held up his hand at the marquess's icy look. "Oh, never fear! It wasn't long enough for scandal, just enough to raise eyebrows."

"I never listen to gossips, frankly."

"Neither do I. But admit it, my old, you've been flitting around that Hathaway chit like a moth to a flame."

"I am not likely to be burnt, believe me!"

Eldon contemplated his friend. The marquess was still concentrating on tying his neckcloth, his movements were still smooth and careful, but there was a tenseness in his answers. He wondered how far he should push Blytheland. He was not exaggerating when he intimated that talk was rife about his friend's seeming infatuation with the lovely bluestocking. Better have it out, he decided. He almost grimaced at the thought. They'd almost had it out when Blytheland was first courting Chloe—his friend had a temper, certainly. But dash it all, for all that it was clear his friend wouldn't listen to him, he'd had to say something back then . . . as he had to now. Miss Hathaway was nothing like Chloe, and Blythe was a marriage-minded sort, even though he tried to deny it. La Hathaway would be perfect for him, if Blytheland would only see it. And if he didn't, he would certainly hate to see the poor girl hurt, for she was clearly caught. Eldon grinned to himself. Well, he never thought he had the romantic in him, but he always did have an eye for a matched pair.

However, Blytheland was too inclined to keep things to himself, and next thing you knew he'd blister you up one side and down the other for saying something perfectly innocent. He could have a nasty temper, Blytheland could, if he didn't air it once in a while. He'd have to watch his step. Eldon sighed.

"Well, I didn't think you were one to change your ways. Why should you? Once burnt, twice shy, after all."

Blytheland gave him a cold, sharp glance—definitely threatening. Eldon mentally retreated and decided to take another tack.

"And Lord knows you could have your pick of the *demi-mondaine*. I hear even Harriette Wilson has cast her eyes your way."

The marquess gave him a pained look. "Really, El, I thought you did not listen to gossip. Harriette Wilson. Good God. I hope I have better taste than that."

Lord Eldon nodded. "That's what I thought. Anyway, it's just as well you don't have an interest in La Hathaway. Rather thought I'd have a touch at her myself."

"What!" Blytheland's hand jerked, and he slewed his head around to stare at his friend. "You?"

"Milor'! Your cravat!" cried the valet, his hands clutching his hair in artistic agony.

"Damnation! Fichet, get me another, *vite*!" The marquess stripped off what used to be an impeccably starched length of cloth and threw it on the floor. He barely seemed to notice his servant's heartfelt groan at this desecration, or the man's muttered imprecations on the vagaries of the English.

Lord Eldon peered at the ruined neckcloth through his quizzing glass. "My, my. I haven't seen you do that since the time you heard Lady Montmorency was increasing—how long ago was that? Before you married Chloe, I think. Luckily it turned out to be Montmorency's brat, all right and tight. Platter-faced little thing—looks just like its father, no mistake. Never did poach on another man's territory after that, did you, Blythe?"

Blytheland threw him a fulminating glare. "Never mind about Montmorency! What the devil does he—I can't believe it. You, El? Setting up your nursery? You are younger than I am—five-and-twenty—if that!"

"Didn't stop my brother."

"That is different. *You* have never been one for chasing petticoats."

Lord Eldon grinned. "Not as much as you, at any rate. Thing is, I'm the eldest. Must do my duty and all that. You might think about it yourself, one of these days." He gave his quizzing glass one more twirl, then neatly pocketed it.

"But why Miss Hathaway?"

"Why not? Lovely girl, good figure, dresses well, good manners. Should do me proud. I don't care much for music, but just as long as it isn't some damned caterwauling I'll listen. By the way, I must thank you for bringing her to my notice. Truly enchanting." He kissed his fingers to the air in salute.

"But damn it, she's a bluestocking!"

"Bothers you, does it?" My, but old Blythe was getting red under his collar, Eldon thought gleefully.

"Yes! No! That's not the point. I've never seen *you* exchanging quotes from Sophocles with anyone! And I'll wager you've never done so with Cass—Miss Hathaway. That would be doing it a bit too brown, my friend."

"True." Cassandra, was it? Well, well. Lord Eldon was

hard put not to smile. "But the world of conversation is large. There are other things of which to speak—her charities, for instance."

"Charities?"

"Terrible situation, my old. There are starving folk all around us. She quite convinced me to contribute to the aid of these poor creatures."

"You?"

"Blytheland, you pain me. Of course, *me*. I may be a Pink of the *ton,* but I am not without heart. And never tell me she hasn't spoken of her charities to *you*."

The marquess looked uncomfortable.

"Ah, I see she has. Laid out any blunt for it?"

"Yes, and I promised to ask my father to speak at the House on it."

Lord Eldon laughed. "Persuasive creature, isn't she? But there you are. We shall rub along quite well together, don't you think? She with her causes, I with the money to fund them."

"You are getting as vulgar as she is," Blytheland retorted.

"I? Vulgar? should call you out, my old, if I didn't know how good you are with the pistols." Eldon moved himself from the wardrobe and sank into a large chair next to the fireplace. "But tell me. How is Miss Hathaway vulgar?"

"I should not have said vulgar," the marquess amended. "She is, certainly, indiscreet."

"Better and better," Eldon leered.

"I did *not* mean to imply she was a light skirt, damn you, El! She's more pure than—than that damnably ill-tied thing you have around your neck! *I* should call *you* out, if I knew you had the smallest ability to drag yourself out of bed before eleven."

His friend looked complacently at his own snowy white neckcloth reflected in the mirror and smiled. "Pure as an angel, I should think. Well, now. Indiscreet?"

"She can't control her tongue. She says whatever comes

to her mind. Lord, the number of times I have seen her give a set-down to some stiff-rumped hypocrite! And sometimes she is not even aware she is doing it!"

"I should be amused, I think."

"Amused!" The marquess grimaced into the mirror. "Well, it is amusing," he admitted. "It is also why I brought her into fashion. I thought it would be entertaining if I did so. That's all there is to it, and so you may tell your betting cronies." Fichet entered with another, freshly pressed, neckcloth. He warily handed it to his master.

"Hmm . . . And not because you are enamored of her?"

"I have known far more beautiful women than Miss Hathaway."

Lord Eldon noticed that his friend did not actually answer his question. He smiled to himself, then rose from the chair. "It's just as well, old Blythe. I just didn't want to step on your toes, you know." He put on his hat at a precise angle and took up his cane. "Think La Hathaway might come to see herself as a baroness? Perhaps I should go see her soon."

"I'd prefer you go to the devil, Eldon," said the marquess through clenched teeth.

"Better than being blue-deviled, my old!" His friend laughed, and left the room.

Blytheland cursed and ruined another neckcloth.

But Eldon's words came back to the marquess, niggling at him, for they were not content to settle in the far corner of Blytheland's mind, where he had consigned them. He glanced at Miss Hathaway, who was at the pianoforte flexing her fingers in readiness for the recital. Thoughts of Cassandra and marriage, of the natural consequences of marriage—the marriage bed, for instance—leapt upon him like a cat upon a mouse and played with his emotions unmercifully and with a killing instinct. They pounced on him when he happened to be near her and looked at the lips he had kissed, and when she played the pianoforte, he thought of how her fingers caressed the keys into soft sound and how they might caress his—

Blytheland took a deep breath and set his violin upon his chest and tried not to look at Cassandra as she began to play the sonata. There were plenty of things to focus upon in Lord and Lady Langdon's house, for it was well lighted and decorated with finely executed paintings, so he need not look at Miss Hathaway at all during the performance. He needed to pay strict attention to the music, for they were before Lady Langdon and her guests, and all eyes were upon them.

It was a piece of music both of them knew well and had practiced before either of them had met, and so it needed only two practice sessions to see if they could play together. There had been an initial awkwardness at first, but they had gone through it well enough, and quickly. He was not sure he could have gone through a third session; he'd been distracted enough during the first, almost as much as he had been distracted when Cassandra first played her pianoforte for him.

He'd look at her only once to signal the beginning of each movement and not look at her while they played. He would concentrate on the music, and that was all.

Silence descended on the guests, he took a deep breath, and nodded to Miss Hathaway. He watched her fingers touch the keys, then he closed his eyes and drew his bow across his violin.

It was a mistake. He should have known not to have selected this Beethoven sonata. If the presto beat made him take in a breath, the first notes in the minor key took it away from him. He had intended to select a difficult piece so that there would be a higher chance of Cassandra stumbling in her performance. He would be able to focus on his own performance then. But she did not stumble now, not as she had done when they had practiced before. She had obviously practiced more, afterward.

And now, now he was lost, for she played it perfectly. The music from the pianoforte twined around his own and pressed itself against him until Blytheland almost gasped and drew his bow across his violin with greater force in defense. But it was as if she would have none of it: her music wrestled with him. Passion gave way to crying sweetness, so tangible and sharp it sat on his tongue and he nearly groaned when he drew in his breath, for it was the taste of lovemaking.

Blytheland opened his eyes and stared at Cassandra. It did not help. Her whole concentration was on the music, and she did not look at him. It did not matter—no, it was worse, for she looked like a woman sunk in pleasure: her cheeks flushed, her eyes heavy-lidded, her breath coming quickly from between her lips. He could imagine it, making love to her, almost feel it.

The music, the music! Think of the music! he told himself, but that did not help either, for the music pulled at him and caressed him like a lover's hand—Cassandra's hands. He looked down at the keyboard, how her slender, delicate fingers stroked the keys and lured the notes from the instrument, so that he wanted to weep with the sweetness of it. But he could not. His violin wept instead and wailed the anguish within him.

The sound caught at Cassandra, and she lifted her eyes and stared at him. The room did not exist—the guests, the house. There were only the notes that pierced her heart, only the way Lord Blytheland looked at her, just as he had when he kissed her at the Marchmonts' ball. Her breath halted in her throat, and she remembered how his lips had moved across hers, how his fingers had traced a scintillating path down her throat, just as his fingers now moved upon the violin and drew out sweet music.

She pulled her gaze away from him, concentrating on the sonata, but she knew he was still staring at her—she could feel it. Cassandra looked at him again; he did not smile, but there was a fiery warmth in his eyes, and his gaze shifted downward to her mouth. She could feel her lips heat as if he had kissed them. She almost missed a note and brought her attention back to the pianoforte. But the music conspired against her, for she could not help looking at Lord Blytheland again when his music moved with hers, and she felt drawn to something she was afraid could not be real.

Joy and fear caught her, and she pounded it into the keyboard, trying desperately to focus on the notes she remembered. But the violin's notes curled around and about her, and touched her in hidden places, seducing her. She had known of emotions that welled up within her when she played or heard a fine piece of music; she did not know music could make her feel these other things. Did he know? She was half afraid of the answer and almost glad the sonata was nearly over. Almost over; it was safe, then, to give in to the music, for it would be done soon. The violin said so— the high, sweet notes whispered in her ears: come, love, listen. Her eyes filled with tears at the sound, and her heart came open as she touched the last chords of the sonata.

Cassandra sighed and felt a drop of wetness upon her hand, and she lifted her hand to wipe at her wet cheeks. She looked up at Lord Blytheland who extended a handkerchief to her.

She smiled and dabbed her eyes with it. "So silly of me! I have never wept before like this. I do not know what came over me."

He said nothing, but only looked at her, a disturbed expression in his eyes. He turned to the guests, then bowed.

The guests! Oh, heavens. Cassandra grew conscious of their silence, and turned also. She felt her hand grasped, and looked up at Lord Blytheland as he pulled her from her seat at the pianoforte.

"Curtsy," he hissed.

Hastily she did. She dared look at the guests, and she could not help blushing. What had she done? She could not help seeing the clearly speculative looks on many of their faces, or sly, knowing expressions. The memory of her feelings during the performance came to her, and she blushed and despised herself for blushing. She hoped that the guests would think she was blushing at their applause, but she had learned enough now—especially with the way they looked at her—that they probably did not. Whatever she might have felt, she did not want anyone else to know. It was a stupid thing to hope, for however many men had seemed to be attracted to her, nothing had ever come of it. Each time she had hoped, and each time she had died a little, inside.

Lord Blytheland turned to her and smiled a stiff smile and bowed low over her hand. "Don't," she whispered.

He looked at her with brows raised, but she only pulled her hand away and smiled tentatively in return. She gave another curtsy to the guests and returned to her seat next to her parents. Her mother smiled and nodded at her, and her father looked at her with searching eyes.

She smiled again, briefly. "How glad I am the performance is over!" she said as cheerfully as possible. "I become quite anxious performing in front of so many people." It was not quite a lie, for though she had lost all nervousness while playing—heavens, she had felt everything except nervousness!—she had felt it at the beginning. But she noticed the speculative looks from the people around her fade, and she was glad of it.

A new set of musicians were tuning their instruments, and the guests looked toward them in readiness for the next piece. Cassandra breathed a sigh of relief and looked cautiously about her for Lord Blytheland. He was nowhere in the room that she could see. Perhaps he had left already . . . although he usually liked to stay for all of a musicale in the past, she had noticed. She sighed again. If he was as conscious of the looks they had received from the guests, she would not be surprised if he had left.

* * *

Lord Blytheland had indeed been conscious of the speculative looks from the guests at Lady Langdon's musicale, and more. He needed refreshment, as he always did after a performance, and had gone to the punch bowl at one end of the room. The musicians were tuning up for the next piece of music, and the guests' eyes were drawn to that corner of the room, and so he doubted he was much noticed as he quickly took a cup of punch and downed it behind a large fern on a pedestal. Certainly he had not been noticed by the ladies who came to stand next to the punch bowl with their backs to him.

"Did you *see* the way he looked at her? Hetty Chatwick said that they were good as betrothed," said one of them.

"*I* cannot see what anyone might see in Miss Hathaway—she is a bluestocking, you know!" the other tittered. "But *she* is a sorry case as anyone can see, for I do believe she has fallen completely in love with him, if looks are any indication." the lady nibbled at a small sandwich, then giggled. "I vow, she seemed almost to pant after him like a dog after a bone! So vulgarly obvious. I feel quite sorry for her. Lord Blytheland can look higher for a wife than she."

The first lady laughed. "Who, like you, Amanda? You may not be a baronet's daughter, but you are not much higher than that."

Lord Blytheland clenched his teeth. He did not like being discussed like a bull to be bought by farmers.

"A viscount's daughter is much more eligible than anything Miss Hathaway can lay claim to," Susan said complacently.

He could stand it no longer and emerged from behind the fern. "For your information, ladies, nothing would compel me to consider either of you as a prospective wife." He bowed curtly and turned on his heel, catching enough of their red and chagrined expressions to feel a savage satisfaction.

But as he went down to his coach and left Lady Langdon's house for his own, he knew he had erred greatly in paying so much attention to Miss Hathaway. If it had indeed been bruited about that they were as good as betrothed—and he would not have put it past Lady Hathaway to have hinted it to her acquaintances—then he was sorely mistaken in how much time he had spent in Miss Hathaway's company. He grimaced. Eldon had been right, and he had been wrong to ignore his friend's warning. For all that Eldon liked to tease and had a damnable way of poking his nose where it shouldn't be, he was a good friend and knew all the gossip around about town. He should have listened to him.

Did Miss Hathaway expect anything from him? He did not know. She had never hinted at it . . . only perhaps wished for his company, for she had never yet refused an invitation to ride with him in his phaeton. But he could not distinguish this from—

He took a deep breath as his coach came to the door of his house, and it only slightly cleared the ache in his chest. If he were a true gentleman, he would at least offer for her. Her birth was respectable, and he supposed so must her dowry be, if her family could afford to stay in a house in the best part of London. She was not like Chloe, he knew that now. She was too blunt, too ignorant of many of the *ton's* rules to pretend and hide behind a facade.

An odd twisting pulled at his gut, and he knew he was afraid. He sneered at himself. It was a stupid thing to feel, for marriages for reasons of inheritance were made all the time, and he need not consider a possible marriage to Miss Hathaway to be anything more than that. And if he was worried that she might ever play him false, he could watch her carefully until she bore him his heir.

He opened the door of his coach with a restless movement and descended. Ah, who was he trying to deceive? He was in love with Miss Hathaway, and he was ten times the fool for it. He did not know what had caused him to fall in love with her—the music, or she herself. Perhaps both. He pulled up his shoulders as if against the cold, although his house was warm enough when he entered it. He thought of how Chloe had fooled him and knew he would not be fooled again.

Of course, if he was careful, he could prevent it. If a woman knew his affections were engaged, she'd take advantage of it. It'd be best if he presented his proposal to Miss Hathaway in a formal manner and said nothing of his love for her. He'd convince her that it was for her own good, for the alternative was more embarrassing whispers, and he was certain she'd not want that. A feeling of relief came over him, and he smiled a little. and of course she'd see the advantage a good position in society could give her. There was much he could offer her, and he'd be rid of his stupid impulses in return. It was really a perfect proposal all around.

He would see what she thought of it tomorrow, and then he'd approach her father about it—no need to do the thing formally if she was opposed to marrying him, after all. They could announce it at the alfresco luncheon to which he'd invited her and her family, as well as his own family and his friends.

A feeling of relief went through him, and his shoulders relaxed. Well, there it was. All he had to do was propose to Miss Hathaway, marry her, and he could stop thinking about making love to her because she'd be in his bed soon enough. That should make his life a great deal more comfortable, he was sure.

Chapter 7

"Only think! Lord Blytheland even offered—he insisted!—that I attend the alfresco luncheon with Mama, Papa, and Cassandra next week. Do you not think he truly is a very kind gentleman?" Psyche bounced upon the sofa seat in happiness.

"Oh, I suppose he is—when he wants to be." Harry sat upon the drawing-room windowsill, his wings pressed against the windows. He shifted uncomfortably, then turned and opened them. He stretched his wings in a contented manner. "There. That's better." He turned to Psyche with a smug smile. "So you see, he is the right husband for her, and she is perfect for him."

"I cannot feel comfortable about it, though. You said he is in love with Cassandra, and he has always been kind to me—though he need not pay me attention, as Mama has said, for I am not yet out. But you have *made* him love her, you see. What if your arrows stop working, and he stops loving her? Then they will be miserable."

Harry looked offended. "My arrows don't stop working."

"How do you know?" Psyche said instantly. "Have you ever been around long enough to find out?"

A brief uncomfortable expression flashed across Harry's countenance, but a slow, crooked grin replaced it. He pulled an arrow from his quiver, twirling it deftly around between his fingers. "I could always shoot some more."

Psyche recognized the grin and grew alarmed. "Don't

you *dare*! You leave Lord Blytheland alone, and Cassandra, too! They are well on their way to marriage, Mama has told me, and need no help from you."

" 'The course of true love never did run smooth,' " quoted Harry. "Besides, if you think the effect of my arrows may fade after a while, then the logical solution would be to apply them again."

Psyche gnawed her lip. What a troublesome thing it was to fall in love! But it was a thing adults did, and she supposed she must do so, too, someday. "Well, Cassandra's love will be true—*if* you leave them alone. No doubt even if the arrows lost their effect, Lord Blytheland will still come to love her, for she is the best sister imaginable, you know. Everything will come out for the best, I think, just by themselves."

"I doubt it. There are too many loose ends left untied."

"And you are the one to tie them up? I *doubt* it."

Harry sighed impatiently. "I wonder when you will understand, Psyche, that I know more about these things than you do? I am much older than you, and have more experience."

"Oh, really? You don't look more than two or three years older than I. Not much experience there, I should think! And when have you fallen in love, pray tell?"

Harry looked taken aback. "Fallen in love? It is not at all necessary that I fall in love to know about it. I need only observe."

"There! That proves it. I admit I have never fallen in love either, but I have read much upon the subject. So I know at least a little!"

"Read what?" Harry flew over to the sofa and rummaged behind the pillows. He brought out a small volume. "This?"

"Harry, give it to me at once!" He tossed it in her lap, then sat next to her. Psyche hugged the book to her chest, then looked at its cover fondly. "Well, yes, it was what I was talking of. It is full of the trials one goes through for love."

"The Tomb of the Accursed," Harry read, peering at the book. "That does not sound like anything to do with love."

"Oh, but it does! Only listen: 'Corimunde! Keep true to your virtue and our love! Do not veer from the true course of our affections!' And then *she* says, 'Though I starve in my dank and gloomy chamber, though my heart and limbs be rend from my body by the evil Orcanto, though demons seize my blood-hued dreams—my soul, my soul, O Gerard, is yours for eternity!' " Psyche recited in thrilling accents, closing her eyes in utter bliss.

There was a long silence. She opened her eyes and looked at her friend. "Well? Was that not truly moving?"

One corner of Harry's lips moved upward, but the rest of his mouth twisted in a pursed sort of way. It was as if he had eaten something sour and was politely trying to pretend he had not. Psyche frowned.

"You must have felt something! What did you think of it?"

"Well . . . I thought it sounded rather gruesome, actually."

"Gruesome!" Psyche felt crestfallen. It was her most favorite book. She had hoped Harry would appreciate it, too. "It *does* end happily, though. Gerard and Corimunde are married after going through horrid trials and adventures, and after Orcanto has a halberd driven through his vitals and dies horribly."

Harry's wings shuddered. "If that is your vision of true love, then I wonder that you care to have your sister and Blytheland married at all." He looked over the biscuits on the table next to Psyche, selected one, then ate it in a contemplative manner, as if wondering if he should have another.

Psyche laughed merrily. "No, you goose! Of course, Cassandra and the marquess are not characters in a book, but you must admit they do not have to go through the troubles that Corimunde and Gerard must! *That,* I am sure, does not happen every day. Now it is not reasonable to think that if Corimunde and Gerard can keep their love through horrible events, that Cassandra and Lord Blytheland can come to find love far more easily when they do not have to defeat villains like Orcanto? *Without* your help?"

"No," Harry replied. He picked up her book and leafed through it. He rolled his eyes and shut the book again, then selected another biscuit.

Psyche let out an exasperated breath. "You are the most odious boy! How can you say so?"

"Corimunde and Gerard are made-up people. Blytheland and Cassandra are not, and mortals need more help than made-up people. That is because characters in books are ideals, and mortals are far from that."

Sometimes Psyche thought it quite unfair that Harry did not have someone keeping an eye on *his* hubris. "What has that to say to anything? Lord Blytheland and Cassandra still have far fewer trials than Corimunde and Gerard. They will do well, I know."

"*If* I help them!"

"*If* you *don't*!" Psyche retorted. "Now promise me you will not shoot any more arrows at Lord Blytheland or any at my sister."

Harry looked at her with an impudent smile and said nothing.

"Harry!"

He made a face at her. "Very well. I will compromise: I will only shoot an arrow if you wish it." He sighed. "I have shot any number of arrows into Lord Blytheland already, enough to make anyone mad with love, but he is a stubborn case. Besides, I am tired of it anyway."

"Promise?" Psyche looked at him warily.

Harry sighed again. "I promise."

The door suddenly opened and Cassandra walked in,

holding the hand of a little boy. Psyche cast a warning look at Harry. He had an innocent expression on his face, which she did not quite trust, but she had to be satisfied with it for now.

"Psyche, where is Mama and Papa?" Cassandra looked a little harried, but turned to smile at the boy—quite dirty and ragged, Psyche noticed, so it must be one of Cassandra's climbing boys. "Tim, you must sit here—or, no, perhaps not there. Mama did not like the soot on the damask cushions the last time. Well, here by the fireplace." The boy shrank away from the fire, and Cassandra grimaced. "Oh, dear! No, no, I will not ask you to climb it . . . see, I will even give you something to eat. That is all I wish from you, do you see?" She went over to the dish of biscuits next to Psyche and gave him one. The boy snatched it and stuffed it in his mouth, then cautiously sat down on the floor by the fire, watching Cassandra and Psyche carefully.

Cassandra turned to her sister. "Have you seen Mama, Psyche?"

"Yes." Psyche nodded. "She went out only a quarter of an hour ago to Aunt Mary's house, and you know they will talk for hours. And Papa is at one of his scholarly meetings."

"Oh, heavens! I don't think I can wait until they come back, for it is getting late, and I wish to start out before dark." Cassandra wrung her hands a little and looked worried.

"Are you going to take the boy home?" Psyche asked. "And may I come with you?"

Cassandra smiled. "No, not this time. I barely have enough of my pin money left to bring myself home again. And I know Mama does not like it when I keep the boys here overnight."

Psyche nodded. The last boy had wailed loudly throughout the night, and the one before that had broken an imported Chinese vase and a porcelain figurine and had stolen

Papa's pocket watch. "I shall tell them you have gone, then—I suppose you are taking the traveling coach?"

"Yes, and a footman, an undergroom, *and* a maid, so Mama need not be worried that I will be unprotected."

"Mama will not like it, even so, Cassandra," Psyche said.

Cassandra sighed. "What else am I to do? The last time I let the servants transport one of my boys, he ran off and another chimney sweep caught him! None of them have run away from me, you see."

Psyche looked at the boy sitting on the floor and believed it. Tim gazed at her sister as if she were a goddess, following her every move with his eyes. All of the boys had been this way, and always minded her. A pang of sympathy went through Psyche. She supposed it was because they had no parents to care for them, as she was cared for.

"Well, I will tell Papa first, and I know he will approve of what you have done, and then Mama cannot say anything about it," Psyche said.

Cassandra grinned. "That should work very well—thank you, love!" She went to her sister and hugged her. "You are the best of sisters." She looked uncomfortable, then said, "But be careful of whom else you tell, please! I cannot like it, but I did promise Mama not to speak of my activities to anyone except those who are family, or close friends."

"I won't, then," Psyche said. "Although I don't understand why anyone would disapprove."

Her sister smiled at her. "Some don't, I have found, but I suppose Mama is right in that we should be cautious." She rang for a servant, then turned to Tim. "Now do be a good boy and stay here. I will be right back, and you may have all the biscuits you want until I return."

The boy nodded and looked so bereft and frightened at Cassandra's departure that Psyche felt sorry for him and brought the whole plate of biscuits to him. He gave one wary look at her and seized the plate, stuffing the food into his mouth and into whatever available pockets he had.

But Psyche was glad that Cassandra came back quickly, though, for once the biscuits were stowed away inside and upon Tim's person, he began to stow away other small items in the drawing room, and Psyche was hard put to keep him from doing it. Harry was no help at all! She gave him a meaningful look, but he merely sat on the sofa watching her take one thing after another from Tim, and shaking with silent laughter.

"No, Tim! Put that back, if you please!" Cassandra said as she entered the room and firmly took a small porcelain shepherdess from the boy's hand. "And the rest of the things you have taken!" Cassandra held her hand out to him. "I have some clothes for you—we will go into the kitchen and you will put them on—and then we will go to the nice place in the country. With horses, Tim!"

The boy's eyes widened, and he hastily took five items from his pockets, then followed her out the room. Psyche sighed, eyeing the crumbs on the floor. Cassandra was a very good sort of young lady, and the best of sisters, but sometimes her goodness was very untidy and inconvenient.

Lord Blytheland had ruined four neckcloths before he was satisfied with the result this morning. He admitted to himself that he was nervous; one did not go about proposing marriage to young ladies every day after all. It was not that he thought Miss Hathaway would refuse him, of course, for he'd present to her the problems of being an object of gossip, and she'd not want any of that. Further, there were all the advantages of being a titled lady of wealth and substance. That, no doubt, would have some weight with her. These were solid, practical things, and was she not an intelligent lady of good reason? But he still hesitated before he raised the knocker on the Hathaways' door and firmly knocked.

"Is Miss Hathaway in?" he asked the butler, giving him his hat and cane.

The butler bowed. "I believe so, my lord. This way, if you please, my lord." He took the card Lord Blytheland offered him, and led the way upstairs. Blytheland could feel his hands becoming a little damp as the door opened to admit him. He rapidly thought over the words he would say, stepped into the room, and took a deep breath.

"Miss Hathaway, I—" He stopped and looked at the girl in front of him. "Miss Psyche! I hoped your sister was here."

"Oh! I am so sorry," Psyche said, her voice contrite. "Was I wrong in not telling our butler not to admit you? I thought perhaps I should tell you myself. I would not want to be rude, you see, in having only a butler tell you that Cassandra is not here."

"Ah." Blytheland felt a little deflated. He had worked himself up to the point, and it was disappointing to have his efforts go to waste. He smiled at Psyche nevertheless. "I will be perfectly content to say pretty things to you while I am here, since your sister is not here."

Psyche shook her head and laughed. "You need not, you know. I know one needs to have blond or black hair to have pretty things said to them, so I know you would only be funning. But Cassandra will return soon. We are all going to your luncheon, after all. She is only going to see to one of her children and should be back tomorrow—" She pressed her lips together, suddenly remembering that she had promised not to speak of Cassandra's climbing boys. But it must be permissible to tell him, since he was becoming quite a close friend? And if he was as close to marrying Cassandra as Harry said, he could certainly be considered almost family.

"Children?" The marquess went suddenly still and his face seemed to pale.

Psyche began to feel uneasy, for an expression of anger had flickered in his eyes before his face became smooth and polite. "I—I'm sorry. I thought perhaps she had spoken

to you of them, because I have heard you are as good as—
That is, you are a frequent caller to our house, and have
been very amiable. I am not supposed to speak of the boys,
because Mama says not everyone approves of such things."

"No, they would not." His voice seemed a little strained.

"You mustn't think she is very unusual for it," Psyche
said earnestly. "I have heard other ladies do it, too. Mama
says it is an eccentric thing to do." She sighed. "But I suppose we are all a little eccentric, and too softhearted to see
any of the children cast off." She peered at him, wary.
"You are not angry, are you?"

Lord Blytheland stared at her for a long moment, and
Psyche felt a little afraid at the darkness that crossed his
face. But then it cleared, and he smiled a little. "No, no, I
am not angry at you." He stood up, and his movements
seemed stiff. "I have another call to make . . . I hope you
will excuse me?"

Psyche nodded and watched her sister's suitor leave the
room. She had a dreadful feeling that she had said something she shouldn't have and hoped it wasn't too awful. But
she was not at all sure of that.

Lord Blytheland strode back to his house, not bothering
to get back into his coach to drive home and telling his
groom to return it for him. He was not at all certain he
could keep his hands steady on the reins, not after the blow
he'd received.

The pattern was there, was it not? Miss Hathaway, deep
down, was no better than his wife had been. Was she not an
intellectual? Was she not a follower of Mrs. Wollstonecraft? And did he not hear Miss Hathaway's own sister say that she had gone to tend her children?

Bile rose in his throat, and he swallowed. He had been
astounded that a young girl would even be allowed to know
such things, or would talk of it with such ease. Not with
total ease! That was clear, for she had stumbled over her

words and looked guilty, as if she had let out a secret she was not supposed to know, much less speak of. He had been mistaken in the Hathaway family . . . he had thought they might be respectable enough, since Sir John was an acquaintance of the duke, his father. But his own father had unusual interests, and his associations were not always of good *ton*. He had assumed—wrongly, for Miss Psyche herself admitted that her family was eccentric—that the association gave the family some cachet, some respectability. It was clear this was not entirely true.

Or, perhaps, in the way of ambitious people—and Lady Hathaway was certainly ambitious—they sought to cover up any indiscretions that might mark their family as undesirable. But to push off an unvirtuous woman as Miss Cassandra Hathaway upon the *ton* was beyond ambitious, it was supremely foolish. They had neither the connections nor the wealth to pull it off. It did explain, however, why the lovely Miss Hathaway was not yet betrothed despite her adequate fortune, and why the Hathaways had left their home to come to London to snare a husband for her.

A hot anger filled Lord Blytheland, and the street seemed to burn in front of him. He walked faster. He'd been a fool—again. He'd been caught—again. God, when would he stop being such a idiot, led by his passions and his obvious lust? For that was what it was, certainly. He should have slaked his lust on some woman long before this, so that he could have chosen his bride with more sense and reason.

He could ruin them. He could let it be known the kind of woman Miss Cassandra Hathaway was, and they'd never show their faces in London again. A small part of him reminded him of his passions again, and he took a deep breath. No, he could not do that. Miss Psyche, at least, was an innocent, for all that she was being raised in such a family. She'd be ruined, too, by association, and that would be unjust.

Then, too, he'd already invited them to the luncheon. He supposed that he could send a note telling them not to come. But again the memory of Miss Psyche's innocent gaze made him think again. He knew what it was to be betrayed, and he was not going to be one to betray a promise of a treat to a child like Miss Psyche. But certainly, he could forgo their company—and that of Miss Hathaway's—after that.

He remembered Cassandra's bluntness, and he frowned. She was different that way. The truth was, he was fool enough not to want to believe Cassandra was like Chloe. Perhaps he had misconstrued Miss Psyche's words, perhaps there was some other explanation for them. Anger warred with reason, and memories of Chloe mixed with that of Cassandra. Perhaps he would give her another chance . . . but he had done this with Chloe, too.

He found himself at his house before he knew it, and walked into the house and up the stairs. He had left his violin in his chambers; he would play it again, and he could get all his anger and passions out of himself and into the music. Then he could think clearly once again.

Blytheland took his violin from the case and slashed his bow across the strings, and the violin wailed in despair and anger. He played the music he knew over and over again, it seemed for hours. But when he was done, the house sounded empty and still, and he knew it was not enough for him.

The late May sun shone brightly and warm upon the group of ladies and gentlemen as they rode in their various conveniences to Marquess of Blytheland's alfresco luncheon. It was not a large group, small enough to make it convivial, but with enough variety in its members to make for interesting conversation. Psyche had been overjoyed when Lord Blytheland had included all of her family in his invitation—except Kenneth, of course, for he was at Cambridge.

How wonderful to be out in the sunshine after a week of being cribbed indoors! Psyche leaned out against the coach's side, staring out at the countryside. She could see the marquess's curricle far ahead of them, and could barely make out his and Cassandra's forms there. They were nearing what must have been one of Blytheland's country houses just outside of London, for they turned off the main road through black iron gates onto a smaller road.

"Do stop leaning out the side of the coach, Psyche, and maintain a ladylike demeanor!" Lady Hathaway said, but it was said without any real reproof in her voice. Psyche nevertheless sat back in her seat.

"Now, I hope you understand, child, that you are to keep out of people's notice," continued her mother.

"Yes, Mama."

"And I do not want you to wander off where you might get lost!"

"Yes, Mama."

"I understand there are other young people about your age, but you are to comport yourself as a mature young lady. Do you understand?"

"Yes, Mama."

Lady Hathaway patted her daughter's hand, satisfied. "You are a good child, Psyche. I hope you will show it today."

"Yes, Mama." Psyche looked up to where the coachman was and nearly burst out laughing. Harry was sitting next to the coachman, behind her mother, shaking his finger at her in a mock-admonishing way. Really, she wished Harry would not do that. It made her want to giggle, and was disrespectful of Mama. But she was glad Harry was coming to the luncheon, nevertheless. It was her first grown-up event, and though she felt excited about it, she was also quite glad there would be someone else she knew. *Would* she be able to do all that she ought?

Looking at Harry, she noted that he had brought his bow and a quiver full of arrows. She felt a little nervous, but remembered his promise. Harry always kept his promises and never lied to her, so she knew she should not worry that he would shoot Blytheland or Cassandra. The thing was, he never promised he wouldn't shoot anyone else. She would definitely have to keep her eye on him. Oh, but the day was too beautiful for worries! Psyche sighed. Perhaps it would not hurt to let Harry have a little bit of fun with his arrows—as long as it was not with her sister or her beau. It seemed to be Harry's nature to matchmake.

The coach slowed, and Psyche found that they were at the doors of the marquess's country house. It was possibly twice the size of her own home in the country, and her father was not an impoverished man by any means. She watched Cassandra descending the steps of the curricle in front of them, then Lord Blytheland escorting her to the house.

Cassandra felt uneasy. The marquess had been very attentive to her, even when driving his curricle. It must have been a difficult thing to maintain an amusing conversation with her while directing the horses, but he did it with an ease that belied the fast pace or the powerful action of the horses. And yet, there was something still and cool about him. No, not cool; that was only a veneer. She gazed at him when he brought his attention to his horses and tried to discern what it was that made him seem so distant, and . . . tense was the best word for it. But she could not elicit much more than common pleasantries from him, and she was no wiser than when they had started out.

When they reached the marquess's house, the ladies and gentlemen retired to their separate rooms to refresh themselves before the luncheon. Cassandra could not help marveling at the fine carpentry of the rooms, the bright brocade tapestries, the fine Aubusson rugs that cushioned her footsteps. It was just, *just* a little intimidating. Her own family had far and above enough funds to provide large dowries for herself and Psyche, as well as maintain a comfortable abode both in town and in the country. But this! This was opulence—in no way vulgar, but the sheer elegance and fine workmanship of the house spoke of a far more than comfortable income, indeed.

Quite, quite above your touch, my girl, said a small voice in her mind. Oh, it was not that she did not come from a respectable and old family, to be sure! It was just that looking at this house brought all the inequalities of their stations to the fore. Her father was by heredity a baronet; the marquess would someday become a duke. Lord Blytheland, of a surety could, and most probably would, look higher than a mere Miss Hathaway.

Cassandra sighed and picked up a wet cloth to freshen her face. She wished she knew what his intentions were. A light flirtation? Something more serious? She did not know if she should let herself—Well, she would think it: let herself love him.

Oh, it would be an easy thing to do. He need only gaze at her warmly, press his lips to her hand, and smile his smile upon her once or twice more. He had paid her more attention than any man had before; she was quite afraid that he would go away like so many others. She had fancied at the beginning of the Season, that she had formed a *tendre* for one or two gentlemen. But they had left for other more lovely young ladies, and it had all come to naught. So she put a guard on her heart, knowing that she was not the most attractive lady in London, and understanding that she would be fortunate, indeed, to find someone who would regard her with affection.

But now, here was the marquess, who escorted her to his home, who danced with her, and took her to the theater.

And with him came his friends—Lord Eldon, Mr. Rowland, and Sir Ellery. They, too, paid her a great deal of attention, although she believed they did so merely for the sake of fashion. Lord Eldon was very much a Pink of the *ton*, a bit more dandified than Lord Blytheland. The marquess, though he took a great deal of care about his clothes, leaned more toward the Corinthians in his preferences, she had discovered.

Cassandra put down the cloth and carefully combed back stray hairs from her face. Perhaps . . . perhaps if Lord Blytheland was merely interested in a flirtation, she could look to Lord Eldon. *He* seemed more and more attentive of late. A little ache seemed to settle in her heart at the thought of looking elsewhere, but she had to be practical, and could not risk being hurt again. She was tired of hoping. Certainly the baron was closer to her station in life than the marquess. And yet, her heart sank when she thought of it.

Nonsense! Lord Eldon was all that is amiable and gentlemanly, she told herself firmly. How could she know if she could feel for him the same—if not more—than what she felt for the marquess? Her mind wandered over the sensations she felt when near Lord Blytheland, and then she thought of Lord Eldon. Well, they were *not* the same. She felt a regard, and a friendship toward the baron. As for Lord Blytheland she, well, she did not know what to make of her reactions to him at all. She despised the way she acted so insipidly around him, blushing and stuttering like an idiot. How could he like her at all? Cassandra sighed, and wished she could comport herself with more assurance and maturity.

Perhaps she should favor Lord Eldon; she had no difficulty acting in an intelligent manner around him. But then, her *experiences* with these two men were quite, quite different. The marquess, for one, had kissed her. Lord Eldon had not. Perhaps if she tried to kiss Lord Eldon also, she would know if she was destined to act like a ninny around men who kissed her. Cassandra felt her face growing warm at the thought, and she put the cloth again to her cheeks.

It would be an experiment, she told herself, and done quite scientifically. If she kissed Lord Eldon and felt the same as she did with the marquess, then she would know whether she would act just as stupidly around men who kissed her. After all, it was something men did with their wives, and how awkward it would be to be such an idiot around one's husband. And besides, Mama did not say kissing was a bad thing, after all, just as long as she didn't do it *often*, and if no one saw.

Cassandra felt much better. There now! She would do her little experiment, and then she could decide what she felt, and if she should encourage Lord Eldon's attentions. Papa was right. One needed only to think things through logically, and one would find the answers. On that thought, she lifted her chin in a resolute manner and left the chamber.

When Cassandra went down to the hall, she saw most of the company were there. Lord Eldon, who was talking to the petite blonde Miss Hamilton, glanced up briefly at her entrance and smiled. There was Sir Jeremy Swift and his lady, and Lady Swift's daughter Georgia Canning (whom she remembered vaguely from her brief stay at the Bath boarding school) and her betrothed, Lord Ashcombe. A few other gentlemen and ladies were also there, but she did not know their names. She looked around the room and caught her father's eye, and he beckoned to her. She smiled at him and her mother as she approached. Psyche, she noticed, was standing quietly behind Lady Hathaway, looking intently at everything in the room. She glanced at Cassandra, gave her a quizzical look, and then continued her perusal of the room. Cassandra almost shook her head. Sometimes she was not sure she understood her young sister.

"Now there," Sir John said, pointing his chin at Lord

Ashcombe, "is a well-informed young man. Educated at Oxford, graduated with honors. He knows Arabic! I must see if I can bring him and Blytheland's father together to work on a translation of the *De Res Medicos*." He sighed. "Wouldn't mind someone like him for a son-in-law."

"Papa! You cannot think that a gentleman's education can be the only consideration for a husband!"

"It would certainly be convenient, though," replied Sir John, looking wistfully at Lord Ashcombe.

Lady Hathaway tapped him on the arm with her fan. "My dear, it is too late, as you can see! Miss Canning and Lord Ashcombe are betrothed and clearly enamored of each other. And your daughter is right. There is more than just education to be thought of in a marriage."

Cassandra looked over at the young couple. If one did not know that the two were betrothed, one could guess it from their demeanor. She watched as Lord Ashcombe tucked his fiancée's hand gently in the crook of his arm, how Miss Canning looked up at him with a tender smile, and how he returned it with a regard that was more than warm. Cassandra felt a small ache in her heart and wondered if anyone would someday look at her in that way.

The door opened once more, and she looked up to see Lord Blytheland enter the parlor. His gaze immediately went to hers, and then turned to the rest of the company. There was little expression in his eyes except for a cool civility.

"If the ladies and gentlemen are ready, we can all proceed to the lake. The servants should have set up our luncheon there by the time we arrive."

There was a general murmur of assent, and everyone went out into the sunlight once again.

"Oh, dear!" exclaimed Psyche, "I wonder if we should have brought umbrellas?" She was looking toward the west, and Cassandra followed her gaze. A thin line of clouds obscured the horizon, although in front of the cloud bank the sky was a brilliant blue.

Cassandra smiled at her sister comfortingly. "I believe we shall be quite comfortable; we have only a breeze blowing from the east, you see, so I doubt we will have any rain at all."

It was not very far to the lake. They walked past the gardens and the maze, which the marquess invited the guests to try later if they liked. The house and gardens were on a small rise, and down the hill and further, for a few yards away the servants had set out the luncheon by the lake.

It took a great deal of self-restraint for Psyche not to run as she wished to down to the luncheon. The day was beautiful and the field was just the sort on which to run until one was breathless. She eyed the other people closer to her age, but they were few and she did not feel inclined to converse with them. One girl looked quite standoffish, and even sneered in her direction. A tall, thin boy walking not far from her own family had eyes for nothing but the luncheon. Not very likely people to talk to, thought Psyche.

Blytheland's servants had set out various tables for the guests, and makeshift sideboards groaning with food. It was a snatch-pastry's dream—not that she, Psyche, was a snatch-pastry. Harry certainly was, however. She watched enviously as he flew swiftly toward what looked to be a sumptuous spread of edible delights. How she wished she could fly, unseen, wherever she wanted! She had never seen him eat much before, and she had often wondered if he ate only for show—or in earnest. Well, she did now know it was in earnest: though he picked at this dish or that, he picked much. There were lobster patties and hams, bread and cakes and tarts. Wine was served as well, although she was only allowed lemonade. Harry, she noted enviously, helped himself to the wine.

Hoping that her parents would not notice her immediate escape, Psyche inched herself toward the luncheon. She no-

ticed the tall, thin boy—older than Harry, she thought—
was already at the table and had picked up a dish. Well,
Mama could *not* say she had made unseemly haste to the
food. That boy was here before her after all, and she had
walked *very* slowly to the table.

She glanced shyly up at the boy. He smiled kindly at her.

"Hallo! Do try the jam tarts. They really are superb," he
said, his voice a little muffled from a bite he'd just taken.
"My name is Garthwaite. Bertram Garthwaite. Oh, and the
lobster patties are first rate!" He put two more on his plate.

"Are they? I do like them, they're my favorite," Psyche
replied. "I am Psyche Hathaway." She looked at his bur-
geoning plate. "Goodness, but you must be hungry!"

"I am," he replied frankly. "I've just come down from
Cambridge on holiday. Never get enough to eat there, let
me tell you! And what they have is pretty poor fare, to
boot."

"Cambridge! Do you know my brother Kenneth Hathaway?"

"Mmmm . . . Oh, yes. Doesn't run with my set—he's a
year ahead of me—but I've met him. He's a great gun, up
for any lark. I imagine he'll come home to you any day
now."

Psyche felt some consternation. No one had received
word that Kenneth was coming home. She hoped that he
was not in trouble again. "Is . . . is he in a scrape, do you
think?"

Bertram looked nonplussed. "Well—That is to say—I've
heard he does have the most deuced good luck—it might
not be as bad as all that."

"Oh, dear." Psyche bit her lip. "Well, I will not worry
about it. It is something Papa will need to deal with, after
all."

"That's the ticket." He nodded approvingly. "No need to
worry about something you can't influence."

She looked across the table and saw that Harry was looking at Bertram intently. She grew alarmed and made what she hoped was a dismissing motion with her hand at Harry. Mr. Garthwaite seemed a good sort of young man, and she didn't want Harry to shoot him with any of his arrows. She wriggled her eyebrows at her friend, hoping that he would take it as a warning to stay away from Mr. Garthwaite as well.

Harry rolled his eyes, then shrugged his shoulders. He reached over and cut off a cluster of grapes from a bowl, and started eating the grapes.

"I say, did you see that?"

Psyche glanced up to see Bertram staring at the grape bowl.

"See what?"

"Those grapes. There was a cluster of them I had my eyes on and then they disappeared!"

She threw Harry a reproachful look and turned to Bertram again. "Are you sure? I did not see them."

He shook his head. "Must be hunger pangs. They are affecting my vision. I must tell Father I need more of an allowance for food." He nodded in a bemused fashion at Psyche and went off with his plate to the edge of the lake.

"Oh, Harry! If you refuse to show yourself to anyone else but me, I do wish you would be more discreet!" she scolded him. She was glad no one else had come to the buffet table yet, so that she could talk to her friend without whispering.

"You needn't worry, Psyche. He did not see me, and only thought the grapes were his imagination."

"Well, that is true, but do be careful! And why were you staring at him so?"

"Oh, you know, just seeing if he was worth bothering with."

"Bothering with?"

Harry popped another grape into his mouth. "Yes. There wasn't anyone around who I thought might be suitable for him. And he's young yet—only eighteen. No need to hurry; he's not wild like your brother. Or stubborn like your sister and the marquess."

"Remember your promise, Harry!"

Harry sighed. "I remember!"

"Besides, Cassandra and Lord Blytheland are doing very well by themselves. You must have seen them in his curricle!" Psyche picked up a lobster patty that the amiable Mr. Garthwaite had recommended.

"Yes. But Lord Blytheland is angry about something, and I think your sister is planning something with Lord Eldon, instead."

"What? How can you say so?" Psyche's lobster patty stopped halfway to her mouth.

"*I* have kept watch on them, if *you* have not. She keeps casting glances at Lord Eldon instead of the marquess. And Lord Blytheland doesn't look happy. But then, he tends to be rather moody, so that may not mean a great deal."

"No. You must be mistaken!" She put her food down upon her plate again and gazed at Harry skeptically. "Besides, how can you tell just by looking at her? She could just be trying to catch his attention."

"Oh, she is catching his attention all right and tight," Harry replied. "And I know because I am very good at reading faces. I learned it from my cousin Hermes."

"Cousin? I did not know you had a cousin," Psyche said, intrigued. Harry only rarely spoke of his friends or relations.

He smiled. "You never asked. Besides, I thought your father would have told you all about me and my family."

"Now that is nothing but a faradiddle and you know it, Harry! Papa telling me of you, indeed! Why you said my father did not believe you existed, and that you were all from my imagination!"

"He does."

Psyche shook her head impatiently at him. "Oh, do stop roasting me, Harry! Now let us get back to Cassandra."

"Yes, do let's," Harry said. "I'll wager you your jam tart that your sister will stroll across the grass with Lord Eldon instead of the marquess. You'll see what comes of my not shooting my arrows."

"Done!" replied Psyche, and she walked quickly back to where her parents were sitting.

She gazed at her sister. Cassandra seemed a little abstracted, the same look she always wore when she would try to puzzle out a problem. She sat on the other side of their parents, but Psyche sat herself down where she could surreptitiously observe her.

She watched as Cassandra glanced at Lord Eldon, not once, not twice, but three times. The third time, he responded with a smile and came over to her.

Psyche bit her lip. Oh dear, she thought. Harry has just won my jam tart. She looked at her friend, then silently held the tart out to him.

Harry looked at the tart but did not take it. He could not. He felt something odd—he'd call it remorse, if he were a mortal. He remembered feeling it once, literally ages ago, when the gods' presence was felt more strongly than it was now, but not since that time. Perhaps he felt it because he had no friend in the world of the mortals, except for this young girl. He did not know, and it annoyed him. "What do you wish me to do?" he asked, and then wished he hadn't said it. It was almost an admission that he had made another mistake.

Psyche sighed and smiled at him, clearly relieved. "Don't shoot any arrows at Cassandra. I would feel horrid if she became all silly like the Mademoiselle Lavoisin and the Comte de la Fer. Could you . . . could you make Lord Blytheland the way he was before you shot any of your arrows at him?"

"It won't work if I do, Psyche."

She pressed her lips together and lifted her chin stubbornly. "They have met already, and have got to know each other. I don't think they need any more help with your arrows."

Harry stared at her for a few more moments, wondering why he bothered with her or the Hathaway family . . . but the thought of leaving them made him feel even more odd than that remorselike thing he'd felt earlier.

"Oh, very well!" he said. He made a face at her, feeling childishly better for doing it—well, was he not in boy-form, after all?—but Psyche merely smiled at him gratefully.

"Thank you! You are a true friend, Harry! You'll see, they'll come about properly!" She looked away from him toward where her sister had sat, but Cassandra was gone.

"Don't worry," Harry said. "Lord Blytheland's gone with them, it seems. I'll find them." He selected an arrow from his quiver, a different one than he'd used before, and rose into the air. He sighed. Perhaps Psyche was right . . . but he doubted it. He was the god of love, after all, and no mortal knew more of love than he did, especially not a young girl.

Chapter 8

Miss Hathaway, Lord Eldon noted, kept glancing at him, and he could not help wondering why. He had never received so much attention from her before.

"I think I need to walk a little—I feel a little stiff from travel still," Miss Hathaway said. She put down her fork on the plate the servant had given her. She had hardly touched the food, although she had taken a little lemonade and then wine. Lord Eldon caught another glance from her. He could see also Blytheland turning toward them at her words, but she did not look toward the marquess at all. Lord Eldon felt a stirring of curiosity. Something in the wind? he wondered.

"I would be most happy to oblige, Miss Hathaway," he said, and smiled at her. He rose and offered his hand. She returned an uncertain smile and put her hand in his. Lord Eldon risked a glance at his friend and almost burst out laughing. Blytheland's expression was a mix of surprise and irritation. So much for his insistence that she was only "a superb pianist," to him, eh? He could tell his friend was madly in love with Miss Hathaway, and she would be perfect for him. He had disliked Chloe from the start, and he often thought she still had her claws in Blythe even though she was gone. Well, there was nothing like a bit of rivalry to get a man to realize what he might be losing.

Eldon turned to the lady at his side. "And where would you like to stroll, ma'am?"

She glanced at him, again uncertainly. "I . . . I think perhaps the gardens, by the maze. It seems very pretty there, and I would like to see the flowers."

"It would be my pleasure."

They walked up the rise to where the gardens formed the entrance to the maze. They conversed about the weather and Miss Hathaway exclaimed over the flowers. Lord Eldon noted with amusement that it was the most desultory and unenlightening conversation he had ever had with her. Something must be bothering her, he thought, and it must have to do with my dear old friend. How amusing. Miss Hathaway must have more than a passing fancy for Blythe, he was sure of it. But why did she choose *him*, Eldon, to escort her to the garden?

He watched her as she spoke of more inconsequential things and noted a rising blush in her cheeks. A mischievous urge rose in him. He would so much like to see how much pinker Miss Hathaway could blush.

"I see you must be a little overheated, ma'am. Perhaps you would like to sit for a little while?" He was rewarded by seeing her turn two shades more pink than before.

"Yes, yes please. Perhaps over there on that bench, where it is private." A guilty look appeared in her eyes, and her cheeks turned positively red.

Private? thought Lord Eldon. Well, well. Now what?

They sat, and Miss Hathaway arranged her skirts around her neatly, and then fiddled with them some more. They were somewhat in shadow, for part of the hedge and ivy that covered the maze overhung the marble bench on which they sat. Eldon removed his hat, looked at her downcast gaze, and waited, suppressing a wide grin. Poor Miss Hathaway! She was no doubt getting up the courage to say something, but what?

She looked up earnestly at him. "Lord Eldon, will you kiss me?" she said, all in a rush.

"Eh?"

"Kiss me. For—for experimental purposes, you see."

Lord Eldon paused before he spoke, trying to put strong control over his overwhelming urge to laugh. Oh, Lord! Was that what this was all about? And why in the world did she feel she had to do this? He thought of Blytheland and wondered if he had kissed her—probably. He certainly had the chance to do so at the Marchmont ball!

"For experimental purposes?" he managed to reply after a short struggle with another upsurge of laughter.

"Oh, please don't be offended, my lord! I like you very well, and I was wondering if, if your kiss would be like— That is, what your kiss would be like."

"Oh, is that it? Well, I would be most happy to oblige, Miss Hathaway. For experimental purposes, of course."

"Would you?"

"Yes."

"Oh." She stared at him for a moment and then put on a resolute expression. She closed her eyes and presented her face.

Lord Eldon gazed at her for a long moment. Oh, he shouldn't. He really shouldn't. But his deeply ingrained mischievousness could not let this priceless moment pass by. Especially when he noted from the corner of his eye his dear old friend Blythe coming up the path. He bent over Miss Hathaway and kissed her firmly on the lips.

They parted, and she looked up at him, clearly puzzled. "That was pleasant, Lord Eldon, but . . . Did it feel pleasant to you?"

"Most pleasant, Miss Hathaway," he replied. He had to admit to feeling a bit warmer than usual. La Hathaway was, after all, a most delectable young lady.

"What the *devil* is the meaning of all this?" The marquess stood before them, his hands balled tightly into fists, fury writ clear in his eyes.

Miss Hathaway rose hastily and pressed her hands to her

mouth. Lord Eldon stood as well, but more slowly, and carefully brushed the dust from his coattails.

"What did it look like, Blythe-my-old?" Eldon replied provocatively.

"It looked damn well like you were kissing Miss Hathaway! I *don't* take well to having any of my female guests molested!"

"Molested? Strong words, old man." He turned to the lady by his side. "Was I molesting you, ma'am?"

"Oh, no! I—I asked him to kiss me, you see," Miss Hathaway replied.

"You what!?" Blytheland's voice rose.

"It was for—for an experiment. I asked him to kiss me."

Poor Miss Hathaway! She looked more and more distressed. Lord Eldon sighed regretfully. He really should put a stop to this.

"Look here, Blytheland. It was all very innocent. In fact, I knew you were coming up the hill and I couldn't help tweaking at you a little. Being a bit of a dog in the manger, don't you think? You never said you had any claim on her—denied it, in fact. And I did tell you I thought I might try for her affections myself, since you didn't say I shouldn't."

"You said you'd have a *touch* at her! By God, Eldon that was a damn sight more than a touch! I should call you out for this!"

"No!" cried Cassandra.

Both men ignored her.

"Nonsense, my old. You know I wouldn't oblige; I detest arising before eleven o'clock. Besides, I know you wouldn't shoot me—I wouldn't shoot you! We've been friends too long, and it would cause a devil of a scandal for Miss Hathaway here."

The marquess turned a blazing look on Miss Hathaway. "Scandal! If she were sunk in it, it would be all that she deserves!"

"Now, just a moment, Blythe!" Eldon said sternly. "If I were so inclined, I would call *you* out for *that*. You heard her. She has no more notion about kisses than an infant. If anything, your argument should be with me."

"No, no! It was all my fault!" Cassandra cried. "I asked him to—truly, I did! It was an experiment!"

Blytheland turned to her and grasped her by the shoulders. "You little idiot! Anyone could have seen you here! *I* certainly did!"

"Idiot! I am *not* an idiot!"

"It was certainly stupid of you to kiss Eldon here in full view of the lake!"

Lord Eldon wondered if it would be discreet or cowardly if he left the two of them to join the rest of the company at the lake. It was clearly a lover's quarrel and a third party would definitely be *de trop*. He gazed at the marquess and Miss Hathaway, both of whom looked furiously into each other's eyes.

"Ahem. If you two don't mind, I thought I might go back to the lake . . . ?" Eldon said tentatively. "I still feel a trifle sharp-set. Thought I might see if there was any of the luncheon left over."

"It was not in full view of the lake! You can see clearly for yourself how we were hidden!"

"Oh? And if so, then why did I notice it?"

They were clearly not interested in his presence at all. Lord Eldon decided that leaving would probably be discreet more than not. And perhaps getting whatever problem was between them aired would be for the better. He picked up his hat, set it neatly on his head, and after an elegant bow in the couple's direction, sauntered back down to the remains of the luncheon.

Lord Blytheland still grasped Cassandra by her shoulders. "I have never known anyone so indiscreet as you, Miss Cassandra Hathaway! By God, if you are not sending people to *point-non-plus* in the most embarrassing way with your blunt comments, you are letting yourself be kissed by all and sundry—and in full view of God knows who! Or perhaps you don't particularly care who sees you."

"I only try to speak the truth, my lord," Cassandra replied furiously. "And as for truth—I do not know how you dare to say I let myself be kissed by 'all and sundry'! You have been the only other one who has kissed me. I asked Lord Eldon to do so only for an experiment."

"An experiment!" The marquess sneered. He stared at her, rage boiling up inside of him, almost choking him. He had wanted to give her another chance, and she took it—showing her true colors. She lifted her chin—Chloe used to do the same thing when she wished to have her own way. How similar were they? He did not truly know, and God, he wished he did.

"You need not sneer, you horrid man! I believed we were private, and—"

"Private! That you should want to be private with—" He released her shoulders, but took her wrist in a tight grip instead. He needed to know, and he would find out, or he would go mad not knowing. A thought flashed through his mind that perhaps he was mad now, for never had he been seized with such anger, such agony, not even with Chloe. But he could not stop, not now. He pulled her toward the maze's entrance, and walked swiftly around one corner and another—right, left, and right again. "Private. You're so deuced indiscreet you don't know the meaning of the word!"

"What are you doing? Where are you taking me?"

"Some place *private,* of course," Blytheland replied through clenched teeth. His steps were swift, and he could hear Cassandra almost running behind him. He turned right again, then left, another left, and two rights, and the enclosing hedges opened up to the center of the maze. A delicate Grecian gazebo stood in the middle of the small garden clearing, but Blytheland strode past it to the hedge behind it. He pushed aside some branches and heavy overhanging ivy, and revealed an old oaken door. He moved the handle, and the door creaked open. Pulling Cassandra through the door, he shut it firmly behind them.

He had not come here in a long time, not since Chloe died. He watched Cassandra look around her in an angry, bewildered way at the riot of blooms and flowering trees around her, and the sparkling fountain that cascaded diamondlike drops of water into a mosaic pool. She turned and stared angrily at Blytheland instead. "And where is this, pray?"

"This, my dear Cassandra, is the heart of the maze. It is a place so damned private that no one would see us together. No one would see *anything* we might do here. What a wonderful way to avoid scandal, yes?" He pulled her to him and lifted her chin so that she stared into his eyes. She was still angry. He felt a queer relief at it—perhaps he was wrong about her. He hoped she felt as furious as he did . . . but he needed to know, dear God, he needed to know. "Tell me, my dear. Why did you kiss Eldon?"

"I told you, it was an experiment! I wanted to find out how his kiss might compare with yours, and that was all!" She stamped her foot. It would have landed on his toe, but he moved it in time. "And I did not give you permission to use my Christian name!"

Anger seized him again. "Oh, my. I think the blunt and truthful Miss Hathaway has told a lie! I definitely remember a ball, out on the terrace—"

Her face flamed red in memory, then paled again in clear fury. "I did not say yes to your using my name!"

"Then what did you say yes to? Kissing me? Do you always say yes to requests like that—or was that an experiment, too?"

"No! Yes! Oh, you odious—!" She stamped her foot again.

"Odious, am I? Are my kisses odious to you, too? Well, how does *this* compare with Eldon's?"

His lips took hers swiftly, hard against her mouth at first, but he let out a deep sigh and moved upon her lips more softly. How could he not? He drew away briefly, staring at her delicately formed lips. They were full and open, and he remembered them the way they were when she had played the piano at the musicale. It would be a sin not to savor them slowly, feeling every little indentation and curve against his own. Her green eyes were wide and startled as they looked into his. He felt he could drown in them. Blytheland gently brought his lips to hers again.

They were as soft as he'd remembered them from the Marchmonts' ball. He tasted the sweet sherry she'd had at luncheon, and breathed in the scent of violets that emanated from her. She opened her mouth on a sighing moan, and suddenly the passion was there—as he had imagined it, as he'd experienced it before. Now her lips moved upon his, her arms came around his neck, and she pressed herself close to him. He deepened his kiss in response and moved his hands to her waist.

He needed to feel her closer. . . . He bent his knees slightly and tried to feel for one of the benches or chairs he knew were in the garden. But then Cassandra leaned forward even more, and they tumbled down upon the grass. She landed half on top of him, and the marquess pulled her fully to him so that she was, indeed, much closer.

"Ah, God, how I've wanted you, Cassandra," Blytheland murmured against her lips.

"Yes . . ."

"Paul. My name is Paul." He rolled to his side, taking her with him and brought his hand up to her breast.

"Ohh, Paul . . ." she sighed, and pressed her lips against his again.

He must have lost his mind—love and fear had robbed him of all reason. He kissed her cheek, her lips, her throat.

She responded with even more passion than he'd thought possible, arching against his hands and his body. Heat moved through him and he shifted his lips from her mouth, trailing kisses on her cheek, her neck, and down to the soft skin his hand had uncovered.

Cassandra shivered as she felt his—Paul's—lips move upon her throat and lower, and lower until—

A drop of water splashed upon her cheek. Then another on her forehead, one on her nose, and another on her eyelid. She opened her eyes. The thin clouds that had appeared at the beginning of their luncheon had gathered to a large thunderous mass. It was raining, and raining in earnest.

Warm kisses coursed across the top of her breasts, trailing downward. She struggled to rise.

"Stop! Oh, please stop!" Cassandra pushed the marquess away from her and sat up. To her horror, her dress gaped open, and one cross-end of it flapped in the wind that had suddenly sprung up. Oh, heavens, how could she have allowed it?

Hastily she closed her dress and looked at the marquess. He, too, sat up. He had a bewildered expression on his face and seemed oblivious to the rain now pouring steadily upon his head. He held out his hand tentatively toward her.

"Cassandra—"

"How *dare* you!" she cried.

"But I—"

"You *dare* accuse Lord Eldon of molesting me when you—*you* went far further than a mere kiss!"

Blytheland's eyes snapped angrily. "Well, I didn't hear *you* protesting!"

"*That* is neither here nor there! What we are discussing are *your* base assumptions about Lord Eldon's actions and my intent. *He* did not force me to the middle of this maze, or force his attentions upon me!" A stab of guilt passed through Cassandra's mind, but she dismissed it.

"Oh, so I forced my attentions on you, did I? Did you scream? My, my, I must be getting deaf in my old age," he replied, his voice ironic. "If you recall, I stopped when you told me to—quite some time after we began."

"Ohhh, you odious—! How *could* I say anything when you—you had your lips over mine?" Cassandra rose swiftly to her feet. Blytheland did as well.

The marquess looked pointedly at her bodice. "I recall instances when my lips were not on yours at all." A slow smile grew on his face.

Cassandra's hands itched to slap that expression from his face. She closed her hands against the sensation and formed two tight fists instead. Oh! How *could* he? She had thought him a true gentleman, but his actions proved her wrong. Why, he was no better than her younger brother Kenneth, who kissed maidservants! And the marquess had no excuse, for he was well over Kenneth's immature nineteen years of age! Well, *she* was no lowly chambermaid! But as she looked at him, his face grew dark and contemptuous.

"Besides, how do I know you don't do this—as well as kiss—other men as well? Your sister told me of your children, after all."

"Children?" Cassandra stared at him, bewildered. "What do my climbing boys have to do with this?"

The contemptuous look vanished, and the marquess seemed to pale. "Climbing boys? Your sister said she had been warned not to speak of it . . . I thought—"

"You thought—you thought—" Cassandra gasped, her breath almost taken away with grief and anger. "I never— how could you ever think I am that kind of—" She clenched her fists tighter, trying to hold back the tears that threatened to burst from her. "You thought I was—And to think I came to love you, while all the time you—" Her voice caught in a sob.

A sudden fluttering sound, a burst of wind pushed the

hair from her face, and a quick twanging hiss of a bow-shot seemed to sear her ear. But Cassandra paid no attention to it, or to the rain that fell hard and fast upon her. She stared at Lord Blytheland, at his clearly confused and handsome face, and for one small moment hatred flared, then turned into white-hot anger. Humiliation and shame warred fiercely with it in her heart, and she could feel her face flame hotly. Anger won.

Her fist flew out. With a right curve that would have gained the approval of Gentleman Jackson himself, it landed directly on the marquess's right eye. Blytheland fell—arms flailing—right into the mosaic-lined pool.

Cassandra stared at him, horrified at what she'd done, her hands clenched tightly against her lips. Lord Blytheland sat in the pool with a stunned look on his face, his eye slowly turning color. A lily pad floated gently across his middle. Rain dripped upon his head, and a tiny stream of fountain water coursed down his forehead and trickled off the end of his aristocratic nose.

Oh, heavens! Never, never had she even thought of violence against another person, much less done it. She had been raised to act like a lady by loving parents, and never had a hand been raised against her as a child, for her parents did not believe in corporal punishment. She abhorred violence, but now she had hit someone—Lord Blytheland. She had thought she had more control over herself than that, even when she had been at her angriest, however she might justifiably be angry. What was wrong with her? Ever since she had met the marquess, she had acted in a manner that she despised: blushing and stuttering like the merest schoolgirl, allowing her passions—yes, she admitted to herself, passions—to rule her instead of her mind, and now this! She turned away and covered her eyes in shame, confusion, and anger now at herself.

"Miss Hathaway, if I may ask a favor of you . . . ?"

Cassandra turned back to him. He was still sitting in the

pool, but was holding a hand out to her. He smiled at her charmingly, and if she did not know better she would have thought that smile on his face was positively merry. Was he mad? She had just hit him, with good reason, it was true, but one did not grin happily upon receiving a flush hit.

"If you would be so kind, ma'am, I believe I need some help from this pond."

"Of course!" It was the least she could do, after inflicting violence upon him, and it would show she had gained control over herself again. She went to him and grasped his hand.

A hard tug pulled her into the pool with a splash. The initial shock of cold water made her gasp, and she choked, spluttering water from her mouth. She fell against the marquess's hard body, and looked up to find her face inches from his. His expression had definitely lightened, and the darkness she had seen in him had fled. He stared speculatively at her face, and then grinned, almost boyishly. "What's sauce for the gander . . ." He bent his head to kiss her.

"No!" Cassandra pushed herself away from him and rolled to find herself sitting next to him in the pond. She struggled to stand up, but fell onto her hands and knees. She had almost been hypnotized by his look, but she pulled forth all the will she had left within her and made herself move. "No. You will not. Not again!"

Her dress dragged against her limbs as she crawled out of the pond. It was ruined; there was no doubt in her mind about that. Cassandra could feel strands of her hair straggling over her face, and though she had managed to tie the wet ends of the dress ribbons together, they had become tangled in her haste and she knew she would have to cut them off when she changed clothes. She must look dreadful.

The rain fell in sheets, and thunder roared in the distance. The marquess rose from the pond, sodden, his hair plastered to his head. His pantaloons adhered to his legs like a second skin. It made no difference; somehow he looked just as elegant as always. It was maddening.

Cassandra pushed a lock of hair from her eyes. "You . . . *horrid . . .* man! I thought you were a gentleman. I thought—I thought you *cared* just a little." She felt tears start to her eyes, but she bit her lip to keep them from flowing. "But you never did. You thought me no better than a—a whore." She forced her voice to be sarcastic.

Blytheland's face turned stormy at her first words, but the look faded, and his expression became confused. "I— Cassandra, I did not mean—I shouldn't have—That is, I thought . . ." He stopped, seeming at a loss for words.

His loss was her gain. Cassandra gathered herself together and said in a dignified tone, "I would appreciate it, Lord Blytheland, if you would escort me out of this maze."

"Of course." The marquess's voice was subdued. He offered his arm to her, but she looked pointedly at it and did her best to sneer. She had never sneered at anyone before, but it seemed she succeeded, for Blytheland's face grew stony and he turned from her.

"Very well, ma'am. Follow me."

Careful to stay close enough not to lose him, Cassandra followed. She was glad she had quelled the impulse to leave by herself, for she knew she would have become quite lost. They turned this way and that, and after a few minutes finally walked into the garden. The other guests were long gone; down the hill she could see the last of the servants carrying away the remains of the luncheon in a sack upon his back.

Cassandra wanted to leave Blytheland as quickly as she could. She almost ran and stumbled in her attempt to hurry. A hand caught her elbow before she fell, and she looked up into the marquess's face.

"Unhand me, sir," she said, and stared steadily at him. Anger flared clearly in his eyes, and she almost thought she saw despair—but it was gone, and she knew she must be mistaken. He pressed his lips together, causing them to whiten.

"Very well, ma'am." His voice was terse and strained, and he let go of her arm instantly.

Walking quickly, Cassandra headed toward the marquess's house and was soon at the doorstep. She could not help looking back at him.

He had not moved from the garden. He stood there, hands clenched at his sides, but for all his clearly angry stance, he looked curiously bereft. Cassandra bit her lip and shook her head. No. She must not let her emotions overcome her reason. He had not said one tender word to her, but had insulted her, and clearly saw her as someone too far beneath him to consider for anything more than a— Cassandra swallowed down a feeling dangerously close to grief. He was a marquess, and someday to be a duke. He could look higher than a Miss Hathaway for a wife. He was not in love with her at all, but had thought her a fallen woman. She was a fool even to have thought he had cared for her.

Taking a deep breath, she opened the door and went up the stairs to the room allotted to her. She ignored the slap-slap of her dress against her legs and the wet trail she was sure followed in her wake. Once in her room, she rang for the maid and carefully took off her dress, even untangling the mess of ribbons at the sides of it with slow, controlled movements.

The maid arrived, exclaimed at the ruin of her dress, and wrapped Cassandra in a warm quilt.

"Please, I would like to rest for a while. Could you make sure I am not disturbed? I believe I have the headache," Cassandra murmured.

"Of course, miss. Shall I get you a tisane?" the maid replied.

"No. No, rest is all I require."

"Very well, miss. When shall I wake you?"

"Before dinner, or if my mother asks for me." The maid left.

Cassandra lay down on the bed and pulled the quilt over her head. Then she cried and raged and cried again, for she knew she still loved Lord Blytheland, against all reason, against all hope. And she had not one idea how to stop it.

Chapter 9

If Lord Blytheland had despised himself for a fool before, he knew he was a hundred times that now. He looked in his chamber's mirror and saw his eye was turning purple. Cassandra had been right to hit him, though he did not expect such a flush hit from a lady. She had said that he had acted worse than his friend Eldon. It was true. He had no right to accuse Eldon of importuning her with a simple kiss, when he had done far worse.

He closed his eyes, and her image rose before him—her eyes full of anger and confusion at his unjust accusation of his friend. And then later, in the center of the maze . . . Mixed in her anger and confusion, he could see disappointment. She had been disappointed in him. The thought made him want to writhe in embarrassment. She had, obviously, believed him a gentleman. Except for those kisses at the Marchmonts' ball (for which he had apologized), he had treated her with all the respect and consideration he would normally give to any lady. Even more than that: he had invited her family to his house as visitors, to the alfresco luncheon and to rest for the night before they returned home. He had never given that sort of attention to any woman. She must know it and her hopes had no doubt been raised. He had insulted her and disappointed her and he deserved the black eye he had received.

Blytheland went to a chair by the window and sank into it, pushing his fingers through his hair. What the devil had prompted him to act in such a totally uncontrolled manner? He could not blame her if she thought him mad, for he had acted like he'd come straight from Bedlam. Was there something about Miss Hathaway that caused it? He'd never acted this way around any other woman. Countless times he'd caught himself staring at her: the way her midnight hair framed her face, the laughter in her green eyes, the elegant line of cheek and throat and bosom, the earnest expression that creased her brow whenever she talked of her charities. She was intelligent, too, and had a sense of humor. All these, other women he had known possessed in part. But the sum of them existed in Cassandra, and he found the whole irresistible.

No, he could not blame her. He had been seized with a madness and had acted like an idiot. Was there a way to retrieve her good opinion of him? He had accused her of a terrible thing . . . and did not know if she would forgive him. Certainly, he could not expect it. He closed his eyes tightly and winced, for his eye ached, and it reminded him all over again of why she had hit him.

But she had said she loved him. Perhaps, perhaps there was some hope.

It was that which must have taken the madness from him: the anguished look in her eyes, and her cry that she had loved him. He had felt it suddenly, as if he had been shot through the heart, and the pain of it cleared the hot mist from his eyes. He saw in that instant how stupidly he had acted, without reason or consideration. For all his anguish at Chloe's betrayal, he had not been as consumed with—yes, he admitted it—jealousy as he had when he thought Cassandra cared for Eldon, and not for him. Well, the scales had fallen from his eyes and he saw everything clearly now, and what he saw of himself he did not like.

But there was nothing for it: he had to apologize and perhaps if she could forgive him, he might have a chance at proposing marriage to her. He glanced in the mirror at his bruised eye and grimaced. He had little right to hope, however. If she refused to ever speak to him again, it was all that he deserved.

A knock sounded on the door, and Fichet entered, carrying a large piece of raw meat.

"If it please you milor', I 'ave brought ze beef steak," the valet announced. His eyes went to the marquess's messed hair, and a pained and sorrowful expression crossed his face.

Blytheland raised an eyebrow. "I thank you, Fichet, but I do not desire beef for dinner, much less raw beef."

"No, no, milor'! It is not for ze meal, but for ze eye. I 'ave noticed it when you came from *le jardin.* It is to put upon ze bruise, *n'est ce pas?*" The man looked at the beef critically. "It is of a very fine cut milor'—not of ze best, but it will make little ze blackness of ze eye."

"*Je ne veux pas*—and *no.* I do not want a bloody piece of meat anywhere near my eye. It will do quite well all by itself."

A look of profound understanding grew upon Fichet's countenance. "Ah! *C'est l'amour!* Why did I not think of it?" the valet murmured, and nodded to himself. "It is ze thing that will make a man mad—even to ze destruction of his coiffure and eye."

"Nonsense." Blytheland shrugged impatiently and turned from him.

"But see, milor'! Your hair! Your eye! They are in a condition deplorable, *hein*? But because it is la Mademoiselle Hathaway blacks ze eye, *la voilà*! You do not take care of these things."

"What did you say?" The marquess swiveled his head abruptly toward his servant.

"Milor' you do *not* turn the head so fast! It will ruin the cravat!"

"The devil take the cravat! What did you say about Miss Hathaway?"

The valet threw up his hands. "English! *Le Diable* will not take the cravat; it is around the neck of milor' le Marquis, and ruined because you jiggle ze head around. Not even *le Diable* would take ze ruined cravat."

Blytheland's glance at Fichet was stormy. "Enough of cravats! How did you know that Miss Hathaway . . . blacked my eye?"

Fichet shrugged. "It was for all to see—if zey looked out ze *chambre* of milor', as I did. I see ze maze, you, and Mademoiselle Hathaway. When you leave, the dress of Mademoiselle is wet, as is milor's coat zat is now in a state ze most execrable. It make me to think. 'Ow is ze clothes so wet, but ze rain just begin?" The valet tapped his head wisely. "But of course! Zere is a pond. Ze beautiful mademoiselle, ze most distinguished marquis—it is a course *naturelle*." The valet put his hand over his heart, and closed his eyes. "*La voilà!* Zey have *l'amour* so violent zey fall into ze pond!" He sighed soulfully.

The marquess ground his teeth. "We did not make love in the pond, Fichet!"

His servant only smiled, bowed, and looked at him skeptically.

"Besides, if—*if* we were so enamored of each other, how is it that I received a blackened eye?"

"Ze English have no finesse, even you, milor' sometimes," Fichet replied placidly. "*La pauvre petite* was frightened of ze violence of ze passions, *hein*? *Eh bien!* She strikes ze eye. With ze Frenchman, it would 'ave been different."

"Oh, really?" Blytheland snarled.

"But of course," the valet said, clearly unmoved by his employer's mood. He lifted the piece of meat expectantly. "Now, milor', ze beef . . . ?"

A grimace of a smile formed on the marquess's lips. "Of course. Do let me take it from you, Fichet." He took the meat between his fingers, went to the window, opened it, and threw it out.

"Milor' Marquis! The beef!" The valet looked offended.

"I do not *want* the beef. In fact, I am beginning to *detest* beef," Blytheland said between his teeth.

"But ze bruise! What are you to do of it?"

"I, Fichet, am going to ask for Miss Hathaway's hand in marriage."

"But zat 'as nothing to do with ze eye!"

The marquess sighed. "It has everything to do with it."

Cassandra awoke with a slight headache. She rose from the bed, and went to the mirror. She looked very much like she felt: her face was pale, her eyes puffy, and there were dark streaks under her eyes. Covering her eyes, she groaned. She simply could not appear like this at supper.

A knock sounded on the door. "Yes? Who is it?" She desperately hoped that it was not her mother.

"It is I, Mary, ma'am. You asked that I wake you in time for dinner."

"Yes, yes of course. Please come in." Cassandra sighed with relief.

The maid looked at her curiously. "Excuse me, miss, but is there aught I can do for you?"

I must really look dreadful, thought Cassandra. "No— yes. If you would be so kind, will you bring some cold water and a cloth for me? I have a bit of the headache."

"Of course, ma'am."

Cassandra sighed and sat down on the bed, looking absently at her hands. She opened and closed them, holding them out flat and then curling them into fists. She closed her eyes and bit her lip, feeling her face grow warm. How *could* she have lost control over herself and hit the marquess? Oh, but she had been so angry! He had been so unfair, so, so accusatory and insulting! As if she had done something horribly wrong. Well, perhaps she should have chosen a more secluded spot for kissing Lord Eldon, but no one else saw! And then when they were in the maze . . .

Feeling her face grow hot, she pressed her hands to her face. What in the world did he think he had been doing? Well, that was clear—he thought her nothing but a light skirt. *What in the world did you think you were doing*, murmured a nasty little voice in her head. It is not my fault! she mentally cried back to that voice. I did not know he was going to do—all that! *But you must have known it was not proper . . . and you did not stop him until you were almost undressed, replied the horrid little voice.*

Cassandra groaned. She felt foreign to herself, she who prided herself on her learning and her logic. Pride was a sin, indeed, for now she had her reward: all she had was confusion and could not see or think clearly at all. He did not make sense to her, and worse, she did not make sense to herself either.

Cassandra sighed and made herself sit up straight. That was the crux of it, was it not? He was not what she thought him. She'd thought him a gentleman, someone considerate of others' sensibilities. Someone who was kind and gentle. It was true that he had kissed her at the Marchmonts' ball, but it bore only a tangential resemblance to what she'd experienced in the maze. At the Marchmonts' the kiss had been gentle and absorbing. But this one! It had been hard—well, at first—and, and overwhelming. She reviewed her past encounters with the marquess and nodded her head. Yes. She had thought once that perhaps there was more to his surface calm, and she had been right. She had been deceived by his manners and outward consideration. Really, it would be better for her to keep her distance from him.

But you love him, and now you are afraid, the irritating voice said, and a responding cry of despair almost wrenched its way past her throat. But Cassandra shook her head and firmly banished that horrid little voice to a deep, dark chamber in her mind. She was afraid of nothing.

Mary returned with the cloth and water and started laying out Cassandra's dress for the evening. Cassandra pressed the cold cloth to her eyes. She simply must go down tonight. She could not stay upstairs, or else her parents—indeed the guests—would think that something was amiss. She could very well plead the headache, since it was true. But her headache was not nearly close to bad at all, and there was no excuse for cowardice.

When Cassandra put on her dress, she looked in the mirror and sighed. Her eyes were no longer puffy, but the light green satin did little to enhance her pale face and seemed to emphasize the shadows beneath her eyes. She pinched her cheeks, but that only brought two high spots of color to them. She sighed again and shrugged. It did not matter. It really did not matter. Hitting Lord Blytheland was perhaps remotely excusable, considering his horrible opinion of her, but she could hardly expect anything more than civility now. What had been between them—what she had thought was between them—was over.

The marquess paced his study and nervously put a finger between his neck and neckcloth. He really should not have tied it so tightly. But it was too late to remedy that right now. Sir John had sent up his note that he would meet with him shortly. Two raps on the door preceded the butler's entrance.

"Sir John Hathaway, my lord." The butler bowed and ushered Cassandra's father into the room.

Sir John gave him a sharp, assessing glance. "You wished to speak with me, Lord Blytheland?"

"Of course. That is, yes. Er, would you like to be seated? And refreshment. Brandy. Would you like some brandy?" The marquess groaned mentally. God, but he must sound inane. How does one set about asking a man for his daughter's hand in marriage?

"Why, thank you, my lord. Brandy would be excellent."

Blytheland was not certain, but he thought he saw amusement in Sir John's eyes. He looked at the older man again, but the expression was gone. He poured a glass for him and then after a short pause poured a small one for himself. The marquess drank it almost without tasting it, feeling the brandy's heat flow down his throat. He did not feel all that much better, however.

"You must be wondering why I requested your presence here today," Blytheland said.

Sir John merely smiled and gazed at him with interest.

"You must have noticed that my attentions to your daughter, Miss Hathaway, have been most marked of late. Indeed, I must confess that I have not always acted as a gentleman ought in her presence."

Sir John's eyebrows rose. "Kissed her, did you?"

"Er, yes." Bytheland could feel his face heating, but damn it, he could not bring himself to tell the man he had done more than that. Surely it was not necessary.

"Thought so."

Lord Blytheland looked a question at him.

"From the way she reacted when she mentioned the Marchmonts' ball, you see. It seemed she was not . . . unmoved." Sir John gave a slight smile.

"Then perhaps she would not be adverse to my suit for her hand in marriage," said the marquess, all in a rush. He felt his face grow warmer. "That is, with your permission, sir."

Sir John waved a careless hand. "Of course, of course."

"Thank you."

Silence ensued. Lord Blytheland cleared his throat. What *did* one do next? He did not remember it being this difficult with Chloe. Becoming engaged was a damnably awkward thing.

"However," Sir John said suddenly, "there *is* the question whether she will accept you." He looked pointedly at

Blytheland's blackened eye. "I assume it was Cassandra who blacked your eye?"

"Whyever do you assume so, sir?" Blytheland replied, hedging wildly. He almost groaned aloud. Damn, did *everyone* know?

"Logic and reason will someday answer the questions of the universe, my lord. To apply the mind's ordered faculties to such matters as your blackened eye is but a trivial exercise." Sir John pulled off his spectacles and paced the room, eyes concentrating mightily on the floor.

"Is it?" the marquess replied, his voice full of ice. He had not until this time thought his eye a trivial matter.

"Of course," Sir John said, apparently oblivious to the marquess's change of tone. "The bruise is of a shape similar to that of a lady's fist—should a lady know how to make a proper fist, that is. I recall, once, my son Kenneth showing Cassandra a few techniques of the art of pugilism—which she despises, by the way. There is the possibility she recalled it from somewhere in the recesses of her mind. Then there was my daughter's absence from the luncheon, and then yours. Lord Eldon returned before you, but since he is your friend and his expression was untroubled and merry and his appetite unaffected, I believe he was not the one who hit you. Prior to your absence, your eye was unmarked. Some hours after we returned to the house, you appeared with the bruise. You mentioned to your guests earlier that you stumbled and collided with a piece of rococo molding in the library. A maid tells my wife that Cassandra is indisposed with a headache."

The baronet paused in his pacing and cocked an eyebrow at Blytheland. "My daughter," he continued, "almost never has headaches. And rococo molding does not protrude to such a distance from the paneling that it would blacken anyone's eye. The most probable conclusion?" He paused.

"You behold me in breathless anticipation," Blytheland said, and could not help his sarcastic tone of voice.

A small smile touched Sir John's mouth. "The conclusion cannot be anything but that Cassandra hit your eye." He gazed critically at the marquess's bruise. "And a rather flush hit, if I may say so myself. I have heard that a slice of beef over the eye will reduce the swelling."

"I do *not* want beef, I thank you, sir," Blytheland replied through clenched teeth.

"Ah, well. But I warn you, my lord, Cassandra is not your ordinary young miss. The things that attract most young ladies do not hold much weight with my daughter. She may not accept you."

Blytheland smiled cynically. "Oh, I concede she is certainly not ordinary. But she cannot be so far different from her peers that a title and all the luxuries of life hold no sway with her."

Sir John gave him a quizzical look. "Ah, but, my dear Lord Blytheland, Cassandra has few peers."

"Of course."

"You think I am a overly fond father, I see." Sir John gave a wry smile that was also kind. "Well, I perceive I cannot convince you. You must find out for yourself whether my daughter will accept you or not. I understand she has risen from her rest. Perhaps she will see you now." He put his spectacles back on his nose, bowed, and gave his leave.

Blytheland stared at the door Sir John had just closed. Perhaps he should go to her now—or, no, did he not have some business with his bailiff—? On the other hand, there was no need to hold Miss Hathaway in suspense. Perhaps she was expecting some declaration or apology from him. It was the honorable thing to do, after all. Yes. Yes, he would ask for her, and declare himself immediately. He sighed. "If it were done when 'tis done, then 'twere well it were done quickly," he murmured to himself. Then remembering the context of that quote from Macbeth, he grimaced. He wished he did not feel he was going to an execution instead of proposing marriage.

Cassandra started nervously when she heard the parlor door open. She stared out the window at the landscape before her, but the gray clouds dulled the trees' and flowers' colors and did nothing to lighten her mood. She shivered, feeling just as cold and colorless as the view.

Her father had said that Lord Blytheland wanted to speak with her, and she could not help thinking that his desire to see her was quite unnecessary. What would he say? Would he apologize? Would he reproach her for striking him?

"Miss Hathaway."

She turned, slowly raised her head to look at him, and could not suppress a small gasp. A broad purple-and-yellow spot colored the area just below the marquess's right eyebrow, the side of his nose looked red, and a dark streak under the eye emphasized it all. The rest of him was, as usual, impeccable. But the eye ruined the effect; it was a blight on an otherwise pure landscape, a marring spot on a perfectly executed painting.

"Oh! Your eye! Does . . . does it hurt much?"

"Er, no, not much." The marquess looked quite uncomfortable, and Cassandra thought he must be in more pain than he admitted.

"I . . . I have heard that a slice of cold beef over the eye will lessen the pain and hasten the healing," she said tentatively.

"I do *not* want any beef!" he snapped.

"Well, you must excuse me, but I thought it *might* help!" Cassandra turned from him and stared angrily out the window again. Really! He was the crossest thing imaginable. She was only trying to help, after all!

"It would have been better if you hadn't been so free with your fist—or your kisses—in the first place!"

Cassandra turned swiftly to face him. "You need not

throw my actions in my face! I well know I should not have used violence against you—but you must admit, my lord, that I was under extreme provocation!"

"And what provoked you to try your little 'experiment,' " pray?" There was a hint of anger in his voice. Anger boiled up within her in response, heating her face.

"Do not start again! I explained it before, and I need not justify my actions to you. What right do you have to dictate to me?" She glared at him. He gave her an icy look in return, but it did nothing to cool her temper.

"Right? I have all the rights of a future husband!"

"What?" Cassandra felt her breath catch in her throat. She stared at Lord Blytheland, uncomprehending.

An uncomfortable look passed across his face, but he lifted his chin and said firmly, "What I meant to say is, will you marry me, Cassandra?"

She clenched her hands. "How *dare* you make mock of me!"

"No, I am not! You must marry me."

"Must? I think I might have a *little* say in this, my lord!"

The marquess impatiently paced the floor in front of her. "Not really. We were seen. My valet saw us go into and out of the maze. I think that is all who might have seen us, but I cannot be sure. Not only that, but your father deduced that we were alone together for quite a long time. I have no choice but to ask that you be my wife."

Cassandra's heart beat madly, but whether it was in grief or anger, she did not know. She had dreamed once, a week after they first met, that he had asked her to marry him. She had dismissed it as a notion beyond probability. Now he asked her to marry him in truth, and she felt it was a nightmare. It was all for propriety's sake—a necessary and bloodless thing that she knew many people lived with quite comfortably, but she knew she could not. She had hoped one day when she received a marriage proposal, that it would be from a man who loved her. But Lord Blytheland had said nothing of love, nothing of respect or esteem.

She looked up at him, putting all the control she could over her emotions. "You have no choice, do you? Ah, but I do. And I say no. No, Lord Blytheland, I will not marry you."

His lips pressed together briefly, as if he clenched his teeth. "And why not?" he asked.

Cassandra drew in a deep breath. "Because, my lord, I know from your words and actions that you neither esteem nor respect me." Or love, she thought. A stab of pain went through her heart at her own words, but she repressed it. "I, at least, can choose with whom I wish to marry and live for the rest of my life. And I choose not to marry someone who has not even one care for me." She turned away from him and looked out the windows, not seeing at all what was before her.

"I . . . care," said the marquess. His voice sounded closer to her.

Don't turn back to him! Cassandra told herself sternly. You cannot give in to him. She shook her head. "No. You care only for your consequence, and your honor, perhaps. I am sorry, my lord, but no. That sort of care is not enough."

"Then if you must hear it, I love you."

Cassandra gasped, then shook her head. No, impossible. His voice had been low and harsh, as if he'd been forced to confess it against his will. How could he love her and accuse her of base things, thinking she was a woman of no virtue? It made no sense! *And your feelings make perfect sense, do they?* said the nasty little voice inside of her. She firmly quashed the voice—it was the uncontrolled and unreasonable side of her, and she felt if she listened to it, she would break apart inside. No, it was best to think clearly, and logic told her he did not love her, but wished only to have his way. Cassandra took a deep breath and once more felt in control of herself. She turned to him once again. His expression was confused and lost.

"No, Lord Blytheland, I think you do not know what love is. My answer is most definitely no." She moved from him toward the door and opened it with what she felt was remarkable calm. "Good day, my lord."

"But wait—!"

The door closed behind her.

Chapter 10

"You did what?" Lady Hathaway's voice rose to a shriek on the last word.

"I refused him," Cassandra said calmly. She carefully put the last pair of earrings into her jewelry box and handed the box to her maid.

Lady Hathaway sat abruptly upon a chair and stared at Cassandra and wondered if a cockatrice was hiding beneath her daughter's apparently unmoved countenance. Certainly she felt as if she'd turned into stone, for Cassandra's words had stopped her heart and she felt numb. She became aware of the maid's interested gaze and waved her hand at her in dismissal. The maid left, her steps clearly reluctant. Lady Hathaway took a deep breath.

"Now, let me see if I heard correctly. Paul Templeton, Marquess of Blytheland, heir to the Duke of Beaumont— Lord Blytheland, who is a young, highly eligible, handsome, talented man of great fortune—proposed marriage to you, and you refused his suit." She held up her hand as Cassandra opened her mouth to speak. "No, no! Say nothing, at least for a few minutes . . . I wish to savor the fantasy that I did not hear the words, that I have reached my dotage at last and have lost all my senses and faculties of mind."

There was an obedient silence as Lady Hathaway closed her eyes and indulged in this hopeless flight of fancy . . . hopeless, indeed, for she opened her eyes and saw her daughter before her, lips firmly closed and eyes downcast.

She could not believe it. Oh, she could believe that all the material benefits of marriage to the marquess would not have weight with Cassandra. But she had been so certain that her daughter's affections had been engaged, and the girl certainly had not objected when the man had kissed her at the Marchmonts' ball! Why, she had even admitted to finding his kisses pleasant!

What had gone wrong? The man had positively haunted the house and Lady Hathaway had been certain he'd propose—and she'd been right! Anyone could see he was clearly enamored of Cassandra; it was the talk of the town, if the gossips were to be believed. *They* had been right, too, for he *had* proposed.

And had been refused. Her daughter Cassandra had refused him. Had she gone mad?

"Come, look at me, Cassandra."

The girl raised her head and stepped forward, and Lady Hathaway could see at last the shadows beneath her daughter's eyes, her pale skin, and her eyes dark with grief. Something was terribly wrong, and Cassandra was clearly miserable. Her heart melted. Silently, Lady Hathaway held her arms out to her. With a sob, Cassandra ran forward and flung her arms around her mother's neck. She wept noisily, as she had not done since she was a child, and Lady Hathaway stroked her hair.

"Hush, hush, child," she murmured. "That's it, love, a little crying will make you feel better."

Her words seemed to make Cassandra cry harder, but it was always thus, thought Lady Hathaway, even when she was a little girl. Cassandra had always been logical, her father's daughter, and tried so hard to emulate his intellectual demeanor. But Lady Hathaway knew she was also like herself, with a deep well of womanly passions, and for all Cassandra's training and studiousness those feelings would surface, will she, nil she. Those emotions always exploded from her, like the steam from a boiling pot too tightly closed, and Cassandra was always better for some venting. Lady Hathaway patted her daughter's back, rocking a little, as she used to do when Cassandra was a child.

At last Cassandra's sobs subsided, and after a few hiccups, she raised her head and smiled weakly at her mother. She searched about her for a handkerchief, then took the one Lady Hathaway gave her and dabbed her eyes.

"Thank you, Mama. How stupid of me! I cannot understand what overcame me. Why, I—"

"Enough, Cassandra! I nursed you myself when you were a babe, unfashionable though it was in some circles, and I remember every tear and smile you gave me since then. I am your mother! Would I not know when you are hurt to your very heart?"

Cassandra's smile wavered, and she shook her head. "Oh, don't—I fear you will make me cry again, Mama."

Lady Hathaway smiled and squeezed her daughter's hand. "Well, I think you have done quite a lot of that already. Perhaps a better idea would be to tell me what transpired between you and Lord Blytheland."

She listened in silence as Cassandra haltingly told her of her "experiment" and how Lord Blytheland had seen it. Lady Hathaway suspected from her daughter's hesitant speech that she did not tell her everything . . . but she would deal with that later. She suppressed the despairing sigh that threatened to burst from her. Heavens! She had not known Cassandra was so naive—she had thought her intelligence would make it easy for her to understand society's ways. Then, too, she'd thought a little naïveté would be an attractive thing in a young lady, but this was more than a little! It was her own fault for not insisting that Cassandra stay in the select boarding school she'd sent her to, but had allowed her husband to teach her instead. And she should have expected that her daughter would turn out so, for she herself had learned discretion and proper conduct at the young ladies' academy to which she had gone when she was a girl.

Clearly Cassandra had misconstrued her instructions and had taken her acceptance of Lord Blytheland's kisses in general terms.

It was clear to Lady Hathaway why Lord Blytheland had lost his temper—he was jealous, and possibly mad with love. Such madness was a rare thing, but she had seen it happen and she was sure it was thus with Lord Blytheland, for he had never been known to act in such a way before, not even in rumor. But it was not time for her to reveal this to Cassandra quite yet. For as she listened to her daughter, there was no hint the girl would admit to loving him, or that her grief and pain came from love, and not from mere insult. She was certain, however, that Cassandra did love him, and was most probably aware of it.

But as Lady Hathaway listened, a burning anger grew in her as well. For however Cassandra had acted, he had behaved in far less than a gentlemanly manner when he took her into the maze, kissed her, and accused her of a lack of virtue. It mattered not whether he was mad with love or was jealous; he should have had better control over his passions than that. And to suspect Cassandra's climbing boys to be her own! If it were not so insulting, she would have laughed. She suspected that someone had referred to the charity in vague terms . . . possibly Psyche, for that literal-minded child had been warned not to mention climbing boys, and only the family referred to the charity as "Cassandra's children." She would definitely have to talk to Psyche soon.

She patted Cassandra's hand and squeezed it in a comforting manner, and her daughter smiled in return.

"Well, we shall be leaving this house soon, and Lord Blytheland need not bother you again. He has proposed—as he should have done, after practically compromising your virtue!—and you have refused. I am sorely disappointed in him—he had seemed so gentlemanly as well as eligible! But that is the end of it, and we need not acknowledge his invitations or his calls to us in town if you do not feel you can face him. And I would not blame you if you did not wish to see him! For all that you were indiscreet—and I will not excuse you on that head!—you did not deserve such treatment from him."

Cassandra cast a tentative look at her mother. "Could we . . . could we leave London and go home, at least for a while?"

"No, that would be admitting you were at fault, should word of this ever come out to the *ton*, as it will, eventually. However painful it is, we must return, and put a good face on it. Besides, *you* were the one to refuse his proposal, therefore there must be something wrong with *him*, not you. If we left London, it would be thought quite otherwise."

Cassandra nodded and was silent, clearly taking in this advice with deep consideration. Lady Hathaway gazed at her, and felt that something had changed, that Cassandra would perhaps show a different face to society than she once had. Lady Hathaway knew a moment of regret and sighed, for she felt torn. Part of her wished that the blunt, outspoken Cassandra had stayed, for it was how she had been since a child, and to see it modified or changed was to see her daughter as a little girl no more. But Cassandra was a woman grown, and to try to keep her from being one was foolishness.

"Besides, you have grown quite popular, have you not? There is no reason why you should not enjoy the entertainments during the rest of the Season. There are other eligible gentlemen in London, too, when you are able to think of proposals again—Lord Eldon, after all, did not refuse to kiss you, after all! But there is time enough to think of that later," Lady Hathaway said hastily at Cassandra's despairing expression. "It is best to think of balls and dresses and other frivolous things."

Cassandra raised her brows. "But frivolous things—"

"No, I do not want any of your homilies about frivolity," Lady Hathaway said. "There is such a thing as balance in one's life, and I think you have had enough of seriousness and disappointments for now, am I not right?"

There was silence, then Cassandra pressed her lips together and nodded. She looked at Lady Hathaway and smiled gratefully. "You are the best of mothers! I know you must be disappointed, for you seemed to like Lord Blytheland over any other gentleman . . . and he is the only one who has proposed, after all. He could be my only—" She swallowed, then smiled again, though it was a smile full of pain. "The only proposal I will receive."

Lady Hathaway patted her hand. "I would not want a husband for you who did not love you as you deserve, my dear. And I am not at all in despair! Why, Hetty Chatwick told me last week that the Viscount Bennington was quite taken with you when he saw you in our opera box! And did not Mr. Rowland and Sir Ellery Heysmith both dance with you at the Marchmonts' ball *and* at Almack's?"

She chattered on, watching Cassandra's face as she outlined new entertainments and future balls. Her expression had lightened a little and she was clearly listening to her mother's advice. But a dark sadness still lingered in her eyes, and Lady Hathaway feared that her daughter's heart might be badly broken.

"It is my fault. It is all my fault," Psyche said, and pressed her hands to her eyes. She had heard her mother's shriek, and had—admittedly—eavesdropped, then ran to her bedroom. She knew she would weep and did not want anyone to see her, and it was close to the time she usually slept anyway. "I mentioned the climbing boys and I shouldn't have, and it made Lord Blytheland angry at Cassandra, and she hit him on his eye and now *she* is angry at him, and they will never be happy again!"

Harry flew down from his perch on the window ledge to the bed upon which Psyche sat and hugged her comfortingly. "No, it was not your fault he was being stupid. Besides, he said it was the rococo molding."

Psyche shook her head and wiped away a tear with the back of her hand. "No, I know she must have hit him, because I saw them come out of the maze and his eye looked terrible. He hadn't walked into molding at all." She bit her lower lip to keep it from quivering but her tears still fell. "Oh, I wish I hadn't told him! I have ruined it for both of them! I am so disappointed in Lord Blytheland. I never, never thought he would be mean to Cassandra, for he has always been kind to me. How could he be so horrid to her? I don't understand! I thought you said he was in love with her, Harry!"

There was silence, and Psyche looked up at her friend. He felt tense next to her, and an odd expression, a mix of affront, surprise, and guilt was on his face. She had seen him affronted before, but she had never seen him look surprised or guilty about anything.

"Is there something the matter?" she asked.

He looked at her, and this time the guilt was clear in his eyes. He swallowed. "I think . . . I think it is my fault a little, Psyche."

"But I thought you turned him back to what he was before you shot him with your love arrows!"

"I did! But, well, I, er, got there too late," he said in a rush. He definitely looked uncomfortable now.

"Oh, Harry!" Psyche said.

"I thought there was no need . . . I thought perhaps it would work well as it was, and I suppose . . . I suppose I didn't go as fast as I should have." He rose from the sofa, went to the fireplace, and fiddled with a few of the ornaments on the mantelpiece. He put them down and walked to the window, then back to the fireplace again, his movements restless. "And . . . and I think I might have shot too many love arrows into him the first time."

"Too many arrows? Why?" Psyche felt a queer ache inside of her, as if something she held dear was quickly sliding from her grasp.

"He was stubborn! He refused to think he could love anyone, or that he could be loved! All he could think of was his stupid dead wife who could never truly love anyone and who he—Who he—" Harry clenched his fists, frowning terribly. "With whom he fell in love because he looked at the wrong woman when I shot him with one of my arrows!"

"You mean you made a mistake."

"No, I never make mistakes. It wasn't my fault he looked at the wrong woman!"

"Not your fault! Why, I would say you should have known he could have looked at the wrong woman if there were more than one about him! Oh, you and your, your *hubris*!" Psyche said hotly. "You say we mortals shouldn't have it because it offends you and your relatives, but I think it's precisely the opposite! If you hadn't been so toplofty as to think you never make a mistake—and you certainly did, don't deny it!—you would have been more careful! You wouldn't have had to shoot Lord Blytheland with too many arrows and—"

She stopped and stared at Harry. "You said too many arrows . . . what did you mean by that? What do too many arrows do?"

"I don't see why I should tell you, especially if you're going to be a witch about it all." A mulish look settled about his chin, and he stared at her angrily.

"You *shall* tell me!" Psyche cried. "It's important! I know my sister has a broken heart—she cried and cried and she *never* cries! If you don't I swear I'll not leave my window open at night, and you will have to stay outside until morning and if you catch a horrid cold it shall be all that you deserve!"

"What do I care? I don't catch colds," Harry said scornfully.

Psyche bit her lip again, for she could feel it begin to quiver and she didn't want to cry again.

"Oh—very well!" Harry said impatiently. "If I shoot too many arrows in someone they become mad. They don't always act as they ought and sometimes they become stupidly jealous. There. I hope you are satisfied."

The ache Psyche had felt earlier grew hard and hurt worse now. She stared at Harry and knew some of the ache was disappointment, for though she knew he was not perfect, a part of her always thought he was. But now his actions had made Lord Blytheland act in a mean way to Cassandra, and now Cassandra's heart was broken. And Harry could not even admit he had made a mistake!

"You horrid, beastly boy!" Psyche cried. "It was all because of you that Lord Blytheland was so odious to my sister! I *told* you, you should not have shot him! I *told* you it was a mistake! But you didn't listen, did you? You knew *so* much more than I! You *never* make a mistake, do you?"

"I suppose your blabbing about Cassandra's climbing boys to Lord Blytheland had nothing to do with it?" Harry hunched a disdainful shoulder. "If you think me so odious, I wonder you care to have me about!"

"Well, I don't!" Psyche retorted. "I hope I never see you again!"

Harry gave her one burning, angry look, and with a rush of wind and feathers he was gone.

"Harry!" Psyche whirled around, looking for him, "Harry, where are you?" No answer, no glowing light, no whisper of feathers or rattle of arrows. He was gone, truly gone. Her lip trembled in earnest now. Oh, heavens. He had been right, really—she was still partly at fault, even though most of the fault was his. But she had been so angry!

"Harry?" she whispered. Silence. She was alone now, and she wished she had not scolded him. And . . . she had told him that she never wanted to see him again. "I didn't mean it! Please come back." She flung the window open wider and strained to see into the night's darkness.

But still there was silence, no sound except the wind outside the chamber window.

Lord Blytheland watched the guests leave in their carriages and watched in particular one coach in which a young lady sat. He lifted his hand and placed his fingers on the drawing-room window. The coach now looked no larger than the width of his thumb. If he could, he'd pluck up the carriage and bring Cassandra Hathaway back to him again.

But he could not, of course. He picked up a glass and swallowed a mouthful of brandy, not tasting it, and hardly feeling the heat of it going down his throat. Grimacing, he put the glass down on the marble-topped table beside him. The madness that had seized him was gone now. How long had it held him? He was not certain, and there was only confusion and despair left in its wake. He had pushed her away with his jealous rage, he was sure.

He pressed his palms against his eyes and groaned. There was no reason Miss Hathaway—Cassandra—should forgive him. He had not only insulted her but his proposal of marriage had been so badly done that no self-respecting woman would have accepted him.

But she had said she had loved him. He should not hope; his actions should have killed any love she might have had for him. And yet . . . and yet she had not said that she hated him, not precisely. It was not much, perhaps, but it was something.

It was, he realized, more than he had had from his wife or from any of his mistresses. None of them had said words of love to him—appreciation, perhaps, for he was fairly skilled at lovemaking and showering those under his protection with trinkets and other expensive gifts. But none of them had said they loved him. He knew now he'd come to expect it: that for all his wealth and title, there was something wrong with him, something in him that was ultimately unlovable. Blytheland half groaned, half laughed. How ironic it was that he'd hear it at last from blunt, outspoken Cassandra, after showing how unlovable he could be. And now she'd left his life—possibly forever, if the cold, haughty looks he received from Lady Hathaway were any indication.

The door opened, and his butler bowed. "Lord Eldon to see you, my lord." Blytheland nodded, and the butler opened the door wider.

Lord Eldon raised his quizzing glass and peered at his friend, his gaze resting for a moment on Blytheland's black eye. "Now that's a wisty castor. Didn't know rococo molding protruded that far out from the wall. Architecture's a damned nuisance, if you ask me."

"It wasn't rococo molding, El," Blytheland said.

"Ah. Thought not. La Hathaway has a handy bunch of fives on her, eh?"

"Flush hit. Knocked me down flat into the pond."

Eldon's brows raised. "Remind me not to have a lover's quarrel with her. Can't hit a lady, after all, and I wouldn't have a sporting chance, then."

Blytheland laughed reluctantly, then looked steadily at his friend. "The field's clear for you, El. She's refused me. Not that I blame her. I'm a villain, a monster, the way I've treated her. She deserves much better for a husband than someone like me." He gave another bitter laugh. "You should have called me out when you had the chance. I deserved it. In fact, feel free to use my pistols now. I promise I won't return the shot."

"Happy to oblige, Blythe-my-old, but I might get blood on my hessians. Can't have that."

"No, of course not."

There was silence for a moment, then Eldon said, "Truth to tell, Blythe, I was hoping to hear wedding bells for you. Seems I miscalculated."

The marquess raised his head and stared at his friend.

Lord Eldon looked a little uncomfortable. "Thing is, you were dancing around the lady so much we all thought it was a promised thing. Betting on it at White's, too. Then you told me it wasn't in the pocket at all. Bad thing to do, friend, especially when she was so clearly top over tails in love with you from the start."

"I couldn't see it, El." Blytheland hesitated. "No, I did not want to."

"Chloe?"

"Yes."

Silence again. Eldon, apparently in deep thought, twirled his quizzing glass on the end of its ribbon.

"Well, I believe you know what I thought of Chloe," he said. "So I won't go into that. But I'll be frank: I had Miss Hathaway figured as the perfect match for you. Everyone did. Music, brains, charities, not to mention a lovely face and form—most everything you like, my old. Thought you could see that, too."

"Had a thought to play the matchmaker, did you, El?" Blytheland said mockingly.

Eldon rubbed the side of his nose and looked a little embarrassed. "You'd been moping about Chloe for, deuce take it, two, three years now? Time to stop mourning for a woman who was little better than a whore."

The marquess stood up abruptly, fists clenched. "I'll remind you not to talk about—"

"Oh, stubble it, Blytheland! What else do you call a woman who came home only to whelp another man's child?"

Lord Blytheland caught his breath. "How do you know—"

"If you'll remember, you lost your way down Pall Mall, after imbibing three bottles of White's finest the night she died. If I hadn't peeled you off the lamppost and brought you to my lodgings to sleep it off, you'd probably have blabbed the whole to the street." Lord Eldon bent a kindly eye upon his friend. "You were pretty badly off, so I daresay you might not remember it. I would have been the same with three bottles in me—in fact, I was, the last time Lightning-Be-Gone placed fifth at Ascot. Lost a deuced thousand pounds, too, and was sick as a dog the next morning.

"Thing is," he continued after Blytheland sat down again, "you're a marrying man. Thought perhaps Miss Hathaway would be the ticket to church for you. But you denied it every time, despite the way you were hovering around her like a bee to honey. So, when she asked me to participate in her, ah, experiment, I thought it'd be just the thing to make you think about what you might be losing." An embarrassed look grew on his face. "Thing was, I didn't think you'd rake Miss Hathaway over the coals, or insult her. You never did that before to a lady, not even with Chloe when you found out about her, ah, indiscretions."

"I'll thank you, El, not to interfere in my affairs in the future," Blytheland said, but he said it with no heat, no anger. He had, after all, no one but himself to blame, and Eldon was quite right. Miss Hathaway was perfect for him, and he'd been making up excuses right and left trying to tell himself she was not. "Well, it's too late now." He rubbed his hand over his face. God, he was tired thinking of it all, and the brandy was not making it any better. "I'll see you in town in a month or so."

Eldon nodded in an understanding manner. "Can't be seen in town sporting an eye like that."

Lord Blytheland hesitated and then gazed at his friend. "Would you look out for her, El? I won't be in town, but she will. She has no more notion about how to go about society than a kitten, for all her intelligence. I suppose . . . I suppose with all the attention I have been paying her, there will be gossip. Let it about that I did propose, and she refused me." He smiled wryly. "If they wish to think I am suffering a decline in the country because of her rejection of my suit, they may do so."

"No, no, not so bad as that!" Eldon protested, clearly revulsed. "But I shall see that she's partnered at every dance, at least."

"Thank you, El. You're a true friend." Blytheland poured himself another glass of brandy and drank it down.

Lord Eldon cleared his throat and looked embarrassed. "Not at all, not at all. You'd do the same for me, should the occasion rise." A look of horror crept upon his countenance. "That is—Good God. I hope not. Not that La Hathaway isn't what a man would want—That is, I wouldn't want to be in the same boat as you right now. No offense meant, Blythe-my-old," he said, looking uncomfortable.

The marquess laughed at last. "No, I know you don't." His smile twisted, and he shook his friend's hand. "Let me know how she goes on, will you?"

"Of course." Eldon turned to leave, but hesitated. "Think you might try again?"

Blytheland sighed and wearily rubbed his unbruised eye with his hand. "I do not know, El. I really don't. Sometimes I think—Well, I suppose it doesn't matter."

Lord Eldon gazed at his friend sympathetically for a moment, then took his leave and closed the door. He frowned. Blythe was in a bad way, but heaven only knew how he'd get himself out of it. He was willing to wager that Miss Hathaway was fair to being miserable, too, by the look of her face before she left. Lord, what a tangle! Well, he'd watch out for Miss Hathaway as his friend had asked, and perhaps put in a good word or two for old Blythe as well.

He'd denied that his friend would go into a decline, but he was not all that certain of it. Blytheland's bottle of brandy was already half empty, and the look on his face was worse than the one he'd had the night Chloe died. He doubted that the man would feel much better in the morning. Worse, in fact. Much worse.

Chapter 11

"And would you know when Lord Blytheland will be returning to London, Miss Hathaway? It has been three, perhaps four weeks since he has been in town, has it not?" Lady Fairway asked.

Cassandra swallowed her anger and bit back an acid retort. She smiled at Lady Fairway. "I have no idea, my lady. I am not privy to Lord Blythcland's activities." She took a sip of tea, glad that her hand did not rattle the cup on the saucer when she put it down again. Perhaps she was not always discreet, but she had learned much control this month. It was important so that she would not scream the hurt and anger she still felt every time someone poked at her for answers to Lord Blythcland's absence from London.

"But I thought you and he . . ." Lady Fairway said, her voice rising at the end in a question.

Cassandra widened her eyes innocently and raised her brows. "Lord Blytheland and I? What have we to do with— Oh! You must mean our mutual interest in music. There was some talk of doing more duets, but I do not know if it will come about. I suppose we might, but I cannot say until he returns to London. It is always a difficult thing to agree upon a piece of music that is mutually satisfactory to both players." She shrugged a little and smiled.

She saw her mother nod in approval at her from across Lady Fairway's drawing room. Her mother had given her support for her spirits and much encouragement, and she was grateful for it. This time she would listen, and try harder to understand the rules of society, however nonsensical and contrary to the philosophies she had learned. There was such a thing as practical application, after all, and one must modify one's theories to real situations instead of to the hypothetical. Even her father had agreed this was true.

Lady Fairway raised her brows and her smile was sly. She tittered. "And to think that there were rumors about your betrothal to him!"

Cassandra could feel herself blush, but she made herself laugh. "As you see, you have made me blush at the notion—it is so ridiculous! How anyone could think such a silly thing, I do not know. Why, Lord Blytheland can look higher than myself for a wife, after all. Everyone must know that."

"A silly notion, of course," Lady Fairway agreed and her smile was odiously sweet.

Cassandra bit back a heated retort, almost losing her resolution to be silent upon the subject—she could easily have mentioned he *had* proposed to her. But she was not at all certain when he would return to London, if at all this Season, and she would much rather deny he had an interest in her beyond mere flirtation. Her mother had thought it might be best to discreetly let people know of the proposal, but though Cassandra agreed to every other one of her suggestions, she could not bear thinking of his proposal, or anyone questioning her about her refusal. Her mother had reluctantly agreed; the subject would be a thing to cause speculation whatever anyone said.

"Oh, hardly silly, Lady Fairway," said a voice behind Cassandra. She turned and swallowed nervously—it was Mrs. Drummond-Burrell, one of the strictest of the patronesses of Almack's. Her cool gaze warmed a little and she nodded approvingly at Cassandra. "Miss Hathaway is clearly a modest young lady of good birth, and that is always attractive in a prospective wife. She is very accomplished as well. Who is to say that a man of Lord Blytheland's breeding and lineage would not look to marry her? I see it as wholly possible that he might propose to her in the future, and be considered most fortunate in his choice."

Cassandra blushed furiously now. "Oh, heavens, Mrs. Drummond-Burrell. Truly, you are too kind. I pray you will not say more. Really, there is nothing between us except an interest in music."

The patroness of Almack's nodded kindly at her. "You are a good, modest girl, Miss Hathaway." She gazed sternly at Lady Fairway. "One does not often see such modesty in young ladies these days, I am afraid."

This time Lady Fairway blushed, and with a hasty curtsy and murmured excuse she left to talk with some acquaintance she had just noticed from across the room.

"Odious woman," Mrs. Drummond-Burrell remarked calmly. She turned to Cassandra and gave her a slight smile. "You did very well. I do hope Lord Blytheland proposes to you and that you accept. He needs someone as sensible as you, Miss Hathaway. His last wife was a horrible woman, immodest and wicked. However, you are wise not to set your sights upon him; gentlemen are not always as sensible as ladies where marriage is concerned. It is remarkable how many of them make the same mistakes again and again." With a nod, she turned to talk to an acquaintance.

Lady Hathaway beamed her approval at her from across the room, but Cassandra felt trapped. Oh, heavens! She *had* refused the marquess. If the *ton*—and Mrs. Drummond-Burrell—heard of her refusal and disapproved, would she be turned away from the doors of Almack's? She almost groaned in despair. It seemed it mattered not what she did or how hard she tried, she could still founder in the murky shoals of society's rules.

And what was she to do when Lord Blytheland returned?

They were bound to see each other from time to time, and it was bound to be awkward. Her mother said that all she needed to do was be civil . . . but such coldness and distance between them would be marked by everyone in the *ton*. Lady Hathaway had shaken her head. There was no escaping it; it would be noticed, and they would have to bear whatever whispers and speculations they heard with aplomb.

A brief silence suddenly stilled the drawing room, and Cassandra knew without looking toward the door that Lord Blytheland had returned. She could see glances from Lady Fairway's guests go between the door and herself; who else would engender such speculative looks? Conversation began again, slightly louder than before, as if everyone were trying to cover an awkward moment.

Awkward indeed. She looked up to see Lord Blytheland before her. The bruise was gone from his eye, only a slight yellowing close to the side of his nose. His gaze was solemn as he bowed to her.

"I trust you are well, Miss Hathaway?" His voice was soft and deep, and she wished desperately she did not feel joy rising in her upon hearing it.

"Y-yes, I am well, thank you. And you?" She could not help glancing at the eye she had hit and her face grew warm with embarrassment.

"I am better, thank you."

Cassandra swallowed and looked away. "I am glad," she murmured.

"Are you?" Was there a slight eagerness in his voice? She was not certain.

"I would not want anyone feeling less than well, my lord." There, that was nothing more than a neutral sentiment.

"Of course." The marquess's voice was cool, and when she looked at him again he did not meet her eyes but seemed to look past her shoulder. She wished she could say something witty or light, but she could think of nothing, and only gave him a brief, weak smile and looked away.

"Perhaps I could call upon you tomorrow or the next day, Miss Hathaway?"

Oh, heavens, what should she say? Cassandra glanced at her mother across the room, but she was talking to the lady by her side. She looked at him; he gazed at her again, and though his face was smooth and cool, he had a questioning look in his eyes. She did not know he would return at this time, she was not prepared for it. At the very least, she needed a day—a few days—to compose herself, to think how she might speak with him from this time on. She wet her lips nervously.

"I—I would be pleased to have you call upon me," she said as calmly as she could. "But not now . . . that is, in a few days. I shall not be home to callers in the next day or so. I have been so busy, you see, and have fallen behind on some of my duties." She hated to give such an excuse, although it was not a lie—she did need to see to some of her duties to her charities—but in truth she was a coward and did not want to face him. She looked down at her clasped hands on her lap. Oh, but she could not, could not speak to him just yet!

She could hear him taking in a deep breath before replying, "I see. Perhaps . . . perhaps in three days?"

"Yes . . . yes, that will do."

"I thank you. Your servant, Miss Hathaway." He sketched a bow and turned away.

Cassandra watched him leave, then caught her mother looking at her questioningly from across the room. She shook her head and then looked down at her lap again. Three days. She wondered what Lord Blytheland would say to her when they met again. Well, she would have enough time to compose herself and rehearse whatever words she might need to . . . what? She did not know. Her hands twisted together and a lump rose in her throat.

She looked at the clock on the mantelpiece—she would have to stay another fifteen minutes before she could go home. And she wished desperately to go home. For right at this moment, there was nothing she wanted more than to fling herself upon her bed and cry and cry until she had no tears left.

Psyche sat and stared dully out at the street in front of the house from her window. She shivered. She wished she could go home to the house in the country—there were many things to do there, not like London. Dull, boring London, with nothing to do and no . . . friends.

Even the scold she had received from her mother upon their return from Lord Blytheland's alfresco luncheon was better than this. She felt a little better about being punished, for she knew she deserved it for ruining things between Cassandra and Lord Blytheland. Well, the marquess *still* should not have acted so odiously, but he would not have if she had not misled him about Cassandra's charity.

A dull, empty ache pulsed inside of Psyche's chest, and she felt like crying again. It was not as if the scolding had helped her sister in any way. She hated how falsely cheerful Cassandra would become when in her, Psyche's, presence, and could see how her sister seemed so listless and sad when she thought no one was looking. Psyche had also heard some weeping in Cassandra's room next to hers . . . whatever Cassandra said, it looked very much as if she *did* love Lord Blytheland anyway. However bad one might argue with someone, it did not mean you hated them, after all.

Psyche sighed. And well did she know that! She wished desperately that she had not argued with Harry. It was awfully lonely without him, for he was always amusing to talk to, and always had a story to tell or would play a game of cards or chess with her. But now there was nothing to do, for she could hardly play chess with herself, and playing

game after game of patience was becoming dreadfully boring.

She heard a door open and shut out in the hallway, and a
rush of activity in the next room. Did Cassandra have a
caller? Psyche gnawed at her lower lip and frowned. She
was not allowed to see anyone who called upon them, and
was more or less confined to her room for the next two
weeks. But a certain rebelliousness rose in her. She had not
totally been at fault for the argument between Lord Blytheland and Cassandra; it was Harry's fault, too, and the marquess's. So her confinement to her room was quite unjust.
Really, it was only fair that she be allowed a little peek at
who was calling at their house, and if she was careful, no
one would be the wiser. Psyche quashed a little quiver of
conscience. No, she had taken on punishment that should
have been Harry's, too. She *deserved* to leave her room at
least a little!

She waited until the voices from Cassandra's room were
silent and the door opened and closed for a last time. She
glanced at the ormolu clock upon the mantelpiece and
waited for another five minutes. There. That should be
enough time.

Carefully, Psyche opened the door to her room and
looked around it out into the hallway. Nothing. She
breathed a sigh of relief and tiptoed silently down the hall.
The stairs went down to a small landing, and there she sat,
peering between the balusters. She could hear someone
pacing below . . . ah! It was Lord Blytheland. His head was
bent, his hands clasped behind his back, but there was no
other gentleman of their acquaintance who had such golden
blond hair and impeccable clothes. He looked nervous, Psyche thought, as if he were trying to think of something to
say. The door of the drawing room opened. He straightened, and his face became smooth, as if he had never paced
or looked nervous at all. Psyche wondered how he could do
that, for she was never able to control her features at all.

Perhaps it was something that came with age. The door closed behind him, then her mother came out, and Psyche shrank back behind the balusters again.

"I will give you fifteen minutes, my lord. That should be quite enough for anything you have to say to my daughter. I shall be in my sitting room across the hall, should either of you need me," Lady Hathaway said into the room, looking very stern, as if she would have liked to have confined Lord Blytheland to his room, too. She left the door ajar, then went across the hall to her room.

Psyche stared at the open door and fidgeted. Perhaps she would go down the stairs to listen at the door. She might as well go back to her room if she was going to let herself be bored by sitting on the landing and staring down at the hall, after all. There was a very large potted fern sitting upon a table just next to the door; if she was very careful, she could conceal herself there and listen.

She rose and tiptoed down the stairs. There was a slight space between the fern and the wall next to the drawing-room door, enough for her to slip behind and curl up beneath the table. She made herself very still, and listened.

Cassandra sat and folded her hands before her in her lap and was glad she could control their shaking. But her palms felt damp, and she took out her handkerchief and surreptitiously dried them. She did not look at Lord Blytheland, for she was afraid of what she would blurt at him if she did, especially since she had no idea what she would say to him. That was what had made her say indiscreet things, she found—not knowing what she'd say in any particular social situation. She had tried to think of potential events before she went anywhere so as to practice what she would say. It had worked well, too, for no one had walked off in an offended manner for a month now, and she had many gentlemen calling upon her the next day after dancing with her.

But for all that she had had three days in which to practice before Lord Blytheland would come calling, she could think of nothing except how she had felt in his arms, how she had kissed him as shamelessly as he had kissed her, his words to her in the maze and how she had hit him. How was one to practice proper responses to thoughts like those? And so here she was, wordless in front of him, twisting her handkerchief into knots, and feeling as if her stomach were twisting into a knot as well.

"Cassand—Miss Hathaway," Lord Blytheland said abruptly, making Cassandra start and stare at him. He had a tight look upon his face, his lips thin and frowning, his eyes tired and a little reddened, his face pale. Was he ill, perhaps? She hoped not . . . although why she should care when he had treated her so badly she did not know. She twisted her handkerchief tighter. She did care, and there was no deceiving herself about that, stupid as it was.

"Miss Hathaway," Lord Blytheland began again. "I . . . I have come to apologize." He began to pace the floor in front of her. "I should have come to town earlier, but was . . . indisposed." He grimaced, then smiled ruefully. "Frankly, I was afraid to show myself with a black eye."

"Oh!" Cassandra closed her mouth tightly to keep herself from saying more. She felt a pressure of words behind her lips, and heaven knew what she'd say if she opened them. Not now, she told herself. Not now. Listen and *think* first.

"I was a brute, I treated you badly," he said, his words coming quickly now. "There was little excuse for it except . . . except I seemed to have gone a little mad. It is not something I have done before—well, I suppose anyone might say that." He raised his hand—a slight, beseeching gesture—then dropped it to his side. "But you may ask any of my friends—Lord Eldon, Mr. Rowland, Sir Ellery."

"I suppose your friends would speak well for you," Cassandra said carefully, trying to keep her voice neutral.

Anger flickered in his eyes, then faded to resignation. "I

wish . . . I wish I knew what to say. I wish to be in your good graces again, so you will not think ill of me . . ."

Cassandra turned away, embarrassed, not really wishing to hear more, for it seemed to be more of the same thing he had been saying before. She had known people who disliked anyone to think ill of them, not because of any remorse, but out of pride, because they could not bear a tarnish on their public mask. It was beginning to seem Lord Blytheland was such a man. She had sensed the passion—no, anger—beneath the surface mask, and he had shown it, and now he wished to hide it, pretend that it would not happen again. But such anger often repeated its performance in one way or another. Did not Mrs. Wollstonecraft say it, also? And Cassandra did not want to see it again. Or be tempted to display your own temper in response, the nasty little voice said inside of her. She firmed her lips. Yes, or be tempted to display her own temper again.

"Please, Cassand—Miss Hathaway—please look at me."

Cassandra turned to him again, gazed into his eyes, and a sharp pain went through her heart. He had stopped before her, his eyes were full of despair, his face pale with strain.

"What I said before was true. I love you. I wish you to be my wife, not because of any scandal, but because I love you. I swear I'll never accuse you falsely of anything, as long as I live." He ran a shaking hand through his hair, messing it terribly, then began pacing again.

Her hand trembled as she pressed it to her lips. There were so many things she wished to say, all fighting for a place on her tongue, all full of conflicting feelings and desires. Anger, weeping, fear. And love? She thought so, but her emotions were so mixed and fiery, they boiled inside like a pot on a stove, and if she put her hand down from her mouth, she knew the feelings would spill forth, confused and heated. She had never felt so much before in her life and did not know what to think, what was right and proper. Nothing her father had taught her of various philosophies helped her, for they were full of theories and hypotheses, and none of them seemed to fit her situation now.

Lord Blytheland stopped again in front of her, gazing at her earnestly. "Please—deuce take it, I know I'm a fool for asking it, and I would not blame you if you never wish to see me again, but I must know. You said—" He hesitated, then rushed on. "You said you loved me, there in the maze. Do you still?"

Cassandra rose, stepped toward the window, and stared blindly out of it. What could she say? Her heart was too full, and she was afraid of what was in it.

"Please, Cassandra . . ."

She turned swiftly around and faced him. "I don't know. I don't know!" She clasped her hands in front of her to still their shaking. "I did, before you—Before we—" Cassandra cleared her throat of the tears rising in it. "I have not been able to think clearly since then." She gave a hesitant laugh, a little bitter, a little sad. "I used to think I was very good at discerning what people were like after I observed them for a while. But you . . . well, I suppose I should not have been so sure of my abilities. And now I am afraid."

"Not of me—I swear—"

"I do not know how you will act in the future, Lord Blytheland," Cassandra said. "If I wed you, how do I know you will not act jealously again? It will be too late, after we are wed."

He gazed at her, frustrated. "How can I prove it to you, that I know I will not do it again?"

Cassandra shook her head. "I do not know how you may prove it. I do not even know what I think or feel." She turned from him, and went to the fireplace. She leaned her head upon the mantelpiece and stared into the fire.

"If I give you time, time to think about it—" Lord Blytheland said eagerly.

"Perhaps," Cassandra said dully. She suddenly felt tired, and her mind refused to work and moved sluggishly. "I think perhaps that would be the best thing, to give me time."

"I see." Lord Blytheland said only the two words, but they were heavy with despair and pain. Something inside Cassandra cracked and flowed hot inside her, and she pressed her hands to her eyes to push down the rising tears. "I am sorry. Perhaps it is best that I leave. You may assure your parents I will not annoy you again, if that is what you wish."

Cassandra could not respond; her whole body felt leaden with the weight of confusion and unshed tears. She almost told him, crazily, that her father had gone out of town, that she would be sure to tell her mother—irrelevant things, for the important ones would not come. She heard his steps, swift, away from her, and she turned at last. But it was too late—he had left, quietly, with no more words.

She stood, mute, staring at the door. Then it opened again, and her heart hammered in hope . . . but it was only her mother, who gazed long into her eyes. Lady Hathaway said nothing, but held out her arms.

With a low moan, Cassandra ran to her and when her mother held her and drew her to the sofa, she moaned again, deep, for the tears she had held back for so long would not come now.

"Hush, child, hush, hush," Lady Hathaway murmured, patting her back gently. "It will come about, you will see. Hush, love, you will see."

She said the words again and again, rhythmically, a soft lullaby like the ones she had sung when Cassandra was a little girl, and at last the tears came, hard and hot and more full of grief than she had ever had since a child. When she was a girl, she could hope. But being a grown woman was a different thing, and hope did not come so quickly, especially when her heart and mind had become that of a stranger's, no longer familiar or sure.

* * *

Psyche crouched behind the potted fern, her fist pressed tightly to her mouth. Silent sobs shook her, for she had heard it all, the hopelessness and love in Lord Blytheland's voice and now Cassandra's weeping. She could not bear that they were so unhappy, and it had been her fault and Harry's. What was to be done now? Their hearts were broken, and it seemed nothing could be done to make it better again. Lord Blytheland was right—he had suffered a sort of madness, for Harry had shot many arrows into him, enough to make him act in a way he would never have acted otherwise. The marquess would not act so again, now that Harry had cured him of the arrows.

It seemed Lord Blytheland might go away, and she wished he would not. He must stay in London, for Cassandra did love him—why else would she cry when he left? He must not give up, he must not leave. Psyche was certain they were meant for each other—did not Harry say so? And he was usually right about that, however they might disagree about his arrows.

Psyche squeezed her eyes shut tighter, thinking of Harry. She did not want to cry loudly, as she wished to, for she knew Mama would hear. But she missed Harry so! If only he were here! She was sure that between them they could think of a way to help her sister and Lord Blytheland.

She took in a deep breath, wiped away the tears with the back of her hands, and hiccuped. She would *not* think of Harry. It would be best if she returned to her room before Mama came out of the drawing room again. Psyche was certain she had not seen her behind the fern, for it was a very large plant, with long leaves that trailed down to the floor.

The afternoon was turning into evening; Psyche could see the sky now dim through the open window of her bedroom. The tears welled up inside her again. She had left the window open, as she always did for Harry. But he was not here. She always hoped perhaps he would return, but he never did, and it was a whole month since he had left. Slowly, she went to the window and slowly closed it, dashing away a tear with her other hand. It was stupid to hope. She had sounded as though she didn't like him anymore when she had shouted at him, and who would want to be friends with a girl who did that?

Psyche crept into her bed and sat against the pillows, hugging her knees. Her stomach grumbled, but she did not really feel hungry, and did not feel like going downstairs to have her dinner or her supper. Perhaps she would ask a maid to bring up something to drink, and then she would sleep. She was not feeling very well, at least not in her heart.

But she would not let herself despair. Cassandra and Lord Blytheland needed help, and even if Harry were not here, she would think of what to do herself. She sighed, feeling very tired, and closed her eyes and leaned against the pillows of her bed. She could do very well without Harry's help, she was certain. Perhaps she would go to Lord Blytheland and explain how Cassandra truly felt about him. Yes, she would go to him tomorrow—properly accompanied by a maid, for she knew Mama would not like it if she were unaccompanied by a maid—and tell him all about it. And if he was not convinced, she could find out where Lord Eldon lived, and make him talk to his friend. Psyche yawned and settled down into the pillows more deeply. Lord Eldon was a very nice man, and because he was Lord Blytheland's friend, he would want him to be happy, too. And then she would talk to Cassandra and tell her all about Harry's arrows, and how it was all a mistake . . . perhaps Harry would come back someday, and tell her . . . himself. . . .

The room was silent, and Psyche turned over to sleep on her side away from the window, as she always did. So she did not see the slight glow just outside, or hear the light tapping upon the window.

The glow hovered about the window, moving back and forth as if trying to see within the room. There was the light tapping upon the window again, but Psyche did not move. The glow stilled, then moved away slowly. For one moment, it seemed to hesitate.

Then it was gone.

Chapter 12

The sun struck Cassandra's eyes and woke her. She kept her eyes closed, for she did not really feel like getting up just yet. Today is just another day, like any other day, she told herself. You will have breakfast, and then you will find Psyche and give her Italian lessons and lessons in geography and mathematics. Then you will do all the other things you have always done since you came to London, only you will not see Lord Blytheland, and it will not matter to you one whit, for you are fully capable of going on as you have before, without him.

Hard words, and they struck her heart like stone. She turned and pressed her face into her pillow. She would not cry. She had done enough of that, enough for a lifetime. Pushing herself from her bed, she rose and pulled the bell rope. Today she would dress and everything would be as it was the day before, and the day before that.

Though she admittedly picked at her breakfast, she ate it, and when Psyche appeared for her lessons, she went through them as she always did. Her sister seemed unusually silent—but though she had received quite a scold from Mama a month ago, and Psyche was very sensitive to scolds and was clearly still affected by it. Cassandra hugged her sister after they finished the lessons.

"Psyche, please do cheer up. I know you did not mean to mislead Lord Blytheland. You see, I do not mind it, for it showed me his true nature, and I cannot wish to wed a man of such violent temper."

Psyche gazed at her wide-eyed and shook her head. "I think you do mind it."

Cassandra looked away and began fiddling with a fold in her dress. "Oh, at first I did, but not now. It was for the best, truly." She glanced up to find her sister still staring at her, her head cocked to one side.

"Well, you may say what you like, Cassandra. But it will turn out well. Lord Blytheland does love you, I know it. Perhaps I could help—"

"Heavens, no!" Cassandra hunched a shoulder. "Please, let us not talk of him. I would prefer not to think of him— or of his feelings." Especially not his feelings. His admission he loved her struck hard every time she thought of it. He *said* it, but what did it mean? He could have very easily—

No. She would not think of him. There were better things to do today. Cassandra waved her hand at Psyche. "I will need to run a few errands soon. Do you wish to accompany me?"

Psyche hesitated. "Where are you going?"

"To the milliner's to see if my hat is finished, and then the draper's to find some ribbons to match the hat."

"No, thank you." Psyche shook her head. "I don't wish to go anywhere right now. Perhaps tomorrow."

Cassandra gazed at her sister for a long moment. "Is there something the matter?" Psyche loved to go to the shops on New Bond Street, and her refusal was unusual.

The girl looked down at her hands clutched tightly to-gether. "I . . . I know you do not like me to speak of him, but I have not seen Harry for a long time. And I wish he were back."

She looked so forlorn Cassandra did not have the heart to remind her that Harry was imaginary. She gave her another hug. "Perhaps he will return . . . or perhaps this means you are growing up, and do not need ima—such friends anymore."

Psyche shook her head. "If growing up means I shall not have Harry for a friend anymore, I do not wish to grow up."

Cassandra gave her a comforting pat on her back. "Well, perhaps he *shall* come back, soon."

"I don't know . . ." Psyche said, dully. She shrugged and rose from her seat. "I am going to read for a while. Do tell me if you see anything amusing when you return."

"Of course," Cassandra replied. She would buy something for Psyche while she was out, a book, or perhaps find some music for her to sing, for her sister loved to sing. She would play the piece upon her piano, and she and Psyche could do a duet—

A book would be better, Cassandra decided, for she did not want to think of music or duets quite yet. She sighed and went upstairs to put on her walking dress. She wished her father would come back to London, for perhaps he could give her advice. He had gone to Cambridge because Kenneth had got himself into trouble again, for her brother detested the place and had often wished—loudly—to join the army. In this one thing, Cassandra thought her father erred. Kenneth was not stupid by any means and if he applied himself he could be quite brilliant. But he hungered for a pair of colors and wished more than anything to fight in Wellington's army against Bonaparte. She could understand her father's wish to keep his son and heir safe in England. But he could speak with someone in government—he had quite a few friends there—and purchase Kenneth a relatively safe position in the army.

As Cassandra finished dressing and tied the ribbon of her bonnet under her chin, she wished life were not so difficult or so hard to understand. Her mother said these things were part of life, what one must bear and from which one must learn, as important as learning of Goethe's ideas or Aristotle's. She had not thought of it in that way before, but she saw practical application of one's theories was always useful. And so she would bear the pain that seemed a constant companion, and put up with the ache in her heart that seemed not ever to go away, and hopefully learn from them.

Psyche waited a whole fifteen minutes after Cassandra left before she rang the bell pull for a maid. It was Gwennie who came to her, and Psyche was glad, because she knew the girl would do anything she asked. She had given her all of her pin money once when she had heard Gwennie's little brother was ill so he could have a proper doctor, and he had become well again. So she had no trouble at all convincing Gwennie to accompany her on her errand to Lord Blytheland's house.

For she had determined, with or without Harry, that she *must* do something about her sister's and Lord Blytheland's broken hearts. It was, after all, partly her fault. And since Harry was at fault, too, and he was her friend—had been her friend—she was responsible for him, too. Making Lord Blytheland and Cassandra understand how wrong they were about each other and perhaps making them be friends again would go a long way to making up for the problems she and Harry had caused.

A brisk wind blew at her and pulled at her bonnet, but she was glad for the breeze, for it was a warm day. It took longer than she thought it would to get to Lord Blytheland's house. Though she remembered where it was, she had only gone past it in a carriage, and it was hard to gauge how long it would take to walk there. At last she was in front of the house. Lord Blytheland's was one of the largest on the street, and the most elegant. Psyche frowned. But there was a traveling carriage near it. The coach had a crest on it, too, and though Psyche did not remember exactly what the marquess's family crest looked like, it looked very much like it could be his. Was Lord Blytheland going away?

She stepped up to the house and knocked at the door, her maid close beside her. The door opened.

The butler did not see her at first, because she was admittedly rather short and he was very tall. But then he glanced down and frowned at her.

"Yes, miss?" he said, looking down his nose, his voice quite frigid.

Psyche pressed her lips together firmly; she would *not* be put aside from her purpose. Besides, everyone knew the best houses had butlers who were always very high in the instep. She needed only convince him she was Quality, and that her mission was serious. "Please," she said, "I must see Lord Blytheland. It is very important. My name is Miss Psyche Hathaway, and as you see I am calling upon Lord Blytheland in a very proper manner, because I have my maid with me. He knows who I am, because he played his violin while my sister Cassandra played the pianoforte, and I was there to listen. He was very kind to me, too, and let me listen along with Mama."

An odd look came over the butler's face, as if he were trying very hard to suppress some strong emotion. His lips quirked up for a moment before turning into a frown, and he cleared his throat a few times before saying, "I am afraid it is not proper for a lady to call upon a gentleman even when she is accompanied by a maid."

"Oh!" Psyche said, and frowned. "Well, I thought a lady might go anywhere with her maid, except Bond Street. Will you please tell him he must come call upon me soon? Today?"

"I, er, I am afraid he is not in at the moment."

Psyche gazed at him suspiciously. "Does that mean he is at home, but he doesn't want to see anyone?"

"No, miss, he is not present in his house at this time." The butler's lips quirked again.

She crossed her heart with her finger and looked at him sternly. "True blue and will never stain?"

The man's stern expression cracked completely and he grinned. He crossed his heart as well. "True blue, miss."

"Oh! Well . . . when will he return?"

"I believe it will be within the half hour. But I doubt you will catch him even then. He will prepare to leave town as soon as he returns."

"Heavens!" Psyche exclaimed. "What am I to do?"

The butler looked at her kindly. "I believe he went to call upon your family one last time—he mentioned he was going to Sir John Hathaway's house. Perhaps if you hurried home, you will find him there."

"Yes, yes thank you!" Psyche gave him a smile, and turned from the house as the butler bowed and closed the door. But her gaze caught the coach in front of her, and she frowned again. She could not be sure she would see Lord Blytheland at her home, for by the time she walked there, he might well be gone. And she could not depend on finding him on the way home. If she waited in Lord Blytheland's traveling coach, she definitely would not miss him, and she could explain everything to him when he stepped into it. She bit her lip and glanced at her maid. It would be awkward to have Gwennie in there, too, for she wished to discuss family matters with Lord Blytheland, and Mama always said it was important not to discuss such things in front of the servants. Well! She would just have to get rid of the maid.

The breeze blew quite strongly, and with a quick tug she untied the bonnet ribbon beneath her chin. The wind obligingly picked up and threw her hat off her head—with only a *little* help from her hand.

"Oh, no!" Psyche cried. "Gwennie, do fetch my hat! Mama will be so angry with me if I return without it!" She was very pleased when the maid ran off immediately after her bonnet. She would give the girl two whole shillings later for her trouble.

Quickly, she climbed into the coach, her heart thumping hard. Did anyone see her? She peered out the coach window carefully. She did not think so. With a sigh, she relaxed against the squabs of the seat.

It was very comfortable in the coach, though very warm. She hoped Lord Blytheland would come soon, for sitting in a coach always made her feel sleepy. However, it could not hurt to close her eyes just a little, and when he did arrive, he would no doubt wake her up. She smiled to herself. Yes, all she needed to do was tell Lord Blytheland how Cassandra really loved him, and how she wept after he left, and he would understand. He seemed to be a rather understanding gentleman, after all, at least to her. He probably would have understood Cassandra, too, if he had not been shot so full of Harry's arrows. Perhaps she would even tell Lord Blytheland about Harry . . . although Cassandra had warned her not to talk of Harry to anyone else. Psyche yawned. It would not be so bad if she closed her eyes, just a little . . . and Lord Blytheland would undoubtedly come soon.

The glow was difficult to see in the daylight even if anyone knew to look for it, and of course no one did. It hovered around the coach in which Psyche sat, hesitated, and then settled upon the groom's seat. Harry allowed himself to take form, though he kept himself invisible. He did not want Psyche to see him just yet, in case she looked out of the carriage.

He found in the month he was away, he could not help thinking of his little friend and he had wondered what she was doing, if she had done anything outrageous lately, or said anything to make anyone laugh. He had left in anger, feeling more hurt than he thought he would. She was just a human, after all, and only a child. But taking mortal form, and a young form at that, always had an effect on him, and he often reacted the way a young mortal would. It was the only way humans could understand his presence, whenever he showed himself. They often became confused when a boy acted like an old man, or vice versa. He grinned. There was no way a human could comprehend an ancient god who could take any form he wished, anyway.

But he had to return and see how Psyche Hathaway fared. While he was away, he had searched a month for his own Psyche, with no success. There were few places these days he could look—he had searched everywhere for any sign of her. He had only twenty more years to find her, before most of the ancient gods faded forever, or so Hecate the Crone, the Secret One, said. They would disappear from the minds of humans, despite the efforts of such worthy men as Sir John Hathaway to preserve the ancient stories. Artemis had already fled to the Americas, where the cities had not yet encroached upon the vast wilderness, and though Apollo had found some contentment with the German and Austrian composers of music, now Ares was strongest, for humans believed in war quite fervently, as they always had.

Many still believed in love as well, so Harry—Eros—had not lost much of his strength. But he was not as strong as he used to be, for he had lost his own love, and he was strongest when he loved as well as when he was loved. When the gods began to lose their power, he had quarreled with his Psyche, for she believed the gods lost their power because they had become too distant from mortals. She would think that, of course, because she had been mortal herself at one time. But then she had disappeared, and only the sound of her voice whispering "find me, find me" had echoed in their empty house at Olympus.

She had been right, or so Hecate had confirmed. And once he found his Psyche, it would save the gods from fading into extinction, forgotten by mortals forever.

So why did he return to Psyche Hathaway? He did not

know. She had the same name, though other mortal females had worn the name, too. Perhaps . . . perhaps she held some clue to the whereabouts of his own Psyche. Who knew why she might! She was a stubborn and argumentative child, and he did not see how she might hold a clue to saving the gods at all.

But if she did, he supposed he should stay to find it out. He had looked most everywhere, after all, and was weary of searching right now. He grinned. Besides, she was a funny child, and it amused him to tease her. It would be especially amusing to see how she went about healing the rift between Lord Blytheland and Cassandra Hathaway without his help.

Something was wrong. Psyche woke up and bumped her head against the side of the coach. It was moving!

"Well, well. The Sleeping Beauty has awakened," said a soft voice.

Psyche gave a little shriek and shrank back into a corner of the coach. "You are not Lord Blytheland!" she said, and stared at the man. He was definitely not the marquess. This man had dark hair, where Lord Blytheland had blond hair, and he was older, too.

"No, I am not. I am Lord Crawforth. And you are . . . ?"

She did not like this man. There was something . . . bad about him, about the way he looked at her. She was used to seeing what people were feeling when she looked into their eyes, but she saw no feeling in this man's eyes, and it made her afraid. But it never did any good to show one's fear, her father always said, so she would not. "I have got into the wrong coach," she said firmly. "I am very sorry, but will you stop it so I may go to the right one?"

"But you have not told me your name, little one." Psyche did not like his voice, either. He made slight hissing sounds when he talked, like a snake—or should have, for he looked at her as if he were thinking whether she should be a side dish or a main course.

"Psyche Hathaway. There! I have told you, so you must stop the coach. Now, please."

Lord Crawforth looked thoughtful. "No, I think I like company on my travels. You shall do very well. How old are you?"

She began to feel very afraid now. "I do not see why I should tell you that, especially since I do not want to go with you. You *shall* stop this coach and I *shall* leave!" She stamped her foot—it was better to be angry than afraid. "If you do not, I shall scream—loudly."

His hand came up and seized her chin, forcing her to look at him. His eyes were cold, cold as ice. "You shall do as I say. You shall indeed come with me, because I wish it. Who are you but a nobody, an insignificant thing? If you scream, I shall simply tell everyone that you are mine, that you are misbehaving. Why should they believe you, and not me?"

Psyche turned and grabbed the carriage handle, almost opening it, but Lord Crawforth pulled her roughly away. She bit him and scratched him, but he was stronger than she, and tore the ribbon from her hair and tied her hands with it.

"There now," he said, breathing heavily from his efforts. "Do be a good girl and stay still."

Psyche glared at him, refusing to cry. She wished she had left a message at home about where she had gone. At least her mother or Cassandra would have known where to start looking for her. Or Harry. She shut her eyes tightly to keep the tears from falling. She wished she hadn't argued with Harry and told him to go away. *He* would have been here with her, if she had not. That would have comforted her and perhaps they would have thought of a way for her to escape.

But perhaps . . . perhaps he had not really gone. Perhaps

he was punishing her a little by not showing himself. Oh, she hoped it was so. For he was, really, her only chance to escape from Lord Crawforth. She took a deep breath.

"Harry! Harry!" she screamed.

Immediately, Lord Crawforth's hand clamped over her mouth. "None of that, my dear. A stupid thing to do. We have traveled quite a way from where we started, and if your Harry was near then, he certainly is not now."

She bit his hand.

"Damn you!" His hand went to her throat instead. "If you do that again, I shall throttle you, depend upon it." His fingers squeezed upon her neck to prove it. "Do you understand?"

Slowly, she nodded, and he released her. He smiled. "That's a good girl. I like good, obedient girls. You will be good, won't you?"

Psyche did not want him to like her, for she felt somehow Lord Crawforth did not treat good girls well at all. In which case, she would try to be as bad as possible.

And hope and wish and pray that Harry would come to her.

Chapter 13

Cassandra was in the midst of untying her bonnet ribbons when her mother burst into the drawing room. "Did Psyche return with you?" Lady Hathaway asked.

"Why, no, Mama. I invited her to come with me to the draper's, but she refused."

Her mother's face creased in a worried frown. "She is not in this house."

A chill went through Cassandra's heart, but she made herself think sensibly. "Perhaps . . . perhaps she decided otherwise, and decided to follow me out?"

"But surely she would have *told* someone?" her mother replied. "I thought to have her do some mending, for she is very good with fine work, but she is not in her room! I knew you were going on your errands, and so assumed she was with you." She wrung her hands and paced the room. "Oh, heavens! Your father *would* be away now, and I shall scold Kenneth when next I see him for making it necessary for your father to go to Cambridge."

"Did she leave a note, or . . . or perhaps one of the servants knows?" Cassandra asked.

Lady Hathaway shook her head. "No, I found no note. The servants do not know, either, although I suppose I could ask—"

A knock on the door took her attention, and when the door opened, Thrimble and a maid entered.

"Begging your pardon, my lady, miss, but Gwennie has

just returned and has some knowledge of Miss Psyche's whereabouts," the butler said and pushed the maid forward. The girl glanced at them nervously and held out a bonnet to Lady Hathaway.

"It's Miss Psyche's bonnet, my lady. We was goin' to Lord Blytheland's 'ouse, and her bonnet flew off acos o' the wind. She asked me to fetch it for 'er, but when I came back, she was gone." The maid hung her head and began to cry. "I looked all over for 'er, I did! But she warn't anywhere! And she wot was so kind when me brother 'ad the flux! I'm afeared somethin' turrible 'as got 'er, my lady. I ran fast as I could, so as you'd know."

"Lord Blytheland!" Lady Hathaway exclaimed. Cassandra glanced at her mother and found her staring in astonishment at her.

"Mama, I have no idea why she would—" A mix of dread and embarrassment crept into her. "She said she thought . . . oh, heavens!" She turned to her mother. "She said she could help—she must have gone to his house to speak to him."

Lady Hathaway groaned. "It only needed this! And of course your father *would* be gone now when we need him! What could the girl have been thinking of?" The maid wailed louder, and Lady Hathaway waved an irritated hand at her. "Oh, for goodness sakes, do go away! And you, too, Thrimble."

"Perhaps we should go to Lord Blytheland's house," Cassandra said tentatively after the maid and butler left. "It is not as if we would enter it, after all, and it is an emergency."

Lady Hathaway shook her head. "I suppose so . . . but your father is supposed to return today. I do not know when. One of us must stay, but it is very awkward, whichever one goes—oh, what is it now?" she said when the butler returned.

Thrimble cleared his throat. " 'Tis Lord Blytheland, my lady."

"Thank goodness!" Lady Hathaway exclaimed. "Perhaps he has brought her home."

But Psyche was not with the marquess when he entered the drawing room. Lady Hathaway sank into a chair and groaned again.

Lord Blytheland strode to her side. "Ma'am, you are not well—is there something I can do to help you?"

"My lord, have you seen Psyche?" Cassandra asked. He turned to look at her, and she felt a blush rising, but gazed at him steadily. He wore a greatcoat of many capes, dressed for travel.

"No, I have not," he replied. "I came to make a last call upon you—I am leaving London."

"Leaving?" The ache that sat so heavily in Cassandra's heart of late turned to pain.

"I thought it best." Blytheland gave her a slight smile. "Country air does clear people's minds, I have heard. But come, what is this about Miss Psyche?"

"She has disappeared," Cassandra said, and wrung her hands. "The maid who accompanied her said she went to your house, and then she was lost, disappeared—I do not know! We thought perhaps you came to bring her back, but you say you never saw her. And my father is not home—he has gone to Cambridge to see to my brother's matters."

"Then you—one of you—must come with me, and we will search for her. I have my carriage outside, but I am afraid it cannot hold more than three." He looked at Cassandra for a long moment, then transferred his gaze to Lady Hathaway.

"Go, Cassandra," her mother said. "Someone must be here to inform your father should he come home early, and what if my poor child should return by herself, to find me gone?"

"I would be here, Mama, for either of them."

Lady Hathaway's lips trembled, and she put a shaking hand to her mouth. "It is not the same as having her mother—what if she should be injured? No, no, you go, Cassandra, I will stay here."

Cassandra gazed at Lord Blytheland and thought she saw hope in his eyes. She swallowed and lifted her chin. I cannot think of myself at this time, she thought. I must think of Psyche, and she must be found. She nodded. "Very well," she said. Quickly, she pulled on the pelisse she had just taken off and hurried to the door.

When they stepped out of the house, Lord Blytheland took her hand and helped her up into the carriage. There was, indeed, not much room in it. If she pushed herself to the far edge of it, she could manage not to have her leg press against his, but to do so would have been awkward. She made herself relax and think of where Psyche might be.

"Shall we start at your house, my lord, since that was where she was seen last?" she asked as calmly as she could.

He glanced at her and nodded. "That was my thought also. She might well have gone inside upon finding I was not there. That must be what happened, and we shall have your sister returned home in no time at all."

"No doubt." It was a comforting thought. She should have thought of this very sensible answer to Psyche's disappearance herself, for the maid had not mentioned asking at Lord Blytheland's house to see if Psyche had slipped inside in an attempt to see him. Cassandra sighed. But then, she hadn't been thinking very clearly lately, had she?

They rode on in silence. Cassandra clasped her hands tightly in her lap, searching the crowded London streets in front of them and feeling thankful Psyche possessed a remarkable amount of bright red hair. She would be easily seen in this crowd. But though her eyes caught every spot of red possible, none of it signaled Psyche's presence. Perhaps she was, indeed, safely in Lord Blytheland's house.

At last the marquess reined in his horses and leapt down, looping the reins upon the iron railing in front of his house. "Wait here—I shall look inside and bring her out again." Cassandra nodded.

A minute passed, then another. It could not take that long to find Psyche, could it? Cassandra bit her lower lip and stared at her hands on her lap, impatiently creasing and uncreasing a fold in her dress. She could not go in, of course, but the waiting was becoming intolerable.

"Cassandra."

She looked up, expecting the marquess, and froze. There, in front of her, delicately perched on the buckboard of Lord Blytheland's carriage, was a boy. She swallowed and felt a little dizzy. "Who . . . who are you?"

The golden-haired boy gazed at her solemnly. "I'm Harry, Psyche's friend." His wings fluttered in an impatient manner. "She needs help, quickly. My arrows are not made for what needs to be done, so you must come, and Lord Blytheland, too."

Cassandra closed her eyes, then opened them. "I *must* be imagining this."

"No, you are not." He reached over and gave her a hard pinch. "There, you see?"

She rubbed her arm—there was, indeed, a red welt on it now, and the crescent marks of two fingernails. "So you do exist," she said wonderingly. She gingerly reached out to touch his knee and felt cloth and warm skin. He allowed it, much like a disdainful cat allowing itself to be patted, tolerant only. She stared at his wings and the quiver of arrows on his back. "And not 'Harry'—Eros, I suppose?" she asked.

He grinned suddenly, a mischievous expression lighting his blue eyes, and she could not help being charmed by it. "Yes. But Harry will do." He glanced impatiently at Blytheland's house. "I wish he would hurry. When he comes, tell him to go to Green Park—they are going in that direction. It's a yellow carriage, and the crest is blue with black swords crossing over a white tower."

"Perhaps you should tell—"

"No. I dislike being seen. You are her sister, and she is in trouble, so I have made an exception in your case."

"Well, I do not see how you can say that! Anyone may see you now."

He grinned, and it was more mischievous than ever. "Only you can see me at this moment. Everyone who has seen you speak to me has been thinking how odd it is that such a lovely young lady is talking to nothing at all."

If this was what Psyche's friend usually was like, it was just as well she did *not* see or hear him, Cassandra thought, irritated. Harry glanced at the house again and made an impatient sound.

"Tell him where to go. I am going back to Psyche and see what I can do." And with a flick of his wings, his shape shimmered and he disappeared.

Cassandra could almost convince herself she had imagined it all, but her arm still hurt where Harry had pinched her. And what if it were true, and she failed to act upon it, and Psyche was hurt? She could not take the chance. She glanced at the door of the marquess's house and bit her lip. There was no time to think of proprieties now, not when her sister was in trouble. Hastily, she descended from the carriage and knocked on the door. A footman answered.

"I am Miss Cassandra Hathaway. Tell Lord Blytheland to come—I know where my sister is, and he need not search his house if that is what he is doing," she said. "Go, quickly, tell him!" The footman nodded and left.

Only a minute passed before Lord Blytheland ran out of the house, looking distracted. "Where?" he said tersely as he gathered up the reins.

"Green Park. A . . . boy saw her climb into a yellow coach and it was going in that direction."

Blytheland groaned as he shook the reins. "There must be dozens of yellow coaches going toward Green Park."

"It has a crest—blue, with two swords and a tower."

"Devil take it." Blytheland's face hardened, then he glanced at Cassandra.

"Tell me!"

"Lord Crawforth. He has . . . fast horses."

His jaw was tight and he would not look at her but stared steadily in front of him, concentrating upon his horses. There was something about Lord Crawforth he did not want to tell her, and she was sure he would not tell her no matter how she pressed him. Please let Psyche be safe, Cassandra prayed, and closed her eyes tightly. She felt a hand close over hers, and she opened her eyes to find Lord Blytheland looking at her with such warmth and kindness that she had to look away, lest the tears she felt rising inside her spill over.

"We will find her, I promise you," he said.

It was only a promise, and he had given her promises before that she did not believe. But she believed him in this now, and felt comforted.

"Psyche."

It was a whisper, and Psyche almost thought she had imagined it, obscured as it was amongst the rumble of coach wheels. But she opened her eyes and there he was, staring at her solemnly. She almost burst into tears of relief, but bit her lip hard to prevent it.

"Harry!" she exclaimed at last.

Lord Crawforth turned from his perusal out the window and stared at her. "How you do persist. Stupid girl. Have I not told you your Harry cannot hear you? If you do not stop, I shall be forced to tie up your mouth as well."

Psyche shrank into her corner of the coach and Lord Crawforth smiled pleasantly. She glanced at Harry and was glad she was not Lord Crawforth. Harry's face was stormy, and his presence seemed, oddly, too large for the coach, though he had not changed in any other way. If she had thought Harry might be dangerous when he was irritated, she had been quite right. His normal glow was pale and translucent, but now he seemed to radiate a hot, almost venomous light when he looked at Lord Crawforth. Psyche shivered. As bad as Lord Crawforth was, she was certain what punishment Harry planned for him would be worse.

But then Harry looked at Psyche, and his expression and his light softened and he smiled encouragingly at her.

"Psyche, I want you to be ill."

She raised her brows in question, not daring to speak.

"Pretend you are about to be sick in the coach. Make loud retching noises."

She looked at him, wondering what he was planning, but nodded. "Oh, dear," she said, and covered her mouth with her hand.

Lord Crawforth gave her a sharp look. "What is it now?"

Psyche closed her eyes briefly, and hoped she looked pale. "I . . . oh, no! I am afraid I feel very—" She pressed her hands against her mouth and coughed. "Ack! Urp!"

Lord Crawforth looked uneasy and moved away from her. "If you are trying some trick—"

She looked at him, making tears form in her eyes—an easy thing to do, for she had been so terribly afraid. "I—I feel ill, my lord, I truly do—Riding in coaches always— Urp!" She lurched forward, as if she were about to give up her luncheon on the coach floor. Lord Crawforth pushed himself into the side of the carriage even more, a look of disgust on his face.

"Tell him you want some milk because it always makes you feel better," Harry whispered.

"Milk? Oh, milk!" Psyche exclaimed, and leaned back in her seat, putting the back of her hand over her forehead. "Please, just a little milk, and I shall feel better."

"Milk? Where the devil would I get milk?" Lord Crawforth said. "I would think water would be better."

"No! Milk, please. Water makes me feel worse." She widened her eyes and pressed her hands to her mouth again. "Urp!" she said, this time with more emphasis than she had before.

"Cretin," Harry muttered, looking at Lord Crawforth. "Tell him there are cows and milkmaids in Green Park, though by the gods he should know it, having passed the place every day of his worm-ridden life." Psyche almost giggled, but turned it into another convulsive lurch and another loud "urp."

"Oh, dear!" she said and heaved a deep, shuddering sigh. "If only we were at Green Park!" She pressed her hand to her mouth and shuddered again. "My mother bought some milk for me there when I felt ill, and I felt better immediately." She gazed at Lord Crawforth as mournfully as possible. "But I cannot hope for that, so I fear I shall be quite—Oh! Urp!"

"Stop!" Lord Crawforth shouted out the coach window to his groom. He gazed angrily at Psyche. "We are at Green Park now. I shall get you your damned milk, but if I find you are tricking me, it shall go very badly for you indeed." He opened the coach door, then turned back to Psyche. "You shall stay here. My groom will be watching to see if you try to escape."

As soon as Lord Crawforth left, Harry untied the ribbon from around Psyche's wrists. "What an idiot," Harry said. "He could have had the groom fetch the milk for him."

"I suspect he wished to get away, in case I should have vomited on him. And I pretended very well, didn't I?" Psyche said proudly.

"Yes. I was hoping you would." Harry grinned, then sobered. "Now, wait here. He needs to be punished."

Psyche gazed at him warily. "What are you going to do?"

The dangerous glow flickered around him again, and he stared at Lord Crawforth's retreating form. "He is a beast, and deserves only the company of beasts," Harry said grimly.

"Oh, dear." Psyche watched as her friend flew toward Lord Crawforth and draw an arrow from his quiver. He fitted the arrow to his bow, and pulled it back. She could not help herself: she covered her eyes and hoped the punishment would not be too terrible.

A plucking, a singing through the air, and then a gasp from Lord Crawforth.

"I say!" Psyche heard him exclaim. "That's a remarkably fine cow you have there." She peeked from behind her fingers.

Lord Crawforth was peering through a quizzing glass at a brown cow.

"Weeell, I daresay Bessie's a good 'un," the cowman replied proudly. "She dropped twins two year ago, and both of 'em sturdy fellows."

"Fertile, eh?" Lord Crawforth said, putting out a tentative hand and patting Bessie on the neck.

"Every year," replied the cowman. "And she never drops 'em bad, neither."

"How much?" Lord Crawforth asked, now petting the cow with more confidence.

"That'll be thrippence, sir," a milkmaid chimed in, and presented a cup of milk.

"No, no!" Lord Crawforth waved the milk aside. "I meant how much for the cow."

"The cow?" The cowman gazed, stupefied, at Lord Crawforth, then exchanged a long look with the milkmaid, who shrugged.

"Yes, the cow," Lord Crawforth replied impatiently. "For how much will you sell it—her—to me? Fifty guineas? Sixty?"

"Er, well, I dunno," the cowman said, scratching his head, but the milkmaid poked him with her elbow.

"I think four hundred guineas would be a good price," the milkmaid said. "Prime bit o' blood and bone, is Bessie."

"Four hundred!" exclaimed Lord Crawforth. "She is a fine animal, I can see, but perhaps one hundred—"

"Three hundred," the cowman interjected hastily.

They continued haggling over the cow, as Psyche watched, wide-eyed. She turned to Harry, who had returned to the coach. "Oh heavens! You have made Lord Crawforth fall in love with a cow!"

Harry grinned and twirled an arrow between his fingers. "He deserved it. At least he will not"—he gazed at Psyche and closed his mouth suddenly, then continued—"frighten girls anymore." He opened the carriage door and took Psyche's hand. "You can come out now. The groom is now madly in love with the milkmaid, and I think she will make him a good wife."

Psyche stepped down from the coach and walked away from it, and still held Harry's hand. She smiled up at him. "Thank you for coming to my rescue, Harry. I am so sorry I told you I didn't want to see you, because it wasn't true at all! I felt awful afterwards, and missed you terribly. It is a lonely thing to be in London without a true friend."

Harry looked at her and cleared his throat. She was right. However ancient one was, it was a lonely thing to be without a friend. There was nothing wrong with having a friend or two while continuing his search, after all.

"Well. Well, I missed you also. And—" He hesitated. "I am sorry, too. It was my fault, I think—the trouble between your sister and Lord Blytheland. Not all," he said. "But at least part of it. There is no accounting for how a mortal may react, after all."

"In which case, you should be careful, Harry!" Psyche

said severely, but she stopped, smiled, and shook her head. "I will *not* quarrel with you!"

"Psyche!" cried a voice from behind her.

"Cassandra!" Psyche cried joyfully. "How glad I am to see you! I did not want to walk all the way back home from here, so I am happy you have come and you have brought Lord Blytheland with you, too! How do you do, Lord Blytheland—I hope you are well?"

Cassandra almost tumbled down from the carriage in her haste to take Psyche in her arms and hug her. "You dreadful girl!" Cassandra cried. "How *could* you leave the house and not let any of us know where you were going? And to Lord Blytheland's house, too! I am *so* embarrassed!" She gave Psyche another hug. "But I am glad to see you safe—I was so afraid!"

Psyche nodded. "I was afraid, too, because Lord Crawforth is a horrid, odious man, but it is quite all right, because Harry rescued me and made Lord Crawforth fall in love with a cow! Was that not clever of him?"

Cassandra hastily glanced at Lord Blytheland, who also descended from the carriage and who looked very grim. "Yes, my dear, but let us not talk of that right now."

"If you will excuse me, ladies, I will go deal with Lord Crawforth," Lord Blytheland said.

"No!" cried Psyche and Cassandra at once.

Lord Blytheland stopped and stared at them.

"Lord Crawforth has been punished already," Psyche said. "My friend Harry did it. He will never bother me again, truly! Or anyone else. He has fallen in love with a cow, you see."

A look of profound revulsion came over Lord Blytheland's face. "Such a foul monster does not deserve to live," he said.

Psyche gave him a puzzled look. "But I think he will treat the cow very well. Only see how kind he is with it." She pointed toward Lord Crawforth. He had apparently concluded his negotiations with the cowman, who was holding a bank note in his hands and dancing in little circles on the grass. Lord Crawforth was leading the cow away, petting its cheek and murmuring into its ear.

"Please, let us go away from here," Cassandra said, touching Lord Blytheland's sleeve. "My sister is not hurt, and it is clear Lord Crawforth is . . . preoccupied." He gazed at her and his expression softened.

"Very well, if you wish it," he said, and extended his hand to Psyche. "Up you go." He lifted Psyche into his carriage, then assisted Cassandra into it as well.

Psyche sighed happily. This was precisely what she needed, her sister and Lord Blytheland together in the same place. Now she would make everything right between them again. She thought carefully over what she would say for many minutes, for this time she did not want to ruin anything between them.

"Thank you very much for finding me, Lord Blytheland," she began. "I wished to speak to you when I came to your house, but you were not there! But it is just as well, because now you and Cassandra are here together, and it is much easier telling both of you what you need to know at the same time."

"Psyche!" Cassandra exclaimed, her face becoming very pink. "Please, do not—"

"No, I will not listen, Cassandra, even though you are older than I. But I want to cry, too, whenever I see you weep, and I don't like to cry, you know."

"Psyche, please—"

Lord Blytheland held up his hand, and he looked curiously at Cassandra and Psyche. "Do go on, Miss Psyche. I suspect I am the cause of your sister's distress, and if I have been the cause of more, I wish to know how I may remedy it."

"It is not precisely because of you, my lord," Psyche said. "You see, Cassandra is very much in love with you, I

know it. Harry says so, too, so it must be so. But he made a
mistake and shot you too full of his arrows, and so you
acted in a bad way toward her. But I made him turn you
back the way you were before he shot you, and you still
love Cassandra anyway, do you not?"

"Yes, of course I do," Lord Blytheland replied. "But who
is this Harry?"

"He—he is Psyche's playmate," Cassandra said hastily.
"You must not mind her, really."

"I do not understand how your friend can know or do
such things, Miss Psyche," Lord Blytheland said, then
turned to Cassandra. "But I do wish to know one thing: do
you love me, Cassandra?"

He had stopped the carriage, for they were at the Hathaways' house. Cassandra stared at him, and his eyes were
warm and anxious, hopeful and full of pain. She thought of
what Psyche had said, remembered Harry's—Eros'—appearance before her. She knew her mythology well: the god
of love could turn a man mad as well as make him fall head
over heels in love. Ane love could heal as well as
hurt . . . Her heart ached and the words gathered behind her
lips, too numerous to choose between.

"I . . . I . . . Oh, heavens, I don't know!" Quickly, she
stumbled out of the carriage and fled into the house.

"Go after her, please, Lord Blytheland," Psyche said ur-
gently.

"She may not wish me to," he said.

"*Please* go in! She *does* love you, I know it. There is no
other reason for her to feel so low when she does not see
you. And if you go away without finding out, how do you
know she will not marry someone and then be miserable
because she loves you and no one else?"

Lord Blytheland stared at the door through which Cassandra had gone, and knew he could not bear it if she married another man. Miss Psyche had said her sister loved

him. Would not a sister know, however young she was? He leaped down from the carriage.

"Here," he said, thrusting a guinea in the Hathaway footman's hand. "Hold my horses." He pushed past the footman and after questioning a few maids in the hallway, went after Cassandra.

He opened a door and found himself in a small flower-and-vegetable garden, next to the mews. Roses climbed one wall, lilies perfumed the air, and pansies crowded the edges of the walkway. He almost did not see Cassandra, for her flower-print dress blended with the colors around her, and she was sitting on a bench, in a shadowed corner of the garden, her face covered by her hands.

He walked to her and sat next to her, feeling helpless. He wished he knew what to do or say, but he had not really ever been a man for words; his music said most of what he had in his heart. But he did not have his violin with him, and he supposed his only recourse was in words . . . though they had not served him well in the past, had they? But she did not move away, and he did the only thing he could think of: He put his arms around her and held her tightly.

She did not stiffen or draw away, but sighed instead. Encouraged, he put his finger under her chin and kissed her lips, gently. "Tell me, Cassandra. Tell me what is wrong."

"I am afraid," she said. "I am afraid I will say the wrong thing, like I always do. And I was afraid you did not mean it when you said you loved me, but then Psyche said Harry shot you and made you act—Well, never mind that. But I do believe it now, and feel horrible because I said terrible things to you."

"It can't be worse than the things I said to you, and I was the one who injured you, you who are totally innocent of all the things I said to you." Lord Blytheland stroked her cheek with his finger, gazing at her with such love that it hurt to see it. She closed her eyes. "I was married once before, you know, and . . . and my wife did not love me. I was afraid, also." He hesitated. "I do not deserve it, but will you for-give me?"

"Yes, yes of course," she said, and smiled at him.

There was silence, and then, hesitantly, the marquess said, "Was Psyche right, Cassandra? Do you love me? For I do wish to kiss you again, but make no mistake—if you do admit it, I shall insist on marrying you soon. And if you don't want that, I suggest you say no. Because, you see, I would not like you to share your kisses with anyone else but me, even in an experiment." There was a hint of laugh-ter in his voice, but a question also.

She turned to him, laughing, and feeling tears as well. "You are an odious man to bring up my experiment! It was a stupid thing, I see it now—"

"But do you love me, Cassandra?" He held her face in his hands, looking at her anxiously now, full of hope.

"Yes! Oh, Paul, yes!" she said at last, and put her hands behind his neck and kissed him fiercely.

With a low groan, he pulled her to him and kissed her with all the love he felt for her. His chest felt tight with wanting, and his heart's defenses shattered at last, causing him to crush her closer to him. She did not protest, but pressed herself to him instead.

"Marry me, Cassandra, please," he murmured against her lips, and he kissed her again, trailing his kisses from mouth to cheek, to chin and down the long column of her throat.

"Yes," she gasped.

"Soon." He moved his hands to her waist and hips, then pulled her onto his lap.

"Yes," she said, and kissed him again.

"Cassandra! Lord Blytheland!" Lady Hathaway's scan-dalized voice echoed in the garden. Cassandra looked up and saw her mother at the door of the garden, her hands on her hips and looking at them sternly.

Hastily, Cassandra pushed herself from Lord Blythe-land's lap and blushed furiously. But Lord Blytheland took her hand and rose from the bench and bowed to Lady Hathaway.

"It is not as bad as it seems, Lady Hathaway," he said and grinned. "You see, your daughter has just consented to become my wife."

"Is this true, Cassandra?" Lady Hathaway asked, her voice still stern.

"Yes, Mama."

"Thank God!" Lady Hathaway said, closing her eyes in heartfelt, grateful prayer. "I thought it would never happen!"

"Mama!"

"You must admit it has been a very trying thing for me, my girl! I have been trying to promote a match between you two this age, and then after that luncheon my hopes were almost completely dashed!" Lady Hathaway beamed happily at the marquess and her daughter. "I must go tell Sir John—he has just returned, Cassandra, and tell Psyche, too, for she was quite anxious about it. I have sent her up to her room to change her dress—she became dreadfully dirty, walking all the way to your house, Lord Blytheland! And thank you for your help in finding her, my lord. We are truly grateful. I *knew* you would be the perfect addition to our family." She turned to leave, then stopped. "Oh, and I should let you know, Lord Blytheland, it is not at all discreet of you to propose and kiss Cassandra in the garden here! It is in full view of the house across the alley, and I am sure any number of persons could see you from there, *and* from our house!" She turned and went back inside.

Lord Blytheland gazed at Cassandra, who was blushing to the roots of her hair, and grinned mischievously. "I suppose that means I should take you inside the house to kiss you."

Cassandra blushed more pink than ever. "Odious man!" she exclaimed, and turned toward the house. He caught her hand and pulled her to him. "Not here!" she said hastily.

"Where, then?"

"I do believe the music room is unoccupied," Cassandra said primly, then grinned and dashed into the house.

Psyche sighed as she gazed down from a guest room at her sister and Lord Blytheland in the garden. "Is that not romantic, Harry? I knew it would work out if I spoke to them. I was right, after all, you see."

Harry shrugged. "Not totally right. I think I helped, also."

Psyche stared at him. "How can you say so? You were the one who shot too many arrows into Lord Blytheland and made him act badly."

"But if I hadn't, he might not have thought of falling in love with your sister."

"You don't know that!"

"And you do?"

Psyche leaped down from her perch at the window and strode to the door of the chamber. "Oh, you odious boy! How can you say that?"

"From experience, my girl, from experience," Harry said, following her.

"Hmph!" Psyche opened the door, then crossed her arms in front of her. But she could not really stay mad at Harry. He was her best friend, after all, and she did not want to lose him again. She looked at him, unsmiling at first, and then she grinned. "Oh, never mind! I am going to the kitchens. Cook has just made up some jam tarts and I am going to get some while they are hot. I know you like them, too!"

Harry grinned. "I'll get there before you do," he said, and flew off down the hall.

"No fair flying!" Psyche called, and ran after him.

Emily Hendrickson lives in Reno, Nevada, with her husband, a retired airline pilot. Of all the many places she has traveled around the world, England is her favorite, and the most natural choice as the setting for her novels. In addition to her Regency romances, she has written a Regency reference book. Readers can reach her at Regencygal@hotmail.com.

Born in Japan, **Karen Harbaugh** was a Navy brat and lived a nomadic childhood, moving up and down the West Coast of the United States. She has a B.A. in English from the University of Washington, collects books of folklore, and grows lots of roses. She lives with her husband and son in Washington State. Karen welcomes comments from readers at her e-mail address, KarenH@sff.net, or by snail mail, P.O. Box 461, Auburn, WA 98071-0461.

Now available from
SIGNET REGENCY

A Lady of Talent
by Evelyn Richardson

Sebastian, Earl of Charrington, is betrothed to a suitable match, but dreams of a beauty in a painting. When he commissions the artist to paint his bride-to-be, he discovers it's a self-portrait, and that the woman of his dreams is much more than a canvas in a frame.

0-451-21009-3

The Lady and the Cit
by Blair Bancroft

In order to properly own her beloved lands, Miss Aurelia Trevor needs a husband. Offering her hand to the infamous businessman Thomas Lanning promises him a seat in Parliament. But soon this marriage of convenience turns to one of love.

0-451-21432-3

Available wherever books are sold or at
www.penguin.com